ILLUSIONS

THE APPLE HILL SERIES BOOK TWO

JENNIFER SIENES

Cover Design by Roseanna White

Celebrate Lit Publishing

www.celebratelitpublishing.com

ISBN: 978-1-951839-03-1

Chapter 1

Corey

Sins, even those buried with time, have the power to destroy. How could I have foreseen, eighteen years ago, that Taylor would be the victim of that destruction? A life for a life. If only I could trade places with her now.

A fluorescent light above her hospital bed spotlights her stark white features, and a lone drop of blood stains her left cheek like a macabre tear. So many tubes. The one attached to her mouth is ominous, plugged to a machine that sucks and whirs, breathing for her. A heart monitor *beep, beep, beeps*, and I'm entranced by the corresponding blips on the screen. One side of her head is shaved, and a neat row of stitches, an inch long or so, stands out against her pale scalp.

Panic crawls up my throat.

What have I done?

Paul storms through the doorless entrance of Taylor's neuro-unit ICU room. "I got here as fast as I could." He wraps me in a fierce hug and pulls away, his eyes darting to her still form and back at me. "What happened?" The pitch of his voice, fear in his eyes, steal what breath I have left. The horror displayed in his features matches that in my heart.

I draw air in through my mouth, unable to abide the stench of antiseptic and anxiety, and shake my head. "I...I don't know." *Liar*. "Car accident."

"I know *that* much!" He grips the side rail, knuckles whitening. Murmured voices float from the hall, and he lowers his voice. "Why was she driving? Did you send her on an errand?"

Send her? I shake my head. She was on a mission, and I was the target. How can I tell him, though? It'll change everything, and I can't face that. Not yet.

Maybe not ever.

Michael moves from the shadowed corner of the room, drawing Paul's attention as he steps up to the bed beside me. The faintest whiff of cigarette smoke clings to his jacket. "Taylor told me she was heading to the church to see you." Accusation, improperly focused, laces his tone.

"Me?" Paul's features are pinched. "But...I...we...was I supposed to meet her? I don't think so. I was preparing for the board meeting..." He stares past me. Is he retrieving his mental calendar?

"It doesn't matter," I say. Another lie. How many have I told in the last ten minutes?

Or the last eighteen years?

I clutch the gold cross hanging around my neck and pray for Taylor to live, bargain my life for hers, even knowing her survival will be the end of me.

The end of everything.

First Michael. Now this.

"It doesn't make sense," Paul mutters. "It's not like her to—"

"Are you Taylor Shaffer's parents?"

"Yes," I say. Hope wars with dread.

The tall man striding into the room glances from me to

Paul, no emotion crossing his tired features, and my heart beats like a bass drum. "I'm Doctor Nielson, Taylor's neurosurgeon."

"Neurosurgeon?" Paul steps toward the man in his usual take-charge manner, and I join him.

The doctor nods. "Has anyone given you an update?"

"No." Paul's one word overflows with impatience.

I place my hand on his forearm, and the muscles relax under my touch. "Not exactly. I was told she'd been in surgery and there's concern about a head trauma?"

"Yes. I've inserted an ICP monitor. Gauges if there's pressure building from the injury."

Michael slumps into the chair beside the bed, watching the interaction with the air of cool only a fifteen-year-old can feign.

Paul shifts from one foot to the other. "ICP?"

"Inter-cranial pressure," Dr. Nielson supplies. "No internal injuries, but the impact to her head..." He looks me in the eye. "It's serious. She's non-responsive."

"Non-responsive?" I shake my head. "What does that mean?"

"She's in a coma."

"*Oh, God.*"

Michael rises, hands slipping into the front pockets of his baggy jeans. "When...I mean...do you know when she'll wake up?"

The doctor turns to him, one eyebrow hitching up. "There's no way to know. Could be days, or weeks. But there's been no swelling, and she's young. Best guess? Days."

As he leaves, I turn back to the bed and slip my hand over hers, pale and still on the bed.

"It's okay." Paul whispers the words against my temple, wrapping his arm around my waist. "She'll pull out of this. She's strong."

"But brain injury?" I look at my beautiful daughter. Tears

pool in my eyes and spill over. If she dies…if she lives…*Oh, God, what have I done?* I swipe trembling fingers at the tears. *You have no right to cry.* I fumble in my pocket for a tissue. With a feather-light touch, I dab it at the blood on Taylor's cheek. No use. It's now a smear.

"You heard the doctor, babe. She's young."

Wadding the tissue, I lick it and try again. Better, but still a trace—

"Mom?" Michael hovers on the other side of the bed, his face as white as Taylor's. "Is she…?" He shrugs, hair spilling over one eye. "I mean, do you think she'll…?"

"I need to call Mark." Paul plants a kiss on my temple before stepping away. A chill invades my bones, like his presence is all that keeps death at bay. "Let him know what's going on. Pray up our girl."

Clenching the tissue, I hug my body and watch while Paul gives Michael's shoulder a squeeze before leaving the room.

Michael moves around the bed and steps into his father's place, eyes on Taylor. Again, a whiff of cigarette smoke. But now's not the time. "She was, like, real mad when she left this afternoon."

I wrap an arm around his shoulders. "It'll be fine, sweetie." But the hateful words that spewed from her lips, the contorted features—the hurt, the loss. My assurance to Michael is just another lie. They're piling up, one on top of the other, burying me alive.

But what difference does it make now? I'm as good as dead anyway.

~

Paul

Chest constricting, cell phone biting into my palm, I slam through the double doors, escaping the ICU. Taylor's face, like a ghost of my girl. Head shaven, a slash of stitches across her scalp. Coma. Brain trauma. What if she…?

I can't go there.

Oh, God, don't do this to her.

Eyes focused on the elevator doors at the end of the linoleum-floored hallway, I pass an elderly couple without a glance. Gotta get out of here before I lose it. Calling the church office was an excuse. Breaking down in front of Corey and Michael…it won't do. At the double-steel doors, I punch the down arrow. Just a little fresh air and I'll regain control. Be strong again.

"Pastor Paul?" A quivery female voice floats from behind me. The elderly couple? Church attendees?

Ignore them. For once, I won't be ruled by my position.

The down arrow lights with a ding before the doors whoosh open. I spot the stairwell to my left and sidestep to it without turning toward the couple I now realize is Grace and Ron Spires. My staunchest supporters, even in the wake of Michael's stupidity. But supporters or not, I can't face anyone. Not yet. Not until I muscle some control.

The stairwell is gray, cold, illuminated by fluorescent fixtures. A giant 5 is painted in black on the wall, in case I miss the coordinating number painted on the drab door. But it's quiet and—thank God—empty. Just in case the Spires try to follow, I jog down a level before pocketing the phone and dropping onto the top step of the landing.

This morning at breakfast, Taylor was excited about some science project for physiology. Blood typing. All she talked about on the way to school was the blood drive. How she'll finally be able to donate, and now…

What if she never wakes up? What if she wakes up, but she's never the same? What if—?

Oh, God, heal her. Please don't let her suffer brain damage.

I rub my eyes, and my fingers come away wet. I can't let

Corey see me like this. She needs to believe, and if I appear afraid, well, then she'll—

A ring echoes in the quiet, followed by the vibrating of my phone against my thigh. Could be Corey. Maybe something's happened…maybe Taylor woke, or…I fish it out of my pocket and check the caller I.D. Not Corey. I shake off the disappointment and thumb the CALL button. "Mark."

"Where are you? The board meeting started ten minutes ago."

"Something came up—"

"Came up?" A sigh blows over the line. "Well, I can put them off for a few minutes. When can you get here? Where are you?"

"Sutter-Roseville Hospital."

"Roseville?"

"Look, Mark—"

"Your position's on the line here. What am I supposed to tell the board members?"

I clench my jaw tight to bite back the expletive. *Let every person be quick to hear, slow to speak, slow to anger.* Breath in, one, two, three and out, one, two, three. "Tell them my daughter's been in a car accident and I need to reschedule."

"*What?*" Mark's voice falters on the word. "Oh, Paul. Man, I'm sorry. What…what happened? How bad is it?"

I swallow down the lump choking off my air supply. "Don't know yet. She's in a…coma."

"Coma? But…how? I mean, what happened?"

"I'm not sure. I haven't had a chance to talk to Corey yet. There might be some brain damage. We don't know. We're kind of in shock here."

"Oh, man." He sounds weary and a sigh comes through the phone.

"What?"

"It's just…you know that group. They're gunning for your position. I don't know how long I can put them off."

A sharp and visceral anger impales me. "Ridiculous. This whole thing's been blown way out of proportion." I slam my fist against the wall, the impact and throbbing pain a welcome distraction.

"It depends on your perspective."

"You agree with them?"

"Didn't say that."

"Then what?"

"It's just…this whole thing with Michael…you know. The way it looks."

"Yeah? Remind 'em of John eight. Might be a good reminder for you, too."

"I'm not making accusations here, Paul. But throwing it back in their faces isn't going to save your butt."

"There's not a man among them whose kids haven't messed up at some point or another."

"Maybe, but none of them are pastoring a church."

With no comeback, I close my eyes. "I can't deal with this right now. My family's got to come first here."

"No. You're right. Sorry. I'll see what I can do."

I hit the end button and fight the urge to hurl the phone.

Chapter 2

Twelve Hours Earlier
Corey

I appreciate when life is perfect, because I know it might only last fifteen minutes. Humming a tune under my breath, I set a pitcher of orange juice on the kitchen table and get busy making French toast and bacon—the breakfast of champions. Tantalizing aromas trickle out of the room, sure to rouse my sluggish family. Just one of my sure-fire strategies to get everyone out on time. Not as obvious as an air horn, but more likely to bring 'em in smiling.

"French toast." Michael plops onto a chair at the table and swings his head to clear his vision. It must be time for a haircut. "Cool."

I wave a spatula at him. "Good morning to you, too." Being taken for granted should be second nature by now—occupational hazard.

He flashes me a cheeky grin, so much like his dad's. "Good morning, Mother. How are you on this fine day?"

I roll my eyes, tween-girl style. "You've been watching *Leave it to Beaver* again." I glance at his baggy jeans and questionable t-shirt—is that a skull peeking from the swirl of black and gray?

Paul steps in, Rambo, killer Westie, on his heels, and catches my gaze. "Tell me, June, whatever will we do about the Beaver?" He nuzzles my neck, warm lips sending a zing down my spine.

Michael hides his scowl behind a glass of orange juice. "What the heck?"

I pop a piece of bacon into Paul's mouth, then take advantage of his momentary silence to run interference. I shift my attention to Michael. "Hey, bud, you might want to rethink the wardrobe." I slide a plate of French toast onto the table and attempt to swipe my fingers through his shaggy hair, but he ducks out of the line of fire. It's no use. The thick mop needs some serious pruning. At least it's not purple. *Thank God* for small favors.

Paul, still chewing, quirks a knowing eyebrow at me and sits. His censorious gaze flicks over Michael's t-shirt.

Before Michael can respond to the non-verbal challenge, a floral-scented cloud floats into the kitchen, competing with the sweet tang of syrup. "Hey, Mom." Taylor scoops Rambo up in her arms and Eskimo-kisses his snout. "Is breakfast about ready?"

"On the table."

"French toast?" She wrinkles her nose and releases the dog. "Total carbs."

Michael snorts. "Just throw it up later, like all your friends."

"Very funny." She plops into a chair and reaches for the pitcher of orange juice. "I'll just have this and a piece of bacon."

I look at Paul to veto that idea, but his face is now buried in the newspaper. No help there. "You're not going to get through the morning on bacon and juice."

"That's all *you're* going to eat."

No point in arguing the truth. "Let me cook you up a couple eggs."

"I'll take a couple, too," Michael says.

Paul folds up the paper. "Of course you will." With a shake of his head, he takes the pitcher of juice from Taylor and fills his own glass. "Where you manage to store all that food is beyond me. By the looks of your jeans, you're wasting away."

"It's the style."

"Style?" Taylor picks off a minuscule bite of French toast from Michael's plate. "Is that what you call it? Why you guys think it's cool to show off your underwear…"

I turn a deaf ear to the banter between Taylor and Michael and catch Paul's attention. "Do you want eggs, too?"

"No time." He downs the juice and slaps the glass back on the table.

"Oh?" I glance at the clock. "I thought you weren't going in until nine."

"The board called for a meeting this evening. I'm not prepared. Not sure I'll be home for dinner tonight."

His tone puts my mother-lion protectiveness on alert. "Problems?" I take a pan from the drawer under the stove and turn on the gas.

"Nothing I can't handle." His eyes hone in on Michael. "So, about the wardrobe, kiddo. You didn't answer your mom."

My eyes flick to Michael as I pull a carton of eggs from the fridge. I bite my tongue. *Stay out of it.*

"There's nothing wrong with what I've got on." His words are garbled around a mouthful of food.

Paul rests his wrists on the edge of the table, his hands loosely clenched. "I'm afraid I don't agree." The words are quiet, but there's no missing the strength behind them. It's not up for debate. Too bad Michael inherited his father's strong will.

"School policy says——"

"I don't care about school policy." Paul takes a breath and softens his tone. "*My* policy says you'll dress appropriately for school." He rubs his brow, no doubt contemplating a compromise. "At least turn it inside out, okay?"

Do I know my husband or what?

"Fine," Michael mumbles.

I move back to the stove and crack four eggs into the pan. "What have you got going today?" I catch Michael's eye. Maybe I can distract him from his defeated mood. It worked when he was two.

"History test."

"What about you, Taylor?"

She pushes back from the table, a piece of napkin-wrapped bacon in her hand. "Blood-typing in physiology today. Mr. Johnson says by the end of the day, we'll know our type. It's so antiquated, the whole blood type thing. I suggested we take a DNA test, like one of those that are popping up all over the place. But Mr. Johnson said it's not part of the curriculum or something like that."

"You already know your blood type," Paul says.

"No…" Taylor draws the word out. "*You* and *Mom* know what blood type you are. And if you'd let me donate blood——"

"Yeah, yeah, yeah." Paul grimaces. "We've been through this. You have to be seventeen, so this year——"

"How fair is that?" Taylor rolls her eyes. "*I'm* the one who came up with the idea of a yearly blood drive for our community outreach."

Paul's lips twitch. "And I'll be eternally grateful."

"Whatever." She shakes her head. "At least I'll know today what mine is."

"Hey, genius." Michael slips a bite of bacon to Rambo. "If you know what type Mom and Dad are, you already know yours. It's simple science."

"Well, Beav," Paul drawls. "I'd be thrilled if your grades

reflected your grasp of simple science. There's no doubt you've got the skills."

Taylor presses on as if the tension level didn't just double. "I also have a prom meeting after school."

"You're on the prom board?" Paul's tone is Papa-proud.

"Me and Genice, Wyatt and Jason." She hops up and pushes her chair in. "Hey, Mom. Can we go prom dress shopping this weekend?"

"Where are you going?" I look at the eggs and back at her. "I thought you wanted eggs."

"No time. Sorry."

Paul rises. "We'll need to discuss this prom dress business." He gives Taylor a mock-stern look. "Maybe we can find something from the Elizabethan period."

"Ha, ha." Taylor throws him a smile. "Don't worry, Mom'll make sure I'm not showing off too much skin." She turns to me. "Won't you, Mom?"

I focus on Michael, hunched over his plate, watching the interaction between Paul and Taylor through shaggy bangs.

Paul hitches his chin at Taylor. "I'll drop you off at school." He filches a piece of bacon. "You want a ride, Michael?"

"Gotta change first. I'll ride my bike."

Taylor snatches up her backpack sitting against the wall. "We can wait a few."

"No thanks."

"I'll call you later." Paul kisses my cheek and hooks a strand of hair behind my ear. "Do you have that women's ministry meeting this afternoon?"

I nod. "And you think a board meeting is tough."

Then he and Taylor are gone.

"I gotta get going." Michael stands.

"Listen, sweetheart." I stop him with a hand on his arm. "I know your dad's a little hard on you—"

"He's being a jerk." He steps away from me.

Well, that's a little harsh. "It may seem that way, but you don't help the situation—"

"It *is* that way." He jams his hands into his front pockets. "It doesn't matter how I dress, he'll find something else to pick on me about. Like my grades. Doesn't he even listen to his own sermons on forgiveness?"

"He *has* forgiven you. He's just worried you'll get into trouble again, so he tightens the leash a little."

"Bet he wishes I could be as perfect as Taylor. Must think he passed that goodie-goodie gene only to her."

"Give it a little more time. He's going through a difficult transition at work right now."

"Whatever." He storms out of the kitchen.

I blow out a breath and push the pan of eggs off the burner. "Well, Rambo. Looks like you hit the jackpot today."

Chapter 3

Corey

Easing the kitchen door closed, I step across the tile floor and flip on the coffee maker. The muffled voices of the women's ministry group, coming from the living room, are punctuated here and there with a laugh—okay, a cackle. Deborah Matson. Why is it her raucous humor hits a nerve today? My pastor-wife patience is a tad stretched.

My cell rings, and I snatch it up, tucking it between my chin and shoulder while whirling around to survey the platter of cookies I'd arranged earlier. "Hello?" The cinnamon-scented candle I lit an hour ago notwithstanding, everyone's sure to know I didn't actually *bake* them myself. They're too perfect for one thing. For another—

"Corey?"

I nip a chocolate chip crumb and slip it into my mouth. "Speaking." Salesperson? Needy congregant? That's just what I need—one more thing to add to my calendar.

"It's Tess Holland."

The tension in my shoulders eases, and I infuse a smile

into my voice. "Hey, Tess. Is the substitute hotline out of whack or what?"

"I prefer the personal touch. Besides, prepping for my students is so much easier if I know you'll be covering for me."

"When?"

"Tomorrow? I know it's last minute, but—"

"Not a problem. It's been a couple weeks, and I need to keep my teacher reflexes intact." A day with students is a vacation compared to ministry duties.

"Your skills are wasted subbing, you know. Although, I'd be lost without you."

Warmth spreads through me, as if I'd just been given a pat on the head from God Himself. "It's all I can manage for now." The lie slips easily from my lips. Too easily. As if the mantra's become my reality. But until Paul sees the value of me working full-time, subbing's going to have to do.

"Well, I appreciate you. And so do my students."

Michael pokes his head through the door and jerks a thumb over his shoulder. "What's with the hen party?" Like father, like son. Since when did he adopt Paul's vocabulary?

"Hold on a sec, Tess." Muting the phone, I glare at him. "What are you, four? Can't you see I'm on the phone?"

His eyebrows disappear beneath his hair. "Coming home to a roomful of women can do serious damage to a young man's psyche, Ma."

A giggle works its way up my throat, and I tamp it down. He's getting much too good at manipulating me. "Make yourself useful and take the cookies in, okay? Tell them I'm coming with the coffee in just a minute."

Eyes wide, his mouth drops open. "Are you kidding me? I barely survived my first pass-through."

"It'll hone your man-skills. Besides, they don't bite. Much." I turn my back on him to hide the grin as he takes the platter of cookies and mumbles something about C.P.S.

"Okay, Tess. I'm back. Sorry about that. Michael just got

home, and I've got a group of women waiting for me in the living room."

"No worries. I don't want to keep you. The lesson plans will be on my desk, and I'll let the office know you're covering for me. I have a doctor's appointment midday but call if you need anything."

"Nothing's wrong, is it?"

"No, no. Just a check-up. Thanks a ton, Corey."

I thumb the END button and lay the phone on the counter. Humming a nondescript tune, I pour the coffee into an insulated carafe and place it on a tray along with five cups, a small pitcher of milk and a bowl of sugar. With an exaggerated grunt, I lift the now-heavy tray and back myself through the swinging door. Even with the load in hand, my steps are lighter. Suddenly, Deborah's cackle isn't quite so grating.

"Sorry for the delay, ladies. The coffee wasn't quite ready."

Linda slides the plate of cookies to the edge of the coffee table to make room for the tray.

Deborah nabs the carafe before the tray hits the table. "What do you think about an Easter pageant?" Starring her little Meghan, no doubt.

I catch a glib response on my tongue and swallow it down. God certainly has a sense of humor if women's ministry is His plan for *my* life. I'd rather eat glass. "I think that's a discussion for another time. Preferably when Kelley can join us."

"But Easter's only two months away." Deborah shakes her head and fingers a couple cookies before landing on one. "If Kelley wanted a say, she should've been here."

Sylvie clucks her tongue. "She's got two sick kids at home, Deb. Cut her some slack."

Deborah's mouth takes on a lemon-sucking twist and her brows arch. "There's trouble in paradise, all right, but it has nothing to do with sick kids."

I stare Deborah down until she's got the sense to lower her

eyes. "Let's stick to the agenda, ladies, if you don't mind."
Why does every group have a resident gossip?

Carolyn shifts to the edge of the couch. "What needs to be
done for the blood drive?" Bless her heart, she's always quick
to defuse the tension. "I'm happy to make some calls and see
if we can get some home-baked cookies. It's always nice to
offer that instead of store-bought." Her smile falters as if she
realizes she's just committed a faux pas. "*Not* that there's
anything wrong with store bought, Corey. I mean—"

"It's okay." I laugh and filch a chocolate chip cookie off
the tray. "I'm not offended. Baking isn't my forte. However,
I'm a whiz at ordering them up at Sweetie Pies."

Sylvie chuckles. "We all have our gifts."

The front door slams, jolting my already-frayed fuse. Now,
what's Michael—

"Mom!" But the screech is all Taylor. Why is she home so
early?

"In here, Tay." I swipe an apologetic smile around the
room. So much for my sweet, charming daughter.

Taylor storms into the room, cheeks red, hair loose, and
comes to a stop so fast, she nearly loses her footing. "I—" Her
face turns a deeper shade of red. "I thought you were alone."

"Can it wait? I'm in the middle of a—"

"No." She shakes her head, eyes welling.

Tendrils of fear let loose in my gut. This isn't an ordinary
school-girl tantrum.

"You know, I was thinking—" Carolyn jumps up and
waves her hands at the other ladies to follow, "—we really
should wait until Kelley can join us. After all, the Easter
pageant is probably the most important item on our agenda
anyway."

"She's right." Linda collects her purse and gives Deborah
a push toward the door. "We'll just table this until next week."

If it weren't for the vacant look in Taylor's eyes, I'd
protest. With a claw working its way up my throat, I walk the

ladies to the door, my heart beating triple time. Whatever could Taylor be thinking?

I close the door, lean my backside against it, and glare at her as she digs through her backpack. "You've managed to chase the ladies away. I certainly hope——"

"Look at this." She tosses the backpack aside and thrusts a single sheet of paper at me.

"What is it?" I reach out for the paper trembling in her hand like a leaf fighting a stiff breeze.

She snatches her hand back as soon as I have hold of it, as if she can't abide my touch. "It's the results of my blood typing." She turns cold, tear-filled eyes on me. "How could you?"

How could I? How could I what? Why is it every time the kids have a meltdown, I'm somehow responsible?

I scan the worksheet, but it makes no sense. Boxes, combinations of letters, along with plus and minus signs. Science does not, nor will it *ever* make sense to me. There's no grade at the top, so it can't be that. "What am I looking at here?"

Taylor machine-gun-taps a shaky finger onto the sheet and stares at me like I'm an imbecile. "I'm O."

Uh, so?

"*You're* O."

"Okay." I draw the word out as if Taylor's five and I need to head off a tantrum. "I'm still not with you."

"Blood type!" The screech, accompanied by the rush of color in her cheeks, has me questioning her sanity. "I *can't* be O."

There ought to be specialized training for parents of teenagers—strategic maneuvers or something. Was I this emotional at seventeen? "Let's sit down, Tay." I try and take her arm, but she snaps it out of reach.

"How can you be so dense, Mom?" Her voice breaks, and tears spill over. "Me and Dad do the blood drive, remember?

Every year." She slaps at the tears with one hand and yanks the worksheet from me with the other. "He's AB. You're O."

A kernel of memory, buried so far in my past it's become non-existent, begins to grow. It can't be. This *lab* experiment is faulty. Isn't it? Breathing is impossible and a hum fills my ears.

"Am I adopted?" Is that hope in her voice? A logical explanation for this ridiculous experiment.

I latch onto a thought like a drowning victim latches onto a minute piece of driftwood. "It has to be wrong." I force my eyes to meet hers and wave at the damning evidence in her grasp. "There's been an error."

She shakes her head, face mottled, mouth set in a rigid line. "No error. We did it three times, and it came back the same." She drops her gaze to the crumpled worksheet. "I'm not adopted, am I?"

I rub my temple where a dull drumbeat's begun and scramble for an explanation—anything but what I fear is the truth. But there's…nothing.

"Does Dad know?"

A hand squeezes my chest—the hand of God? — reminding me of my sin. If I couldn't confess it to Him, how could I possibly confess it to Taylor? And Paul?

"You cheated on him." Disgust twists her features, fists her hands, before she turns away and snatches up her backpack.

"Where are you going?" The question works its way past my constricted throat.

"What do *you* think?" She spins to pin glacier eyes on me as she reaches the front door. "To tell Dad." Her voice cracks.

Go after her. Stop her. But my legs have no substance, no strength.

No fight.

The door slams and a sob escapes. I clap a hand over my mouth to hold in a scream and shuffle into the living room. *Why, God, after all these years?*

But He's silent. Letting me stew in my sordid circumstances.

Do I call Paul? And tell him...what?

The front door slams, and a surge of something—hope, reprieve—shoots through me. She's changed her mind. We can work through this somehow. I rush to meet her, but it's not her.

Michael throws his hands in the air. "What's Taylor's problem anyway?"

I shake my head and turn away. "What did she say?" As if it matters. Everyone will have a front-row seat to my shame. To the death of my relationship with my children. The death of my marriage.

"Who knows what she was ranting about? All I know is she was ticked and going to see Dad."

As long as I can muddle through mundane tasks, the world hasn't yet ended. I load the tray that sits on the coffee table—cups, saucers, cookies—as Michael fills the void with a monologue. Aside from an occasional grunt, no response from me is necessary.

"So, get this." His arm snakes around me to snatch a cookie from the tray as he shadows me to the kitchen, Rambo dancing at his feet. "Mr. McGinty says we have to use at least *six* sources to back up our research. You'd think it's a friggin' college class."

A reprimand forms in my head, but my tongue is too thick to communicate it. It's only a matter of hours before my parental moral compass will cease to carry any weight. What's an indelicate word compared to the heaviness of my past? Even Michael's brush with the law last year will seem trivial.

"You okay, Mom?" Michael's worried blue gaze penetrates the protective fog.

How long have I been standing around like a loon, with the tray nearly dissecting my middle? I ease the knuckle-whitening grip and set it on the counter. "Don't you have some homework?"

He rolls his eyes. "And you guys say *I* don't listen." He grabs two more cookies and backs out of the kitchen. "Research. *Six* sources. Mr. McGinty. Any of this sound familiar? Geez."

Once he's out of range, I press my hands against my belly, which is performing acrobatics of Cirque du Soleil proportions. A whine draws my attention. Rambo sits at my feet, black eyes accusing me. "I have to call Paul. There's no way around it." He cocks his head as if in agreement.

I fumble with the phone. It takes three tries to punch in his cell number. What will I say? I take a deep breath and close my eyes. *Hello, sweetheart? Taylor's on her way, and she has this crazy notion…* Except it's not so crazy. *I'm the crazy one.*

When his phone goes to voicemail, I hit the END button with enough force to chip my nail. What if he's talking to Taylor right this moment? I thumb the church office and scrape at a spot on the counter with my now broken nail.

One ring—my heart's thrumming in my ears. Two rings— I draw in a full breath. Three rings—I let it out with a *whoosh*.

"Crossroads Community Church, this is Dorothy. How can I help you today?"

"Hi Dorothy." My voice belts out a wobbly soprano, and I clear my throat. "This is Corey. Is Paul available?"

"Oh, hi, Corey. He left about ten minutes ago."

"Did he say where to?"

"Not exactly." She *tsks*. "I think he's a little anxious about the board meeting tonight. He said he had to clear his head. You know what *that* means."

Yeah, a reprieve. If Paul's anxious, he'll run a good five to ten miles. "I'll leave him a message on his cell, but in case he doesn't get it—"

"I'll be sure and have him call."

I busy myself bagging the cookies and washing the coffee cups and carafe while listening for the sound of a car in the driveway or the slam of the front door. Taylor will have no choice but to come home when she finds Paul isn't at the church, won't she? Can I convince her to let me tell him myself? And then what? There's just no easy way to break something like this.

When the kitchen's spotless, I snatch up the phone and try Taylor's cell. It rings four times and goes to voicemail. Why isn't she home yet?

I fill Rambo's food bowl and check in with Michael. He's slumped on the bed, tinny music coming from the buds crammed in his ears. A history book lies unopened at his feet while he's focused on his cell phone. Unless one of his friends is texting research material, he's off task.

Waving a hand from the door, I get his attention.

He yanks at the wire coming from his ear and his eyebrows shoot up. "What's up?"

"I thought you were doing homework."

"Taking a break."

"Working at the speed of molasses won't get much done, son."

He nods. "Good one, Mom. I got it covered."

I've heard that one before. But compared to what is sure to come, this isn't a hill worth dying on. Instead, I pace the family room and, every thirty seconds, peer through the front window—which is where I'm standing when the police car pulls up at the curb.

Please don't come here. But even as I whisper the prayer, the officer looks up at the house, a grim set to his mouth, and heads up our walkway.

Dear God. How is it possible this day could get any worse?

Chapter 4

Corey

After three days at the hospital, the house is a wreck—unopened mail piled on the dining room table, a mountain of laundry in the basement, and the innards of two pillows that fell victim to Rambo's boredom blanketing the family room. Why did Paul insist on down?

It was easy enough to ignore the mess late last night after another uneventful day at Taylor's bedside. I even pretended not to see it when trudging to the kitchen for my early morning coffee fix. But I can't ignore the pristine white feather floating on my mocha-laden concoction before I even have my first sip.

Tears well, an overreaction for sure, unless you're Sarah Bernhardt. It's not just the coffee or the mess, I swear. But Rambo is repentant. He drops at my feet, resting his chin on his front paws with an apologetic whine.

"My fault." I crouch down and scratch his perky ears. "I should have found someone to keep you for a few days."

He rolls onto his back, offering up his soft belly for a rub. I know when I'm beat.

"We going to the hospital?" Michael stands in the kitchen doorway, dressed in baggy jeans and a wrinkled T-shirt he must've collected from the laundry pile. At least it's goth-free.

"*We're* not going to the hospital." I stand to reword Paul's command before leaving earlier. "*I'm* going—you're going to school. You've missed too much as it is."

"I can get the work from Dan. I want to be there if Taylor wakes up."

"Even if she does, she won't know you." I can at least rest in Dr. Nielson's prediction that Taylor will wake any day now, even if he says she won't recognize us.

Michael's jaw clenches and rebellion lights his eyes before he opens his mouth. "It's Dad, isn't it? He's the one saying I gotta go to school."

I stifle a sigh. Here we go again. The battlefield is occupied by opposing forces, and I'm playing mediator-in-the-middle. "Taylor's going to need you more when she's home, Michael." I'm talking to a dolomite rock here. "*I'll* need you more when she's home."

"You know I can make up the work. It's a cinch."

I'm tempted to call him on it but bite my tongue. We both know he can pull off straight A's without breaking a sweat. So why doesn't he?

"Come on, Mom." The little-boy whine is reminiscent of his four-year-old self.

Shaking my head, I spot a backpack on a chair at the kitchen table. Taylor's backpack. Ignoring Michael, I step over to it and my stomach clenches. "Where'd that come from?"

"Dad brought it in last night. He picked it up from the impound lot yesterday. It was in Taylor's car."

That's right. How could I forget he went to look at the car? I reach for it but hesitate. Did Paul look inside the backpack? Did he find *it*? Maybe, but if he did, he didn't let on. I'd have known. His kiss…his touch…something would have clued me in.

"What's wrong, Mom?" Michael's brows draw together.

"What?"

"You look——"

"No…nothing." I scrape my hair behind my ears. "You need to get to school."

"What about the hospital?"

"I'm going. A little later. When Dad gets done with a few things at church." After I do a thorough search of Taylor's backpack.

"But what about me?"

"Huh?" Even if I find the paper, then what? How can I explain it to Paul?

"Breakfast?"

"What? Oh, yeah." I snatch a brown banana from the fruit bowl and slap it into his hand.

"That's it? No French toast?"

"You'll be late for school."

Shaking his head, he mumbles something about child abuse and leaves. If he only knew.

I wait, breath held, until the front door slams. Plucking up the backpack, I set it on the table, my heart beating like I've just completed the fifty-yard dash. *Oh, God, why did this have to happen? Why now?*

The *pzzzt* of the zipper is loud in the sudden quiet of the house. Rambo hops up onto the chair and watches with the fascination normally reserved for the neighbor's three-legged cat.

"Here goes nothing," I mutter, pulling out the contents and placing them on the table. A physiology textbook, a bright red binder with pictures tucked into the plastic cover, a tattered green notebook. That's it? I tip the backpack toward the window and search its innards. A folded paper lines the bottom. Breath short, heart beating in triple time, I reach for it.

The doorbell peals, and I jump. Rambo goes into

watchdog mode, tearing across the kitchen, barking to warn the invader he's on the job.

Paper clutched to my chest, I groan. Who in their right mind shows up at someone's house before eight? My tattered robe isn't the most flattering—only exemplifies the extra ten post-pregnancy pounds I've settled into over the last fifteen years. Maybe I can pretend I'm not home. It's not like anyone can hear me over Rambo's incessant alarm.

"Corey!"

It can't be. I cram the paper in my pocket and schlep across the kitchen on slippered feet to peer around the corner. Rambo stands at attention in front of the door, tail wagging, body shuddering with each bark. Even though the figure is as distorted as a Picasso painting through the leaded glass, the blonde bob is impossible to mistake for someone else.

"Tricia?" Speaking her name dissolves my emotional fortitude. I rush to the door and throw it open to be swallowed by a warm embrace and Oscar de la Renta.

"I got here as soon as I could," she tells me over my sobs. "It'll be okay. Everything will be okay."

Bless Tricia, she doesn't even give the family room a second glance, as if clumps of feathers spread about are part of the decor. With a flick of her hand, she clears a spot off the couch and settles. "So? How's Taylor? What's the prognosis?"

I swipe at my eyes, hook my hair behind my ears, and set my frumpy self on the other end of the couch. I could be dressed to the hilt and still feel as classy as a gawky thirteen-year-old—not that I even own anything hilt-like. "I thought you were still in New York."

"I was. Until I got your message. Placerville's just a quick detour to home. I rented a car at the airport, and I'll head down to Carmel when I'm sure everything's good here."

"Define *good*." I slump back and rub my face.

Tricia's brows furrow. "How bad is she?"

"Still in a coma. Doctor thinks she'll come out of it any day now. But—" I shake my head as my eyes well. "We're not sure what to expect. Brain injury, amnesia…"

"So, you take it a day at a time." Sensible words, but her eyes swim every bit as much as mine. "My goddaughter is strong. She'll be just fine."

Until she remembers.

"It's my fault." The words hang out there, and a decision must be made. Do I confess it all? Oh, what a relief it would be to say it aloud.

"That's ridiculous. Unless you were behind the wheel." She reaches out and takes my hand. "You always did take on too much. Remember sixth grade P.E.? That was the year—"

"No." I shake off her hand. It would be so easy to let her smooth it all away, to take my sin and water it down until it resembles nothing more than the melodramatic mutterings of overwrought emotions. "It *is* my fault. We…Taylor and I…we had an argument. She was upset. I should have stopped her, but—" I press my fingers to my lips to still their quivering. "I was…in shock, I guess."

"Shock? About what? The argument?"

I reach my hand into the pocket of my robe and finger the folded sheet of paper. Although I haven't yet looked at it, I know what it is. And I can't expect Taylor to forget. At least not for long.

"Corey? What's this about?"

"A science experiment, of all things." I try to laugh but it gets stuck on a sob.

"You and Taylor fought over a school project?"

I shake my head and leave the veil of messy hair over my face as I pull the paper from my pocket and offer it to Tricia. Holding my breath, I watch her unfold it then smooth it out on her linen-clad thigh. Taylor's name, discernible even upside-down, is written in the top right corner. I can't make out everything she's printed in the boxes, but I recognize it as the same worksheet she waved in my face not four days ago.

"Okay." She looks at me and shrugs. "I don't get it."

"Her physiology lab. They did an experiment on blood typing."

"So?"

Good grief. Do I have to spell it out?

The snick of the front door opening, and Paul's voice rings out. "Corey."

Heat suffuses my face as I snatch the sheet from Tricia. *Act normal.* I suck air into my lungs. "In here." Voice too high. I clear my throat and crush the paper in my pocketed fist, praying Tricia won't say anything about it to Paul.

"Are you ready?" He stops at the threshold of the family room, eyes widening. "Tricia. Hey. I didn't know you'd be here." A tired smile accompanies his words.

"I didn't wait for an invitation." She meets him halfway for a hug. "I got Corey's message and here I am."

"Well…" He steps back. "That's…great. Corey can use your support."

The hesitancy in his voice alerts me. Did something happen at the church? "I didn't expect you back so soon."

"I can't concentrate at work." He rubs an eyebrow. "Thought we might as well get down to the hospital. But… well…I can see you're not ready." Impatience laces his tone.

"Give me ten minutes." I turn my back to him and give Tricia a little head shake. Will she get that I need her to keep this between us?

Their voices fade as I slip down the hallway and enter our bedroom. Rambo's curled up in the muss of the unmade bed, and I long to snuggle beside him and sleep until this nightmare is over.

But I don't deserve oblivion.

Growing up, my father's favorite mantra was, "You reap what you sow." Well, I'm reaping now.

My fingers tremble as I pull the crumpled paper from the pocket of my robe. My sin is stamped there, as sure as a big red *A*. I smooth it out and refold it. Snatching a pair of panties from my drawer, I slip it beneath the underthings then muss them up to be sure it's hidden.

"Corey?"

I jump at Paul's voice right behind me and slam my finger in the drawer. My heart's hammering clear up my throat, choking off the cuss word that trips across my mind. "Almost ready." I can see his reflection in the mirror atop the dresser, just standing in the doorway, and my face heats. How long has he been there?

"You okay?" He crosses the room and comes up behind me, wrapping his arms around my waist. Okay, good. Normal's good.

"Yeah. I just need to get dressed."

"What're you hiding in here? A note from a secret admirer?" He reaches out and grasps the handle of the drawer and I freeze.

I can't think.

I can't breathe.

Chapter 5

Paul

Corey's acting...strange. To be expected considering the circumstances. I don't even know what normal is anymore. She took my head off for teasing about a secret admirer. I get she's tense, but the whole drive down to Sacramento, she didn't say two words. Tricia sat in the back seat and rambled on. I made the appropriate responses. I think. Then again, maybe I didn't. Either way, she wasn't deterred, just kept rambling. About a buying trip, her shop, whatever.

Walking down the hall toward ICU, I wrap an arm around Corey, give her shoulder a gentle squeeze. She melts into me for only a moment, but it's long enough to reboot my senses, reconnect. It would help if I knew what she was thinking. "You okay?"

"Fine." The word's whispered, but with a tired smile, so I don't push. I have enough problems of my own. Don't need to borrow more.

We're admitted into the ICU, approach Taylor's room, and Corey pulls ahead.

"Oh, God," she says, braking at the entrance, covering her mouth with a hand.

I step up behind her, half expecting to see Taylor awake. Instead, I'm slapped with the image of my daughter, hands mitted and tied to the bed railing, gown bunched up around her thighs.

Corey rushes to her side, Tricia right behind, and I turn in search of a nurse or doctor. Someone who can tell me what the heck's going on.

Two nurses are at the front desk. I don't bother to wait for their conversation to cease. "Why's my daughter tied up?"

They look at me. "She's been restless," says one. Janet? Yeah, according to her name tag. "We're afraid she might pull out her feeding tube and ventilator."

That must mean… "She's waking?"

"Coma patients sometimes become agitated. It doesn't mean they're waking up."

"Oh." It would be good if *something* positive happened.

"But it's only a matter of time, Pastor Shaffer. We're confident Taylor will come out of it soon. Her vitals are stable, no swelling…all good signs."

I pray she's right. My spunky daughter, so full of life…well, it doesn't do any good to go there.

Entering Taylor's room, I see her gown is back in place. Corey stands at her side, fingers touching the stubble on Taylor's scalp. Tricia watches from the other side. They don't notice me, and I take the opportunity to observe.

An odd couple, Corey and Tricia. Was it this obvious back when I married Corey? Has she changed so much? Or was it Tricia? Corey's settled into the thankless job of a pastor's wife, blended into the background, while Tricia…well, she's anything but settled. But it's Corey's heart I see when I look at her. What she is, not what she isn't. I wouldn't trade her for the world.

"Well?" Tricia stares at me, hand on hip. "Did you find out anything?"

"She's been restless." I step up next to Corey, slide my hand under her hair, rest it on her neck. Warm. Soft. She looks up at me. "They were afraid she'd pull out the tubes."

"I wish she'd wake up."

"I know, babe. Me, too."

"What a mess," Tricia mutters.

Corey's shoulders tense under my hand. Her eyes remain fixed on Taylor.

"This could be my fault." I disengage my hand from Corey's hair. "Michael said she was upset when she left the house. He said…" The accusation in his eyes still burns in my memory. "He said she was coming to see me at the church." Was I so focused on the Simpson mess I forgot an appointment with my own daughter?

Corey slips her hand into mine, rests her head on my shoulder. "It's not your fault, Paul. Don't even go there, okay?" She looks up at me, tears swimming in her blue eyes.

Would I be so quick to dismiss blame if it were the other way around? I'd like to think so.

"Good. You're here." Dr. Nielson strides into the room, white coat flapping. His presence fills the space. I would love to reproduce that energy from the pulpit. He diminishes my six-one frame by mere authority.

"Is something wrong?" Corey asks, then winces, eyes closed. "I mean besides the obvious."

He glances at Tricia but faces Corey and me. "I'm concerned about the damage the ventilator might do to her vocal cords if we leave it in much longer. I think it would be wise to perform a tracheotomy tomorrow."

"Trach…tracheotomy?" Corey turns to me, panic brightening her eyes.

I hug her to me. "That seems a little extreme."

"Standard procedure in a case like this. We don't know

how much longer she's going to be non-responsive. I think being proactive is our best defense against complications that could arise."

I nod and hope he knows best.

Corey

I can't get the vision of the upcoming tracheotomy out of my head. There has to be a better way. The thought of Taylor's throat being slit so a tube can be inserted...well, it's nauseating. How quickly life can take a sharp turn from normal to madness.

We take our positions around the bed, like voyeurs at the zoo. Taylor's legs flail on occasion, and she pulls at the bindings around her mitted wrists. She's going to wake soon. I just know it.

"I'm going to get some coffee," Paul says an hour into our visit. "Either of you want anything?"

"A mocha, if you can find one." I never did get my morning fix.

"I'll see what I can do. Tricia?"

She shakes her head and watches while Paul leaves. As soon as he's out of sight, her head whips around and she pins me with a narrowed glare from the opposite side of Tay's bed. "I got it."

Got it? Got what? Did I miss something?

"The experiment. Blood typing."

My heart leaps. "Shush." I look at Taylor.

"She can't hear us." But Tricia lowers her voice. "And even if she can, it's not like she doesn't already know."

"We can't talk about this now," I whisper. "Paul could—"

Tricia comes around to my side of the bed and leans into me, her perfume assaulting my nose. Oscar de la Renta doesn't blend well with sterility. "You told me nothing happened that night. You swore to me."

"I never imagined—"

"Mrs. Shaffer?" A nurse stands at the entrance. "Taylor has visitors. Looks like maybe a friend from school and mom."

"Oh?" How much did she hear? "Well, that's fine."

"Do you want to step out while they visit?"

"Step out?"

She points to a sign above the doorway. *No more than two visitors at a time.* "We've been a little lax," she says, "but if you want to allow them both to come in…"

"Yes, of course." I snatch my purse from the chair next to Taylor's bed and lead the way out. If Tricia's going to berate me, I'd rather she not do it in front of Taylor anyway. Coma or not.

Stepping through the double doors to ICU, I'm stopped short in the hallway. Why am I surprised? Josh Andrews and Taylor have been close since the beginning of high school— maybe too close. Although, it's not the kid who makes me feel about as awkward as a pimply-faced teen, but his mother. Alexis. The name fits. I'd bet my last meal she was a high school cheerleader.

"Josh, Alexis." I paste on my pastor's-wife smile. The one I pull out in dire emergencies. I may not look like I have it together, but I can fake it pretty well. "So good to see you both."

Tricia steps forward, hand extended. "Hi. I'm Tricia Sewell. Corey's friend."

"This is Josh and Alexis Andrews," I tell Tricia. "Josh is Taylor's…friend." At least that's what Paul wants to believe— all he can handle at this point. I resist the urge to gather my hair up and straighten my clothes. Not that I can do much with the jeans and sweater I'm wearing. Alexis is wearing the same combo, but like Tricia, she could be wearing a flour sack and it'd look good.

"So nice to meet you, Tricia." Alexis flashes her beauty-queen smile, then turns to me, not a brunette hair out of place. "How's our girl doing?"

Our girl? That's a little too familiar for my liking. I tuck resentment aside and give them a quick rundown. "Talk to her," I tell Josh, who nods and appears to be on the verge of tears, which softens me. "I'd like to believe she can hear us."

Tricia nudges me with a shoulder as we watch the two enter the ICU. "What's with the mom?" she whispers.

I grit my teeth to hold back the snarky remark that sits on the tip of my tongue. Why don't I trust Alexis? She's never been anything but…nice. Okay, maybe a little condescending, but I suppose if I looked like that, being humble wouldn't come naturally.

"Don't bother answering. I can see it in your face."

"What?"

"Does she attend your church?"

"She used to." What can I say that doesn't land me in gossip?

Tricia's eyebrows disappear behind flaxen bangs. "Pretty friendly with the pastor?"

I grimace. With the sin of adultery hanging on me like a nasty leech, gossip is the least of my worries. "She went through a divorce last year and wanted Paul to counsel her."

"I'll just bet she did."

"Hey, guys."

I jump at Paul's voice and turn to see him with a Starbucks coffee cup in each hand. "I thought you were going to find a vending machine." I take the cup he offers me with a trembling hand. Maybe coffee isn't the best choice right now.

"They don't have mochas."

"Oh, sweetheart, you didn't have to—"

"It wasn't a problem. How come you're out here?"

"Taylor has visitors," Tricia says.

"Josh and Alexis." I watch Paul's face for a sign when I say,

"Alexis." A man would have to be half dead to not be smitten with her—as obvious as she is. But Paul's scowl isn't of the smitten variety. "What?"

"Do me a favor. Call me on my cell when they're gone. I'm going for a walk."

"But Paul—"

"I'm afraid I don't have the patience for her right now."

I watch as he retreats. "I wonder what *that's* all about."

"Maybe you're not the only one with secrets," Tricia says.

Chapter 6

Corey

A burning band of tension tightens along my shoulders as I work alongside Paul in the kitchen. Alone. Well, except for Rambo, who's scoping out the floor like a bottom-feeding catfish. Tricia's off on some errand, and Michael's locked away in his bedroom. Doing his homework? I hope so, because Paul will check on him and I can't take any battles tonight. The scents of garlic and basil compete with the lit cinnamon candle that sits on the counter—my ill attempt at a room deodorizer.

We have enough food in the freezer to feed us for the next six months, thanks to the Helping Hands ministry at our church. Food is a universal comforter, for both the giver and the receiver. I don't have to plan meals or take the time to cook. The only downside is that I'm not quite sure what it is we're eating most of the time.

I don't want to think about Taylor's tracheotomy scheduled for tomorrow. I don't want to think about the lab sheet I hid up in the closet after Paul caught me slipping it into my underwear drawer. And I don't want to think about Paul's strange behavior around Alexis Andrews.

What's left?

Tricia's crack about secrets keeps playing over and over again in my head. I want to ask Paul about it, but what right do I have to question him? My own dark secret, looming like the shadow of death, is big enough to choke the life out of all of us.

"Who's handling the women's Bible study next week?" Paul takes the dripping pan from my soapy hands and wipes it with the same quick efficiency he applies to every task.

"Rebecca Simpson."

"What?" The pan clatters to the floor startling a yelp from me and a bark out of Rambo. Paul retrieves it, pulling it into his stomach like a football. "Why would you pick *her* of all people?"

What's his problem with Rebecca? First Alexis, now Rebecca. "She's helped me out in the past, so when she asked—"

"Asked? You mean she came to you?"

I take the dishtowel from Paul and dry my hands. "What's this all about?"

He shakes his head and puts the pan in the cupboard. Why won't he look at me? Is Tricia right? "There are women better qualified than Rebecca. What about Karen Jacobson?"

"She doesn't have time to prepare with all the kids. I haven't had a chance to lay out everything, and Rebecca's okay with that. She'll do fine."

He grunts and fiddles with wiping up the sink.

"What's wrong with Rebecca?"

"You'd be better prepared if you'd give up that substitute position…"

I stifle a sigh. Here we go again. "First off, I'm ill-prepared because I've been living at the hospital, *not* teaching. But even if I was, you agreed I could work part time—"

"If it didn't get in the way of your duties with women's ministry."

Closing my eyes, I rub at the headache forming between my brows. "We've been through this, Paul. If I want to keep my credential valid—"

"You already have a full-time job."

"So, I should let all those years of college just go to waste?"

"You're teaching."

"Women's Bible study wasn't what I had in mind."

"Whatever you do, do it for the glory—"

"Don't." My tone comes out sharper than intended, and I rein it in. "Please, don't quote scripture when we're in the middle of an...of a discussion. It's not fighting fair."

Paul steps close, slips his hands around me and flashes his placating smile, the one that lights up his hazel eyes. "You're right. Sorry." He presses a kiss on my forehead. "I just want you to be content with the work God's called you to."

"The work God's called *you* to," I say against his chest. Why can't he understand? "I didn't major in theology. I majored in liberal studies."

"It doesn't matter at this point anyway. Taylor may need full-time care for a while once she's out of the hospital." He gives me a quick squeeze before stepping back. "But I'd rather you find someone other than Rebecca Simpson to handle things for now."

I'm being manipulated. "Why?"

"It's just—"

"Mom." Michael breezes in and plops an open textbook onto the counter. "You gotta explain this algebra equation again. I'm not getting the same answer that's in the back of the book."

I hold my hand up to stop him. "We're in the middle of something here."

"But—"

"No," Paul says. "That's fine. We're done." He walks past Michael and out of the kitchen.

"Hang on, Michael," I say, following Paul.

I find him in his office, a room that reminds me of my father. He sits behind his heavy oak desk surrounded by shelves full of books—volumes of *Systematic Theology* and commentaries on every book of the Bible by authors like MacArthur and Henry.

Judgement sits heavy in this room.

I don't cross the threshold. "What's your issue with Rebecca Simpson?" And Alexis Andrews, I want to add.

He sighs and shakes his head. "I don't want to get into it right now. It's church politics and—"

The phone rings. He checks caller ID and snatches up the receiver. "I have to get this."

"Is it the hospital?" Maybe Taylor's awake.

He looks me in the eye. "No. Yeah, Mark," he says into the receiver.

And I've been dismissed.

Stepping from the doorway, I hesitate when Paul mentions Drew Simpson's name in a tone that's less than pastoral. Eavesdropping is wrong, but I ignore the prick of guilt and lean against the wall, tilting my head close to the doorframe.

"There you are."

I whip around, heat shooting through my body, to see Tricia. "Oh, uh, you're back."

"I'm back." Her mouth twitches and I know she knows. "I was just...I mean, Paul and I..."

"Yeah. So I see. You have a few minutes? We need to talk."

Great. The last thing I want to talk about is the night of my Great Shame. "Michael needs help with his algebra home-work. I told him I'd be right back."

"I feel responsible," she says, planting hands on slim hips.

I latch onto her arm and pull her into my bedroom,

closing the door behind us. "What's the matter with you?" I grind out between clenched teeth. "Paul was in the next room."

"I talked you into going to that stupid party that night. Remember?"

I drop onto the bed and fight the urge to climb in and hide. "You didn't force me to be stupid that night." I scrape both hands through my hair and look into her sympathetic eyes. "What am I going to do?"

Paul

Gut clenching, I resist the urge to hurl the phone across the room and, instead, drop it on my desk. The elder board's pushing a meeting—new complaints about the worship music, and the children's ministry leader isn't getting the support she needs.

The dissension growing has nothing to do with either. I'm half tempted to walk away, but I've worked too hard and too long to give into a few dissenters. Community outreach has never been stronger, membership is up, collections are up. What more do they want—my blood?

From cradle to grave, that's what they want. Middle-of-the-night phone calls when someone's sick, fighting, or depressed. I'm everyone's best friend except when I'm not.

And my daughter's in a coma.

I push up from the chair, back protesting from neglect. I would love to get a run in tomorrow, but we'll need to leave early if I'm to have time to work on Sunday's message and be prepared to defend myself at Monday night's board meeting. Nothing like being called on the carpet. What do they have in mind? A hand slapping or a request for my resignation?

I need a distraction. Maybe Corey'd like to take a walk.

Michael sits alone at the kitchen table, textbook open, head resting in one hand while the other taps out a beat with the eraser end of a pencil. Rambo's planted under his chair and raises his head when he sees me. "Where's your mom?"

He shrugs. "Not my turn to keep track of her."

I grind my teeth and bite back a reprimand. When did he morph into a smart aleck? It seems like every comment I make is met with disdain. "I thought she was helping you with homework."

"And I thought she was with you."

I start to walk away and stop. Someone has to be the adult here. "You need some help? I know I'm not as good at algebra as your mom, but—"

"I'll wait for her." He doesn't bother looking at me, like I don't warrant even that respect.

"You want to talk about it?"

"What?"

"Whatever it is that's eating you. Been eating you for months."

"Nope."

I shake my head. "This attitude's got to stop, Michael. Whatever your problem—"

His head snaps up. Well, at least I got his attention. "My attitude? You started it."

"*I* started it?" Stepping up to the table, I plant my hands on it and lean in. "I'm not the one who vandalized the elementary school. That was you, my friend."

"How many times do I gotta say I'm sorry?"

"It's not enough."

He snorts. "So much for repentance."

Clenching my fists, I check my temper. "If you were truly sorry, you'd cut the attitude."

"One's got nothing to do with the other."

"How can you say that? Every action has consequences. You trash the school, you've got to pay the consequences."

With both hands, he shoves his textbook toward me, pencil flying into the air. "And you're not gonna let it go."

"Let it go? You have no idea the repercussions of your little stunt. What you do effects other people, Michael."

"Like you?"

"Yeah, like me. Like your mom. She subs at that school, you know. How do you think the teachers are looking at her?"

"You're such a hypocrite. You don't even want her there."

"That's beside the point. We're not talking about me here. We're talking about you and your thoughtless actions."

"Forget it," he says with a sneer, jumping up from his seat. "You guys should have stopped after Taylor. Seems she got your goodie-goodie gene." He shoulders past me.

Breath short, I hang my head and search for scripture to grasp onto. What is his problem? We've been over this so many times I've lost count. When will he learn to take responsibility?

"What was that all about?"

Tricia's voice behind me draws me up. "Nothing."

"It looked like something to me." She arches an eyebrow. A challenge?

Heat crawls up my neck. "He's…difficult."

"You've all been through a lot lately." She steps past me and retrieves a glass from the cabinet. "I'm guessing Taylor's accident is just as hard on him as it is on you and Cor."

"It's not that. This has been going on—" The ringing of the landline cuts me off. It's after nine. I don't think I can take another church emergency. When it stops, I assume Corey got it in the bedroom. "Anyway, his behavior isn't recent. I'm sure Corey told you what happened last year. You know, the vandalism—"

"Yes." Filling her glass at the sink, she glances at me. "But that was out of character for him, wasn't it?"

Pushing a hand through my hair, I rest my hip on the door jamb. "That's when it all started. But since then… He was always on the honor roll until then." I shake my head. "It doesn't make sense. He could get straight A's without any effort. In fact, he has to work at flunking out."

"It's obvious he's angry with you. So, what'd you do?" Is that suspicion lurking in her eyes?

"Nothing. I mean, maybe I've been a little busier at work, but nothing to warrant this attitude. I don't know, I—"

"Paul." Corey's panicked tone has my heart tripling. She rushes into the kitchen, arm flailing as she tries to shove it into the sleeve of a sweater. "That was the hospital on the phone. We need to go."

Chapter 7

Corey

Taylor doesn't look any different than she did when we left the hospital late this afternoon, and disappointment has tears burning my nose and eyes.

"I tried to explain to your wife on the phone that she's still unresponsive," the on-call doctor tells Paul. "Taylor gave the staff quite a scare tonight."

"I don't understand how this happened," Paul says.

"The nursing staff can't be in the room at all times," the doctor explains, his attention on Paul. "Somehow, even with her hands mitted and tied down, she managed to rip out her feeding tube and ventilator. This isn't the way we would have liked to test her capacity to breathe on her own, but it doesn't change anything."

He doesn't bother to look at me. Does he think I'm some kind of a moron for rushing down here tonight? "Will she still have to have a tracheotomy?"

"No, of course not. She's breathing fine without the ventilator." His tone reminds me of a kindergarten teacher explaining the basic fundamentals to a five-year-old.

"Then something's *changed*, hasn't it?" I ignore Paul's warning nudge. Maybe it's exhaustion prodding me to challenge this man, or maybe I know my daughter better than he does. "She heard Dr. Nielson earlier today and decided to take matters into her own hands."

Paul tucks me into his side. "It really doesn't matter. What's done is done."

Doctor Snooty leaves as a nurse steps up to check Taylor's vitals. "Be encouraged," she says. "This is a great sign. Taylor had the nursing staff a little freaked out, but the physical therapists are celebrating."

I reach out and stroke Taylor's pink cheek. "Why's that?"

"It shows us two things. Strength of character and healthy brain activity." She flashes me a smile that makes up for the doctor's attitude. "We're calling her Little Houdini." She flicks the tube running from the drip bag and resets the machine before leaving.

Slipping a finger around a strand of Taylor's silky soft hair, I look up at Paul. "She's going to wake up anytime, Paul, I just know it." The thought of it quickens my pulse. Will she remember everything that led up to her accident? Dr. Nielson told us that she won't wake up talking and walking, like coma patients do in the movies, but who knows how long before her memory returns?

"I'm sure she will, babe," he says around a huge yawn. "But I doubt it's going to happen tonight. Let's go home and get some sleep. We can come back first thing in the morning for a couple hours."

I shake my head. "She'll be scared if she wakes up and I'm not here."

He rubs the back of his neck. "Corey, I still need to work on the message for Sunday. And the board's called a meeting for Monday night I'm not prepared for."

"Why don't you have Mark do the message? Isn't that the whole point of an associate pastor?"

"I can't. This is something I need to do."

"*This*," I say, tilting my head toward Taylor, "is something you need to do." How can his job be more important than his daughter?

"Visiting hours are over, babe."

"I'm not a visitor. I'm her mother." And I want to spend every moment possible with her before my Great Shame comes crashing down on us.

"Look, Cor—"

"You go." It'll be easier with him gone anyway. Keeping up pretenses with him watching my every move makes me edgy.

"What?"

"No, really. I'll be fine. If you can't come back in the morning, I'm sure Tricia will come down the hill and pick me up. Besides, Michael will want to come tomorrow, since there's no school."

Paul stuffs his hands into the front pockets of his slacks. "He has community service tomorrow."

"He's almost done. I'm sure the manager at the thrift store will cut him a little slack."

"I want him to finish it up so he can start working to pay back the restitution."

I keep my eyes on Taylor when I roll them big enough to draw envy from an eleven-year-old. Why does Paul have to push Michael so hard? And why, for heaven's sake, does he *always* have to win an argument? "I'll call you when she wakes up."

"Fine. I'm too tired to argue with you." He drops a kiss onto my head, and I keep my back to him as he shuffles out.

Tension I wasn't aware of eases from my shoulders. I lean over Taylor's bed and buss her cheek with a kiss before following Paul out in search of a nurse. There must be some kind of chair-bed available and maybe a blanket and pillow.

As tired as I am, I could curl up on the pristine linoleum floor and sleep about a year.

Within ten minutes, a young man in scrubs rolls a pink vinyl-upholstered chaise into the room. "I'll be back with some blankets and a pillow."

"Oh, this'll be fine. I don't want to be a bother."

"No bother. It gets pretty cold here at night."

"Well, if you're sure."

He's halfway to the door when he turns around. "She's going to be fine."

"Excuse me?"

He points to Taylor. "Your daughter. Everyone's talking about what she did earlier. We see restless coma patients, but what she did took some strategy. Very cool."

He's back in a few minutes with bleach-white blankets and a pillow. "You won't get much sleep with the nurses popping in here constantly, but at least you'll be more comfortable."

After he leaves, I rummage through my purse in search of the toothbrush and floss I stashed there on our first visit to the hospital and slip into the sterile steel bathroom. The fluorescent lighting above the mirror is unflattering, but even knowing that, I'm shocked by my appearance. Forty-one isn't looking good these days, with exhaustion etched in the bags beneath my eyes and my pale complexion.

But it doesn't matter, because Taylor will be awake before morning.

Aside from the glow of a soft light above Taylor's bed, the room is bathed in darkness. The chaise brings back memories of the futon in Paul's first apartment, with its serviceable upholstery and lack of cushion. Everything was so simple back then. I knew right from wrong, drilled into me by my staunch, by-the-book father.

And yet, here I am facing the consequences of disobedience. And I've dragged my daughter right along with me. But then, if things were different, she wouldn't even be here, would have never been born. Somehow, I don't think Paul's going to see the irony in that. Tricia urged me to tell him everything. *Now*. But how? His reaction toward Michael after getting into trouble is just how my dad reacted whenever my brother got out of line. How my dad would have reacted if he'd known of my Great Shame.

A shiver skitters up my spine.

Did I sense that about Paul? Is that why I got cold feet at the last moment and almost backed out of the wedding only a week before we said our vows? Is that why I was so easily swayed to party with Tricia when I should have been working on seating charts and wedding favors? Paul preaches forgiveness, but there's a side of him that seems to take every mistake as a personal affront. Michael is the perfect example.

If he can't forgive Michael for a juvenile mistake, how will he ever forgive me? Maybe he'll never speak to me again. What if he wants a divorce?

Questions swirl around in my mind, accompanied by the beep, beep, beep of Taylor's heart monitor, making sleep impossible. I'm so tired, it hurts. Tension hums throughout my body and my head won't stop spinning. Scenarios play, one after another, of Paul's reaction when he learns of my unfaithfulness. When he discovers Taylor isn't his biological daughter.

My stomach roils.

God forgive me, please. I've made such a mess of things. Please don't let Taylor suffer for my sin. I know I don't deserve it, but I beg You to walk me through this nightmare. But God's silent. A fog of guilt separates Him from me.

Reaching into my purse on the floor beside me, I rummage around for my cell phone. It's been three hours since Paul left, so I must have slept some, even though exhaustion still crushes me like a lead weight. Thumbing through the apps, I tap the little Bible and wait for it to load—all of ten seconds. Incredible. Psalms is where I go when my mind is too fuddled to find the words for prayer. There is comfort in David's brokenness and sin. A man after God's own heart—that's how he's described—and yet he was unfaithful too.

But there's no comfort to be had for me tonight. The verses flitter away, forgotten, as soon as I read them. Condemnation is a heavy cloak snuffing out any peace I might draw from God's Word.

"Repent," my dad would say.

Tricia said the same thing, sort of. "Tell him. You're making yourself sick with worry. The sooner he knows, the sooner he'll get over it."

Or not.

I'm so lost in my own little pity party, the noises coming from Taylor's bed don't register at first. Not the shuffling of limbs and sheets I've grown accustomed to, but instead grunts and groans. Is she trying to talk?

I stumble off the chaise and trip over the blanket encircling my stockinged feet as I rush to Taylor's bedside, my phone skipping across the floor.

"Taylor?" Leaning over the metal rail, I place my hand on her forehead then on a rosy cheek, my heart hammering so hard, I can't draw a decent breath. "Wake up, sweetheart."

Her eyelids flutter. Have they done that before? Maybe. I don't know. Then a grunt escapes tightened lips. Okay, that's new. I glance at the monitor, as if I know what to look for. Everything I know about hospitals I learned from reruns of *House*. Not at all comforting.

More grunts and groans. Head moving. Legs pumping.

I don't want to leave Taylor's side, but I can't find a call button. "I'll be right back, sweetheart. Hang on." The ridiculousness of my command shocks a giggle from me.

Rushing out of the room, I scramble for balance on the slick hospital-polished floor and grab the attention of two nurses—neither of whom I recognize—working behind the low lights of the station. "She's waking. I think my daughter is waking up."

"Let's have a look," the older nurse says.

"Don't you think you should call the doctor?"

"I will, Mrs. Shaffer. Let's just be sure first." She moves at an easy pace to align with her calm tone, but I don't bother to wait for her to catch up.

My eyes search out Taylor's before I reach her side, breath held, willing her to be awake. Her eyelids move again, but this time, I see a slit of an opening. "Hey, Tay. Wake up, sweetie. Can you hear me?"

The stout nurse, identified as Joan by her name tag, steps up to the other side. She glances at Taylor then focuses on the monitor. "Heartbeat's increasing," she mumbles.

"That's good, right? That means she's waking." Excitement climbs up my throat and I fight the urge to squeal like a little girl. In this precious moment, I push away any thoughts of doom and gloom.

Love trumps fear every time.

Joan adjusts Taylor's blanket before moving to the end of the bed. "I'll page Dr. Reynolds."

Dr. Snooty, she means. "Can't we call Dr. Nielson? I mean, isn't this important enough—"

"Don't let Dr. Reynolds rattle you. Dr. Nielson will be here first thing in the morning. I'll be right back."

Taylor's hand moves beneath mine, just the tiniest flutter, like the butterfly kisses I once brushed on her cheek to work a giggle from her. I'm grinning so big, my cheeks hurt. If only Paul were here.

Glancing around the floor, I spot my phone. I snatch it up and move back to Taylor's side. Taking her hand in mine, eyes on hers, I thumb our phone number. It rings once, twice, three times.

∼

Paul

The circle of light from a reading lamp is the only thing that dispels the shroud of darkness in my office. I check the clock —three a.m.—and press my fingers against blurry eyes. Sleep's been sporadic, filled with anxiety—over Taylor, issues at church, arguments with Michael, Simpson, Alexis. Can't remember the last time I slept a full night—long before Taylor's accident—and weariness fogs my brain like a drug.

I shove at the papers that pool my desk—disorganized notes for Sunday's message overshadowed by letters that reek of blackmail. Corey's right. Maybe I should pass the responsibility to Mark. He can whip up something to speak on in no time. That's his job, right? But then I'll look weak when facing the board Monday night. Of course, if I speak unprepared and the message bombs—

The ringing of the phone startles me, and adrenaline pulses through my veins as Rambo materializes from beneath the desk. It can only be Corey. A quick glance at the caller ID proves me right. "Yeah, Cor?"

"She's waking up." Her tone hovers at a level only dogs can hear.

I smile past the sudden moisture that blurs my vision. "You're sure?"

She sniffles. "Positive. Can you come?"

"On my way. Give her a kiss for me."

Coffee. Black. That's what I'll need to get down the hill. Gathering up the mess on my desk is all it takes to wipe the silly grin off my face. I should have told Corey, but with everything else...it doesn't matter. Somehow, someway, it'll get handled. I shove the notes into my laptop case, lock the vile letters in the bottom drawer, and push out of my seat.

I'm tempted to forget the coffee and head out, but I'll

regret it before I'm ten miles down the highway. Setting the coffee to brew, I jot a note to Tricia and Michael, check the thermostat, and collect my coat, Rambo shadowing my every move. Rain and wind pelt the windows sending a chill up my back.

But Taylor's awake, which is more than enough to dispel the dreariness of the night.

Standing over the coffee maker, I tap impatient fingers. Come *on*. The spit and gurgle tells me it's about done, and I snatch up the pot. After filling two travel mugs with hot coffee, I doctor one with chocolate syrup and milk, just as Corey likes it.

Rambo rushes to the door with me, tail wagging, black eyes watching me with expectation—like he shares in the excitement. "She's awake." I ruffle his head before heading out.

The car's parked in the driveway, and I duck my head against the cold, fat raindrops as I cross to the driver's side. It takes some maneuvering to secure the armload—coffees in holders, iPad, coat—and my impatience increases the challenge.

Traffic's non-existent. Who in their right mind would be out at this hour in this weather? I tune the receiver to talk radio and let my mind drift. The windshield wipers *thwump* back and forth, mesmerizing, hypnotic, and I roll the window down just enough to feel the chill on my face. One accident per decade's enough.

It's all I can do to stay alert enough to make it to the hospital, but forty-five minutes after backing out of the driveway, I pull into the parking lot, coffee mug empty. Lights beckon me, and I gather up Corey's travel cup and my iPad—in case I have a chance to work on the message.

The hospital is eerily quiet, the silence occasionally punctured by the squeak of a nurse or doctor traversing the corridors on rubber-soled shoes. The lights are low, shadowing the recesses of the halls and waiting rooms. No one hanging out at this hour. I press the elevator call button, its immediate ding startling. My heart picks up a beat with each floor I ascend. When the doors whoosh open on the fifth floor, my stomach flips, like I've just topped the peak of a roller coaster.

Breaching the closed doors of the Neuro-ICU department slows me down. I press the call button and wait. Feels like an eternity. I tap my phone against my thigh, patience thin now that I'm so close. Should I call Corey? Would that speed up the process? I dial her number then hit END before it rings through. Just wait. When the doors open, I'm greeted with the sight of staff scurrying in and out of Taylor's room.

So, it's true. *Thank You, God.*

Corey's standing in the same place I left her over five hours before. Difference is, now a smile lights her face. After giving her outstretched hand a squeeze, I wrap an arm around her and concentrate on Taylor. Her eyes are open, but no focus or recognition.

"Taylor?" I choke out her name and try to make eye contact. There's a nurse taking vitals, another checking her drip line.

"She's awake," Corey says, hugging my arm. "I told you she'd wake up."

She's awake. But that's it. There's no spark of recognition. No life behind the blank look. Fear knots my stomach and lodges a rock in my throat. "Is she okay?"

"She's awake," Corey whispers. "Dr. Reynolds says it's perfectly normal for her to look…well…" She turns teary eyes on me. "For her to look lost. Remember Dr. Nielson said she wouldn't wake up talking."

But he didn't say she'd appear brain dead.

Chapter 8

Corey

The "step-down" unit Taylor's in to await transfer to the rehabilitation hospital is much smaller than her ICU room. Maybe it just feels that way because there are too many people crammed into it, like a tin of sardines. Rain runs in rivulets down the lone window, obscuring the parking lot view. Taylor sits up in bed and looks almost normal, aside from the mitts on her hands, neck brace, and spiked hair on one side of her head.

And the fact that she doesn't talk—at least not in any language we can decipher.

"Zetipo nishimini chabot," she mutters, as I drape the pink bathrobe I brought from home around her shoulders, leaving her arms free. A PICC line runs from her right forearm, connected to a drip line, and I'm careful not to disturb it. Taking her hand in mine, I run a thumb across her dry and jagged cuticles.

"What'd she say?" Michael stands at the end of the bed, camera slung around his neck, and looks at her like she sprouted wings.

Paul and I flank one side of her, Josh the other, and Tricia occupies the only chair. We all look at each other—I suppose, with the hope that one of us can translate.

Paul grips the bed rail. "Dr. Nielson said it'll take some time for her to find her voice."

Josh shrugs. "I think it's kinda cool."

The neck brace will be her constant companion until she can tell someone she doesn't need it. Does it make it hard to swallow? My own throat constricts in sympathy. I reach out and hook a strand of silky brown hair behind her ear, hoping to draw her attention. But she stares straight ahead, a slight catatonic daze. No recognition. Her face has taken on the resemblance of a Picasso painting I remember from college— eyes that are askew, a smile that doesn't work.

Guilt makes it hard to breathe, hard to look Paul in the face. And if I can't look at him, how can I ever bear to face Taylor?

The utter joy I felt when Taylor woke is being chipped away, minute piece by minute piece, like an artist sculpting to the core of his masterpiece to reveal deep-seated anxiety. She's awake, yes, but she's not my daughter. How can my daughter possibly come back from this shell of a girl? I don't dare utter my fears, as if to do so will make them true.

"You know," Michael says, pointing at Taylor's hair, "she might like that. It's kinda the in thing."

"Don't give her any ideas," Tricia says.

The two visitors at a time rule doesn't apply here, and word's gotten out—Taylor's awake. Her friends have been parading in, one after the other, sporting excited grins and stuffed animals. But when reality hits a scant few minutes later, they stare at their feet and make excuses to leave, grins gone, arms empty after depositing their furry friends on any available surface.

It's Sunday, which I imagine contributes to the number of kids able to make the forty-five-minute drive from Placerville.

It didn't take much persuasion to talk Paul into skipping church this morning and accompanying us to the hospital. He's been quiet—too quiet. I'd like to chalk it up to exhaustion or the fact that Taylor has a long road ahead. When my own guilt leeches in, I think maybe he found Taylor's lab report, that I didn't do such a good job of hiding it in a shoe box on the top shelf of the bedroom closet. But if that were true, he'd be anything but quiet.

Lorraine, Taylor's nurse, hustles into the room, shaking her head at the row of colorful animals propped in the corner. "How're we all doing here?"

Michael grunts out a chuckle. "Taylor's learned a foreign language since she woke."

"If only we could interpret," Lorraine shoots back. She edges her way past Josh, who steps against the wall to give her space. "Just want to check her fluids." She fiddles with the I.V. "Is she being transferred to the on-site rehabilitation center?"

"There's no room," Paul says. "We've chosen Mercy General. I think they're moving her Tuesday."

Lorraine nods. "She'll be in good hands. The folks there know their stuff."

Michael looks through the lens of his camera and snaps a couple pictures.

I shake my head. "Taylor would be pitching a fit if she could."

He snaps a couple more. "I'm going to put together an album for her. A kind of before and after. Smile," he says to me. *Snap.*

Tricia reaches out and pushes the camera down. "Just because she can't protest…I certainly wouldn't want someone taking pictures of me at my worst."

"But that's the whole point." He lifts the camera again, pointing it at Josh. "When she's back to her old self, she'll want to see what she went through."

"Don't count on it," Lorraine mutters.

"I gotta go," Josh says. "I told my dad I'd meet him in the lobby five minutes ago." He reaches out to touch Taylor's arm, but she pulls away and tucks her fist into her armpit. He drops his eyes and shrugs, backing away from the bed. I want to say something to let him know it'll be okay as I watch him exit. But my own doubt will communicate a hollow assurance.

Focused on Josh, Lorraine's shout of, "*No*," has my heart leaping as my head whips around to see Taylor gripping the PICC line, the mitt on her lap. Before I can stop her, she rips it out, eyes glued to Lorraine's horror-stricken face as blood spurts from her arm.

We all shuffle into the elevator like a herd of cattle, stunned into silence. At least, I'm stunned. Who would have thought Taylor could shift from catatonic to rebellious in the time it takes to light a match?

"This is a good thing," Lorraine had assured us earlier, as we stood around the bed, mouths gaping.

"She could have done serious damage," Paul responded, incredulous. "How is anything about this good?" I gripped his hand in warning.

Lorraine didn't seem to take offense as she swabbed Taylor's arm. "She had to think through every step to get that PICC line out. First, she knew she couldn't succeed with the mitt on, which is pretty clear thinking as far as I'm concerned. Then to get it off?" She looked at Paul and grinned. "Brilliant."

"Well, I'm glad you're amused." Paul's smile took the sting from his words. "How are you going to be sure she doesn't do it again?" He took Taylor's hand, bending down as if attempting eye contact with her.

"There are no guarantees, but we'll do the best we can."

"That's not good enough," Paul growled. I was with him on this one.

"It never is," she said.

It was Tricia who suggested we leave. The sooner there were no distractions, the sooner Taylor would sleep. We thought that would slow her down until Michael reminded us that she was in a coma when she pulled out her ventilator and feeding tube.

Now we step out of the hospital, a stiff wind battering us as we make our way to the car. I shiver and pull my coat tighter, sinking into Paul's side when he wraps a protective arm around me. But it's not the February weather that has me dragging my feet.

"I don't want to leave her," I confess through chattering teeth.

"You keep pushing yourself, babe, and you'll make yourself sick. She's going to need you more when they transfer her to Mercy."

"Paul's right," Tricia says. "She'll be fine."

I'm not convinced. Mother's intuition or an overactive imagination? The visual of blood spurting from her arm makes my stomach flip. Maybe if I stay—who's going to watch over her?

We reach the car and Paul takes his arm from me to retrieve the keys. I hesitate, eyes back on the hospital.

"Come on, Corey." Paul fingers a loose strand of hair from my face. "The staff are trained for this."

"It didn't stop her from ripping out that line."

"You can't watch her every minute." He opens my door and waits.

We pile in, me in the passenger seat, Michael and Tricia in the back. Paul gets behind the wheel and starts the engine.

"Besides, Mom," Michael says. "You told me you'd help me with algebra."

Paul looks over at me, eyes widening, then peers into the

rear-view mirror. "Glad to see you're taking your homework seriously."

I wince, sure Michael's going to take that comment wrong, and wait for the comeback. It seems everything Paul and Michael say to each other has some underlying meaning I'm not privy to.

"I'm not doin' it for you."

There it is.

"Good," Paul says, maneuvering through the parking lot. "I'd rather you do it for you. College isn't that far off."

"It is for me, 'cause I'm not going."

Paul pulls out into traffic. "Of course you are."

"So, Tricia," I say, shifting in my seat to see her. "What do you think about putting together a little care package for Taylor?"

"What do you have in mind?"

"Well, her cuticles are pretty ragged. I thought we could pick out some nail polish, give her a little mani-pedi."

"Sounds great. I have a new color I picked up in New York."

"That's right, you must be anxious to get home. How long have you been gone now?"

"Three weeks. My assistant is feeling a little overwhelmed. Once Tay's in the rehab hospital, I'll head home. I should have had the spring line out by now."

Paul and Michael are blessedly silent, and I breathe a sigh of relief. The queen of distraction. I've spent the better part of my life playing the shell game of life. Keep changing the subject and pretty soon, the thread of conversation is shifted.

"You can't make me go to college."

Or not.

Paul's knuckles tighten on the steering wheel. "What do you expect to do with your life without college?"

"Uh, photography." There's an edge to his voice—an intonation that communicates with crystal clarity that Paul is clueless. The height of disrespect.

"Michael," I warn. "You might want to—"

"Photography?" Paul snorts. Oh, why does he allow Michael to push his buttons? "I'm not supporting some starving artist."

"I don't expect you to."

"Hey, Cor," Tricia cuts in. "Maybe once Taylor's out of rehab, you girls could come down for a long weekend. We could take walks on the beach. There's a new restaurant I'd love to take you to."

Bless Tricia.

"Sounds great."

Paul clears his throat. "How do you propose to support yourself, Michael? Photography, just like any other artistic endeavor, takes time to perfect."

"I'll get a job." He all but tacks on a "duh."

"A job? Why don't we start with the restitution you promised to pay off? A thousand dollars."

Rubbing at a headache forming between my eyes, I scrunch down in my seat.

"You'll get your money," Michael says. "What's the big deal, anyway?"

"The big deal?" Paul slams the steering wheel, and I jump. "The big deal is that I might lose my job thanks to your lamebrain stunt. Is that big enough for you?"

Silence.

It takes a moment for me to put all the pieces together—Paul's inability to forgive Michael for vandalizing the school and the anger that's evident whenever the issue comes up. His distraction when at home and preoccupation with work. It all fits.

And if Paul's job is on the line because of a juvenile act, what will happen when the truth of Taylor's accident comes out?

~

Paul

The first time Corey and I got into an argument, a month into our marriage, she gave me the cold-shoulder treatment for days. It didn't bother me too much—I preferred quiet anyway. But now, eighteen years into our marriage, her stony silence makes me nervous. She's not just stewing, she's thinking. And when she's done thinking, she'll have plenty to say.

When we get home, I pull the car into the garage and glance at Corey, but she's got avoidance down to a science.

"Get your algebra book, Michael, and meet me in the dining room in ten," she says, climbing out of the car.

"Will do." He passes me like I'm invisible, and I follow him to the door leading into the house and hold it open for the ladies.

Tricia pats me on the arm as she passes and gives me an apologetic smile. I don't know what *she* has to be sorry about, but the fact that she is doesn't bode well for me. She and Corey are connected like Siamese twins. Whatever Corey feels, Tricia's aware of it.

"Dinner will be ready in about forty-five minutes." Corey doesn't bother to look at me. The ETA on dinner is the only thing she's said to me since I lit into Michael.

There's not much point in trying to talk to her yet. She's not done processing, and I have a little of my own to do, so I hide out in my office.

Easing behind my desk, I click into my email and watch message after message load. The usual Sunday evening activity—perusing the reviews. What grade will Mark get for his efforts? Critics happy to share their opinions. In one of my lighter moods, I thought about tacking a grading chart on the back wall of the church along with a stack of stars to be placed by the members: one star—poor; two stars—fair; three stars—good; four stars—excellent. But I'm not secure enough to share my reviews with the entire congregation.

Of course, a chart's not necessary for most. They're not shy about letting me know how they feel. Only ten emails today—and nine of them are positive. I have to admit, it stings to see my associate get better reviews. What does that say about the body? What does that say about *me*?

I whittle away the better part of a half hour returning emails and planning how I'll answer to the board tomorrow night. I glance through the letters I'd locked in my bottom drawer. Better to keep them to myself for now.

I'm not looking forward to dinner. Not with the silent treatment I'm sure to face. But skipping it? That'll show weakness.

The smell of cooking wafts down the hallway the moment I open the office door. We've been living on mystery casseroles since Taylor's accident, thanks to the kindness of the church ladies, and I'm grateful. But what I wouldn't give for a recognizable meal. I can't tell if I'm eating chicken, tuna, turkey…tofu.

The table's set with cloth napkins, cut flowers, and lit candles. Maybe I'm not in as much trouble as I thought.

"Well, isn't this nice?" I say to anyone who'll acknowledge me.

Corey carries in a casserole dish, hands covered by hot mitts, much like those Taylor's wearing. "Tricia did it." She sets the food onto a trivet and returns to the kitchen, passing Tricia on her way out.

"I thought we should celebrate Taylor's transition." She sets a salad and rolls on the table. "I'll go get Michael."

I follow Corey to the kitchen, where she's scrubbing at the tile counter with enough gusto to take out the grout, and stand at the entrance. "Look, Corey, we need—"

"Are we gonna eat?" Michael calls from the dining room, plopping into a chair.

"Hold your horses, kiddo," Tricia says, ruffling his hair.

It's then I notice his hair. When'd he get it cut and how did I miss it? I'm tempted to comment on it, but all it'll get me is more attitude.

Dinner's an awkward affair, and I'm grateful when it's interrupted by a phone call from Mark. I excuse myself and escape back into my cave until the house is quiet.

The wood floor squeaks as I step into our bedroom, expecting to find Corey sound asleep—or at least faking it. Instead, the room is bathed in soft light emanating from the pair of reading lamps on our nightstands. Knees drawn up to hold her book, Corey's propped up on pillows, head down, hair spilling forward. Her reading glasses, black-framed, sit on the end of her nose. And she never looked cuter.

"Hi," I say, testing the waters.

She takes the frames off and looks at me, her blue eyes filled with something I can't quite read. Concern? Sadness? Whatever it is, it's not anger.

"Why didn't you tell me your job's in jeopardy?"

Closing the door, I move across the room. The bed frame squeaks when I sit at Corey's feet. "I shouldn't have said anything."

She slams her book closed and tosses it aside with a sigh. "You're so missing the point. How long has this been going on? Close to a year?"

"What? No. It's only been a couple weeks."

"Then how can it be Michael's fault?"

"Simple. The board received letters from some of the families in the church who are asking for my resignation. Their main issue is that I can't control my kid."

She leans forward, brows marred. "But, Paul, that was almost a year ago."

"So?"

"So, why did they wait this long? If it's such a concern,

wouldn't they have been up in arms about it right after it happened?"

Realization hits me upside the head like a sledgehammer. As a rule, dissension spreads through a congregation with tornado-like speed, churning everything, or every*one* in its wake. But if Michael wasn't the catalyst, what was?

Suspicion sours my stomach. But at least knowing my opponent gives me a fighting chance. No way I'm going down without a fight.

I take hold of Corey's shoulders, lean in and plant a big kiss on her lips. "You're brilliant, babe."

Chapter 9

Paul

Conversation and laughter float down the hall as I step through the side door of the church offices—voices of board members I handpicked. Men whose lives I've been part of for going on ten years. Chuck, who shoots hoops with me twice a month. Gary and Bill, my staunchest supporters when enacting changes. Dan, who I counseled along with his wife through a tough time in their marriage. Jeff and Wayne, miracle workers with the finances. And Ben, my accountability partner. These men are my friends.

And yet, it feels like I'm walking to my execution.

Mark moves past me. "You ready?"

I grunt a non-committal answer and follow him into the meeting room. The guys mill around, doctoring their coffee and dipping into danishes from a pink bakery box. Dorothy, super secretary, strikes again. She seems to think no meeting would be official without carb-loaded sweets.

"Hey, Paul." Ben's voice booms out. "How's Taylor doing?"

Conversations cease and the focus homes in on me, like I

have a bullseye on my forehead. "She'll be transferred to Mercy General tomorrow. In-patient rehab." I move through the bodies to the coffee carafe as the guys within arm's length pat me on the back.

Dan reaches past me to dip into the bakery box and pulls out glaze-covered dough. "Mark said she shows promise as an illusionist."

I can't help but chuckle. "Yeah. The hospital staff's nick-named her Little Houdini." The horror of watching her rip out her PICC line yesterday's been replaced with a keen sense of pride at her spunk. That's my girl.

I'm asked a few more questions about her progress as we take our seats around the table. Although there's plenty of space in the room, the walls close in on me. I don't want to think about all I have to lose. They can't force me out, but without their support, staying would be tough.

Chuck, who keeps the minutes, plops a notebook on the table, takes a sip from his cup, and clears his throat. "I'm sure Paul would much rather be with his family right now, so the sooner we get this meeting started, the sooner he's back with them." His balding head is glistening with sweat. Not a good sign.

"You know," Mark says, "this meeting wouldn't even be necessary if it weren't for Simpson trying to usurp authority here."

"True." Gary pushes his hand through graying hair, shoulders slumped. "But the fact remains, his accusations aren't without biblical merit. And he's got eleven other families backing him in this."

Resting folded hands on the table, I rein in my temper. Biblical merit? I can't argue with that. But it reeks of a set up, and I'd bet my last meal the real culprit isn't Simpson.

"First Timothy three, four and five," Gary continues, opening his well-worn Bible and marking his place with a finger. "One who rules his own house well, having his children in submission with all reverence—for if a man does not know how to rule his own house, how will he take care of the church of God?"

"I hate to say it," Wayne scratches a brow, "but these twelve families, well, they're the financial backbone of this church. Without their contribution—"

"We're sunk," Jeff finishes.

"Sunk?" I scan each member in the room. "A little melodramatic, don't you think? I started with about a hundred and fifty members ten years ago. We've got, what?" I look at Mark.

"About a thousand, give or take."

I nod. "A thousand. And you're going to tell me twelve families are the financial backbone?"

Jeff leans in. "Unhappy members are like a cancer. It might start small but look out. It'll spread."

Mark pounds a fist on the table. "You guys seem to forget who's really in charge here, and it's not Simpson or his army." He points a thumb at me. "It's not even Paul."

"That may be." Dan shakes his head, eyes downcast. "But like Gary said, his accusations have biblical merit, even if we don't agree with his methods."

I straighten my shoulders and take a deep breath. "So, why now?"

"What's that?" Wayne asks.

I lean on my elbows. "Michael messed up, I'll grant you that. And it's obvious I didn't have control of the situation." I make eye contact with each man and hold their attention for a beat before moving on. "But that happened almost a year ago. So, why'd it take so long for Simpson to bring this to the board?"

Dead silence for a moment.

"Good question," Mark says, thrumming his fingers on the table. "Anyone bother to ask Simpson that?"

Grumbling ensues around the table but brings no clear answer.

"That's not the only complaint, Paul." Gary slides a sheet of paper across the table to me. A bulleted list of offenses along with two rows of six signatures at the bottom.

I peruse the accusations, most of which are laughable. "This is ridiculous." Then my eyes light on number seven. "They want me out because my wife works part time."

"Their logic is that if Corey had been home instead of teaching, Michael wouldn't have gotten into trouble in the first place," Gary says.

I flick the paper back at him. "Look, guys, you know this is bogus. Attack me all you want but leave Corey out of this. She's a great mom. They want to push me out, fine."

"No one can push you out," Mark says. "Unless you let them."

Pinching the bridge of my nose, I weigh my options. A little time, that's what I need. "With Taylor just coming out of the coma and facing weeks of rehab, Corey's not going to be working for a while."

Gary clears his throat. "She's not going to be able to do much for the women's ministry, either."

Chuck raps his knuckles on the table. "Even Simpson isn't going to raise a ruckus because Corey's tending to her recuperating daughter."

Maybe not. But Taylor's recovery is only a short distraction. What we need is a permanent solution.

Corey

The rainstorm of the weekend has passed, and the clear night sky is bathed with stars—a proverbial light show for anyone who takes the time to look up. If it weren't Tricia's last night with us, I'd be researching traumatic brain injury from the websites Taylor's doctor gave me today. Or maybe I'd be snuggled under my down comforter, the latest romance novel keeping me company along with a cup of hot chocolate. For certain, I wouldn't be walking in the thirty-five-degree chill of the night.

I zip up my down coat, take hold of Rambo's leash in gloved hands, and look at Tricia. "Which way?"

"Let's walk downtown. It always looks like something out of a Thomas Kinkade painting at night."

"Where do you think he got his inspiration?" A slight breeze carries with it the comforting aroma of wood burning, puffs of smoke drifting from the neighbors' chimneys. I draw the scent into my lungs and hold it there for the brief moment it allows me to forget the spiderweb of lies I'm living.

Stopping to let Rambo sniff, I look at Trish. "I wish you weren't going home tomorrow."

"Taylor's going to be fine, you know."

I can't do more than nod for the lump that cuts off my words when I remember leaving Taylor at the hospital earlier today. She was sitting in a wheelchair, tugging at the neck brace still in place. It has to remain until she can tell them she's okay. Will that day ever come?

I ran my hand over the shorn part of her head, praying she would make eye contact with me, look at me—something.

"It'll be easier after they move her." Paul slid his hand up under my hair and squeezed my neck.

"Do you...do you think she'll ever be the same again?"

Before Paul could answer, Lorraine came in with an armful of clean sheets. "You'll be amazed," she said. "I'm telling you, the girl's got spunk."

"We have to go, babe," Paul whispered against my temple. "I have to get some things done before the board meeting."

Leaning down at eye level with Taylor, I kissed her forehead. "We'll see you tomorrow. Okay?"

"Okay," she said, clear as day.

With a squeal of excitement, I looked from Paul to Lorraine then back at Taylor. "Did you hear that?"

Paul grinned. "She talked."

"Automatic response." Lorraine dumped the sheets on the end of the bed. "She didn't have to think about it. That's normal. Once she's in rehab, it'll happen more and more until she's jabbering away like always."

Cupping Taylor's chin in my hand, I looked into her eyes. "I can't wait."

I shake my head now to dislodge the memory. "It's not just Taylor."

Tricia nudges my arm with an elbow. "You're going to be fine, too."

"You know what Paul's doing right now?"

"Attending a board meeting. At least that's what he said when he left tonight."

"It's not just a board meeting," I say. "He's defending his position. There's a group demanding his resignation."

"Because of Michael?"

"How'd you know?"

"Aside from his outburst driving home from the hospital yesterday, Paul said something when I walked in on him and Michael arguing the other day that clued me in."

I sigh. "It sounds like you knew about this before me. They're *saying* it's because of Michael."

"But?"

"It doesn't make sense. It's been almost a year. Why would they wait this long to make such a stink about it?"

"Did you ask Paul?"

"Yes."

"And? What'd he say?"

I smile and tuck away his affectionate response for a later time. It might come in handy when he's spitting mad at me. When he might view every past intimate moment as an act of betrayal, because that's what went through my mind as we made love last night. Every day I hold back the truth is just one more deception.

"He said I was brilliant." I shrug. "I'm not sure what he meant by it. I can't imagine what it'll do to him if he's forced out. He's spent the last ten years building up that church, working ridiculous hours for even more ridiculous pay."

"You guys have weathered storms before."

"It feels like a tsunami's coming." I blow out a breath and watch the cold of it evaporate into the dark. Our lives are as fragile as that puff of air. "Paul asked me to find someone besides Rebecca Simpson to handle the ladies' Bible study. In fact, he *told* me to find someone else. I was irritated because it felt like he was manipulating me."

"So? You find someone else. It's not worth a battle, is it?"

"It's too late. I'd already given her everything." I glance at her. "What was I supposed to do? I had no idea what his problem was, and I wasn't about to get in the middle of something."

"I'm sure he'll deal with it."

"It turns out Rebecca's husband is the one who's raising such a stink about Michael."

"That's not good." She nudges me with her elbow. "When are you going to tell him the truth?"

"About Rebecca?"

"No."

"It's been a year since Michael's incident." I glance at her. "A *year*. Did Paul sound like he'd forgiven him yesterday in the car?"

"It'll only get harder."

"Paul's not the only one who's going to have a fit over this —not that he doesn't have every right. But how will I explain it to Taylor?"

We turn the corner to Main Street, lit up with old-fashioned streetlamps—iron and glass domes—that give an air of a simpler time. Aside from the occasional restaurant, the shops are closed, but interior lights glow to showcase unique window decor. And the bell tower, Placerville's historic nod to the volunteer firefighters more than a hundred and fifty years before, looms large in the middle of downtown.

We stop in front of a clothing boutique that reminds me of Tricia's. "You'll be happy to get back to your shop, I bet."

"Have you told your family about Taylor?"

I keep my eyes on the vintage-style dress draped on an emaciated mannequin. "It's complicated."

"That's what I thought. I thought it was strange that there haven't been phone calls back and forth."

"I told them she'd been in an accident but didn't let on how serious it is. I can't face them right now."

"Your dad can't read minds, you know."

Tugging on Rambo's leash, I start walking again. "Maybe not, but I don't doubt he can read my face."

"And when they learn the truth?"

"I might as well save it all up and hit them with it at once. Who knows? I might have to move back home."

"That'll never happen."

"You don't know that."

"If it gets that bad, you can come live with me. It'll be like the old days."

I laugh despite myself. "We didn't live in luxury in the old days."

Tricia shrugs. "That's just location. Carmel, Placerville, or Indiana—it doesn't matter much. Wherever I am, you always have a home there."

Chapter 10

Paul

The first time I heard Corey laugh, it hit me—she's The One. It was a crisp fall day—the kind that makes me think pumpkins and leaf raking. Wheaton College, Indiana. A time when anything was possible. Liberal Studies and English—a double major—and the excitement in her voice when she talked about wanting to teach...well, it was the same for me and preaching. But over the years, the demands of my calling took precedence over the dreams of her youth.

And last night, I all but agreed the status quo would remain. To keep the dissension beasts at bay, I threw her to the lions.

Pulling on a sweatshirt, I pad out of the bedroom on bare feet. I close the door, but leave it unlatched and make a straight shot for the thermostat. The house is cave dark and about as cold. I would much rather stoke up the wood stove, but we won't be around long enough to keep it stocked.

Taylor will be moved to the rehabilitation hospital today. Her doctor assured us that this is where the real work begins. It'll be a full-time job for Corey over the next several weeks.

She won't have time to even think about going back to work. And when the time comes that she can...we'll deal with it then.

I turn on the hood light above the stove and get the coffee brewing. After unplugging my iPad from its charger, I pull up Yahoo and sit at the kitchen table to check out the headlines. Some are pertinent, others just a waste of space. But isn't that the way of the world?

When the coffee maker beeps, I get to work on Corey's mocha. I would have braved the cold to hit Starbucks, but it's not worth the risk I might run into a church member. Last night's meeting went my way, but I'm still hanging by a thread, and it leaves me raw.

Coffee mug in each hand, I toe open the bedroom door and almost trip over Rambo in a hurry to get out. Corey's still sound asleep. Maybe this wasn't such a good idea. Placing both cups on her nightstand, I look at her in the dawn light turning the room into shades of gray. She's on her back, only her head poking out from the layer of blankets, hair in a tangle on her pillow.

I finger a strand of hair off her face and nudge her cheek with my lips. "Babe?" I whisper.

"Hmmm?" she sighs.

"Brought you a mocha." I sit at her hip. "Extra chocolate."

"Why're you whispering?"

"Didn't know I was."

"What time is it?"

"A little after six."

"We're not going to the hospital for," lines of concentration appear between her brows, "five hours."

"I'm heading to the church to get a little work done first. I thought you might want to know how the board meeting went."

"Oh." Eyes now open, her arms emerge from her cocoon

to push the covers back. Sitting up, she blinks a couple times. "You should have woken me when you got home last night. I never heard you come in."

"I didn't have the heart. You were zonked." I retrieve her coffee and hand it to her.

"Mmm. Thanks." She takes the mug in both hands, sips, and sighs. "Now tell me what happened."

"Bottom line, the board's backing me. Thanks to you."

"Me?" With the mug still in one hand, she pushes a strand of hair behind her ear. "What did I have to do with it?"

"You," I say, planting a kiss on her nose, "asked the question we should have all thought of. Why wait this long to make such a stink about Michael?"

"So it's over?" It's not relief in her voice, but what? Concern? Fear?

"Well…for the time being. Simpson's not going to just back off."

She scowls. "What's his problem anyway?"

"I don't know." But I've got my suspicions. One who's quick with an accusation often has the most to hide. "We're not going to worry about it right now. Our baby girl's going into rehab today. We need to focus on her."

Corey places her mug on the nightstand and takes my hands. "Listen, Paul. There's something I need to tell you." Her eyes flicker away from mine, and I tense. "I…I didn't get someone else to facilitate the Bible study class."

"But—"

"I know you told me to." She holds tight to my hands when I try to pull away. "Please listen."

Slow to anger. Quick to hear. It hasn't been my go-to verse lately. I take a deep breath. "I'm listening."

"I'd already given everything to Rebecca. I had no idea her husband was causing problems in the church. But even if I had, I don't know how I could have asked her to return it all without making things worse. And really," she adds, tugging on my hands, "I don't think she has anything to do with this."

"How could she not, Corey? She must know what he's up to."

She drops her eyes and shrugs. "Not necessarily. It's not like you shared this whole mess with me until you were in the thick of it."

The truth of it is too logical to argue. And I don't want to argue—there's no point. "You're right. I should have told you."

"I…"

"What?"

She shakes her head. "Nothing."

"You sure? Everything out in the open from now on. Remember?"

"I was just going to offer to make you some breakfast while you shower."

"That'd be great." But as I head into the bathroom, the tension I felt earlier remains. Could be because I still haven't told her everything, but…

What isn't Corey telling me?

∾

Corey

We slip through the double glass doors and down the long hall to reach the reception area. The walls are painted what once might have been a soothing green but now appears tired—like a woman faded with the loss of her youth. The decor wasn't important to us when we chose this hospital for Taylor's rehab —we focused on the professionalism of the staff and the quoted success rate. This is not an institution that puts more value on appearances than it does results.

The U-shaped front desk is ripe with activity as receptionists, nurses, and therapists, dressed in colorful hospital scrubs, interact. The wall across from the desk is plastered with a whiteboard to rival any classroom—charted activity for patients. When we viewed the facility last week, we were told that we could walk in and be informed about Taylor's whereabouts at any given time—once she starts therapy. Although I'm not expecting to see her name, I scan the whiteboard, nonetheless.

"Do you think Taylor's here yet?" I ask Paul, shifting the overnight bag from one hand to the other.

"In her room," a receptionist informs us, pointing to the room within eagle-eye observation range from the reception desk.

"Let me take that." Paul reaches for the bag, but I hold tight.

"It's fine." There's some comfort in carrying Taylor's things.

Taylor, wearing a hospital gown, neck brace still in place, sits in her wheelchair across from the speech therapist we were introduced to on our previous visit. Veronica. Dark hair, olive complexion, and a very white smile. She's holding a piece of what appears to be a sandwich. As we step up to the doorway, I hold my breath. We were told yesterday that the first thing they'd do is a swallow test. If Taylor was unable to pass that, a feeding tube would be reinserted.

"Do you like egg salad, Taylor?" Veronica offers the sandwich.

Taylor opens her mouth like a baby bird, accepting the food.

She's eating. Thank You, God. My hand covers my lips to stifle the whoop of sheer joy. But I can't stifle the tears as Paul's arm snakes around my waist and pulls me close. Not wanting to distract Taylor from the first meal she's had in more than a week, we don't move.

Before Veronica can offer another bite, Taylor leans

forward and opens her mouth. Her eyes don't appear to be
focused on anything. Veronica gives her another bite then
turns to flash us a smile.

"Good news," she says. "Looks like we can forgo the
feeding tube. Taylor's passed the swallow test."

Paul and I step into the large, private room as Taylor
finishes her sandwich. In the center is a hospital bed with a
blue cage attached—it looks like a miniature version of a
bounce house—next to a hospital-issue nightstand. A toilet
and sink are tucked into one corner with only a curtain for
privacy. Dresser drawers take up half a wall, an empty cork
board above it.

"Not quite like home," I murmur to Paul.

He gives me a one-armed hug. "It could be worse."

"I think that's enough activity for one morning," Veronica
says. "I'll call a nurse in to put Taylor to bed, and we can
discuss her care."

I kneel in front of my daughter and attempt to make eye
contact. "Her eyes…" I glance at Veronica, who's observing.

"They're a little askew," she says. "Right now, it's causing
double-vision which makes it hard to make any kind of eye
contact. That'll change with a little time."

Double vision? I can't even imagine it.

Paul points to the bed. "What's with the cage?"

"It's to keep Taylor protected. She's not able to walk on
her own yet, so we don't want her to stumble out of bed.
Once she's mobile, the cage will be removed."

Paul's eyes widen. "It seems to me that she'll be better
protected tucked into a cage once she's mobile."

Veronica grimaces. "It's considered inhumane to cage a
mobile person. We have to adhere to the letter of the law.
Ahh. Here's Nancy now."

A young nurse takes my place in front of Taylor. "We're
going to put you down for a nap now, okay, Miss Taylor?" She
wheels the chair to the far side of the bed and points to the

bag I'm still holding. "Did you bring her some things from home?"

"Oh, yes." I place the bag on a chair in the corner next to the nightstand. "We were told to bring a few pair of sweats and socks." Rummaging in the bag, I pull out Taylor's stuffed dog—a childhood toy she keeps on her bed. "And Toto."

Nancy unzips the cage. "Toto?"

"Her *Wizard of Oz* phase," Paul says.

Veronica touches my arm and waves her hand toward the doorway. "Why don't we step out into the hall?" she suggests. "I'll answer any questions you might have."

Nancy wraps her arms around Taylor and pulls her into a standing position. "I'll get her changed."

I reach into the bag. "I put some underwear in here, too."

"It'll be a while before she needs those," she says. "She'll be wearing diapers for some time."

"Diapers?"

"Just until we get her potty trained."

Paul grasps my upper arm. "It'll be fine, Corey. Let's step out and talk to Veronica."

Diapers? Potty trained? How could I have been so naive about how bad this is?

"How can you guarantee her safety?" The tone of Paul's voice pulls me from my own stupor. "Do you know they called her Little Houdini in the ICU? And that was while she was still in a coma."

"You have to understand, Mr. Shaffer, that we deal with all stages of rehabilitation from both traumatic brain injury and stroke. We're equipped to deal with whatever challenges Taylor throws our way."

"How can you be sure she won't escape?"

"We have a monitor attached to her chair. If she opens any of the three doors leading out of the hospital, an alarm will sound."

Paul rubs his forehead. "I don't know."

"How..." My voice catches and I have to start over. "How is it possible that she'll ever be normal again? I mean, diapers, and...and..."

"Let's sit." Veronica waves her arm to indicate a group of chairs at the other end of the reception area.

Paul takes my hand and squeezes.

"You'll be amazed at Taylor's progress," Veronica says. "It seems overwhelming right now, but day by day, the neurons in her brain will regenerate. If she were ten years older," she shrugs, "the outcome wouldn't be so positive."

Paul nods. "That's what we were told at the hospital. But to see her this way..." He looks toward Taylor's room as if he can see her through the wall.

"Taylor is young, which is in her favor, but it's still a slow process. You'll see great improvement here, but there will be months of rehabilitation after she's discharged."

"Months?" Somehow, I thought once Taylor left here, she'd be recovered. More naiveté.

"Has anyone discussed the complications that may occur during the recovery period?"

I shrug. "We were given a website, so I've done some research. But to be honest, the information was pretty subjective."

"That's because each patient is different, depending on the degree of damage."

Paul clears his throat. "We read that there can be issues with anger and depression."

"Yes. Traumatic Brain Injury causes a chemical imbalance, so that's possible. Also, once the recovery begins, it's hard for the patient to come to terms with the loss, which also causes anger and frustration."

"The loss?" I glance at Paul then back to Veronica. If only she knew how much Taylor lost.

"Yes. The more intelligent the patient, the greater the frustration. She'll be aware of her limitations and will know that it wasn't always this way."

"But that's temporary, right?" Paul asks.

Veronica nods slowly. "To some extent, yes. But some things aren't temporary, such as problems with short-term memory, maybe some long-term memory, as well."

"Long-term memory?" Was it possible Taylor may not even remember what set this off?

"Initially, yes. She'll regain most of it as she recovers. Chances are she won't ever remember the first few weeks here at the facility or even the accident itself."

"What about before the accident?" Guilt makes it difficult to look at Paul. My own shame as well as the selfish hope that this could all blow over without me saying a word to Paul.

"It just depends. She may have permanently lost time before the accident."

Relief slows my breathing. Is it possible?

"Of course, if there's an emotional attachment to those memories, chances are she'll recover them in time."

An emotional attachment is an understatement. How can I be so selfish as to even imagine this accident can benefit me? What kind of a mother thinks that way?

"She may also exhibit issues with impulse control and social coping skills."

Paul rests his elbows on his knees. "Like what?"

"The loss of a filter system, so to speak." She rests her elbows on her knees and clasps her hands. "We sometimes have thoughts enter our minds—that woman's dress looks terrible on her, or he's overweight—but we don't voice those out loud because we know it would be inappropriate. When someone suffers a brain injury, that system is often haywire for a while."

Paul offers me a weak smile. "Just when you think you have them raised."

Chapter 11

Corey

Within a week, our routine is set. I drive down to Sacramento each morning to spend the day with Taylor while Paul goes to work. Saturdays we'll both go, and Sunday, which is visitor's day, Michael will join us. Visitors aren't allowed on any other day—those are workdays, and patient routines cannot be interrupted.

The first day of week two, I arrive at the hospital just as Nora, the physical therapist, is wheeling Taylor into the gym.

"Would you like to join us?" Her smile is engaging.

"What's on the agenda today? Kickboxing or weightlifting?"

Nora laughs. "I think we'll start with rolling the ball back and forth. You can be the third. We'll start weightlifting next week."

Nora settles Taylor onto the carpeted floor while I watch, unsure what to do. "Can I help?"

"Yeah. Why don't you sit down here?" She indicates a spot across from Taylor before retrieving a ball resembling one the children use at school to play four-square. Nora joins us on the floor with a groan and a smile. "You ready, Taylor?"

Taylor moves her head and tugs at the neck brace. Is it a nod of agreement or coincidence? She appears anything but ready, her legs straight out in front of her, hands fidgeting with the brace.

"Here goes." Nora nudges the ball to Taylor, aiming for her right side rather than allowing it to hit her feet.

It sits at her hip and she looks at the ball then to Nora then me, as if asking for directions.

"Take the ball and roll it to your mom." When the spot between Taylor's eyebrows wrinkles, Nora crawls over to her and places the ball in her hands. "It might be easier if you open your legs." She eases Taylor's ankles apart and places the ball in the V of her legs. "Let's roll the ball to your mom." She places Taylor's hands on the ball and helps her push it to me.

"Good job, Tay." Amazing how such a simple act fills me with excitement. I stretch to my side to reach the ball then return it. This time, Taylor knows what to do.

Twenty minutes later, we wheel Taylor back to her room. "It's a slow process, isn't it?" Even though Veronica warned me, it's disheartening.

Nora gives me a sympathetic smile. "You'll be amazed how fast she'll progress. It didn't take her any time to catch on to the ball rolling. That will only improve. She was fortunate she didn't sustain any physical damage in the accident. The more active she is now, the more oxygen moves through her brain and regenerates those important neurons."

When we're left alone in Taylor's room, I sit on the bed and smooth her bangs off her forehead. "I wish I knew what you're thinking, sweetie pie. You've always been such a talker, this new you is a little daunting."

Taylor's eyes catch mine for a moment and hold. She opens her mouth as if she's going to speak, and my breath catches in anticipation. But all that comes out is soft gibberish

—baby talk. Her eyes are beginning to lose the catatonic glaze and, even though they're still a little off kilter, her focus seems improved.

"Guess what I brought?" Retrieving my purse from the dresser, I pull out a large envelope and settle next to her on the bed. I take out the 4 x 6 photos I collected the evening before and offer them to Taylor.

She doesn't take them but gazes up at me.

"They're pictures." I shuffle through them and find one of her. "Do you know who this is?"

One side of her mouth lifts as she touches it.

"That's you. And this one—" I slip the last photo to the top. "This is your brother, Michael." No response. We go through the other three, but again, no response.

"That's okay." I gather them up, fighting the tears that clog my throat. "We'll put them up on your bulletin board. You'll remember them in time." Using the push pins lined up along the edge of the board, I pin them up in a row, taking a moment to appreciate each one.

I sit through another of the therapy sessions, this time with the occupational therapist, Mason. He sits on the floor with Taylor and places a Tupperware Shape-O-Ball in front of her —a toy she had when she was eighteen months old. She picks up a plastic square and attempts to force it through the octagon shape, twisting it back and forth, her chin thrust out in determination. Her accuracy rate was much better as a toddler than it is now.

"If it doesn't fit, Taylor, you need to try another hole." Mason puts his hand over hers and, along with the death-gripped shape, moves it to the proper opening and guides it through.

Taylor snatches an oblong block from the floor and tries to shove it into the circle hole. When Mason attempts to pull her hand away, Taylor's chin thrusts out again and her eyebrows draw together—a look of determination I recognize from her terrible-two stage. She pulls away from Mason and continues to twist the shape until she has it partway in, then pounds it with her fist until it goes through.

"I guess that's one way to do it," Mason says with a shake of his head. "The hard way."

I swallow a sigh. So much to relearn. How will she ever be the same as before her accident?

By three o'clock, Taylor's exhausted. The nurse tucks her into bed and smiles at me. "She's a breath of fresh air around here."

I look at my daughter, her face so young and innocent, and a well of emotion swells in my chest. It's getting harder each day to walk away from her.

I thank the nurse as she leaves, then move to the side of the bed. "I have to go now, sweetheart, but I'll be back tomorrow." I bend down to kiss Taylor's cheek, and her arms come around my neck, pulling me into a tight hug—as if my leaving is just as hard for her as it is for me. I hold her close, eyes brimming with tears of joy. This is the first contact Taylor's initiated since the accident. And just as quick as she hugs me, she lets go.

"I love you, baby." I kiss her forehead and lay my hand against her cheek as she gives me a funny half smile.

∼

Paul

With the board's decision to back me, the tension that's been my constant companion over the last few weeks eases. I set aside my concern over Taylor for the time it takes to get through yet another counseling session with the McCartys. I'm not an advocate of divorce, but if I were...

"You didn't listen to a word I said." Jenna McCarty's voice bounces off the walls of my office. After twelve years of screaming at Craig, I'm sure she's right—he's not listening anymore. My suggestions for professional counseling have been met with blank stares of confusion.

"Not true." Craig might be talking, but he's checked out. A mere vestige of the man Jenna married. "We've been over this so many times, Jenna. I don't know what you want."

"Want?' The pitch of her voice shoots through the roof. "What I *want* is for you to never have slept with that...that tramp." Her spittle speckles my desk.

Time to take charge. Be the voice of reason. Again.

"Listen, folks." I check my tone—strong, but compassionate. "We're not getting anywhere. You two have gone round and round with this." I give Jenna a pointed look. "Until forgiveness begins, there can be no healing."

Jenna slumps back in her chair, head down, like a rag doll. "I've tried." Her voice wobbles, and I check the edge of my desk for tissues. I should buy stock. "But every time I close my eyes, I see"—she waves a dismissive hand toward Craig —"them. Together."

Craig grabs the edge of my desk and leans toward me. "The affair, that's not the real issue here."

Jenna looks at him like he's morphed into Satan. "Of *course* it's the issue. If it hadn't happened, we wouldn't be here."

"If it hadn't happened, *I* wouldn't be here," Craig growls at her.

"What's that supposed to mean?"

He shakes his head, defeat in the droop of his shoulders.

"Jenna." I wait until I have her attention. "I think what Craig is trying to tell you is that the affair is a symptom of something deeper. If your marriage had been healthy, he wouldn't have slipped."

She's shaking her head before I even finish. "That's his excuse."

"It's the truth," Craig mutters. "You harp on me all the

time. I can't do anything right. I don't bring home enough money *and* I work too much. You can't have it both ways. And when I *am* home, you talk to me like one of the kids." He shrugs. "I can't win."

"I don't—"

"And the worst part is the kids. Why should they respect me if you don't?"

"No," Jenna whispers, eyes welling. "That's not true. The kids love you. Nathan thinks—"

"Nathan talks to me like you do." Craig shoots her a glare. "Like I'm nothing."

Now we're getting somewhere.

A rap on the door, and Dorothy pokes her head in. "I'm sorry, pastor, but there's someone here who insists on seeing you."

You've got to be kidding. "I'm a little busy here."

"I told her, but," she throws a glance behind her and lowers her voice, "she's insistent."

Leaning over in my chair, I look through the crack in the door made by Dorothy's head. Is that...? It is.

Alexis Andrews.

"Tell her I'm not available. If she needs to see me, she'll have to make an appointment." One I don't intend to keep.

Dorothy looks at me like I've sealed her doom before closing the door. I should give serious thought to raising her pay.

"Sorry, folks. Craig, finish what you were trying to communicate."

I try to tuck away my irritation with Alexis, but a rock sits in my gut. Does the woman have no boundaries?

The session continues for another thirty minutes, and for the first time, I'm optimistic.

"We've made some strides here." I stand to let them know we're done for now. "I know I've suggested it before, but I think you might be better off finding a marriage counselor. I have the names of a couple great Christian therapists."

Craig looks at Jenna, eyebrows raised. She responds with a slight head shake, and I know I'm in for the duration. Not my forte.

I walk the McCartys out of my office, afraid Alexis is camped out on Dorothy's desk. But aside from Dorothy gathering up her things, the coast is clear.

"You make that appointment for her?"

Dorothy sighs. "She wouldn't make one. Just said she'll come by another time." She throws the strap of her purse over a shoulder and looks at me with a shake of her graying curls. "What is it with that woman?"

I'll take that as a rhetorical question.

"She's not even a congregant anymore, but she has no problem bossing people around." She marches around her desk, indignation stiffening her spine. "Oh." She stops and turns to me. "I called Drew Simpson like you asked. He wouldn't make an appointment, either, but said he'll drop by and talk to you soon. No one makes appointments anymore," she mutters.

"Thanks." I'm not looking forward to that confrontation, but it has to be done.

"I'd watch my back with that woman," Dorothy says. "She's trouble with a capital T."

That's what I'm afraid of. Just maybe, Simpson will shed some light on that situation.

Chapter 12

Corey

I'm schizophrenic. Maybe paranoid, too. There are moments I'm sure of what it is I need to do—go to Paul, tell him everything, and trust that God will catch me when I fall. But do I truly trust Him? Then in the next instant, fear makes it difficult to walk and breathe, let alone lay the whole sordid mess out for Paul's evisceration—maybe God's too. It makes it easier to focus on Taylor and get lost in the fantasy that her phys lab report isn't burning a hole in a Keds shoe box up in my closet.

I drag myself through the door at 4:45 to an exuberant Rambo. "Hey, boy, aren't you getting enough attention around here?"

"As if," Michael mumbles from the corner of the family room, where he sits in front of the computer. "He's relentless."

"Relentless?" I drop my purse onto the couch and grimace at the layer of dust that covers the coffee table. "What is that, a new vocab word?"

"Very funny."

Stepping up behind him, I try to ruffle his hair, but he

dodges my hand. Is that cigarette smoke I smell? "What are you doing?"

"Did you know Benjamin Franklin played a huge part in us winning the Revolutionary War? He was, like, the ambassador to France or something."

Okay, who is this kid? "What's with you lately? Every night I come home and you're doing homework. I mean, don't get me wrong, I'm thrilled."

He shrugs. "I like history."

"And math? And English? And if I'm not mistaken, you were writing a report for science yesterday."

"Thought that's what you and Dad wanted."

"Just makes me a little suspicious is all." I'm starting to sound like Paul. "Keep up the good work. I'm going to get dinner started."

After a detour to the bathroom, I head for the kitchen. Dishes from the morning are still piled into the sink. Does no one else know how to load a dishwasher? With a heavy sigh, I squirt dish soap onto the mess and wait for the water to turn hot.

"Hey, Mom." Michael's voice from the entrance startles me. "I gotta talk to you about something."

His furrowed brow and serious demeanor has me turning off the water and facing him, hip resting on the counter. He's hiding something behind his back—an F paper that needs signing, or a detention notice? I prepare myself. What other reason could he have for this sudden interest in homework?

Take a deep breath and stay calm. "Okay, I'm listening."

Instead of an official notice or graded assignment, he hands me a brochure. "What's this?" Black, red, and orange jump out at me—pleasing to the eyes. It's titled SOCAPA in large black print. Underneath is *School of Creative & Performing Arts*.

He shrugs. "Mr. McGinty, my history teacher, gave it to

me a couple weeks ago. He noticed how much I like photography and thought I could go."

I flip through the brochure. "Summer camp?"

"I know it's kinda expensive, but they have financial aid—"

"It's not just that, Michael." I trace my finger over the campus cities. "The closest is Los Angeles."

"Yeah. But New York would be way cooler."

"And way more expensive," I say with a sigh. There's no way Paul's going to approve this. Not by the way things have been between them. "What about last year? Will they let you in with that on your record?"

"Mr. McGinty's offered to write a letter of recommendation. If I get my grades up."

"Ahh." I nod. "This sudden interest in school."

"Yeah." He shrugs. "But I checked with all my teachers, and with extra credit…"

The last time I saw his baby blues light up like Christmas morning was…never. How can I disappoint him? I do an internal cringe when I think of how Paul will react. "Your dad —" That's all it takes to snuff out the light.

"Yeah, I know." There's an edge to his tone. The muscles in his jaw tighten, and he looks like the spitting image of a young, angry Paul. "But you can talk to him, can't you?"

"Your timing stinks, son."

"Mr. McGinty said this could open doors for me."

I tap the brochure on the counter and study my shoes. What I wouldn't give to assure Michael that he stands a chance. "You want to tell me why you're so angry with your dad?"

He drops his head, feet shuffling. "I told you before, he doesn't understand me."

"To be honest, neither do I."

"Yeah, but you're not on me all the time."

"He's worried about you." I wish I believed that was the only reason. "He loves you, you know."

"He cares more about what people think if I mess up."

"He's living in a fishbowl, kiddo. We all are." And once the truth about Taylor is out, the focus will no longer be on Michael.

"Please, Mom."

I look up at his pleading eyes.

"Just talk to him for me."

"What about the restitution you owe?"

"I only have ten more hours of community service, then I'll get a job."

"I don't know, Michael."

"Craig at the Pit 'n' Stop's already told me he'll hire me as soon as I get my work permit stuff done."

"It's not just that, sweetie." I turn to rest my backside on the counter and fold my arms, the brochure hanging from one hand. "All this stuff with Taylor—"

"It won't take any of your time. I promise. I'll even help around the house more."

I picture Michael with a dust rag, but it's too bizarre an image to hold onto. "Okay, I'll talk to your dad."

He grins, stuffing his hands into his pockets.

"But don't get your hopes up."

"Okay." He turns to leave, and the stale scent of cigarette is unmistakable.

"And Michael?" I wait until I have his attention. "If your dad says no, promise me you won't go back down that road?"

His brow furrows. "What road?"

"This road of self-destruction you've been flirting with over the last year."

He scowls. "That was, like, a year ago."

"I don't mean the vandalism."

"Then what?"

I hesitate. He doesn't need two parents on his case, but to

ignore it won't do him any favors. "Cigarette smoke. I've smelled it on your clothes off and on lately."

"What?" He waves a dismissive hand. "I don't smoke."

I want to believe him and just leave it at that. My usual M.O. "It's kind of hard to miss. I'm surprised your dad hasn't called you on it."

"Dan smokes. You know, Dan Porter? I hung out with him after school today."

I choose to believe him. To push further would be tantamount to calling him a liar.

I'm a lot of things, but a hypocrite isn't one of them.

~

Paul

It's after eight before I pull my car into the driveway. Long day, long night. I got a call earlier that John Pendleton, a long-standing congregant and loyal supporter, suffered a stroke. His wife, Beverly, feared the worst and was inconsolable after sixty-two years of marriage.

"What will I do if he dies?" Her faded-gray eyes had swum with unshed tears as we sat in the hospital waiting room surrounded by their five children.

"Let's not go there yet," I said. A month ago, I would have been practical—if he dies, he'll be in his eternal home. What could be better for him? And that still holds true. But after Taylor's accident...well, it's not so easy to think in practical terms. Great for John, but what about Beverly?

It reminds me of Dad raising me and Justine alone. I never thought about how hard it was on him. I just knew it was hard on me.

I'm pondering this as I turn off the car ignition. If Corey were to go before me, how would I handle it? And it's not the cooking and the cleaning and the laundry—the everyday mundane tasks she accomplishes without a whisper of complaint. It would be like losing a huge chunk of myself.

The house is quiet when I enter through the garage door. Corey told me on the phone that she needed to talk to me, and I half expect her to be waiting for me, along with Rambo. But nothing. The living room is dark, but a dim light shines from the kitchen. The toaster oven hums, and inside, a foil-covered plate. My dinner.

No Corey in the bedroom or my office. I open the basement door to a pitch-black void. The last place I expect to find her is in Taylor's room, but light's beaming on the hall carpet past the door that's ajar. I push it farther open and poke my head through. Corey's sitting on Taylor's bed hugging a stuffed animal to her chest, Rambo sleeping along her thigh.

"Hey." I step inside.

She looks at me and blinks, as if coming awake. "Hey."

Rambo's head pops up and he gives a little yip of greeting. I scratch his ear while bending over to give Corey a kiss.

"Are you hungry? I kept your dinner warm."

"In a minute." Sitting at Corey's other side, I slip my arm around her hip. "What're you doing in here? Not worrying, I hope."

She shakes her head and smiles. "Just thinking about Taylor. I thought I might repaint her room before she comes home."

"When're you going to squeeze that into your schedule?"

"I don't know. But we talked about it before...you know. Lavender and mint."

"Excuse me?"

"The colors she wanted. Lavender and mint."

"Sounds like potpourri."

She laughs and pulls away to look at me. "What do you know about potpourri?"

I nuzzle her neck, breathing in the clean shampoo scent of her hair. "I know it smells." Lavender and mint. I can't quite picture it. Taylor's room's been pink since forever. Pink and white—girlish and innocent. Just the way I like to think of her.

"How's John?"

"It doesn't look good. Beverly's a mess."

"I'm not surprised. They've been together their whole lives." She reaches out and fingers my wedding ring.

"Sixty-two years."

"Sixty-two years." She sighs.

I take a deep breath. "So, is that what you wanted to talk to me about?"

"Hmm?"

"Painting Taylor's room? Is that why you're hiding away in here?"

"Oh, no. I came in here to collect a few things to take to the hospital tomorrow."

"So, what'd you want to talk about?"

Putting a little distance between us, she rubs her hands down her thighs and looks up at me. "Promise you'll hear me out before jumping in?"

Great. I'm on the defensive before we even begin. "Since you put it so eloquently, how can I resist?"

"Promise?"

I put three fingers up. "Scout's honor."

She blows out a breath. "Michael has an opportunity to attend a great summer camp program."

What? Not at all what I expected. "Summer camp?" I can't picture our teen sitting around a campfire singing *Kumbaya.*

"Summer camp with an arts program. His history teacher suggested it. He can learn more about photography—"

"No."

"You promised to hear me out—"

"I can't believe you want to support this asinine idea, Corey." I push up from the bed and stand over her, hands on hips.

"Please, Paul," she says through gritted teeth. "Hear me out."

I throw a hand in the air. "After all we've been through with him, you want to reward that behavior?"

She jumps up and stands her ground. "He's been working really hard to get his grades up. Haven't you noticed?"

"I've noticed that he's taken the initiative to do the work he should have been doing all along. I should have known there was a hidden agenda behind it." Take, take, take. That's all that kid knows.

"What difference does it make if it motivates him to do well?"

"Because as soon as he has his way, it's back to the same crap all over again."

"You can't be serious, Paul." Her voice rises, and Rambo jumps off the bed and hightails it out of the room.

Not a bad idea. I start to follow, and she grabs my arm.

"So, he messed up," she says. "Once. Are you going to punish him for it forever?" Her voice wobbles and tears swim in her eyes.

I harden myself against her emotions. "He owes us a thousand dollars, Cor, and he hasn't even made an attempt to pay it back."

"He has every intention of doing so. He's got a job all lined up, and—"

"Great. Then when the money's repaid, we'll talk."

"Do you have any idea how long it'll take on minimum wage?"

"Not my problem. He should have thought about that before he destroyed someone else's property."

"Wow. Really?" She looks at me like I'm the bad guy here. "What happened to the forgiveness you preach on Sunday mornings?"

"It has nothing to do with forgiving him." My words reverberate off Taylor's cotton candy walls. Seems sacrilegious somehow. I take a deep breath and lower my voice. "I'm trying to teach him about consequences. You want him to think he got away with something?"

Corey stares at me, eyes swimming, face ghost white.

Why do I get the feeling this is about more than Michael?

Chapter 13

Corey

Natural consequences. I was raised on this concept from the time I could walk. There were no shades of gray as far as Dad was concerned—everything was a stark black or white. No equivocating. No negotiating. He had the Old Testament down cold. But grace? That was altogether something different. The fact that redemption came along with Jesus Christ was lost on him.

After my battle with Paul, the old adage that a girl marries someone like her father has never felt truer.

Sleep was sporadic, and I wake dreading the moment I have to face Michael and report back that his father is about as pliable as Mount Rushmore. Although Michael promised no negative repercussions, I'm not hopeful. Being angry enough for both of us makes slinking out of the house while Paul's in the shower seem almost chivalrous. He doesn't want to face me in my current mood.

"You're going with me today, boy," I tell Rambo, who spins in excited circles. I don't know if he understands or is just happy that someone's talking to him. Veronica feels that interaction with a pet will be positive stimulation.

With Rambo's crate loaded and a collection of Taylor's favorite things packed, I make a beeline for Starbucks and a Venti mocha. I need the caffeine just to get my eyes to open. Drive thru or fight the line inside? I opt for going inside so I can contemplate the best pastry selection to kick off the caffeine.

Starbucks is the hot spot before seven, the hoard of people suffocating. Young and old crowd the small coffee shop, some in some semblance of a line, others gathered around tables. The noise level rivals any high school classroom, so when I see Tess Holland flagging me down, it feels as natural as if we'd met at school.

She squeezes in next to me. We're like a before and after photo—and she's the after. Oh, to be young and vibrant again. "Hey, Corey. It's so good to see you. How's Taylor doing?"

"I'm actually on my way to see her now." I give her the condensed version of Taylor's recovery thus far.

"It must be so difficult to watch her go through this."

She doesn't know the half of it.

Her eyes tear and she presses a hand to her flat stomach. The emotionalism, protective move, youthful glow. She's pregnant.

Moving to the front of the line, she orders a decaf mocha.

"How far along are you?"

She flashes a beatific smile. "Thirteen weeks." Her answer floats an octave below the noise level, but I've gotten good at lip reading. It's my secret weapon in the classroom.

"Congratulations. You must be ecstatic." It seems like forever ago I was expecting Taylor. She nods and moves ahead to await her order.

"What can I get you?" The female barista, no more than twenty, sports piercings and tattoos to rival a me rock star.

I order my mocha and a bran muffin—when what I want is a chocolate old-fashioned. She hands me a bag with my muffin, and I join Tess.

"We've sure missed you at school." She leans close to be heard. "It's funny that you're here. I was going to call you."

"Well, if it's about subbing, it'll be a while." Has it only been a few weeks since I was in a classroom? "Maybe not until next school year."

"Next year works for me." She collects her drink from the coffee bar and fingers the lid. "I want to go part-time next year and was hoping you'd be open to team teaching."

Team teaching? "I...well...wow." How perfect would that be?

"You're credentialed, aren't you?"

"Venti mocha for Corey," a faceless voice calls as my drink is placed on the bar.

I take the cardboard cup and cock my head toward the door. "Let's talk outside. It's too noisy in here."

The air is cool but refreshing after the stuffiness of the coffee shop. I walk to a patch of sunshine at the edge of the small parking lot and wait for Tess.

"This is much better," she says. "So, what do you think?"

What do I think? What will *Paul* think after his frustration with my sub position? But I may be getting ahead of myself. "What makes you think I'd be approved for this position? Aren't there tenured teachers waiting in line?"

Sipping her coffee, she shakes her head. "You'd think, wouldn't you? But even if there were others to choose from, you'd be my first choice."

I find that hard to believe.

She pats her still-flat tummy. "I'd need you to be full-time for the first couple of months while I finish up maternity leave, but after that..."

"I haven't even taught, Tess."

"Subbing is way harder, if you ask me. All the work of a teacher without the perks."

"Or responsibilities." Planning, grading, parent-teacher conferences. Paul complains about the time involved with subbing. How will he react to an actual teaching assignment?

"You're the only sub I request, Corey. We teach the same and share the same philosophy. It would be perfect." Raising her eyebrows, she grins. "Well?"

"May I think about it?"

She raises her hand as if to stop me. "No pressure. Take all the time you need."

"All the time I need?" She can't be serious.

"Okay, not *all* the time you need, but I'll try to be patient."

"Give me until Easter break?"

"You got it. And just in case you need a little incentive, come by my classroom any time you want. I'll show you what we've been doing. Maybe you have some ideas for next year."

Paul

Gathering up the stack of papers from a chair in my office, I invite Mark to sit, then dump the whole mess onto my desk to join piles from the previous week. Clutter makes me...edgy. Reminds me of how far behind I'm falling. I haven't even started on Sunday's message. It's hard to be motivated when I'd rather head down to the hospital first thing instead of glad-handing congregants, some of whom would like nothing better than to see me removed.

So much for loyalty.

"So, what's on the agenda?" Mark plops into the chair and shoves aside a clear spot to place his yellow legal pad, then runs his hand across his shaved head.

Flipping open the blinds, ladders of sunlight spotlight my

incompetence—and a layer of dust. "The blood drive is next weekend. You okay with overseeing it this time?"

"Not a problem." He makes a notation on the pad. "You have any idea how much longer Taylor'll be in?"

"We have a meeting with the staff tomorrow. I should know more after that."

"And Sunday?"

"I've got it handled." Not true, but I will. "Back to the blood drive. Maybe Jim can get some help setting up in the sanctuary Saturday morning. If not—"

"We have the men's breakfast. I'll recruit some of the guys before they head out. Then Jim only needs a cleanup crew to prepare for Sunday. He's got it down by now."

"Good." I rake a hand through my hair and peruse my list. "Maybe check with Simon and see if he's okay with toning down the volume for worship on Sunday. Got ten complaints that the music's too loud."

"Too loud, too soft, too contemporary, too many hymns, not enough hymns." Mark shakes his head. "There's always someone complaining."

"What are you going to do? It is what it is."

"That meeting you have with Drew next week. You want me to sit in on it?"

"I could use the support. No telling how things might be misconstrued without a witness."

"Glad to do it."

"I know Easter's still six weeks away, but we should check with Becky and see if she still wants the kids to put on an Easter program."

"She does. I have a list of her thoughts here." He flips through his notes. "First off—"

A knock on the door and Dorothy's face is framed in the opening. "You have a...visitor."

The grimace. The tone. I don't have to ask. "Busy."

"I told her, but—"

"This will only take a minute." Alexis Andrews' voice precedes a momentary struggle for control of the door, and then she appears—perfect hair, perfect makeup, and her perfume stinking up my office.

Dorothy looks to me for direction, determination stamped on her features. Given the word, she'd take Alexis down in a heartbeat. I'm so tempted. "It's okay, Dorothy." But the flip of my stomach tells me different.

Dorothy throws up her hands and, muttering, marches off.

Mark turns from Alexis to look at me, eyebrow raised in question. "You want me to give you a few minutes?"

Not a good idea. "No."

"Yes." Alexis crosses her arms and cocks a hip encased in jeans tight enough to suffocate. "It's personal."

Mark stands, looks from me to Alexis and back again. "Well?"

"Your funeral," Alexis says with a shrug.

Which is worse? Speculation over the meeting or an audience? "Five minutes," I tell Mark. "And leave the door open."

Alexis doesn't sit, but instead places her hands on my desk, arms straight, breasts jutting.

"Have a seat, Ms. Andrews."

"I'd rather stand."

Jaw clenched, I rise from my chair. The last thing I need is her towering over me. No doubt a manipulative move to show power. "You want to tell me what you're up to?"

"Excuse me?" Her eyes go all wide—fake innocence—as she draws herself up to full height. Still working the angles.

I cross my arms, fists clenching. "This business with Drew Simpson."

"I'm not a church member anymore. Or don't you remember asking me to leave?"

This woman could try the patience of a saint. And God knows, I'm no saint. "Get to the point."

"You know Josh and Taylor are pretty tight, right?"

The change of subject has me faltering. What's she getting at? "Uh, yeah."

"*Good* friends."

"Cut the innuendo and tell me why you barged in here."

"You left me no choice."

"Ever hear of making an appointment?"

She shrugs. "We both know you would have wheedled out of it if I did."

I can't argue with that. I make a point of checking my watch. "You have three minutes."

"Fine." She huffs out a breath, mocking my impatience. "It's about Taylor."

I grit my teeth. "Who's not capable of defending herself right now."

Her mascaraed eyes go wide. "You don't think I'm here to talk trash about your precious daughter, do you?"

She'd like nothing better, I'm sure. "Two minutes."

"Okay, okay." She rolls her eyes. "Taylor and Josh are in the same physiology class."

Will she ever get to the point? "So?"

"The day Taylor was in the car accident, her last class was physiology."

I wait.

"With Josh."

"Point?"

"They were doing an experiment on blood typing," she says. "And Taylor wasn't happy about the results. In fact, she argued with the teacher about its accuracy."

I shrug, shake my head.

"Taylor told Josh the experiment *had* to be wrong. There's no way she could be type O."

True. "So, the experiment was wrong."

"Or not." She taps a finger on my desk. "I know how hung up you are on morality. Thought you'd like to know."

Heart thumping so hard it constricts my breathing, I wave

her toward the door. I want to believe she's just spreading lies, but my mind races with all the times I've wondered what Corey isn't telling me.

It doesn't matter. The accusation is ridiculous, and the sooner I talk to Corey about it, the sooner I can put it to rest.

Chapter 14

Corey

It takes a miracle to find a parking space in the covered garage if I don't get to the hospital before 8:30. And thanks to my conversation with Tess, I'm running late. Instead of circling the garage praying for that miracle, I park on the street. It's a hassle to feed the meter every two hours, but what choice do I have?

Tess's offer took the edge off my foul mood after the argument with Paul. Even so, I thought about skipping the day with Taylor—she wouldn't know the difference anyway—but I couldn't. Even if Taylor doesn't need me, I need to see her. Each moment with her cleanses me in some way, makes me a better person just by virtue of being in such an innocent presence. I'm seeking forgiveness for something Taylor has no power to forgive, yet I can almost believe we're starting from scratch—that anything is possible.

Lowering the windows a few inches, I push my sunglasses on top of my head and gather the things I'd collected for Taylor—a pair of pink, fuzzy slipper socks, a drawing pad and colored pencils, and a strawberry crème, which required a detour to yet another Starbucks. But it's Taylor's favorite and allowed by the staff only because it contains no caffeine. Stimulants are bad.

"I'll be back for you in a few," I tell Rambo, who's curled up in his crate at the backend of my CRV.

Arms full and sunglasses back in place, I speed walk down the street toward the hospital. The weather's taken a wonderful turn, almost spring-like in its warmth—a teaser of what's to come. Now if the breeze would just settle.

Mind occupied with the day's agenda, I almost miss the yellow daffodils exploding in the neighboring yards, nearly extinct in the midst of winter-worn garden beds and bumper-to-bumper cars parked along the curb. Traffic's horrendous, everyone in such a rush they can't be bothered to stop at the crosswalk. Do I have to step out in front of moving traffic to get across the street?

Then I see her.

Dressed in baby blue sweats, Taylor heel-walks her wheelchair toward me on the opposite side of the street, oblivious to speeding traffic and the danger she's approaching. Where's her therapist? They didn't bring her out and leave her alone, did they?

Heart pounding, I step into the crosswalk, ignoring oncoming traffic, and receive an angry toot from someone's horn. Without a glance in the direction of the offensive blaring, I keep my focus on Taylor, reaching her less than five feet from the curb. Dumping my stuff onto the sidewalk, I kneel in front of her wheelchair and pull her rigid body into a fierce hug.

"What in the world are you doing out here alone?" I draw back to look at her, my hands running down her arms, touching her cheeks. She seems unharmed.

Taylor's eyes meet mine—no fear, but no recognition either.

My eyes catch a blur behind her. Veronica and Nora are running full speed toward us, relief evident in their eyes.

"Mrs. Shaffer," Veronica says, breathless. "I can't tell you how sorry we are this happened."

"I don't understand." I stand to face the women, my hand resting on Taylor's shoulder, unable to break the connection. "How could you leave her out here unattended?" I wave my free arm toward the ceaseless traffic. "She could have wandered out in that. Or, or…" My mind and heart race in fierce competition, breathing labored. "Or what if some pervert came along and snatched her?" My voice rises with each word until I'm shouting.

"No one left her here." Nora's voice is calm, as if trying to inject some of the same attitude into me. "She walked her chair out of the hospital. It is inexcusable that no one noticed, but that's what happened."

"No…the monitor." I look from one to the other. "You assured us that Taylor had a monitor that would set off an alarm. Didn't it work?" I throw my hands into the air, fear and frustration battling for supremacy. Swallowing the anger and threatening tears, I take a deep breath.

"We're so sorry, Mrs. Shaffer." Veronica pats my arm. "We do have precautions, and given the circumstances, I'm not sure you'll be able to appreciate this." She waits a beat, hesitant. "This is actually a positive move. Don't get me wrong," she rushes to say when I start to argue. "It's not the way we like to see it manifested, but you have to understand. Taylor took off her monitor."

"What?"

"Yep," Nora says. "She's not even walking without assistance, but she located the monitor and removed it from her chair. She had to know what she was doing."

"What are you saying?" My heart rate slows to almost normal level as I stroke Taylor's head.

"She had to *plan* her escape," Nora says.

Veronica jumps in, her eyes lighting with excitement. "She had to make several connections to pull this off. First, when we noticed she was missing, one of the housekeepers told us she'd been staring out the window, as if she wanted to be out here."

"Also," Nora says, "she had to figure out how to get from her room to the outside, which required her to know the configuration of the hallways and outside doors." The enthusiasm in her voice rises. "Not only that, but she must have known the monitor would hinder her escape, then figured out how to eliminate it. We found it on the floor of her room, the strap ripped."

Understanding dawns like the slow rise of the sun, their excitement contagious, and I stare at Taylor in wonder. What's going on in that amazing mind of hers?

"She certainly lives up to her nickname." Veronica squeezes Taylor's shoulder. "Little Houdini."

"Of course, this will require reinforcements." Nora takes the handles of Taylor's chair and turns her back toward the hospital. "She'll need to be on constant watch, the monitor on her chair hidden where she can't see it, and a second one put on her person."

I gather up the discarded items and strawberry crème, which Taylor reaches for without a word. Yesterday I would have been thrilled that she identified it. Today, it seems like a no brainer after her intricate escape. Maybe that stubborn, rebellious nature in my daughter is a gift after all. Taylor's fighting her restrictions, which will only help her improve faster.

But an instant later, that bubbling joy wavers.

Recovery means revelation. And revelation? Well, that could very well be the end of our relationship.

∾

Paul

The wind whips up a pile of dried oak leaves that cling to my slacks like leeches as I head for Marshall Hospital to visit John Pendleton. The sun's about set and the pleasant temperatures of earlier plummet, reminding me it's still winter. I'm itching to get home, put Alexis's ridiculous accusations to rest. Corey and I'll have a good laugh about it. Maybe it'll lighten the tension brought on by last night's pointless summer camp argument. But I promised Beverly and—I check my watch—Corey's just now getting home.

Stepping into the hospital, I cross the lobby and push the up arrow for the elevator, but before it dings, I head back out the door. No way I can focus on the Pendletons with asinine questions crowding out coherent thought. I'll come back out after dinner, after Corey assures me that Alexis is stirring the pot with innuendo and outright lies.

Back in my car and impatient to get home, I gun the engine at a yellow and push the speed limit until I turn onto our tree-lined street. Corey's Honda sits in one side of the driveway, leaving the other open so I can pull my Toyota into the garage. I cut the engine, sit for a moment, and try to pray. Corey will want to know why Alexis is being vindictive. I've kept her out of the loop this long, how will I explain?

The *tick, tick, tick* of the cooling motor fills the otherwise dark silence. Prayers don't come—my head's too full of questions that have no good answers.

Rambo's muffled greeting rouses me from my stupor, and I climb out of the car, briefcase in hand. The barking continues until the door opens just as I reach for it. Rambo pours out, spinning in circles and demanding dibs while Corey steps back to allow me entrance.

"Hey," she says, grinning.

"Hey yourself." I give her the expected peck on the cheek and brush past her. "Do we have time to talk before dinner?"

Closing the door, she leans her backside against it. Her hair's pulled back into a ponytail, lines appearing on her forehead. "I...I guess so." She narrows her eyes. "Is everything okay? You seem upset."

"Is Michael home?"

She shakes her head. "He's talking to Craig at the gas station. You know, he's serious about starting that job. He needs to finish about ten more hours of comm—"

"Let's talk in the living room." I lead the way, dropping my briefcase as we pass the hall and discarding my jacket on the back of the couch. I toss the newspaper I'd left on the couch before leaving for work this morning onto the coffee table and sit.

Corey joins me. "You won't believe what happened at rehab today."

"I want to talk about something else first."

"You *are* upset. What's going on?"

"I had a...a visitor at the church office today."

"Oh?" Brow furrowed, mouth turned down, hands wringing—why should she be nervous? I'm the one dealing with the Wicked Witch of the West.

"It's crazy, really." I fold my hands and rest my elbows on my knees, eyes down. How to explain this. "You know Alexis Andrews. I mean, of course you know Alexis. Anyway, she has this crazy notion—" I shake my head. Ridiculous. How's Corey going to react to such an insulting accusation?

"I...I thought she didn't go to our church anymore." The waver of Corey's voice hits me, her face whitening. Does she know about Alexis?

"Well, she doesn't. But that's beside the point." I wave a dismissive hand. "This is crazy, really. You're going to laugh. She has this asinine notion that Taylor was upset about something that happened in physiology the day of her accident. I mean, she all but blamed the accident on...on this...incident."

"Incident?"

"Something about a lab on blood testing. It's a mistake,

I'm sure. We've been doing the church blood drive for some time, and we both know Taylor's blood type has to be A or B. You're O and I'm AB. It's a class lab, for crying out loud. Of course, it's a mistake."

So why isn't she agreeing with me?

Corey's posture crumples like a deflating balloon, fingers covering her lips, eyes down.

Realization hits. "You know."

"I was going to tell you."

Her tone is so low, I have to lean forward to hear. "Tell me? Corey, this is a mistake." I grab her wrist and tug on it until she looks up, face ashen, eyes welling.

She shakes her head. "I didn't know. I mean, until Taylor showed me, I didn't know."

No. This is some bizarre fluke. But then, Corey would have assured Taylor. "You...I..." Dizzy and breathless, I stand. "What...what are you saying? That Taylor's *not* my daughter? That you...?" I point an accusing finger. "You cheated on me?"

A sob steals her words.

"Look at me."

Her red-rimmed eyes meet mine then flitter away. She wraps her arms around her stomach. "It happened before we were married."

"No." My legs give out, and I drop back onto the couch. "You were a virgin when we married. I...we vowed to wait..."

"I can explain."

"Explain? *Explain?* There is no explanation. You...you slept with someone else right before me."

"I was confused." Face wet, nose running, she lays pleading eyes on me.

"Then you should have come to me, not slept with someone." I'm not Taylor's father. But someone is. "Who was he?"

Sobbing, she shakes her head.

"You won't tell me? Or you don't know?"

"Trish and I, we went to a party. I was drinking. I…I don't remember."

An ache builds in my chest, constricting my breath. "You…I…" Lightheaded, I draw in a deep breath and stand. I stare down at Corey, fists clenched. Words won't come, although questions ricochet through my brain like a runaway bullet.

Corey's tears disgust me, nothing more than a ploy to manipulate. A visceral need to enact violence stabs through me—a red hot knife—and I step back before the temptation to follow through is too much.

Nothing is as it seems.

~

Corey

After Paul storms out of the house, I lock myself away in the bedroom with Rambo. There is no end of tears—just when I think they're spent, I remember the look of disgust on Paul's face…the tone of his voice…the accusations…

My throat is raw, eyes swollen to slits, and I've gone through a half box of tissues when Michael's voice calls out.

"Anyone home? Hey, Mom?"

Locking the bedroom door, I press my face to it. "I'm in here, Michael," I shout, my voice cracking.

"You okay?" His voice comes from the other side of the door.

"I think I have the flu or something. I don't want you to catch it. You'll have to fend for yourself for dinner, okay?"

"Oh. Okay." He hesitates. "Can I get you anything? Soup or tea or something like that?"

"No. Thanks," I manage through another onslaught of tears at his thoughtfulness.

"Where's Dad?"

I swallow and muster a normal tone. "He's working late. Lots to do to catch up."

We have our meeting at the hospital in the morning. Surely, he won't miss it.

"Well, yell if you need anything."

"I will." I take two steps toward the bed and oblivion.

"Oh, Mom?" His voice is just outside the door again.

"Yeah."

"Craig says I can start at the station next weekend. It's only minimum wage, but it's something."

"That's—" I steady my voice. "That's great, sweetheart."

"You talked to Dad, right?"

"Not yet," I lie. "It's…it's been a little busy."

"Oh." He sounds disappointed. "Well, I'll be around if you need anything."

Diving under the covers, I pull Rambo's warm body into my chest and bury my face in his wiry fur. He struggles against me, pulls away, and plops down by my face, his little black nose snuffling at the tears on my cheek.

My cell phone rings, and I ignore it. But maybe it's Paul. Does he feel bad for the way he slammed out of the house? I snake my arm over Rambo and pluck the phone from my nightstand. Tricia. How could she have known?

"Trish?" My voice croaks.

"Cor? Is that you?"

"Oh, Tricia." Snaking my arm out again, I snag a few tissues from the box on my pillow and swipe at my nose. "He knows."

"You told him?"

"No." I sniffle and wipe my eyes. "He found out from someone else. Alexis. You know, the woman you met at the hospital. He's so…angry. Worse than angry. Livid."

"How did this Alexis chick know?"

"Josh." My nose is plugged, my voice nasally. "Taylor's friend. Boyfriend. Whatever."

"He was going to have to find out sooner or later, sweetie." Sympathy laces her words.

"You should have seen how he looked at me. Like I'm… the dirt beneath his feet. Lower than that. The dust mites beneath the dirt beneath his feet."

"He'll get over it."

I shake my head, but she can't see. "I don't think so. I've never seen him like this." Tears well again, and I try to choke them back. "He was shaking, he was so mad. What am I going to do?"

"Give him time, sweetie. He'll come around. He loves you."

"Think about it, Trish. I try to imagine myself in his shoes. But it's worse. It's not just that I slept with someone right before I married him, but Taylor…she's not his daughter."

"Yes, Corey, she is. Biology doesn't matter."

"He wanted to know who he was. The guy, you know?"

"And?"

"Somehow it makes it worse that I don't know. Of course, it makes it worse. What kind of a…" I wave my arm around, looking for the right word.

"Don't go there."

"It's true." I blow my nose, and Rambo escapes to the end of the bed.

"Do you want to come down here for a few days, maybe give him some space?"

"I can't leave Taylor."

"No, I don't suppose—"

Taylor. "Oh, no."

"What?"

"Taylor's going to want to know. How am I supposed to tell her I don't even know who her father is?"

"Look, Cor." Tricia's voice hardens. "*Paul* is her father. The other was just a sperm donor."

"And her mom's a sl…slu…slut," I sob.

"You want me to come up there for a few days? I can get my assistant to cover things here."

"I don't think your being here will help. I don't think anything will." I swipe at the tears. "He's going to leave me, I just know it."

"No, he's not."

"No…I suppose not. What would that do to his image? But if he can't forgive me—"

"You've known about this for how long? Eighteen years?"

"I didn't know Paul wasn't Taylor's dad."

"You had to wonder."

"When I first found out I was pregnant, yes. But it was so long ago, and Taylor's so much like Paul. I just kind of forgot." Out of sight, out of mind. Ignorance is bliss. A number of clichés fit the situation. I suppose that's what makes them clichés.

"Well, Paul's had all of, what, a couple hours to process? Give him time. Besides, he has a few things to answer for himself."

"Like what?"

"Like what's the deal with this Alexis chick? Didn't you wonder why he got all weird when he saw her at the hospital? And why's she coming to him with this information anyway?"

A sledgehammer's going off inside my head, it's hard to breathe, and my eyes are raw from all the crying. I can't think about this right now. Whatever Paul's up to, it can't be any worse than what I did.

Can it?

Chapter 15

Corey

Huddled outside the hospital doors, I push the sleeve of my sweater coat back to check the time. 8:55a.m. I was so sure Paul would come home in time to drive down to Sacramento with me. I waited until the last possible minute before leaving the house. Where did he spend the night? Did he wait until he knew I'd be gone? Is he at the house right now, packing up his things?

Drawing in a deep breath, I push through the glass doors and enter the sterile halls of the rehab center. I'll just have to handle this meeting on my own.

"Mrs. Shaffer. You're right on time." Joy, the patient advocate, waves me into what appears to be a staff lunchroom, where Veronica, Nora, and Mason sit at a table. "Will your husband be joining us?"

"Uh, no. He had an emergency to attend to." I avoid eye contact while taking a seat. Can they tell I'm lying? Probably not. I'm getting pretty good at it.

"Well." Joy sits to my left and lays a folder —Taylor's chart? — on the table in front of her. "We're glad you're here.

Unfortunately, Dr. Holland, Taylor's neuropsychologist, is unable to attend, but we have her notes here."

"Sorry I'm late."

Paul's unexpected voice shoots a rocket of adrenaline through me as he takes the empty chair to my right. The only unoccupied chair in the room—lest I think it means something.

"We were just getting started," Joy says. "We thought… well, it doesn't matter."

Now they all know I lied. Great. Heart beating in my throat, I chance a glance Paul's way, but he's not biting. Hands folded on the table in front of him, he bestows his pastorly smile on each person in the room.

Except for me.

Joy opens the folder and taps her finger on what I assume is the meeting's agenda. "I'm sure the number one issue for the two of you is how we're going to be sure there won't be a repeat of yesterday's incident."

"Excuse me?" Paul leans forward. "What *'incident'* are you referring to?"

"I—" My voice catches, and I clear my throat. "Paul worked late last night, so I haven't had a chance to tell him." Lies, lies, lies. Maybe I should try to remain invisible during this meeting.

"Oh." Veronica shares a glance with Nora. "Well, it seems your concern about Taylor escaping the hospital had merit."

"What?"

I want to cover his hand with mine but clench my fist instead. Comfort from me won't be appreciated at the moment. "She was fine."

"But she got outside?"

Nora hooks a strand of blonde hair behind her ear. "It won't happen again." She and Veronica go through their litany of reasons Taylor's escape was a good thing, in retrospect.

The tension coming off Paul is palpable. Is it because he's worried about Taylor? Angry with me? Frustrated with what he'd see as incompetence with hospital procedure?

"Let's move on to another matter," Joy suggests once Paul's questions are answered. "We'd like to have a goal for Taylor's release." She flips through her notes. "Dr. Holland thinks Taylor might be ready in another four weeks."

Four weeks? "That soon?" Forget being invisible. "She's not even talking yet."

"No," Nora says. She whips a quick look at Veronica and Mason, who are both shaking their heads. "We appreciate Dr. Holland's confidence in Taylor's ability for recovery, but by our calculations, it'll be closer to six weeks. And even that can't be determined for certain until she's talking again. It's hard to assess what she's retaining when she can't communicate."

"Even six weeks doesn't seem very long." I look to Paul for confirmation, and although his eyes don't meet mine, he nods. "And what about school? Will she be able to return when she's released?"

"Her rehabilitation doesn't stop here," Mason says. "She won't need much in the way of physical therapy, but definitely speech therapy, and maybe occupational therapy."

Joy touches my arm. "There will still be a lot of work ahead for Taylor. She'll need 24-hour supervision for a time and a chance to reintegrate back into normal living. There is a residential rehab facility in Santa Clara. They only take six patients at a time, and they set up real life scenarios."

"You mean like playacting?" Paul asks.

Joy nods once. "That's the gist of it—"

"Why can't we do that?" I say. "I'm sure there are things we can do at home to achieve the same end."

"24-hour supervision," Joy reminds me. "And she'll still need outpatient therapy if she stays home."

"I understand." There's no way I'm going to ship Taylor

off once she's released from here. "But if we can manage, wouldn't it be better if she's in a familiar, loving environment?" How loving, at this point, I'm not sure. But an absentee father is still better than a facility.

"It's worth discussing," Joy says. "Now, next on the agenda."

I try to stay with the meeting, but my mind takes off in directions I can't control. It takes every ounce of strength to keep the battling tears at bay. But after another fifteen minutes, I sense things are winding down.

"Just so you understand," Paul says as he stands and gathers his coat, "there *cannot* be a repeat of yesterday's *incident*, as you guys called it. I don't even want to think about all that could've gone wrong."

"But it didn't," I can't help but point out. He can be as angry with me as he wants, but the therapists caring for Taylor are top-notch. Stuff happens. If anyone's aware of that, it's me.

Paul flicks a quick glance my way before focusing on the team again. "I appreciate all you do for my... *our* daughter." His tone is a little contrite, as if he's aware that his anger with me is poorly focused. "I just want to be sure she's safe."

Veronica nods. "We completely understand your frustration with us, pastor. We have an alternative plan in place for Taylor. It won't happen again."

He gives her a brief nod before moving toward the door.

That's it? He's not even going to talk to me? I throw a "Thanks" to the team and follow him out the double glass doors. "Paul."

His step falters, but he doesn't stop.

I look around to be sure we're alone, then pick up my pace. "You can't ignore me forever, you know," I say to his back.

He doesn't bother to turn around or even slow down, but his voice floats back to me. "I can't do this right now, Corey."

∾

Sleep didn't come last night. I was too preoccupied with make-believe scenarios of how I would break through Paul's cold front when given the chance. The words *I'm sorry* seem so…inadequate. Years ago, I attended a weekend Christian conference—one of those affairs where pastor's wives learn to serve better alongside their husbands. Paul thought it might motivate me, make me long to be on Team Paul. One of the speakers taught on the art of asking for forgiveness. It went something like this: I'm sorry, _____, that I _____ and made you feel _____. I will do everything in my power to not _____ again.

Somehow, I don't think this approach will work with Paul. I tried it out in my head—I'm sorry, Paul, that I cheated on you before we were married and made you feel, what? Bad? Sad? Angry? Deceived? I will do everything in my power to not cheat on you again.

There is no formulaic approach to repentance. Not true repentance, anyway.

So, I'm almost relieved that Paul didn't give me a chance to speak to him after the meeting. He cut me off with one sentence and a wave of his hand and didn't even bother to look at me when he walked out. I'm dead to him, and it doesn't look promising for a resurrection.

I lose myself in Taylor's rehab appointments. We've progressed from rolling a ball to bouncing it, and she's able to get eight of the ten shapes into the Shape-O-Ball—a record. Lunch is macaroni and cheese, which she can't identify. Or maybe she can but doesn't know how to verbalize it.

What I wouldn't give to hear her talk.

At three o'clock, it's time for her nap and for me to say good-bye. I dread going home. How will I explain to Michael why his dad's not home for the second night in a row? And if, by some miracle, Paul *does* come home, then what?

"Okay, sweetie." I sit in Taylor's cave with her and tuck a thin blanket beneath her chin. "It's time for me to go." I give her butterfly kisses on her cheek, and she blesses me with a nudge of her shoulder and a smile. "I love you."

Her arms snake around my neck and pull me down. What's she doing? A kiss? No, a butterfly kiss. Her lashes tickle my cheek. "I love you, too, Mommy."

My throat closes up as the tears well and spill over. The sweetest words I've ever heard. I brush back the hair from her face—a face contorted with such anger a few weeks ago, it was unrecognizable.

But I fear it will be the same again once she remembers.

~

Paul

Open door policy or no, I lock myself away in my office. After refusing to answer the fourth call of the morning, Dorothy gets the hint and handles them herself. Not the best timing for caveman mode. Not the best timing for Taylor's accident. Not the best timing for yet another blight on the Shaffer name—with Simpson and his crew seeking out reasons to usurp my position with the congregation.

Computer open, notes scattered in front of me amid two different Bible versions, I make a great show of working. If someone comes in, I can at least fake it. But that's the best I can do. I can't wrap my head around the fact that Taylor's not mine. Not biologically, anyway. Could it be a mistake? She's more like me than Michael. But hey, who's to say Michael's mine? I cringe at the cynicism.

A family picture sits on my desk—Taylor's about five, tucked under my arm. Michael, sitting on Corey's lap, was three. It was one of those Sears promo photos. Posed, color coordinated, cheap. But it's my family. *My* family. Except it's not. Someone else impregnated Corey. Someone she doesn't even remember. Sounds like some cheesy nighttime soap opera. Not what's expected of a pastor's family. Not what I expected of *my* family.

Taylor's been a daddy's girl since she could walk. It was her idea three years ago to start the yearly blood drive at the church. Right here in my office. She came by after school to share her brainchild with me.

"It'd be a community outreach," she'd said.

"Outreach?" I chuckled. "What do you know about outreach?"

"Hey, you're always talking about bringing more people to the church. Maybe we could give away hot dogs or something, then slip scripture into the wrapping."

"A cheap rendition of In-N-Out Burger." I liked the idea. "And if we build on it…" Blood donation. Blood of Christ. Could work.

"I'll even be first to donate." She bounced on her toes in her excitement. "That way, I can show everyone how easy it is. I mean, if a kid can donate blood—"

"I love your courage, kiddo, but one problem."

"What's that?"

"You have to be seventeen."

"What? But that's, like, three years away." Her face was so crestfallen, I had to laugh.

"Never have I seen someone so eager to face a needle. And it's a *big* needle." Not to discourage her, but maybe make her rethink the enthusiasm a bit.

"That's stupid. Why do I have to wait if I want to give blood? It's *my* blood."

"You're right. But the truth is, you probably don't weigh enough yet, anyway. Enjoy your youth while you can."

"Well…" She grumbled under her breath as she picked up a paperweight from my desk and studied it. "Fine. But we could maybe sell t-shirts, too." Her eagerness reignited. "I mean, after people donate, they find out what type they are, right?"

I nodded.

"We can have something like 'I'm type O' or 'I'm type A.' You know? Maybe next year, so whoever donates this year can buy one."

And so, we did. The blood drive was her baby, and she worked every year to improve it. Corey and I'd wear those silly t-shirts—which is how Taylor knew what her blood type should be. And this year she would have been able to donate for the first time, but now—

A rap on the door has me reaching for my notes as Dorothy sticks her head inside. "Drew Simpson's here to see you."

I bracket my forehead with my hand and rub. Does no one know how to make an appointment? Not a good time. But if I put him off...

"Give me five minutes," I say. "Tell him I'm on a phone call." I pick up the phone receiver to make it true. Like God's not going to see right through that.

Dorothy shuts the door and I give up the subterfuge. What do I know about Simpson? He's influential. Has at least ten families following in his wake of dissension. Married with three kids—two of them out of the house. Wasn't there something about his son a few years back? What was it? DUI? College hazing? Mark was supposed to be here for this meeting.

Another rap on the door. Too late. I'm on my own.

"Send him in, Dorothy." I stand as Drew enters.

His six-two height tops me by an inch. Prematurely white, military-style haircut, white mustache. Looks more like a marine than a junior high school principal. He clears his throat. "Pastor Shaffer."

"Mr. Simpson." I extend a hand to offer him a seat in front of my desk.

"Your secretary called, said you wanted to meet."

Yeah, but an appointment would have been nice. I sit at my desk. "I thought it was time to get whatever issues you have out in the open. I would have appreciated it if you'd come to me before approaching my board."

"Habit, I'm afraid. I'm used to mediating between my teachers and parents. I thought of your board the same way."

He's lying, but it won't achieve anything to call him on it. "You've been a member here longer than I've been preaching."

He nods an acknowledgment.

"This...issue with my son, Michael—that was almost a year ago. Why the sudden interest?"

He looks me in the eye. "Vandalism's a serious crime."

"And he's paying the price. We're not shirking the conse-quences."

"Maybe not, but how can you lead a church if you have trouble with your own kid?"

Drinking and driving. That's what Simpson's kid was kicked out of college for. Nearly killed a couple other kids in the car, too. "Some might ask you the same thing."

His eyes narrow, mouth hardens. "Excuse me?"

"You're supposed to be a role model at the middle school, yet your kid got kicked out of college and almost faced invol-untary manslaughter charges."

Face reddening, he comes out of his seat. "How dare you—"

"I dare because you dare." I keep my voice low and stand to face him. No sense in turning this into a shouting match. "Check the plank in your own eye before you come in here throwing around accusations. Neither of us is innocent. I blew it with my kid, you blew it with yours."

"Except I'm not playing hanky-panky on the side."

My mind scrambles to make sense of his charge. Is he referring to Corey and her past? No. He can't know of that yet, and even if he did...the dissension started before Taylor's accident. "You have me at a disadvantage. I don't have a clue what you're talking about."

"Yeah?" He marches to the door and throws it open. "Tell it to Alexis Andrews." And he slams out before I can respond.

Chapter 16

Paul

Where's the peace promised in God's Word? I've served the better part of twenty years in one capacity or another, and now this. Accusations. Dissension. Anger. And it's not all coming from my congregation. My family's crumbling around me faster than my church. When others are in difficult circumstances, I tell them to not ask why, but what? What's God working in and through your life?

But all I can ask is, why?

The office is cloying—responsibilities and discontent closing in on me. I grab my jacket and keys and head out before one more phone call can come in, one more expectation foisted on me. Yeah, I'm feeling sorry for myself, but I can't seem to get past it.

The air's brisk as I cross the parking lot, a gust of wind whipping my jacket open, chilling me to the bone. Once in the car, I start the engine, crank the heat. And sit. Where am I going? I'm not ready to face Corey—I have nothing for her. The life's been sucked out of me and there's nothing left. But if I sit in the parking lot, the staff will start talking. The last thing I need is more speculation.

I drive with no destination in mind.

Too late to haul down to Roseville to see Taylor. My daughter. But not my daughter. I just can't wrap my head around this new reality. I don't *want* to wrap my head around it. It makes me rethink everything. Every comment made by Corey, every vow, every endearment. Every intimate encounter.

Who is this woman I've been married to for eighteen years?

I pull the car into the lot of Main Street Cafe and sit while the engine cools. This'll have to be my sanctuary. iPad tucked under my arm, I head inside where it's quiet and point out a back table to the waitress who looks as if she's been a fixture here since the Reagan era. "Mind if I sit there?"

"Be my guest." She follows and plops a plastic-covered menu in front of me as I settle into the booth. "Would you like to hear our specials?" Her enthusiasm is underwhelming.

"Nah. Just a cup of coffee and a piece of pie, if you have it."

She retrieves the menu. "Cherry, apple, or peach?"

"Fresh peach?"

"In February?"

"Apple. A la mode."

"You got it."

Powering up my iPad, I start to check my email. But what's the point? There must be two hundred unread messages, each more pressing than the one before. I'm drowning here. Instead, I click on the Bible app to begin preparation for Sunday's message.

"Cream?" Little Miss Sunshine slides a thick ceramic mug toward me. By some miracle, the coffee doesn't slosh over the edge.

"Black's good."

"Apple pie, a la mode." She slaps the plate down, along with the check. "Anything else I can get you?"

If life could be that simple. "I'm good. Thanks."

Coffee's hot, pie's sweet, and I take a moment to appreciate both before getting back to work.

"Hiding out?"

The question's so reflective of my thoughts, it takes me a second to realize it's not God asking. Instead, Kent Richardson stands over me—my easy-going, mild-mannered competition. The epitome of grace.

"I could ask the same of you."

"You'd be right. Cheryl has me on another diet. Thought I'd come in and snag a snack before dinner." He pats his paunchy midsection.

"Want to join me?"

"Sure, I'm not interrupting?" He slides in across from me before I can answer. I guess it was a rhetorical question. "How's Taylor doing? I heard she's been moved to a rehab facility."

I nod. "You heard right. It's a slow process, but we're grateful she's going to make a full recovery. God willing. I got your messages at the office, just haven't had a chance to call you back."

"No problem."

Little Miss Sunshine reappears. "What can I get for you, pastor?" Her enthusiasm's gone up several notches.

"Hey June. You got any of that cherry pie left?"

She smiles. "Yup. Coffee and cream?"

"Perfect. How's your husband doing? His surgery go okay?"

Hand on cocked hip, she shakes her head. "Stubborn old goat. It's like pulling teeth to get him to do his physical therapy exercises."

Kent grimaces. "We men aren't good patients. You keep on him, you hear?"

"You betcha. I'll be right back with that pie and coffee."

I watch her rush off to do Kent's bidding. "Church member?"

"No. Not that I haven't tried. I've been coming here for years."

"Is Cheryl aware that June's sabotaging her dietary efforts?"

"They balance each other out." He folds his arms onto the table and leans forward. "How're you doing?"

"Well, Taylor—"

"I'm not talking about Taylor, although God knows that's gotta be difficult."

Small town gossip strikes again. I take a sip of coffee. A stalling technique. "You ever think about chucking the whole thing? Just walking away from preaching altogether?"

Clenching a fist, he raps his knuckles on the table. "Only about once or twice a year. This job isn't for wimps."

"It's like I'm on a sinking boat, and every time I get one hole plugged—"

"Another springs a leak. I know." He scratches his thinning blond hair. "But there's always someone out there working on the side of the devil."

"What happens when there's just too much stacked against you?"

He raises an eyebrow. "Something the gossip mill hasn't got hold of yet?"

The truth's almost too ugly to say out loud.

"I—"

"Here's your pie and coffee, pastor." June slips his order on the table along with his check. "Coffee's on the house."

"Thanks, June. Appreciate it," he says to her retreating back, then looks at me. "You were saying?"

"For one, accusations have been made." I look him in the eye. "Untrue accusations."

"Then you bring them out into the light."

"But——" How much do I tell him? To say it out loud makes it true. And once it's out there, I can't take it back. "Pastoral confidentiality?"

"You have to ask?"

I push my pie aside and fold my arms on the table. "Exposing them will pose another threat." Could I sound anymore cloak and daggerish?

"Lay it on me."

Corey

A lone 60-watt bulb looming from the low asbestos-covered ceiling of the basement is poor light for the claustrophobic space. I retrieve a musty cardboard box from the corner and, toeing a stack of dirty laundry aside, place it in front of the washer. Then I return to the corner for two more.

My collection of teacher books.

All of them outdated by now, I'm sure. But each of the volumes packed within were gifts—the bearer's belief that I would one day step in front of a classroom of youngsters. I flip through pages, some moldy with age. How could it be otherwise in this dank basement? I should have taken more care when storing them.

I close my eyes and picture Tess's classroom and the freshman kids that were my charge the last time I subbed for her. Is it wrong for me to feel more fulfilled when working with kids than I do facilitating a ladies' Bible study? Why would God put the desire in my heart if He didn't intend for me to follow it? Of course, I followed another desire eighteen years ago and look how that ended.

"What're you doing?"

Michael's voice startles me, and the book flies out of my hands, landing on the concrete floor with a *thwap*. "Do you *have* to sneak up like that?" I shoot him a glare as I retrieve the book.

"I didn't sneak." He drops an armful of clothes onto the already insurmountable pile.

"Didn't you say you were going to start helping out around here?" I nod at the pile. "Maybe it's time you learned how to do laundry."

He shrugs. "Sure. How hard can it be? You just throw it in the washer with soap, right?"

Leave it to a teenager to trivialize a never-ending chore. "There's a little more to it than that, but I think you've got the smarts to learn."

He points to the boxes. "So, what's all this?"

I kneel down in front of an open box and search through it. "Outdated books."

"Yeah?" He moves beside me and peers over my shoulder. "Teacher books?"

"Maybe I'll take them to the thrift store on Saturday when I drop you off. You are going in, right?"

"Last ten hours of community service."

I scrape my hair back and look up at him. "They're not open ten hours."

"I start at six."

"Six? A.M?"

He nods.

"I didn't know you were aware there's such an hour."

"I wanna get done so I can start my new job next week. They said if I'm willing to come in and sort out the donations, I can. If you don't want to take me in—"

"No. I'll take you. Maybe you can haul these boxes up and put them in the back of the Honda."

He lifts a box and rests it on the washer. "Hey, did you ever talk to Dad about summer camp?"

I knew this was coming, but I hate to disappoint him. "I did." Folding my arms, I rest a hip against the dryer. "Look,

Michael, I want you to know that I see how hard you're working. Not just at school, but with the community service and getting a job and—"

"He said no. I get it." He hugs the box and hefts it from the washer. And although he shrugs it off, I hear the hurt in his voice.

"Wait, sweetheart." I touch his arm before he can leave. "Let's talk about this."

"Nothin' to talk about, Mom. Dad's not going to let me go. He's still ticked. I get it."

I wish *I* did. "Don't give up."

He drops the box back on the washer and looks at me like I've lost my mind. "Dad doesn't change his mind."

I pray he's wrong. "Don't give up, Michael. Your dad… he's going through a rough spell right now. It's not you."

He snorts and rolls his eyes.

"I swear it's not. Let's take it one step at a time. I'm sure if you get your grades up he'll be more open to talking about it."

Resting his arm on the box, he drops his eyes. "He didn't come home last night, did he?"

It would be easy to lie, to say he came in after Michael went to sleep, but how can I expect him to trust me to tell him the truth if I'm not honest about everything? "No, he didn't. He's…he's dealing with something. That's all I can tell you."

He shakes his head and says something I can't hear.

"What's that?"

"Nothing. I'll get these boxes in the car."

We're halfway up the stairs when the doorbell peals and Rambo goes into guard dog mode. Michael drops the box in the hallway at the top of the stairs and reaches the front door before I do.

I grab Rambo's collar and pull him from the door as Michael opens it.

"Grandpa. Grandma. Hey, I didn't know you guys were coming."

Am I lightheaded because I'm bending over the dog, or is it the knowing look in my father's eyes when they latch onto mine?

"This is a surprise," I manage. Lovely. I have a husband who won't speak to me, a daughter who *can't* speak to me, and I'm now faced with a father I've been avoiding for weeks.

Isn't life just grand?

Chapter 17

Paul

The glow of a streetlamp spotlights an unfamiliar car smack in the middle of my driveway. I can't pull into the garage, but I'm more irritated that I don't know who it belongs to. Simpson? Or worse, Alexis? Maybe I should have stayed at the church office again, but Kent...well, it's not smart to ignore wise counsel.

"You can't fix it if you can't face it," he'd said after I vomited my problems all over him.

I'm not ready to fix it, but avoiding it isn't a solution, either.

I park at the curb, gather my things, along with a little fortitude, and head up the walk. The car's a rental—Hertz—which provides no clue. Corey had turned on the exterior lights —for me or our guest? — and it takes some of the edge off. Not much, but some. No idea what I'm facing. There were no text messages or voicemails from Corey, so I'm going in blind. I toss up a quick prayer and push through the front door.

"There you are." Corey crosses the family room, smile

strained, face pale, to greet me. "Just in time for dinner." Eyes pleading, hands wringing, she reaches my side and escorts me to my in-laws, Richard and Marlene, sitting together on the couch.

I'd rather deal with Simpson or take my chances in the lion's den.

"Marlene, Richard. This is a...surprise." I bend down to kiss Marlene's cheek, and she gives me a warm smile. How such a gentle soul ended up with Richard Carroll is one of life's mysteries.

Richard stands, unfurling his imposing stature, and offers a hand. His grip is firm and quick. "We were a little surprised ourselves to find out Taylor's accident isn't the triviality Coraline made it out to be when she called a few weeks ago."

"Yes, well—" I glance at Corey, who's now perched on the edge of the love seat. Angry or not, I'm not about to throw her under the bus. "That's my fault. I didn't think it would do any good to worry you. Certainly didn't expect you to fly out here from Indiana. At least, not without calling first."

"What good would calling do?" Richard shakes his head. "You might just have lied to us again."

Jaw clenched, I move next to Corey and squeeze her shoulder. "What can I do to help get dinner on?"

"Oh." She pops up from her seat. "Why don't you get Michael? He's in his bedroom doing homework."

Thrilled to escape the room, even if only for a moment, I comply. Richard's overbearing tone follows me down the hallway. Ticked with Corey or not, I'm grateful she got her mother's genes.

Rapping on Michael's door, I push it open. He sits at his desk, hunched over a textbook, under the glow of a desk lamp. Rambo, lying on the bed, sits up and yips a greeting.

"Mom asked me to come get you for dinner."

I expect attitude, so his look of dismay throws me. "It's my fault they're here." Tossing his pencil down, he pushes up from the desk.

"How's that?"

"They called here a few days ago. I thought they knew, and I said something about Taylor's rehab and how I couldn't wait until Sunday when she can have visitors." He shrugs. "Totally lame."

"It's not your fault."

"Grandpa…he was *mad* at Mom when they came in. I don't get it."

"It's complicated, Michael, but there's a reason we live here in California instead of Indiana. Your mom…well…it's complicated."

He turns off his desk lamp and follows me. "Where were you last night?" There it is, the attitude I've grown accustomed to.

"That's complicated too."

"Yeah, whatever."

We both fall silent when we enter the dining room and take our usual places at the table. Richard and Marlene are seated on one side, Corey at the end. A church casserole sits on a trivet surrounded by a few side dishes. I should ask Richard to lead us in prayer, but I'm not opening that door. Instead, I do the honors.

While Corey serves up the casserole, I scramble for something to say. Keep the focus on them, because there are no safe topics on our end. "So, where are you two staying?"

"Here, of course." Richard takes his plate from Corey.

"They're…um…" Corey waves the serving spoon in the direction of the hallway and a chunk of noodles plops onto the table. "They're going to stay in Taylor's room."

"Taylor's room?" I look at Corey. Is she insane? The strain in her eyes tells me it's not her idea. "She's just got that old double bed in there. You two would be more comfortable at a hotel."

Marlene touches Richard's hand. "Paul's right, sweetheart. Besides, I'm sure they don't need us underfoot here."

"Underfoot?" Richard's gray caterpillar eyebrows shoot up. "We're family for crying out loud." He rakes his eyes to Corey then to me. "What's going on here, anyway? What is it you're hiding? First the lies about Taylor's accident, now this."

"Richard." Marlene's tone is sharp.

Michael hunches over his food, no eye contact. Smart boy.

"We told you, Dad. We didn't want to worry you." Do they hear the strain in Corey's voice?

Richard's not buying it. His black and white mentality leaves no wiggle room.

I clear my throat. "We're sorry as we can be that you were hurt by this. That's the last thing in the world we wanted to do. Corey's trying to do the right thing here, even if you don't like her methods. Taylor will be just fine. I promise you that. But Corey's under enough strain dealing with Tay's rehab." Would he get the point?

"We shouldn't have come without calling first," Marlene says. "We're happy to stay in a hotel tonight."

"But we're not flying home." Richard pounds a fist on the table. "Not until we can see our granddaughter."

It can't be soon enough for me.

Corey

Why is it some people can lie with every breath they take and come out on top? Not me. No. I just dig myself into a deep well of a hole. If Paul hadn't stepped in…

But he did. Hope worms its way into my soul. Does this mean he forgives me? He must, or why else would he be so quick to jump to my defense? The lead ball that's been growing in my stomach eases up a bit.

Hotel arrangements made, my parents leave, and I sigh in relief. Michael escapes to his room using homework as an excuse, and Paul mumbles something about work and retreats into his office. Should I follow and see if he'll talk to me? Better to not push. Maybe when he comes to bed...

I check my emails: one from Tess prodding me to accept the team-teaching assignment, and one from Tricia. What's the latest scoop, she wants to know? Too much to convey in an email. I'll call her on my way to the hospital tomorrow. I finish up the dinner dishes, wipe down the counters, and refill Rambo's water dish.

Before heading to bed, I knock on Michael's bedroom door.

A muffled, "Yeah?"

I poke my head in. "What are you doing?" Silly question, since he's sitting on the floor, back against the bed, book propped on his knees. The answer's obvious.

He lets the book drop. "I'm sorry."

"About?"

"Grandpa." He groans. "You should've told me you were keeping it a secret."

I pull the desk chair out and sit, the hardwood seat a rude reminder of my age. How does he focus in this thing? "I didn't mean to keep it a secret." Another lie? "Okay, maybe I did. It's just...Grandpa can be—"

"A jerk," Michael supplies.

Mental cringe. "Respect, bud. He's your grandfather."

"Has he always been so, I don't know, harsh?"

"Always."

"How does Grandma stand it?"

Good question. "I think she knows how to handle him. After forty-some odd years, she should."

"You think they'll really stay until they can see Taylor?"

"Afraid so."

He nods and picks up his book again.

"What're you reading?"

He holds it up so I can see the cover. "*To Kill a Mockingbird*."

"Great book."

"You've read it?"

"Sophomore year of high school, just like you."

He smirks. "I didn't realize it was that old."

"Funny." I stand and take a swat at his head, but he ducks. "On that note, I think I'll turn in. See you in the morning."

A half hour later, I'm tucked into bed with Rambo by my side, trying to focus on my own book. Every noise outside the bedroom door has my heart jumping. When will Paul come in? What if he doesn't? He wouldn't sleep in his office, would he? But the door opens, and he slips through, closing it again. A drum corps does a solo in my chest, and it's hard to breathe.

"Hi." All I've got is a weak olive branch. Will he accept it?

He crosses the room and sits on the end of the bed to remove his shoes. "Figured you'd be asleep by now."

Well, that's not promising. "I...I thought we could talk."

Big sigh. "There's nothing to talk about. Not yet, anyway."

"But," I swallow down the lump in my throat, "I just thought, after tonight..."

He stands and turns to look at me. "One has nothing to do with the other."

Tears burn my eyes. "Look, Paul, can't we talk about this? I mean, give me a chance to explain."

"Explain what?" He throws his hands up. "Explain how you didn't want to marry me, so you slept with some... stranger...and then married me anyway?"

"It's not—"

"Explain that the daughter I've always thought was mine, isn't? Or that you've been lying to me for eighteen years?"

"It's not like that. You're twisting—"

"*I'm* twisting? Seriously, Corey?" With each word, he

yanks at a button on his shirt, jaw muscles tightening. "That one lie's made everything that followed a lie. Everything."

"No." Tears spill over and I swipe at them. "It's not like that."

"And how are you going to explain it to Taylor? Have you thought of that?" Balling up the shirt, he throws it into the corner with enough force to expel a grunt.

"Of course."

"And Michael? You don't think that this isn't going to get back to him? Or maybe you think you can hide this from him like you have from all of us."

Each word he hurls at me is another link in a chain of bondage. There is no freedom in truth.

"We can get through this, Paul." But I'm pleading in vain. I'm dead to him.

"If you didn't want to marry me, then why the did you?" He snatches a pillow from the bed, then marches to the door and yanks it open. "I'm going to sleep on the couch."

"Wait." I scramble from the bed, tripping over the covers, and grab his arm, my nails biting into his bicep.

"I don't even know you." Yanking his arm from my grasp, he pins me with such a look of loathing, it forces me back, then he slams out of the room.

I drop my head on the closed door, a sob rising up my throat. "I don't know you, either."

Chapter 18

Corey

When I was seven or eight, I went with my brother Brian to the corner store to pick up something Mom needed for dinner. Sitting outside the store was a kid with a cardboard box and a sign that said FREE KITTENS written in big, black marker. Natural shyness forgotten, I rushed to the box to peer inside. There was one left.

"Can I hold it?" I asked.

"He's a boy," the kid said.

Brian grabbed my arm. "Don't do it."

But I was smitten. Little black fluff, blue eyes, pink nose. I kissed him on the head and inhaled kitty smells. His heartbeat against my hand, engine-revving purr rumbling against my chest. I'd never wanted anything more. How could Mom and Dad say no? And so I ignored Brian's warning and tucked Prince, as I named him, under my jacket.

"Better give him back," Brian said. "Dad'll never let you keep him."

My father didn't even look at Prince, just told me to return him. "A lesson in asking permission."

I pleaded with him, but it did no good.

"You take that animal back where you got it."

How could he look at Prince and not see what I did? Heart breaking, I positioned the kitty under my arm and started for the door.

"And Coraline?" He'd changed his mind. I knew he would. "Don't come home with that cat. If the boy is no longer there, find another home for it."

By the time I got back to the store, cursing my father under my breath, tears streaming down my cheeks, the kid was gone, along with his box and sign. Now what?

I stood outside the store for what seemed like forever and asked everyone going in, and again coming out, if they wanted a free kitten. But no one did. Prince was getting cranky, and so was I. It was getting late, the sun dropping behind the store, streetlights coming on. My stomach reminded me it was dinner time. Although it was getting cold, Prince's fluff was damp in my sweaty hands, his mews growing more insistent by the minute.

What would Dad do if I couldn't find a home for Prince?

Crazy Charlie, who lived at the end of Cherry Lane, had a big orange cat named Tasha. The kids at school swore that whenever she delivered a litter of kittens, he drowned them. Dad wouldn't do something that cruel, would he?

I couldn't take any chances.

Walking the long way home, I stopped at the first house that had lights on inside. The grass was surrounded by a white picket fence, and there were kids' toys scattered around. A bicycle lay on its side next to a tricycle, a four-square ball, and a red bucket.

I unlatched the gate, crouched low, and ran up the walkway. After kissing Prince on the head, I whispered, "You stay. I bet nice people live here." Then I set him on the black welcome mat, rang the doorbell, and ran as fast as I could down the brick walkway. My jacket got caught on the gate latch, but I tugged it loose and kept going.

When I got home, Dad asked if I'd returned the kitten. I said I had. But I couldn't eat my dinner. What if no one answered the door and Prince wandered onto the street? He could get killed by a car. Or a bigger cat. Or maybe Crazy Charlie would find him and drown him, just like he did Tasha's kittens.

By the time I was ready for bed, I was sure Prince had met some horrible fate, and it was all my fault.

"I know you wanted that kitten, Coraline," Dad said as he kissed me goodnight. "But it's better to learn early that we don't always get what we want in life."

All the worry over Prince came bursting out of me. "Oh, Daddy. I lied."

"What?" He pulled back, his face stern. "What are you talking about?"

"No one would take Prince," I sobbed. "I left him on a doorstep and ran."

He shook his head and sighed. Somehow, he'd make it all better, wouldn't he? "A harder lesson to learn than asking for permission is living with consequences. Remember this the next time you do something foolish. You're not the only one who could get hurt."

That lesson took root in my soul. But a deeper reality hit me when I was old enough to understand it—don't expect grace and forgiveness in the wake of foolish mistakes.

The foolish mistakes I'd made as a child paled when compared to that fateful night I questioned my decision to marry Paul. Somehow, I forgot that first lesson. But the second? If I couldn't be forgiven for Prince, how could I expect to be forgiven for a selfish night of oblivion?

Regardless of what Paul might say, I've never been good at lying. Burying my head in the sand, yes. I've honed that to an art form. A flock of ostriches have nothing on me. Rather than confess that sin and plead forgiveness, I'd chosen to ignore it.

So why did I marry Paul? The truth of it is too painful to face, let alone share with my husband. I ponder this on the drive down to Sacramento, Michael in the passenger seat, my parents following in their rental car. For once, I don't resent the ear buds in my son's ears, making conversation impossible. Today, it's an answer to prayer.

Another answer to prayer is Paul's absence. Church was his excuse. And I'm grateful, because I don't have to fake it in front of my parents. Faking it is just another form of lying.

Parking is a cinch today. Although Sunday is visitor's day, there are few cars clogging the covered garage. The first Sunday we were here, I was relieved that there wouldn't be the usual parking chaos, until we walked into the hospital. It was as quiet as a funeral. Where were the other patients' families? Aside from some old man yelling, "I gotta go pee. Help me. Someone. I gotta go pee," there was little activity. A skeletal nursing crew, no therapists, no doctors, no schedules.

I lead my parents down the long entry hall. Mom has packages, gifts for Taylor, dangling from one arm. The fire-engine red and sunflower yellow bags clash with the hospital-worn colors of faded green and industrial gray.

Michael forgets to be cool and rushes ahead to be the first in Taylor's room, holding the camera around his neck so it doesn't bounce.

"Good morning, Mrs. Shaffer," a nurse greets from behind the reception desk. "We've been keeping a close eye on your girl today."

"Hi, Erica. How's she doing this morning?"

She grins. "Chatty."

Is she kidding? "You're not serious."

Her eyebrows shoot up. "I'm totally serious. She demanded breakfast early."

Anxious to get to Taylor's room, I make quick intro-
ductions.

"When will she be released?" Dad looks at the worn green
decor with the same distaste I imagine he'd view prison walls.

"We don't know yet. They can't assess her until she's talking." Which might change now. I quicken my steps.

Mom tugs on my arm, halting my progress. "Will she
know us?"

I wrap an arm around her shoulders. "I don't know, Mom.
It's just been recently that she's recognized us."

"Well, let's get in there and find out," Dad grumbles.

Taylor, her back to the door, sits in her wheelchair facing
Michael, who's made himself comfortable on her bed. The
room, which appears larger since the removal of the cage over
her bed, has morphed over the last couple weeks. Pictures of
family and friends fill the cork board above her desk. Stuffed
animals and art supplies crowd the surface.

Michael holds up his camera. "What's this?"

Taylor's shoulders hunch up in a shrug. "I don't know."

"Sure you do. I take pictures with it."

"Cards?"

He rolls his eyes. "It's a camera, Tay."

"It's a camera, Tay," she repeats.

"Taylor?" I take an arm of each of my seemingly reluc-
tant parents and walk them forward. They demanded to see
Taylor, now they're hesitant?

Michael hops off the bed and spins Taylor's chair around
so she's facing us. Her neck brace is gone.

Walking up to her, I touch her hair. "Hi, Tay."

"Hi, Mom." Will I ever get tired of hearing her voice?

"Do you know these people?" I point to my parents.

"Hi, Tay-Tay." Mom drops her packages and kneels in
front of Taylor, unmindful of her peach slacks. "You look
beautiful."

Taylor smiles at Mom, then looks up until her eyes latch

onto Dad standing military straight. Visits with the grandparents have been few and far between, so I don't expect much. "Grouchy Grandpa," she says, pointing to him.

Michael's laughter barks out from behind Taylor.

I hold my breath, unsure of Dad's response, and catch Mom's eyes. He'll be offended, and rightly so. How will I explain the nickname the kids thought up years ago?

"That's right, granddaughter." Dad's eyes light up with laughter. "Grouchy Grandpa."

~

Paul

The rehabilitation hospital is as quiet as a church when I step into the entry hall late in the afternoon. One short text from Corey and I know she's heading for the airport to see her parents off. I somehow managed to dodge *that* bullet. Even so, I can't help the slice of guilt that cuts me. I didn't have her back this morning. That's not how we operate. Operated.

I can't reconcile the two Coreys—like an internal before and after picture. Except, as I studied our wedding picture late last night—or maybe it was early this morning—it hit me. It's not all internal. The Corey I remember from Wheaton College was…audacious. She exuded vibrancy, a passion for life that I haven't seen since. Maybe I could have believed the drudgery of marriage was the catalyst for change—until I studied that picture. Even then, on our wedding day, something was different.

Was it guilt or resignation? Which is worse?

I find Taylor napping on her cage-free bed. When did that happen? It must mean she's mobile. And the missing neck brace? I would know that if I'd had a conversation with Corey that didn't focus on the past.

Taylor's curled up in a fetal position, arms hugging a

stuffed animal, feet encased in purple and pink toe socks.

"Hi."

My gaze flies from Taylor's feet to her face. Did she just initiate conversation? "Hi, sweetheart."

"See?" She holds out a stuffed bear clothed in what appears to be a yellow hospital gown, its head wrapped in gauze.

Walking toward her bed, I reach for her offering. She's talking. A miracle that rivals Jesus walking on water as far as I'm concerned. "Where did you get him?" I take it in my arms while she pushes up and sits cross-legged. What I want to do is dance an end-zone jig.

"Don't know."

"Does he have a name?"

She nods. "Grouchy Grandpa." The kids' nickname for Richard.

"Did you have lunch?"

"Crispy olives."

"Crispy…what?" I laugh. "I think you're confused."

"How're we doing?" Erica stands in the doorway.

I touch the bear to Taylor's nose before giving it back. "She's talking."

"There's no stopping her now. I was telling your wife before she left that therapy will kick into gear now."

Taylor tugs the bandage off the bear's head.

"What was on the lunch menu?"

Erica wrinkles her nose. "Why?"

"Because Taylor said she had crispy olives."

She shakes her head and laughs. "No worries. We fed her real food. Spaghetti, salad, and garlic bread."

"So, crispy olives comes from where?"

"We'll never know. But get used to it. Her brain can't retrieve the right words yet. That'll change. Let me know if you need anything."

"Fix it." Taylor holds the bear in one hand and the

bandage in the other.

"Okay, but you have to leave it alone if I do." Deja vu hits like a two by four between the eyes. Taylor at three, dismembering one of her dolls and making the same demand.

How is it possible she's not my daughter? How many times have I heard, "She has your eyes"? And what about our shared personality traits? Proof that nurture wins over nature, or faulty lab results?

"Fix it." Taylor slaps my hand.

"Did you see Grandma and Grandpa?"

"Grouchy Grandpa." She picks at a loose piece of skin on her lip. Her nails are bitten down to the quick. Since when?

I pull her hand away from her mouth. "You biting your nails?"

She shrugs.

Okay, now what? I spot a thick newspaper on the desk— Sunday edition?

"Want to read the comics?"

She shrugs again, focused on chewing a nail.

I snatch up the paper and flip through it until I find the colorful comic section. Sitting next to her on the bed, I take her hand from her mouth.

"Stop it." She slaps my hand and goes to town on another nail. It's like three-year-old Taylor all over again. Strong willed and defiant.

"It's going to bleed if you keep that up. Look." I pull her hand away again and wave the paper under her nose. "You like *Garfield*, don't you?"

We settle at the head of the bed, our backs against the wall. I lay the paper across both our laps and point to the pictures as I read the captions.

What was I expecting? She'd one day wake from her stupor and be her old self? Maybe if I'd spent as much time with her as Corey, I'd be better prepared. I didn't think we'd be raising her all over again.

Would I trade Taylor for the wife I thought I was marrying? The virgin bride? If Corey hadn't been pregnant, Taylor wouldn't be here now. It hits me that I can't have it both ways.

I move onto *Born Loser* and Taylor lays her head on my shoulder. Before I've finished the comics, she's sound asleep.

Slipping from the bed, I ease her into a more comfortable position and cover her with a blanket. Aside from her size, she looks much like she did as a toddler. Acts like it, too. I fold up the paper and drop it where I found it before planting a kiss on Taylor's forehead.

My daughter.

Whatever Corey did, this can't be taken from me.

Erica and another nurse—Holly? Polly? —stand behind the reception desk.

I rap my knuckles on the desk. "It's quiet around here."

"That it is," Erica says. "Our patients work hard the rest of the week. It's all they can do to handle visitors."

I glance around the empty room. "Doesn't look like you've got many of those."

"It's nice you and your wife broke up your visits today. Taylor had quite a bit of stimulation with your son and in-laws earlier."

"Yeah." Might as well pretend it was intentional. "What's with the nail biting. Is that new?"

"Focus issues," Polly or Holly says.

Nail biting. Lip picking. Walking. Talking. What else have I missed?

Pushing through the hospital door, I pull my cell phone from my pocket and thumb Corey's number.

"Paul?" Corey sounds hesitant.

"Have you started dinner yet?"

"Uh, no. Will you be home?" What's in her voice? Sarcasm? Resentment?

"Let's go out. We need to talk."

Chapter 19

Corey

Wind and rain pelts the bedroom window, dreary gray light peeking through the blinds. I bury my head deeper beneath the covers, no energy to face the day after a sleepless night. I don't have to reach across the bed to know it's empty. Even with Paul's cold presence last night, his absence leaves a profound ache. Will we ever move past this? Is it even possible?

"Hey, Mom?" Michael raps on the bedroom door.

I force enthusiasm into my tone. "Yeah, kiddo. What's up?"

"Can I come in?"

"Um…yeah." I push the covers back and sit up. Goosebumps skitter across my bare arms.

Michael enters, his usual baggy jeans absent. Instead, he's wearing a pair of khakis he got for Christmas and a dark blue sweater. "Oh. Thought you were already up. You feeling okay?"

"What's with the G.Q. look?"

He shrugs. "Ran out of clean clothes."

"Remind me to forget the laundry more often." I yawn and rub the sleep from my eyes. "What's up?"

"I'm leaving early for school. Make up test. I'm working at the Pit 'n' Stop this afternoon, so I'll be late."

"Khakis and grease don't mix, you know."

"I'll change before heading over." He hitches his chin at me. "You going to see Taylor today?"

"I'm going by school first. Mr. Hamilton wants to see me."

Michael smirks. "Getting called to the principal's office, huh? What'd you do?"

"You're a regular Bob Hope."

"Who?"

"Oh, come on!"

"Kidding," he sing-songs. "Anyway, I left a couple CDs on the table for Taylor. Thought she should remember what music sounds like."

"I'll make sure she gets them."

Once he's gone, the house is bathed in eerie silence. I hurry through my shower, then dig deep into my closet to find something presentable to wear. Before leaving the house, I throw a load of laundry into the washer and lock Rambo in the garage. White dog and a muddy backyard mix as well as khakis and grease. My stomach rumbles, but there's no time to fix breakfast. Starbucks it is.

I pull into the school parking lot and sit for a moment while rain drums on the roof of my car. Mr. Hamilton's going to want an answer regarding the team-teaching assignment, but I don't have one. My heart tells me, "Take it," but my head isn't on board. I haven't even talked to Paul about it yet, so how can I make a unilateral decision?

With a sigh, I throw open the car door and make a dash for the office.

"Hey, Val." I push a strand of damp hair from my face while water drips off my raincoat.

Val looks up from her work, lacquered dark hair, model

perfect makeup. The only woman I've known to wear false eyelashes. "Hey, girl. Mr. Hamilton said you'd be coming in this morning. He's down at the bus stop but'll be up in a minute. You can wait here or go the to the staff room, if you want."

"I'll wait here." I peel off my coat and groan at my water-logged shoes. An umbrella would have been a good idea. I peruse the bulletin board tacked to the wall and the sign-in sheet for late arrivals, listening as Val answers two phone calls, until Mr. Hamilton arrives. The hint of a scent prevalent in every school I've ever been in takes me back to childhood. Is it old books or musty kid-bodies?

"Good morning, Corey." Mr. Hamilton is as wide as he is tall, gray fringe surrounding a bald pate, full beard and mustache to rival Santa Clause's. "Let's go back to my office, shall we?"

I follow him down a narrow hallway and we enter his chaotic office. I was told that it was the staff room years ago, long before he became principal. It was a time when teachers were allowed to smoke on campus. A faint whiff of tobacco lingers, or maybe it's just my imagination on overtime. Now it looks more like an archeological dig site, with the skeletons of small animals taking up prominent space on books shelves. His strategy to gain a psychological edge over his students? Or maybe the former science teacher in him isn't yet laid to rest.

"Tell me, how's Taylor doing?" He indicates I should sit with a wave of his hand before positioning himself behind his desk.

"She's coming along."

"Will she be returning to school soon?"

"It's possible, although I'm not sure she'll be able to grad-uate in June with her class. I'm meeting Mrs. Kendall on Wednesday."

He nods, bushy brows lowering over baggy eyes. "Well,

some of the teachers have been holding a prayer session before school each day. Taylor's at the top of our list."

I'm warmed by his words. With the separation of church and state, prayer in a public school is discouraged. "We…Paul and I…appreciate that. If you could pass that on."

"Will do. So, then…" He slaps an open palm on the desk. "Tess Holland tells me you're considering the team-teaching assignment for next school year. Just wanted you to know that we'd love to have you on board. I've been trying to find a way to finagle you onto our staff for some time now."

"I…wow." I clear my throat of the lump that rises. With Paul's defection, every kindness is a gift. "I'm sure you understand that it's been hectic at home. With Paul juggling his pastoral duties and me practically living at the hospital."

He nods. "I'm not pushing you for an answer, Corey."

An uncomfortable laugh slips. "Good, because I don't have one for you. I haven't even had a chance to discuss this with Paul yet. I'd love to say I'll take the position, but until I know what Taylor's needs will be…" And if my marriage will survive.

"I understand." He slaps his hand on the desk again. "Well, I don't want to keep you. Just let us know if there's anything we can do to convince you to take the position."

I brave the rain to reach my car, start the engine, and sit. I thought I'd have a chance to raise the topic at dinner last night, but Paul's agenda had been set.

Bella Cucina had been moderately busy for a Sunday night. My stomach revolted at the thought of eating the antipasta the waitress deposited on the table as an appetizer. Was Paul going to grill me about the past? Ask me for a divorce? No, his place in the community trumped a faithless wife.

"What'll you have?" He sat across from me in the red vinyl booth, head buried in the menu.

I fingered my own menu. Aromas that were tantalizing the

last time we were here only made my stomach turn. "Mine-strone soup."

"Soup?" He looked at me then, eyes widening. "Since when do you have soup here?"

There was no sense telling him I couldn't stomach more. I'd just be opening myself up for some sarcastic comment on how I made my own bed, something my dad used to say, too. "I'm not very hungry."

The waitress materialized in a white blouse, black apron, and black slacks. I didn't recognize her and vaguely wondered if she was new. She couldn't have been much older than Taylor. Paul ordered for both of us and she collected our menus, leaving us with nothing to focus on but each other.

Paul folded his hands on the table. "Good to hear Taylor talking again, isn't it?"

Was this a truce, then? I nodded and waited. We could have had this conversation at home. There was sure to be more.

"Taylor," he cleared his throat. "Is there any way those lab results could be wrong?"

How I wish I could tell him yes. But then, it wouldn't change the real issue here. "Would that change how you feel about me right now?"

"At least I'd know she's my daughter."

Foolish man. Couldn't he see the truth of it? "She's your daughter regardless of what the lab results say. How can you think anything else? You've raised her and she adores you. If it hadn't been for that test—"

"It would have come out anyway. If she hadn't been in that accident, she would have donated blood. Did you think you could just keep this a secret forever?"

"How many times do I have to tell you?" I leaned forward and lowered my voice. "I. Didn't. Know."

Paul mirrored my position. "You didn't know you cheated on me?"

I clenched my fist. Better that than slapping him, which is what I itched to do. Slap that smug look right off his face. The thought stole my breath. This was not me, tempted to enact violence on my own husband, or *anyone*, for that matter. "I didn't know I was pregnant, Paul. It never entered my mind that it could be possible."

"And when you discovered that you were? Did it enter your mind then?" The muscles in his jaw tightened, a sure sign of his tested temper.

"No." But that wasn't completely true. I'd refused to believe it. It was easier to play the ostrich card. "Not...not for long. It was too hideous to imagine."

"Here we are." The waitress's cheery disposition, juxtaposed against our agony, was jarring. It was as if the world around us had disappeared to black and white, and now the chatter, laughter and clinking of dinnerware exploded around us in full color.

I didn't dare lift my tear-filled eyes from my minestrone soup. The scents and steam wafting from it bathed my face in moisture. There was no way I could choke down a bite. Could Paul? Dipping my spoon in and swirling the broth, I stalled for some direction from him.

With a weary, resigned tone, Paul said, "I don't know how we can resolve this, Corey."

So, he did want a divorce.

"I'm...I'm trying to find forgiveness. I know it's what I'm supposed to do." He sounded like a petulant child being forced to use good manners.

Is this the way our life would be from now on?

"But I need more time."

"And until then?" Would we live in limbo, him gone every night, me crying myself to sleep?

"Let's just take it one day at a time."

We suffered the rest of our meal in silence. It wasn't until we stood to leave that I became aware of Alexis Andrews in the booth behind me.

Chapter 20

Paul

There have been seasons in my life where I've put my feelings on hold. Emotionally stunted. The year my mom fought and lost her battle with breast cancer. I'd been thirteen, Justine only ten. Twenty years later when my dad killed himself. The official diagnosis was cirrhosis of the liver, but we knew it was a slow and steady choice to die.

And now.

It's in these times it hurts too much to feel. I go into my "nothing box" as Corey likes to call it—a place where I can function without thinking. I return phone calls and emails. I write inspirational messages even when I'm spiritually bankrupt. I focus on the required mundane tasks without letting on that my personal life is falling apart.

Corey and I are merely cohabiting.

"I went to see John and Beverly last night." Mark tosses his legal pad on my desk and sits. "Looks like he'll be going into rehab today."

Opening my iPad, I shake my head at the Post-It notes lined up along the edge—dutiful soldiers awaiting their orders.

"Maybe he'll end up in the same place as Taylor. Then I can visit them at the same time."

"Any word on when she's coming home?"

I grin. "Today."

Mark's eyes pop open. "Today?"

"Just for the night. We wanted her home for Easter. I'll drive her back down tomorrow evening. If all goes well, possibly next weekend for good."

The door flies open and Becky, face flushed, rushes in. "Sorry I'm late."

I wave her to the empty chair next to Mark. "No problem. We haven't started yet."

"Can we make it quick? I have lots to do to be ready for tomorrow."

"We'll start with you, then. Are the kids ready?"

"Yes." The one word is infused with enthusiasm. Just what we need in our children's ministry leader. "Or they will be by tomorrow. We have one more practice in," she checks her watch, "about forty-five minutes."

Mark's eyebrows shoot up. "How'd you get all those parents to bring their kids in today?"

She blinks. "I asked." Then a grin bursts forth. "And threatened. Every parent wants their child to be the best in the program. No practice, no performance."

He snorts. "Wish that approach worked with everyone."

"You just have to know how to charm them," Becky says.

I shift in my chair. "I don't think it's charm you're using, but whatever it is, keep up the good work."

"I hear Taylor's going to be here tomorrow."

"That's right."

"I really could have used her expertise with this," Becky says with a sad smile. "She always gets the kids to perform better. Not sure how, but she does." She finishes the update, then excuses herself.

Mark and I go over the next month's schedule: spring

break activities for the youth, signups for the summer camp-out, Vacation Bible School schedule.

"Anything else?" I shuffle through my notes.

"There is one thing."

His tone has my adrenaline kicking into gear. Gun shy, I guess. "What's that?"

"I wish you'd had me sit in on your meeting with Simpson."

"We've had this discussion. He didn't give me a chance—"

"There's talk, Paul."

I scowl. "There's always talk. It doesn't mean anything."

"I want to have your back, but—"

"Then do." My tone is abrupt, impatient. I hope it communicates I'm sick to death of the whole sordid business. "This thing with Alexis Andrews is a serious fabrication in her evil little mind."

"Alexis?" He shakes his head. "What's this about Alexis?"

A lead ball drops in my gut. If it's not about Alexis… Gossip travels faster than a runaway train—and is just as deadly.

"Paul?" Dorothy knocks on the door while opening it. "Kent Richardson is here to see you."

Mark gathers up his stuff and stands. "We need to talk."

"Agreed." I check my watch. "But I've got to head down to Roseville after I meet with Kent. Can it wait until Monday?"

"Monday it is. See you in the a.m." He and Kent greet each other as they pass.

"Long time no see." I nod at Kent.

He shuts the door. Is it my imagination or is the click of the latch ominous? Pulling a folded sheet of paper from his pocket, he tosses it on my desk.

Dare I open it? Every move is now shrouded in a dark covering. Veiled messages. Double meanings. False motives. Better to have a heads-up first. Rather than pick it up, I point to it. "What's this?"

"An opportunity."

"Great. We're talking in riddles now?"

"Look at it." He takes the chair Mark vacated seconds before.

Snatching up the paper, I unfold it. On it, a picture of a small church—some would say quaint—with statistics. "I don't get it."

"A friend of mine sent that to me. Their pastor took a position down in the Bay Area, and they're looking for someone to come in and do some reconstruction. Bring it back to its former glory."

I peruse the numbers. "I'm not a contractor."

"We're talking reconstruction of the human variety. The building's in sound condition."

It looks like something out of *Little House on the Prairie*. Instead, it's a mere thirty minutes away. "Georgetown?"

"Yep."

I hand the paper to him. "I still don't get it."

"A chance to start fresh. Leave all this backbiting and innuendo."

"Afraid the gossip travels with you."

Kent, eyes on the paper, says, "It doesn't have to be that way."

"I'm not turning tail and running. Not when I've done nothing wrong."

"So, you'd rather wait around here while they crucify your reputation?"

With a sigh, I drop in the chair. "How many members?"

"Does it matter?"

More than I'd like to admit. "I've worked hard at building this church up over the last ten years."

"And there are people out there who'll do everything in their power to take that from you. Is that what you want?"

"The lies they're telling about me—"

"It's not just you anymore."

First Mark, now Kent. "Corey's past…mistakes are none of their business."

"They don't see it that way. And even if they did, it's not going to stop them if they can use it to get what they want."

I rub my face and blow out a sigh. "Why's this happening?"

"That's between you and the Big Guy." Kent points to the ceiling. "I'm sure He's got something to say about it all."

"Maybe. But He's not talking lately."

Kent pushes up from the chair. "Might be you're not listening."

∼

Corey

Taylor's found her voice and there's no stopping her. Her chatter fills the silence and tension between Paul and me as we pull into the driveway with a checklist of instructions. Keep television and music down to a minimum. 24-hour supervision. Not too much stimulation. Church is fine, but if she seems to get agitated, escort her to a quiet area to recoup. Be prepared for her to speak whatever comes to mind—no filter system.

It's either inspiration for a sitcom or setup for colossal failure.

"We live here?" Taylor holds her injured bear tight against her chest. "I don't remember this house."

Unbuckling my seat belt, I turn to look at her. "We've lived here for eight years."

"Oh, yeah." She stares out the window at the yard. "I kinda remember that." She points.

"What?" Paul ducks his head to look out my window.

"That…flower. No. What is that?"

I follow the line of her finger. "The oak tree?"

"Yeah. The oak tree."

We were told to expect this, but still…it's disconcerting to realize how much Taylor's lost.

I open her door and help her out while Paul collects her bag from the back.

Every experience is new and daunting. Rambo jumps up on her when she walks through the front door, and she steps back with a squeal.

"That's Rambo," Paul says. "Do you remember him?"

"I brought him to see you a few weeks ago, remember?"

She ignores the dog and wanders into the house, as if searching for something. Or someone. "Where's Michael?"

At least she hasn't forgotten her brother. "He's at work, but he'll be home for dinner. Let's get your stuff unpacked." What will she think of the new colors in her bedroom? I spent three late nights painting the former pink walls lavender and mint. But will she remember?

The lack of memory is both a blessing and a concern. When she begins to put the pieces together…I'm not sure how we'll handle it. Unless Paul moves to my side of the camp, it could be detrimental.

"This…this is my room?" Stepping through the door, she drops the bear on the bed and runs her fingers along the wall. "I…I don't…wasn't it a different color?"

That's a good sign. "I repainted it last week. Do you like it?"

"I…I think so." Walking the perimeter of the room, her eyes scan the posters on the wall, books in the case. Her eyes are drawn up to the high shelf encompassing two walls— every conceivable space crammed with china dolls she's received every birthday since the day she was born, thanks to Mom.

She moves on to her desk and picks up the photo that takes center stage—her and Josh mugging for the camera. "Who's this?"

Paul pokes his head in the door. "I'm ordering a pizza. What do you want on it?"

It took several minutes to navigate her through that decision. We settle on sausage, mushrooms, olives, and artichoke hearts.

"Why don't you rest until dinner," I tell her. "I'll go put a salad together." Tucking the bear in her arms, I cover her with a light blanket and leave her to nap.

Rambo's at my feet the minute I start chopping vegetables. I toss him a small piece of broccoli as Paul appears. Every interaction with him is rife with tension. The ability to communicate has become foreign to both of us.

"What do you think?" He snatches up a piece of red pepper and pops it into his mouth. The moment feels almost normal.

"About?"

He jerks a thumb in the direction of Taylor's room. "It's going to be a little tougher than I thought."

"She won't be able to go back to school this year, will she?"

"I wouldn't hold my breath."

"Mrs. Kendall told me homeschooling's a possibility, but I don't see how she can pass physiology or calculus."

"Hey, guys, I'm home," Michael's voice reverberates through the house. "Where is everyone?"

"Tone it down, Michael." Paul's voice rivals his son's. "Taylor's napping until dinner."

Forty-five minutes later, we sit down to a semi-warm pizza and salad.

"This is your spot, Tay." Michael pulls out her chair and my jaw drops. Since when did he acquire manners?

Taylor grabs a slice of pizza and takes a bite before we're settled into our places.

"Hey, Taylor," I say. "You probably forgot that we give thanks before eating."

"Thanks?" The word's mumbled around a full mouth.

Paul, who sits at her right, reaches out and takes her hand, and we all follow suit while she chews, and he gives the blessing. Taylor's "Amen," echoes a beat behind the rest.

Michael bypasses the salad and takes two slices of pizza.

I hand the salad bowl to him and ignore the eye roll.

He scoops a minuscule serving onto his plate. "Can I take the leftover pizza for lunch tomorrow?"

"Lunch tomorrow?" Paul says.

"Yeah. I'm working. Hey, Tay." He turns to his sister. "Did Mom tell you I got a job? Working at the Pit 'n' Stop."

Paul serves himself salad. "You can't work tomorrow."

Michael's head whips around. Here we go again. Why is everything between these two a battle? "I gotta work. I promised Craig."

"Sorry, but it's not gonna happen. Have you forgotten it's Easter?"

"So?" Michael scowls.

"So? What d'you mean, so? You're expected to be there. Regardless, you're not going to be working on Sundays."

"You do," Michael fires back.

Taylor's eyes widen as she tracks the argument, her own food forgotten.

"Listen, guys." I place a hand on Paul's arm.

"I *have* to work on Sunday, smart guy. That's my job."

"And I told Craig I'd work on Sundays, so that's *my* job."

"That's enough." I shoot daggers at Paul and Michael, but they're so embroiled in their battle, they don't seem to notice my raised voice.

"It's not the same, Michael."

"This sucks," he shouts. "You want me to get a job to pay back that stupid money, but you won't let me work. So, what am I supposed to do?"

"You can work on Saturdays. Or maybe after school, if you keep your grades up."

"You guys…" Taylor's face scrunches up, greasy hands covering her ears. "You're…noise…stop."

I rush to her and kneel at the side of her chair, tugging on her hands… "It's okay. They're done. Aren't you?" I glare at Paul as he kneels at her other side.

"No…fight…fighting." Tears swim in her eyes. "It's too…boom."

"Sorry, Tay," Michael mumbles.

"Your brother and I will finish this discussion after dinner," Paul says. "In my office."

Michael scowls. "What's the point?"

Chapter 21

Paul

Church is packed with visiting families and bi-annual attendees to the Big Two—Christmas and Easter. Tons of kids,
since there's no Sunday school today. Boys with slicked back
hair, miniature suits, and ties. Girls in pastel and lace. A
banner hangs across the altar—*Happy Resurrection Day!*

My message has been prepared for a month, but I'm not
feeling it. Too many battles in my head and heart. Too many
disappointments. After dinner last night, Michael and I took
ours to my office. I'm not a hundred percent sure he'll accom-
pany Corey and Taylor this morning. I left early.

Taylor home for the weekend stirs things up. I'm grateful
she's recovering but can't shake my resentment toward Corey.
Just when forgiveness seems possible, my head's filled with
sordid scenes of her and some faceless guy. Visions that turn
my stomach and fill me with anger all over again. And yet,
I've never needed her more.

Where does that leave us?

Warnings from Taylor's therapists weren't enough. I
wasn't prepared for the extraordinary work involved for her to

hold up her end of a conversation. She chattered all the way home, but more random rambling than actual conversation.

The worship team starts up the opening chords of their second selection, *I Will Rise*, and I take in the sea of familiar and not so familiar faces. Beverly Pendleton, sans John, with some of their children and grandchildren Drew and Rebecca Simpson, Mark's parents—third row, center—with his wife and young son. Corey, her arm around Taylor who's covering her ears again, and, yes, Michael's with them. Could he appear any more bored?

He had the nerve last night to tell me I'm hung up on what people might think.

"Who cares if I'm in church or not?" he'd said. "If you weren't the pastor, *you* wouldn't care."

"Not true." But was it? Was I more concerned about appearances than truth? I hated to admit the first thing that entered my mind was what Drew Simpson and his bullies would make of Michael's absence.

"So, you're saying I can't work on Sundays at all?"

"Give me tomorrow."

A glare was his only answer.

"Better yet, give your sister tomorrow. It'll be hard enough for her. She could use your support."

His features softened. Couldn't fault his loyalty.

"You can work one Sunday a month."

"Three."

"Two."

"Done." His smile was triumphant. He'd worked me and I'd played right into his hands.

If we could only hone his manipulative skills for good.

Mark's nudge brings me back to the here and now. "You about ready?"

I glance behind him where Becky's got the kids arranged, ready for their performance. "Let's get this show on the road." And that's what it feels like today. A show.

Mark introduces Becky, who marches the children out for their Easter performance. White-gowned bodies in angels' wings. The cute factor more than makes up for the voices so far off key it makes my fillings ache. From my hidden position, I watch Taylor's reaction with some trepidation. The noise level's on par with the argument at the dinner table last night. I can imagine the reaction to her stepping up to halt the performance. But Corey's got it covered.

Closing my eyes, I search for God's presence. *Are You there, Lord? Can't do this on my own here.* I've spent so much time pushing Him away, and now when I need Him...

It's my turn to step up to the mic, and I find three friendly faces and focus on those for the duration. It wouldn't do to get hung up on Drew Simpson's scowl.

"Welcome to all of you in celebration of Resurrection Sunday. Some of you may wonder why I refer to it that way rather than Easter. This day is a celebration of the resurrection of Jesus Christ. Easter, with its European origins in a Pagan goddess, is identified more readily with a bunny and egg hunt. We want our focus to be where it should be—on the person of Jesus Christ."

As I near the end of my message and the worship team gears up to retake the stage, a shuffling of bodies catches my eye. Corey and Taylor make their way to the aisle. Who is that following them? Alexis? Stumbling over the closing prayer, I plan my exit. I've got to get to Corey and Taylor before Alexis can spread more of her poison.

Disconnecting my mic, I step from the podium. The worship team files up, blocking me from stepping down. Nerves zinging up my back, I push through the bodies with as much grace as an elephant on ice skates.

I can't let Alexis get to my family.

~

Corey

I shuffle Taylor out into the sanctuary and shut the doors to muffle the music. Her face is scrunched up, hands pressed tight against her ears.

"You can let go now," I say. It would be funny if she didn't look so upset. Two months ago, she complained that the music needed to be louder, more contemporary. I suppose she won't be making that claim again anytime soon.

Her hands come down in slow-mo, cautious. "It's too loud. It hurts my head."

"That's fine. We can wait out here until the service is over." Maybe we'd better wait in the car. Her entrance caused quite a stir—like some kind of rock star. To her credit, she'd only shrunk back a little.

I can't even imagine what's going through her mind. Getting dressed this morning had been a challenge.

"Can't I...just...just wear...sweats?" She'd clutched the powder blue cotton set to her chest as if it were a treasured doll.

"Wouldn't you like to dress up a little? It's Easter."

She shrugged. "I don't have to wear a dress, do I?"

"No." She'd lost weight in the hospital. A dress would be an easier fit than slacks, but the crease between her brow was reminiscent of her toddler tantrums. Taylor hadn't had the terrible-twos—nothing halfway for my girl. She'd liked the expanded version that lasted until sometime in the middle of first grade.

We went through at least ten different outfits before finding something acceptable. Gray leggings with layered tunic-length shirt. Loose fit, but not so much they looked like hand-me-downs.

"Now, what about your hair?" We stared in the bathroom mirror together to assess. The silky-soft hair of two months before was dull and course. And that wasn't the worst of it.

What to do with that quarter patch of military-style outgrowth?

"It's…ugly." Tears pooled in her eyes and I scrambled for some way to make it better.

"We'll do a comb over. If old, bald guys can get away with it…"

She glared at me.

"A hat?"

We settled on a scarf tied gypsy-style. I heated up her curling iron and created magic. An overstatement, but it passed muster with Taylor, so that's all that mattered.

We'd gathered up a grumbling Michael and run out the door only five minutes late. Not bad.

Now, as we walk across the foyer, the noise level explodes for a brief moment. Someone must have exited the sanctuary.

"Taylor?"

With a protective arm around my daughter, I turn to face Alexis Andrews looking like a runway fashion model. How does she stay so thin? Hair and makeup impeccable as usual. I'd love to have seen how she handled Josh's infancy. Baby puke on her shoulder, in her hair. Just the thought of it brings some kind of sick satisfaction.

"What are you doing here?" The question is out before I can filter it through my pastor-wife persona. My face heats and I pull my foot out of my mouth. "I mean, I thought you were no longer attending here."

She cocks a penciled eyebrow. "I haven't quite found my niche yet." Her eyes travel over Taylor. "You look wonderful, Taylor."

Taylor smiles and pats her thighs. "Yeah. My shirt matches my toys."

A snort escapes through my nose as Alexis's eyebrows draw together in confusion.

"Your…toys?"

"Leggings, sweetie," I whisper to Taylor, the smile still

pulling at the corners of my mouth as Michael barrels through the door.

"Can we go now?" He scowls at Alexis, so like Paul. What *is* the deal with this chick, as Tricia dubbed her?

"Just one moment." Alexis rests acrylic-covered nails on Taylor's arm. "Are you home now? I know Josh would love to see you."

Taylor turns panic-stricken eyes on me.

"A weekend visit," I tell Alexis. "It might be better if Josh waits until Taylor calls him. She's a little overwhelmed right now. Let's go home guys."

Michael takes Taylor's other arm, and we turn to leave when the doors open again. Paul, mouth set, charges out as if the hounds of hell are on his heels. He passes Alexis with a brief glance and encompasses us with outstretched arms.

"Are you going to take Taylor home now?" It's a command couched in what? Concern? Anger? "I'll be there soon, and we can drive her back down to the hospital."

Paul in manipulation mode. He wants me out of here. I'd fight it just on principle, but Taylor would pay the price. And what's with the show? Tender kiss on the cheek, squeeze of the shoulder? I'm not the only one with secrets lurking in my past. Or *is* it his past? Does Alexis have anything to do with his present?

I think back to the night at Bella Cucina. Alexis in the booth behind us. Did she hear anything? If so, she knows that Taylor isn't Paul's daughter. And if that's true, it won't be long before it's spread all over town. It won't matter if Taylor remembers the day of her accident or not.

What was it Benjamin Franklin said? Three can keep a secret if two of them are dead.

Chapter 22

Corey

The week has been packed with therapy "benchmarks" to assess Taylor's readiness to come home. Seven weeks of one step forward and two steps back hasn't changed in these last five days. So, when it comes time for Dr. Holland to do her final evaluation the day Taylor is to be released, I find it impossible to take a full breath.

"We would generally refer Taylor to another six-week occupational rehab facility," Veronica told me earlier in the week. "But most young people in Taylor's situation are not being returned to a healthy home life. She not only has that going for her, but you have experience in the classroom." She smiles. "Nora's felt a little intimidated on the days you sit in on her therapy."

"Intimidated?" I laughed. "By me?" That's a first. But somewhere deep inside, it felt good. Pastor Paul intimidates by virtue of his position. Not me. I'm just the housewife. I suspect it's one of the reasons Taylor connected so early in her life with Paul. What kind of a role model was I to a young girl— unless she wanted to blend into the background?

But as I sit in the corner while Dr. Holland does her last assessment, I pray, I feel anything but intimidating. The chair bites into my butt cheeks as I perch on the edge, too keyed up to sit back and even attempt to pretend I'm relaxed. What if Taylor fails? What if they decide to keep her another week? Or worse, make her go to the other rehab facility for six weeks? Even Veronica, who recommends the facility all the time, said it wasn't the best environment for someone like Taylor.

"More often than not," she'd said, "these kids are doing something they shouldn't be in the first place, which lands them in here. Driving under the influence of drugs or alcohol. They don't handle the brain injury with Taylor's sweet, smiley-faced disposition. They're angry to start with, and the chemical imbalance of the injury doesn't make it any better."

It was our concern over what that environment would do to Taylor that had Paul fighting against it. It was my worry about Taylor's memory returning while there that made me determined she'd come home.

And we won.

Taylor now paces back and forth in her room, a tub of yogurt in one hand, a spoon in the other. Dr. Holland rests her backside against the desk, clipboard in hand, taking notes after every question she fires at Taylor.

"Are you nervous about going home?"

"Uh-uh," Taylor grunts around the spoon in her mouth. She licks it clean and continues the pacing. "Well. I guess a… little…bit. I can't remember things. And Josh…he makes me feel weird."

Dr. Holland makes eye contact with me before making a notation in the chart. We talked about this. The brain injury may cause difficulty with discernment. Taylor could perceive sexual advances where none exist, and it could repel her or attract her. Either way isn't healthy. So, no Josh for a while—at least not unsupervised.

"Would you rather be admitted to another rehabilitation facility or go home?"

I don't dare breathe for the moment it takes Taylor to answer. I asked Taylor this same question last week, and she assured me she wanted to come home. But will she remember?

"Home." She dips her spoon in for another bite of the cherry-pink yogurt. "I don't want…to be…with a bunch of… strange…strangers."

"You realize you still need to attend therapy sessions twice a week."

"There's nothing wrong with me."

"If that's the case, then you should have no trouble putting your spoon where it belongs."

Taylor looks at her spoon. "Okay."

"Where does it go?"

"Dish thingy." She waves it around. "You know. To be washed."

Dr. Holland nods. "Why don't you take it there then?"

Taylor looks around the room as if the dishwasher will appear out of thin air. She walks to the bathroom sink and deposits it.

"That's not the dishwasher," Dr. Holland says. "In what room do we keep the dishwasher?"

"With the fridgerator."

"Where do we keep the refrigerator?"

Taylor walks over to her bed and places the spoon on the top of the fluorescent light fixture that tops the headboard. "There?"

Dr. Holland shakes her head. "Let me walk you to the kitchen. We'll be right back, Mrs. Shaffer."

When they're out of sight, I reach into my purse for my cell phone and punch in Paul's number.

"What's up, Corey? Are they letting her come home?"

"I'm not sure yet. She just put her spoon on top of the

light fixture. And I didn't tell the doctor this, but when I first got here, she tried to brush her hair with a toothbrush."

"At least she's got the brush part down."

Anyone listening to our conversation would never guess that we've fallen into the dysfunctional family category. Veronica wouldn't be so quick to assume Taylor's going back into a healthy home life when it feels anything but. We're polite. Cordial. But underneath the veneer of civility is a host of unspoken words—accusations and mistrust that, if allowed to reign, would spew out with the impact of a level 5 volcano.

"Well, give me a call when you know."

"I wish you were here—" I bite off the rest. The resentment that he chose a staff meeting over being available for Taylor's discharge. The resentment that he looks for any excuse not to be alone with me.

"It can't be helped. I'll pick up dinner tonight, so don't worry about cooking."

As if that makes up for it.

I disconnect without saying more. What else is there to say?

"…painted it a purple and green color." Taylor's voice floats down the hall before she's visible. Is it my imagination or is she louder now?

"That sounds lovely," the doctor says. "We'll get you discharged lickety split, and you can sleep in your own bed tonight."

I let out a sigh. She's coming home after all. *Thank You, God.*

Paul picks up Chinese—a celebration for Taylor's true homecoming—and I give Taylor her first assignment. Set the table.

She's had this chore since she was four, but she looks at the utensils bundled in her hands as if she has no clue what to do with them.

I watch from the kitchen entrance, the scents of garlic chicken, hot oil sauce, and spices I can't name wafting from the white take-out boxes sitting on the dining room table. My stomach rumbles. Did I forget to eat lunch today? "Do you remember which side the fork goes on?"

Spreading the forks, knives, and spoons on the table, she stares at them. Maybe a better question would be, "Do you know which are the forks?"

"We're having Chinese." She frowns. "Where's the chopsticks?"

Okay, maybe I'm not giving her enough credit. "Are you up for the challenge?"

She nods once, an emphatic snap of her head. Every now and then, there are nuances of her toddler self I want to hold close to me. There's no telling when it will come to an end, when she'll recoup her almost-adultlike self.

Word got out, most likely through Michael, that Taylor would be coming home. There are a stack of phone messages for her. Of the six, three of them are from Josh. So much for waiting for Taylor to call him. But then, who knows if Alexis bothered to pass on the message.

The front door slams, Rambo gives a welcoming yip, and Michael storms in. What now? But when he appears in the dining room, he looks like he just won the lottery, grinning from ear to ear.

"Hey, Taylor."

She glares at him. "Do you have to be so loud?"

"Sorry." But he seems unfazed and not at all apologetic when he homes in on me. "Where's Dad?"

Who are you and what have you done with my surly son? "Why?"

"I gotta show him something." He waves an official-looking sheet of paper over his head.

Paul appears, rimless glasses pushed up on his head. "What's up?"

"This." Michael hands him the paper, standing close enough to read it along with Paul.

"This is great, Michael." He clamps a hand around the nape of Michael's neck and gives it an affectionate shake. "I knew you could do it."

"What is it?" I take the sheet Paul holds out to me.

"Progress report," Michael says.

Scanning the grades, my grin matches Michael's. "Sweetie, this is outstanding." Three A's, three B's and a C.

"Also," Michael says, pulling something from his pocket and slapping it into Paul's hand, "the first payment toward my restitution."

Paul fans out the three twenties and nods. "Good job, son."

"So." Michael looks from Paul to me and back again, hands jammed into his jeans' pockets. "Can we talk about SOCAPA?"

"What?" Paul shrugs, brows drawn down in confusion.

"Summer camp."

Oh no. I should have seen this coming.

"I don't get it," Paul says. "What's this to do with that camp thing?"

"Everything." Michael's grin slips. "You wanted me to get my grades up, so I did. You wanted me to start paying back that money." He nods at the money in Paul's hand. "There it is."

"Michael's going to summer camp?" Taylor stands in the entrance to the kitchen, an assortment of chop sticks in her hands.

Paul slips the money into Michael's shirt pocket. "No. Michael's *not* going to summer camp." He's addressing Taylor, but his eyes remain on Michael. "For one thing, we can't afford it. And if you think you can make a token effort and get whatever you want—"

"Whatever I *want?* Are you *kidding* me?"

This will go nowhere fast. "Michael, let's talk about this—"

"No, Corey." Paul glares at me. "We're not going to *talk* about this. We've already discussed it."

"That's so not fair." Michael's face reddens, jaw clenching. "If it was Taylor, it'd be different."

"Fine." Paul turns on Michael, his face every bit as red as his son's. "You want to talk about Taylor? Let's do that. Taylor didn't go out and vandalize a school for no reason. Taylor's had stellar grades—"

"Paul, stop!"

He turns on me. "He wants to talk about Taylor." Then back to Michael. "Everything she's worked for was lost with one stupid car accident. Thanks to your mom, she won't even be graduating high school this year. You want to be like Taylor?"

Heat fills my face, nails biting into the palms of my hands. How *dare* he.

"I won't...grad...graduate?" Taylor stands against the wall, tears swimming in her eyes, arms tight across her stomach.

"Mom?" Michael scowls. "What's Mom got to do with it? It's not her fault Taylor got in that accident."

"That's enough, Paul." The words reverberate through the room, resulting in dead silence. My hands shake as I reach out for Taylor, anger thrumming through every nerve ending. I can't look at my husband, can't stomach his betrayal—a betrayal every bit as damaging as my own.

Wrapping an arm around Taylor, I hold her close and walk her to the table. "Everything will work out just fine with school, sweetie. I'll make sure of it. I'm working with Mrs. Kendall, and we have some ideas." I glance at Paul and

Michael, so alike, so uncompromising and stubborn. And selfish.

With a deep breath, I will my tone to not belie the underlying violence. "Let's eat. It is, after all, Taylor's first night home."

Chapter 23

Paul

The kink in my back's a rude reminder of a sleepless night on the couch. Corey's ticked. So much she's not talking. Not even looking at me. How did the tables get turned? *I'm* the one who should be angry.

So why does guilt eat at me?

Up before the sun, I showered in the kids' bathroom and threw on my clothes from yesterday. No way I was going to face the lioness in her den to get clean underwear. Then I snuck out of the house like a danged thief. My own house. Bought and paid for by the sweat of my father's brow.

We should be celebrating. Taylor's home. Michael's grades are up. Instead, there's a pall of darkness looming over us all. I kind of get how Job felt.

I park in front of Kent's house and kill the engine. I called earlier to see if he could meet, and this was his idea. Modest home, well-tended yard. I recheck the address before climbing out. The scent of fresh-cut grass reminds me it's spring as I approach the front porch.

The door flies open before I can knock. "Hey," Kent says.

"Right on time. Come on in. It's a little crazy right now, but Cheryl'll have the kids out the door in a jiff."

"No problem." I step inside to the cacophony of voices coming from somewhere beyond my vision. Boys' voices superseded by that of a young girl.

The scents of coffee and bacon remind me that I left the house with my tail between my legs. No caffeine and no food.

"Let's go to my office. It'll be quieter there. Can I get you some coffee?"

Does my desperation show? "That'd be great." I follow him into the kitchen and see remnants of breakfast on the kitchen table, dishes in the sink, cereal boxes on the counter.

"Milk? Sugar?"

"No, thanks."

I wrap my hands around the full mug he gives me, while he clears off the table. "Appreciate you taking the time to meet with me."

"Glad to do it. Here, have a seat." He pulls out a chair for me. "Afraid this is my office. With four kids, we needed all the bedroom space we could get."

"I don't know how you manage four kids." Life's crazy enough with two. We settle at the table, and I take an appreciative sip of coffee.

A little girl with curly brown hair rushes in and stops short when she sees me. "Oh, hi."

"Hi yourself." She reminds me of Taylor when she was little. "What's your name?"

"Ruthie. What's yours?"

"Pastor Paul." I offer my hand. "It's nice to meet you Miss Ruthie."

She giggles and puts her miniature hand in mine. Tight grip for such a little thing. Turning to Kent, she says, "Mom said to tell you we're going now." She throws her arms around his neck and gives him a loud kiss on the cheek.

"Okay. Have a good day, and learn something."

She nods, curls bouncing. "'Kay." Then she rushes out the way she came in, pink pack bouncing against her back.

"My youngest," he explains, "and only girl."

I shake my head. "Three boys? Ever feel like a battle zone around here?"

"We have our moments." He sips his coffee and waits like he's got all the time in the world. The noise level escalates for a couple heartbeats, and then the house is silent except for the ticking of a clock and the hum of the refrigerator.

"I guess you're wondering why I wanted to meet with you."

Quirk of one eyebrow, but still he waits. Patient man. Enviable.

"I could use some wise counsel."

"I'm listening."

"The female instigator I told you about last time?"

He nods.

"She made an appearance at the service Sunday." Staring at the dark liquid in my cup, I hesitate. "She's up to something. It feels like I'm waiting for the other shoe to drop."

"You have truth on your side. Nothing to hide."

I shake my head. "I haven't told you everything."

"Oh?"

"If this blows up, it's not just me who'll be hurt. Corey and Taylor. Michael, too, for that matter."

"If what you told me last time is true—"

"It is. But I didn't tell you everything. Alexis...she has information...about Corey and Taylor. Whatever she's got going with Drew Simpson, she's willing to use it to get me to step down."

"So, what do you want to do?"

"Do?" I shake my head. "I'd like to stand up to her. This whole sordid mess started because I stepped on her precious pride. I had a front-row seat to her humiliation, and she wants me to pay. But in the process, Corey and Taylor will pay too."

"I can't tell you what to do here, Paul. But I will say that it's not going to end well if you let them bully you."

"And it's not going to end well if I don't." Impossible situation. I can't quite remember why I wanted to be a pastor in the first place. But to let them railroad me out...I have my pride too.

"What can I do to help?"

I shake my head. "Would you be willing to go with me to talk to her? I don't think it's smart to do it on my own."

He nods. "You shared this with your associate pastor?"

"No."

"Might want to bring him in on this. While you're at it, consider gathering anyone who's taking part of this lynch mob mentality. Get it out in the open, once and for all."

"Makes sense." I rub a thumb across the rim of the mug. "But first, I need to tell Corey."

Kent's eyes widen, and he shakes his head. "You've kept all this from your wife?"

"You don't know the whole story. You see—"

"I don't have to. Ever hear the saying divide and conquer? You know as well as I that it's Satan's favorite strategy. Every day you go this alone makes you both more vulnerable."

"I get that, it's just..."

"Just what?"

"It may be too late."

∾

Corey

After weeks of spending every morning in a rush to get to the hospital, the idea of time to myself feels unsettling. I should feel free, unencumbered, maybe even renewed. Instead, the change in routine is clouded by doubt. Nothing is as it should be. What did I do before Taylor's accident? Paul and I would get the kids off to school and sit together with a cup of coffee, share the day's schedule.

After last night, I couldn't stomach looking at Paul, let alone sharing small talk with him. How dare he tell Michael that Taylor's accident was my fault? I can't deny the truth of it, but to throw it out there, as if he had no concern for the ramifications…

What happened to that man who'd lay down his life for me? Or was that all talk? Now, he's more than happy to throw me under the bus and take out a couple innocent bystanders in the process—Taylor and Michael. And what if Michael had asked about Paul's accusation? I waited for it this morning, nerve endings frazzled, until Michael left for school. But he was quiet while he ate his breakfast. Probably battling his own demons.

I dump Michael's breakfast dishes into the sink and wrap all but one of the leftover chocolate chip pancakes in foil for Taylor. The kids' favorite. With little energy and even less enthusiasm, I forced myself to make a batch this morning while glib sayings played a mantra in my head, spurring me on. Fake it 'til you make it. Loving actions produce loving feelings. Just do it.

I bite off a piece of the pancake I left out for myself, Rambo moving in to beg. "Chocolate's not good for you, pal." The truth is, I'm not willing to share. I load the dishwasher and wipe down the counters, forcing myself to complete a few mundane tasks before sneaking down the hall to check on Taylor. Again. Just like I did when she was an infant.

I slip into her room and close the door, so Rambo won't wake her. Sun pours through the lavender sheers on her window, bathing the room in warm light. Twelve hours, and she's still sleeping. Is this normal? I dangle my hand in front of her face. Okay, she's breathing. I'm just being a worrier.

Better use the quiet time to make a game plan, because the one I have now isn't working. I will have to face both

Taylor and Michael with the truth, but I can't do it with St. Paul raining judgment on me. I have enough of my own to deal with—eighteen years' worth.

Whatever is going on between Paul and Michael, I'm a hindrance. They both use me as a go-between and refuse to deal with whatever the true issue may be. Michael's rebellion. Paul's inability to forgive him. It's not that simple. It never is.

While Paul slept on the couch last night, I couched myself in prayer. When it comes to praying for others, I'm a world-class champion. The words flow through my mind and out my mouth. Whether it's for Paul or the kids, a friend, our country, or any other for that matter. But when it comes to praying for myself? I hear my father's words, "A harder lesson to learn than asking for permission is living with consequences." I've made my bed, so what right do I have to ask God to clean it up?

Last night was different. Was it my sobs that had Him responding? Or maybe He's been speaking all along, but I've not been listening. Well I was listening last night. He wasn't prolific, but He laid on my heart a verse: *Better to live in a desert than with a quarrelsome wife.* Or a quarrelsome husband. After more prayer, I knew what I should do. Needed to do.

When Paul and I started dating, I had such stars in my eyes that they blinded me to any comparison I might have made with my father. Paul was sweet and affectionate. I'd never seen either trait in Dad. Paul was focused and passionate about his calling but could shift that laser focus onto me so fast it took my breath away. This would not be a man who put work first.

And he courted me. That was romantic enough to dispel any of the underlying red flags I might have noticed otherwise.

~~Because they'd been there.~~

A month before our wedding, Paul's sister, Justine, came to him in tears, pregnant. What should she do?

"What did you tell her?" I'd asked him. We were sitting in "our" booth at the back of a small cafe. The red vinyl seats were faded and cracked with age. Fake daisies, set at every table, tried to muster a little dignity in their dime store vases. Student budgets didn't allow for us to eat anywhere fancy, but that was fine with me. There was comfort in knowing the people who worked there. Comfort in the familiarity.

"What do you think? I told her she'd need to marry him."

Marry Glen? I tried to form a picture of it in my mind, but it wouldn't stick. Justine was sweet and vulnerable. Glen was…not. I was no Freud, but it didn't take a psych major to see something was off about him. He was a con artist with narcissistic tendencies.

"You can't be serious, Paul."

Head down, focused on the menu he could quote in his sleep, he said, "What're you going to have. I was thinking the burger." He glanced at me and must have caught my glare. "What?"

"Glen's…Glen! Justine doesn't belong with him anymore than she does Jack the Ripper."

One eyebrow hitched up, a move I'd thought was cute the first time I saw it. But it didn't take long to figure out he used it to communicate disdain. "Don't you think you're being a little melodramatic?"

"Don't you think you're being a little dismissive? She came to you for advice."

"She should've come to me before taking up with that loser. What choice does she have now?"

"With a little help, she could raise him on her own. Maybe your dad—"

"Dad can't take care of himself, let alone Justine and a baby."

"Well, what about adoption?"

"She doesn't need me for that."

"You know she looks up to you, Paul. If you suggest adoption, she'll consider it. But if you tell her to marry that jerk, that's what she's going to do."

"She'll do what she wants. Obviously."

"You're wrong about her. She wants your love and acceptance, but instead, you give her a set of laws. Talk to her, tell her you—"

"I warned her about him. She chose to ignore that warning. Now she's going to have to live with the choices she's made."

I was paralyzed by his words. If this was how he responded to the needs of a sister he claimed to adore...

Shaking off the memory, I step through the sliding glass door to the back deck. Inhaling the earthy scent of spring, I assess the winter-worn backyard. The lawn is in serious need of a cut. Dead plant stalks mingle with browning daffodils and freshly blooming tulips. My favorite time of year, and instead of the joy the season brings, I'm acting like Eeyore—a gloomy cloud hanging over my sorry head. Maybe Taylor and I could spend some time outside this afternoon. It's going to be a beautiful day, and a little activity will be good for both of us. Reconnect her neurons and my God relationship.

But first things first.

I pour a cup of coffee, doctor it up so it's palatable, snatch up the phone receiver, and tuck myself into the corner of the couch before dialing Tricia's cell number.

"Hey, girlfriend." Her voice explodes across the line, a welcome reminder of normalcy that has me reaching for a tissue. "I was going to call later today. When can I come see Taylor?"

"I have a better idea," I say through my tears. "How would you like a roommate?"

Chapter 24

Paul

Everything's in play.

After my meeting with Kent, I went back to the church to track down Mark. Time to get everything out in the open. The only way to handle a bully is to stand up to him. Or in this case—them. But the best laid plans and all that. Two irate parents, three "emergency" phone calls, and one attitude from an Awana leader later, I was finally able to confess all to Mark —Alexis's vendetta. Simpson's accusations. Corey's betrayal. Taylor's accident.

"Whoa." Mark had slumped back in his chair. "You've been dealing with this how long, and it's the first I've heard of it?"

"Thought I could get a handle on it."

Mark was silent for a heartbeat or two. Probably questioning my discernment. "So, what's the deal with Alexis and Simpson?"

I shook my head. "I don't know, but it's time we find out."

"We?"

"I should have brought you in on this from the beginning.

I've also asked Kent Richardson to join us. Thought it would be good to have an unbiased observer."

"When?"

"As soon as we can get a meeting together." I drummed my fingers on the desk. "But first, I need to talk to Corey."

Hours later, the meeting's set and I'm ready to face the lioness in her den. I'm not sure what I'd been expecting when I walk in the door at five, but it sure wasn't the tantalizing aroma of Italian herbs and garlic. Lasagna? Why would Corey make my favorite dish when she's angry? Arsenic in the sauce?

"Hi, Dad." Taylor comes out of the kitchen carrying plates. "Mom made some noodle thingy."

"Lasagna?"

She nods. "Yeah, that's it."

"It smell's great. How was your day?"

"We worked in the backyard."

"You get your first therapy appointment scheduled?"

"Mom's taking care of it."

Corey comes out of the kitchen, utensils in hand. "Hey, Paul."

"Hi, Corey. Dinner smells great. Lasagna, huh?"

"Yeah." She turns to Taylor and hands her the silverware. "You set the table. Michael's finishing up the salad. Dad and I need to talk for a minute."

"What's this about?" Did someone tip her off?

Taking my arm, she steers me down the hall and into our bedroom.

"Look, Corey, I know you're angry about last night. I shouldn't have—"

"No, you shouldn't have." But her eyes swim with tears, not anger. "We're in an impossible situation here, and—" scrapes her hair back then folds her arms "—I'm leaving."

A lance to the gut. "What do you mean, leaving?"

"I don't see how we can resolve this while I'm here."

Crazy talk. "So, leaving me is the answer? What? You want a divorce? On what grounds?"

She barks out a humorless laugh. "Divorce? No. But I also don't want to live out our marriage in a combat zone. You and me. You and Michael. And if I'm not careful about how I handle this, Taylor and me."

"What *about* Taylor? You're going to just leave her when she needs you the most?"

"Of course not." She looks hurt that I would even suggest it. But what are her options? "I'm taking her with me."

"Wait." I put my hands up, a traffic cop stopping the flow of her lunacy. "Taking her where?"

She looks down, arms tightening around her middle. "Tricia's. We'll leave tomorrow."

"And what about school? And rehab? She's supposed to go twice a week."

"I've spoken with Mrs. Kendall. Taylor will be on independent study, since she can't go back to school yet. It doesn't matter if she's here or in Carmel."

"And rehab?"

"I spoke with Joy, and she—"

"Who?" The word comes out a near-roar.

Corey glares at me. "Joy. The nurse advocate at the hospital. Anyway, she says there are a couple good outpatient rehab centers down in Monterey."

I shake my head. "You've got this whole thing figured out, haven't you? You're just going to make a unilateral decision to leave, not bother to consult me?"

"I'm doing this for you, Paul."

I let out a snort and throw my hands up. "You've got to be kidding."

"I *am*. For you and Michael and Taylor. And yes, for myself, too."

"What does Michael have to do with this?"

She shakes her head, pins me with a look. Determination.

"The two of you use me like some kind of mediator. You need to figure this out for yourselves. But as long as I'm here, you'll default to me."

"You don't know what you're talking about."

"I think I do."

"If you'd just told the truth from the beginning—"

"Like you don't have any secrets of your own?" Her eyebrows hitch up, eyes wide. "There's something going on between you and Alexis Andrews."

"I was going to talk to you about that tonight."

"How convenient."

"No, Corey. It's the truth."

"It doesn't matter. Not really. The issue isn't Alexis."

"You can't think there's something going on between us."

"Of course there's something going on."

"No, Corey."

She waves a dismissive hand. "Oh, don't worry, Paul. I don't think you're having an affair or anything. But there are other ways of being unfaithful, and you haven't trusted me with it. Maybe a little distance will help make things clearer."

Arguments line up in my mind, one after the other. But before I can voice even one, I'm stopped by the determination etched into her features with Mount Rushmore-like proportions. She's made up her mind, and nothing I can say will change it.

Corey

Once Paul realizes he can't change my mind, he paves the way for a normal evening, engaging Taylor in conversation, asking Michael about his schoolwork and job, and even helping with the dinner dishes. *This* is the man I fell in love with—the man I was prepared to lose myself for so many years ago.

I awake to predawn gray seeping through the bedroom windows and know without opening my eyes that Paul isn't in bed. Sliding my bare leg across the mattress, I'm met with lingering warmth. He hasn't been up for long then. Does he regret the tenderness he showed me last night—a tenderness that brought tears to my eyes? Is he regretting the distance that's grown between us, brought on by misplaced motives and a guardedness that has no place in a marriage? Or was his lovemaking a last-ditch effort to change my mind?

If it was, it's working. For better or worse...

Am I abandoning ship merely because the water's a little rough? What if this is a colossal mistake, leaving Paul and Michael? If Paul's willing to work through this stuff, to trust me again—

"I was hoping you were awake." Paul stands in the doorway, chest bare, pajama bottoms resting low on his hips, and a cup of coffee in each hand. He looks anything but pastorly, and my heart leaps. "Heard you moving around and thought a caffeine fix might set the tone for the day."

I've stepped back in time—before Taylor's accident. Before the truth of my past ripped our life in two. Maybe—

"I doctored yours just the way you like it." He waits for me to get settled against the headboard and hands me the steaming mug.

"Mmm." I inhale the heady combination of coffee and chocolate. "Thanks." Warmth spreads through me that has nothing to do with a hot drink. Paul always knew how to tap into the farthest reaches of my heart.

How can I leave now?

"I thought we should talk." He places his mug on my nightstand and sits at my hip. Scratching his cheek, I hear the rasp of his whiskers, blond and barely discernible in this light. Whiskers that had shivers skittering down my spine in the dark of night.

I reach up and touch his face, run my fingers over the

stubble. "It's been so crazy." I wait for him to agree, to make promises. Make me change my mind.

He takes my hand from his cheek and kisses my palm, the stubble tickling, before lowering our joined hands to his lap. "I think your decision to leave for a while is…"

His hesitation fills me with hope.

"A good idea."

My heart stops. "I'm sorry?" I must have heard wrong. "But I thought—"

"It'll do us both good."

He made some other excuses, but they drifted away the moment they left his lips. Excuses. Logical reasons for a separation. After last night? What was that all about then?

Maybe I should have pushed to know what, exactly, his issue was with Alexis Andrews.

I haul all the suitcases I can find from the basement and take two of them to Taylor's room. She sits on her unmade bed, sleepy-eyed, Rambo nestled in the V of her folded legs.

"Okay, Tay. Let's get you packed."

"We can't go today. Josh is coming over." She rubs Rambo's ear and makes no move to get off the bed.

"I'm afraid that's not going to work out."

"But I don't get it. Why are we leaving? I just got home."

"A little vacation. Tricia's very excited to see you."

Michael leans in the door, scowling. "Dad says you're leaving."

With a sigh, I tug on Taylor's arm. "Help me out here, kiddo. I don't know what you want to take."

"Nothing. I want to stay here."

"You love Carmel."

"Mom," Michael says. "What's going on here?"

"Taylor, get started, please. I'll be in my room packing my

things." I pass Michael on my way out, fully expecting he'll follow. I'm not disappointed.

"Are you and Dad getting divorced?" He sounds like a four-year-old.

I toss my own two suitcases on the bed. "No, Michael. We thought this would be good for Taylor. She can focus better on her schoolwork and rehab."

"So, you're just going to bail on me?"

"Look at it as an opportunity to reconnect with your dad."

He snorts. "Whatever."

"Attitude," I throw at him over my shoulder. Wrenching at the zipper, I mutter a word better left unheard under my breath. Why am I so upset? This was *my* brilliant idea. Shouldn't I be thrilled that Paul's backing me instead of fighting me?

"Why can't I go on independent study and come with you?"

"Hmmm. Let's see." I pretend like I'm actually thinking it over. "For one, you just started working at Craig's. Not to mention it would be pretty tough for you to deal with whatever issue you have with Dad long distance."

"I could say the same for you."

Smart aleck. I glare at him, fully prepared to set him straight, but he looks so little-boy-lost, shoulders hunched, mouth downturned, I don't have the heart. "It'll be okay, sweetie. This is just temporary."

"Promise?"

"Promise. And I do think you should use this as an opportunity. Whatever it is that has you angry with Dad, you need to work it out."

He scowls, cramming his hands into the front pockets of his jeans. "What if it can't be worked out? What if he did something...you know...that can't be forgiven."

So, there *was* a reason behind his behavior. Folding my

arms, I sit on the edge of the bed. "Is that why you vandalized the school last year?"

He drops his eyes, staring at the vicinity of his size 11 shoes.

"You want to tell me about it?"

"No," he mumbles.

Whatever it is, it can't be worse than my own sordid past. "Give him a chance to explain, kiddo. Then remember that we're all guilty of unforgivable sins of one form or another."

His head snaps up, brow furrowing. "You don't want to know what he did?"

"It'll come out sooner or later," I say with a sigh. "It always does."

Chapter 25

Corey

Springtime in Carmel-by-the-Sea is as close to heaven as I've ever been—as long as I stay away from the tourist radius around Ocean Avenue. Once I've maneuvered Highway 1 at turtle-crawl pace, the back roads to Tricia's is a snap. Her "hobbit cottage," as I like to call it, sits back from the quiet street, shaded by majestic Monterey cypress. And for a brief moment, I'm Frodo.

Pulling into Tricia's narrow cobblestone driveway behind her red Mini-Cooper, the tension from my shoulders eases, and I inhale the tang of the sea, less than a half mile away as the crow flies. Taylor's asleep in the passenger seat, her head lolling at an odd angle that has my own neck aching with sympathy pains. Rambo, sensitive to the lack of movement, yips from the back, galloping across the bench seat to check out the view from both windows.

"Hey, Tay," I whisper. "We're here."

Raising her hands, she rubs at her pink cheeks, eyes blinking at the sun spotlighting down through the branches of a tree overhead.

I reach behind her seat and snatch up my purse. "Do you smell the ocean?"

"Mmmm," she groans, stretching her arms high enough to touch the headliner.

The arched, weather-gray plank front door opens, and Tricia comes out, shouting words of welcome. Faded jeans and a fuchsia-colored sweater hug her trim body as she runs down the walkway on bare feet. My frump-factor rises several notches as I climb out of the car to accept her welcoming hug. When was the last time I felt as young as she looks?

"It's so good to see you." She gives me a quick squeeze, eyes darting to Taylor through the windshield. "How was the drive?"

"Long." I push the mop of hair behind my ears. "The air feels wonderful here." A soothing balm to a wounded soul. Okay, maybe a little melodramatic.

"You brought great weather with you. We've had lots of rain the last few days, but today—hey, have you lost weight?" She takes my hands, opens my arms, and inspects me.

"No," is my automatic response. But...my jeans *have* been looser. Who can eat with all the stress? "I don't know. Maybe."

"No 'maybe' about it, girl," she says as she rushes to open Taylor's door.

"Hi, Auntie Trish."

"There's a rumor going around that you were in a car accident." She takes Taylor's hands and repeats the inspection process. "Must be a lie. You look great." She pulls Taylor in for a hug as Rambo hops off the passenger seat.

Taylor steps back and looks at the house. "I remember here." The smile and excitement in her eyes are a good sign.

"Of course you do," Tricia says. "You've been here a hundred times."

I don't bother pointing out that she didn't remember the house she's lived in for eight years.

We get everything unloaded from the car, and Tricia

shows us to our rooms. It's luxurious living, bordering on the decadent. A four-poster queen bed sits in the middle of Taylor's room, covered in a white, embroidered quilt and about a million pillows in bursts of color. Three windows, all covered in cream-colored wooden blinds, allow slatted sunlight.

"I'm going to lie down, okay?" Taylor doesn't wait for an answer, but plops into a wing-backed chair in the corner to remove her shoes.

"Aren't you hungry?" Tricia asks. "I have lunch."

"No, thanks. I'm really tired."

We leave her to her nap.

Tricia closes the door as we exit. "Must be the excitement, huh?"

"She sleeps a lot. The stimulation's hard on her."

We deposit my bags in another guest room. Slats of sunshine filter through the blinds here too. Soft green and white—like mint ice cream.

"You sure know how to live." I run a finger across the pine footboard and fight the urge to snuggle into my own nap, like Taylor.

Tricia leads me to the kitchen, Rambo following. "Are *you* hungry?"

I wince at the spread laid out on the table in the dining nook. "Not so much."

"That's okay. It'll keep. Let's get something cold to drink and go out to the back deck."

The backyard, like the front, is cocooned in its own little world by cedars and foliage. Easing into the cushioned deck chair, I sigh. "It wouldn't take long to get used to this." Rambo explores the fence line, making himself right at home.

"It's little compensation for no husband."

"Oh, please." I roll my eyes, Taylor-like. "You could have a husband like that." I snap my fingers. "Just look at you." I take her in from her blonde bob to her fuchsia-painted toenails. "It's been what, six, seven years since Steven died?"

"Eight," Tricia says. "Having all this," she spreads her hands out to encompass the yard, "is little comfort."

"Don't you think it's time to move on? Surely there must be someone out there who's husband-worthy material."

"Yet you have one and don't seem much interested in keeping him." Her tone is light, but I don't miss the admonishment, and it stings.

"What's that supposed to mean?"

She sips at her iced tea and shrugs. "Aren't you a little concerned about leaving Paul in the clutches of that Alexis chick?"

"A little."

"Then why?"

"I didn't know what else to do. It was an impossible situation. Or at least I thought it was."

"So, where do you go from here?"

"I don't know." Did I make a mistake? I was so sure last night it was God's voice urging me to do this, but now... "I thought Paul was going to talk me out of it this morning, and I was ready to let him."

Tricia's eyes soften. "What happened?"

Shaking my head, I swallow the sudden lump in my throat. "He agreed it's a good idea."

"Well, maybe he's right. A little time apart..."

Or maybe "that Alexis chick" has more to do with it than I want to believe.

Paul

When Corey said she was leaving, the bottom dropped out of my world—for the wrong reasons. Concern over what others will think—Simpson in particular—left a pit in my gut. What kind of a husband am I? Guilt softened my attitude. And it hit me—Corey and Taylor are better off gone, out of the line of fire.

"So, why'd Mom really go?" Michael stares me down from the doorway of my home office, brow furrowed, arms crossed. If he could, he'd blame me for all the ills of the world.

"What'd she tell you?"

He snorts and swipes at the hair hanging in his eyes. Time for another trim. Or, if I had my way, a buzz cut. "Said it was better for Taylor. She can focus."

Good as any reason. "There you have it." Conversation over, I shuffle through my sermon notes.

"The other night," he waits until I'm looking at him again, "you said Taylor won't be graduating because of Mom. You meant the accident."

I know better than to throw Corey under the bus a second time. "People say things they don't mean in the heat of an argument."

He shakes his head, hair slipping to cover one eye again. "You meant it."

"No, Michael. I didn't." Why is it this kid pushes every limit of my patience? "Things have been a little tense is all. Your mom had no more to do with Taylor's accident than I did." Now if only I can believe it.

"It seems like you're mad at everyone. Except Taylor."

I can't argue with that. "There are things you don't understand, more complicated than you think, Michael."

"Yeah? Well, explain it to me then." He crams his hands in the pockets of his jeans and leans on the doorjamb. "You're always preaching truth and love and forgiveness. But all I get is lies and anything *but* forgiveness. You know what, *Dad?* Stuff's more *complicated* than you think on this end, too."

"Yeah?" I flick a hand to the chair across my desk. "Sit and explain it to me, then."

"Forget it." He turns to leave.

I push up from the chair. "Michael. *Michael.*"

"What?" He turns back, a scowl on his face.

"We aren't going to resolve anything if we can't talk about it."

"What's to talk about? I screwed up. And you're gonna keep punishing me for it."

Stepping around my desk, I sit on the edge of it. "I'm not punishing you—"

"Then how come I can't go to the photography camp? You said it was 'cause I vandalized the school. That's punishing me for something I did, like, a year ago."

Not this again. "There's more to it than that."

"Like?"

"Like your attitude for one. You'd think *I* was the one who messed up. You're angry, disrespectful, and—"

The phone cuts in. Could be Corey, and without looking at the caller I.D., I snatch up the receiver. "Hello?"

Michael tosses another scowl before walking out.

"Paul?"

"Uh, Marlene?"

"Yes. How are you?"

"Good. I'm afraid Corey's not here. But you can reach her on her cell."

She hesitates. Probably because I'm rushing her off the phone. "I'll do that. How's Taylor settling in?"

I rub my temples with a thumb and forefinger. Hate to lie, but it's not my place to explain Corey and Taylor's absence. "She's…she's doing well. Tired, but that's expected."

"Well, I'd love to talk to her."

"Oh, well, she's with Corey. Like I said, you should try her cell phone."

"Is something wrong?" Her tone sharpens. Must be mother's intuition.

"Wrong? No. But Corey took Taylor down to Carmel. We

thought it would be easier for her to focus on rehabilitation without all the distractions here."

"Oh?" She's not buying it. "Well, then, I suppose I'll call her cell."

We finish up with our good-byes and I hang up with a groan. If it's not one thing, it's another. And speaking of which…my conversation with Michael.

His bedroom door is closed. Two quick raps and I open it. He sits at his desk, textbook open. "Hey, Michael, I want to explain…" He doesn't acknowledge me. Looking closer, I see ear buds and discern the tinny sound of music. It'd be easier to let it go. Why continue this fight when it gets us nowhere?

What happened to the days he'd follow me around like my constant shadow? Is it teenage rebellion? I've been on the counseling end of parents' complaints about their kids distancing themselves. It's natural, I'd tell them. And it is. But this…this is something else. If only he'd talk to me.

Stepping up behind him, I tap his shoulder.

He jerks, as if I startled him, and yanks on the wires hanging from his ears as he turns.

"Thought I'd order a pizza for dinner. What d'you want on it?"

"I have to work." He doesn't bother looking at me, just turns back to his desk.

I've been dismissed. I should know—it's a tactic I use often myself.

Back in my office, I shuffle through my notes. Where was I before Michael came in? We've been working through the book of Acts. It continually amazes me how much the apostle Paul accomplished in his life, given where he started. I struggle to find inspiration for my next message, and he wrote more than half the New Testament.

Glancing at the clock, I do a quick calculation. It's eight east coast time. Early enough to call Justine. I retrieve my phone from the edge of the desk and punch in her number.

"It's about time you called, big brother. I've left a gazillion messages."

Smiling at her exaggeration, I sink back in my chair. "Three. You've left three."

"It feels like a gazillion. Is Taylor out of the hospital? How's she doing? I bet it's been hard on Corey."

"Whoa." I laugh. "One thing at a time."

Her sigh reaches my ears. "Okay. How're things going?"

I update her on Taylor's condition.

"Rehab twice a week, huh? Is Corey taking her down to Sacramento for that?"

"Corey's taken her to Carmel. You know her friend Tricia? They're staying at her place for a while."

Nothing. I didn't think it was possible to stun my sister to silence.

"You there?"

"What's going on?" Suspicion and a hint of admonishment laces her tone.

"We've hit a…rough patch."

"What'd you do?"

"Me? Why do you assume it's me?"

"I know you and I know Corey."

So much for her having my back. "How's Nathaniel? He must be about done with his first year. Has he declared a major yet?"

"You're changing the subject? Really?"

"I didn't call so you could chew me out, Justine. I get enough of that here."

"You didn't call to check on Nathaniel. He said you talked to him last week."

Somewhere along the way, my baby sister grew up. Pride for her softens my tone. "I don't want to get into the details, but I didn't do anything." Not entirely true, but close enough.

"I deal with enough baggage here to know it's never one-sided. But you gave me some good advice once."

"Yeah? What was that?"

"Put the past behind you and move forward with a fresh slate. It's the only thing that keeps things civil between the two of us. So, if you and Corey are having problems—"

"It's not quite that simple."

"It never is. There's something else you once told me. You have to live with the consequences of your actions."

Somehow, I knew that one would come back to bite me one day.

Chapter 26

Corey

I'm on a deserted island. Not the kind I'd imagine being stranded on after a plane crash or the sinking of a cruise ship. Nothing even remotely romantic. This island looks more like one of those ice floes in the midst of the Alaskan glaciers. And everyone I know is on dry land, watching me float away. I've had this dream at least five times since Taylor's accident. But this time it's different.

This time, Alexis Andrews is by Paul's side. Smug smile in place.

An insistent trilling drills into my head, a dull pounding behind my left ear, pulling me from the nightmare. Awareness of my surroundings makes a slow appearance. It's my cell phone. And I'm not in my bed. Tricia's. I'm at Tricia's. *Thank You God.* It was just a dream.

Reaching for my cell on the nightstand, my heart picks up. *Please, be Paul.* I squint at the caller I.D., my eyes not yet focused. But it's not Paul. Richard Carroll. My thumb hesitates over the 'ignore' button. How long can I put him off? At least long enough for a caffeine fix.

Pushing the covers aside, I shiver in the early morning cold and shuffle up to the window, then peek between the wooden slats into Tricia's backyard. The sun's not yet up, but the sky is a predawn gray—no fog. A perfect morning for a walk.

Now if I can just convince Taylor.

Yesterday we made a token visit to the beach after church with Tricia. Just enough to whet my appetite. Today will be busy—Taylor's first outpatient rehab appointment, unpacking to finish, and a little wallowing in my self-inflicted pit of doom. Paul didn't call yesterday. I was so sure he would, but why should I expect he would? I left him.

And he didn't fight me.

Snatching up my robe from the end of the queen bed, I don it as I leave the room. The tantalizing scent of coffee lures me to the empty kitchen. Just a note from Trish to greet me —*Gone in early to the shop. Stop by for lunch.* But bless her, she made coffee. Being alone works for me. I'm not quite ready for conversation anyway.

I rummage through the fridge but find nothing more interesting than low-fat milk to doctor the strong brew. It's better than nothing. Searching through cabinets, I come across a box of individual packets of raw sugar. It's not chocolate, but Tricia hasn't stayed in such amazing shape by indulging. I can't say the same for myself.

Twenty minutes later, I'm ready to hit the beach. Dressed in baggy sweats, I converge on Taylor and Rambo, both sleeping the morning away.

"Hey, kiddo." I sweep Taylor's hair away from her eyes as Rambo maneuvers behind her to give her ear a sniff. "Let's go to the beach."

"Hmmm." Taylor's eyebrows rise, but her lids seem to be glued shut. She mumbles something incoherent.

It takes ten minutes to get her up. Another ten to talk her into a walk.

"I'm tired," she groans.

Rambo spins in circles in front of her, as if he knows where we're going.

"It's good for the neurons."

"What?" Her nose crinkles.

"Veronica said you need to get some exercise every day. It'll help the neurons in your brain reconnect."

She scowls.

"Oh, come on, Tay. You love the beach."

"It's too early, Mom."

"We need to go now if we want to get it in before rehab."

Once outside, the tang of the sea tickles my senses. A briny, salty scent not altogether unpleasant. The air is moist and cool, a slight breeze raising a chill beneath the light sweatshirt I'm wearing.

"It's cold." Taylor folds her arms tight across her chest.

"You'll be fine once we get moving." I tug on Rambo's leash. "Let's go."

We walk the half mile down 8th Avenue, passing multimillion-dollar homes no larger than cottages. Cobblestone driveways, copper-roofed eaves, custom gates and garage doors. Each one its own little wonderland. The residents must have high-powered jobs—no pastors among them—or have had their homes passed down, generation after generation. Like Tricia's late husband. Still, it'd take a fortune just to pay the property taxes.

Taylor's not quite awake, so there's no point in engaging her in conversation. I'll have to tell her about my past—the past that was a roundabout cause of her car accident—but that won't be the worst of it. How will she react when I tell her Paul's not her biological father? She'll want to know who is, won't she? The fact that I can't produce him—not even a name—sickens me with shame. If I can't bear to look at myself in the mirror, how can I expect *her* to forgive me? Or Paul, for that matter? And then there's Michael.

A deserted ice floe sounds pretty good right now.

The thunder of the ocean reaches our ears before it does our eyes as we cross San Antonio Avenue, then a patch of weedy grass, and finally step onto Scenic Drive. Frothy, white waves slow-roll, crashing in a tumble of power before skittering across the sandy beach below, dotted with pieces of driftwood and seaweed. Dogs run free, followed at a leisurely pace by their owners. Rambo tugs at his leash with a yip, and I bend down to release him.

Taylor whips her head around. "What if one of the other dogs attacks him?"

"I think they're pretty seasoned."

"But Rambo's not." She tromps through the ice plant and slides down the sand dune in his wake.

I follow, my eyes tracking back and forth between Taylor and Rambo, who's stopped to greet a sleek golden retriever. The wind tugs at my ponytailed mop of hair. I zip up my sweatshirt and pull the hood over my head as I maneuver the shifting sand.

"Beautiful morning, isn't it?"

I turn to reply and am taken aback by the vibrant blue eyes that greet me. They belong to an elderly man—silver hair, weathered skin, and the kindest face I've ever seen. "Yes. A beautiful morning."

"I've never seen you here before. Tourist?"

"No. Not exactly. I'm staying with a friend."

He nods toward Taylor. "Your daughter?"

I look at Taylor, who's now on her knees in the wet sand, face-to-face with the retriever, Rambo sniffing its other end. So much for worrying about Rambo being attacked. "Yes."

"Well." He starts to say something more, then stops. "I hope to see you again…?" It takes me a moment to catch the question in his tone.

"Corey." I offer my hand. "And you are…?"

"Jonas." He clasps my hand in both of his. "A pleasure, Corey." As he turns to leave, he whistles once—a quick, piercing call—and the retriever Taylor and Rambo befriended sprints up from the beach to follow.

A brief encounter with a stranger. Nothing out of the ordinary, yet—I glance back, but he's gone.

Curious.

Dottie Newman greets Taylor and me with a broad smile and firm handshake before leading us to her office. After working with Veronica for weeks, I half expected Dottie would be a clone of the younger woman. But Dottie's older than me by a good ten years, her short, dark hair streaked with gray. She's confident, but friendly.

"First thing we'll do is assess the severity of Taylor's injury." She rounds her desk in the cramped office and waves a hand at the two chairs facing it. "Have a seat. The hospital faxed a copy of her chart, so I have a place to start. But before I do, any questions?"

Only a million. But I look at Taylor. This is her gig. "Well, Tay. Any questions?"

"I don't know what I'm doing here."

"I explained about speech therapy," I say. "Remember? We talked about it the other day?"

Taylor shrugs.

Dottie folds her hands on the desk and waits for Taylor to make eye contact. "The term 'speech therapy' is a little confusing in your case. My job, along with an occupational therapist, is to help you with focus and memory issues."

"I don't have any."

Dottie makes eye contact with me and I nod.

"Well," she says with a smile. "If your mom talked to you the other day about why you were coming here, and you don't remember—"

"She forgets stuff, too." Taylor's tone is defensive—not unlike the Taylor of before. Strong willed.

Dottie laughs. "Good thing she's here then. She can learn a thing or two that'll help her, too. But let's focus first on you. What year were you born?"

"Umm." Taylor looks at me, eyebrows raised, like she wants me to give her the answers.

"You're on your own, kiddo."

"I think 1952."

"Wow." Dottie laughs. "You're older than I am."

"Okay," Taylor says with a sigh. "Maybe I forget some things."

"Perfectly normal under the circumstances. I'll be working with Heidi, the occupational therapist. It doesn't look like physical therapy will be an issue, but we should let Jacob run an assessment before making that decision."

I clear my throat. "A couple questions, if I may?"

"Of course."

"What is the expected outcome of therapy? I mean, Taylor was supposed to graduate in June."

Dottie shakes her head. "Unless you've made some special arrangements with her school."

"She's on independent study. She has enough credits to graduate, but she needs to pass physiology and pre-calculus."

Dottie's eyebrows disappear behind her bangs and we share a look that says it all—there's no way Taylor's graduating in June. That'll go over about as well as my confession that Paul's not her father. "Let's take it one day at a time, shall we?"

Our next session is with muscle-bound Jacob. I'd bet my last meal he's a surfer. Sun-bleached hair, deep tan, and a loose gait. "Looks like we can forgo physical therapy," he says, thirty minutes later. "Although, she might have sustained some injury to her shoulder. I'll put together some exercises she can do at home."

We leave with three shoulder exercises, computer-generated homework, and an appointment on the books in three days. Twice a week for who knows how long? It could be months.

Taylor buckles her seat belt. "I'm not finishing high school, am I?"

"Of course you will, sweetheart."

"In June?"

It's so hard to disappoint. "Probably not."

"This is stupid! I got good grades in school."

I place a gentle hand on her arm, hoping it'll calm her as it often does Paul. "There's a lot of memory involved in Precalc and physiology. In time—"

"That's not fair, Mom. I want to," she flaps her hand about, "oh, what's the word?"

"Graduate?"

"Graduate with my friends. Not that *they* care. No one came to see me at the hospital."

"You had lots of friends come to see you. Remember all the stuffed animals we showed you?"

Tears swim in her eyes when she looks at me. "But they didn't come to the house. Not even Josh."

"You weren't home long enough. That's my fault. I brought you here—"

"Why?"

"What?"

"Why'd we come here?"

Now's not the time for the truth. Not when she's emotional and tired from therapy. Or am I just making excuses?

"I thought it would be good for us to get away. You love the ocean." *Lame.* "It'll be easier for us to work on your rehabilitation here. Your dad and Michael...well, they aren't getting along." *Yeah, blame them.*

"No high school. That means no college."

"I'm sorry, sweetie. I know this is hard."

"Why's God punishing me?"

"God's *not* punishing you. You've done nothing wrong. And even if you had, that's not how He works." But haven't I believed this more than once since the accident? That I've somehow not repented enough, not *paid* enough for my sins? Why is it I can assure others of God's grace when I can't accept it for myself?

"I'm hungry," Taylor says.

"You want to get an ice cream before we go back to Tricia's?"

Swiping at the tears, she nods. And just like that, she's assuaged.

If only ice cream could fix everything.

Chapter 27

Paul

It's been two days since Corey left. I should call. I meant to, but the lies and innuendoes hanging over me—over us...of course it's not all lies. Alexis has just enough truth to change the game.

I pull into the parking lot at Kent's church—a safe zone—and head around the back where his office is located. Mark's beater car sits in the back lot along with others I don't recognize. We scheduled a strategy meeting first but could be Simpson and Alexis have their own strategic plans. Arrive early, get the upper hand.

Stepping through the double glass doors, I attempt to tamp down the comparison game, with little luck. The bane of my existence. Nicer digs than mine. Larger church. Larger staff. I'm greeted by Janice McPherson. I know her because she once attended Crossroads. Was it the music or my deliverance of the message that motivated her to leave?

It's always something.

"Janice. So good to see you," I greet with a forced smile. "How're Nathan and the kids?"

"Pastor Paul." She gives me an awkward smile in return. Situations like this are never free from embarrassment from one party or the other. Or both. "Pastor Kent told me to send you on in." She points to the door behind her. It's not until I'm opening it that I realize she never answered my question.

The room I enter isn't Kent's office, as expected, but a small conference room not unlike the one where I hold my board meetings. Kent and Mark sit at a round table with three empty seats.

I slide the folder I carried in across the table to Kent before sitting. "Appreciate you mediating, Kent."

"Glad to do it. Are these the complaints presented at the last board meeting?"

I nod, then turn to Mark. "You ready for this?"

"Is anyone ever ready?"

I'd like to assure him I am, but the knot in my stomach says different. Nothing more disconcerting than having accusations thrown at you. Is it righteous anger that makes me uneasy, or that there's enough guilt in the mix?

Kent looks up from the file as I sit. "So, how much of this is true?"

"It's all lies," Mark says. His defense of me eases my breathing some.

"That's not true," I say. "Yes, Michael vandalized the elementary school last year. Yes, I'm living in a house that, by all appearances, is above my pay. The truth is, I inherited the bulk of it from my father."

"So, the real issue is what?"

I shake my head. "Simpson made some cockamamie claim that I am now, or have been, messing around on the side. No doubt information he gleaned from Alexis."

Kent looks me in the eye. "And you've already assured me that's not true."

"A woman scorned." Mark snorts. He never even questioned the truth of it. Will Corey be so loyal to my reputation?

"So, let's go over it again," Kent says. "You can be sure Simpson will."

"Okay." I clear my throat. "Last May, Alexis and her husband, John, separated. I suggested counseling, to see if they couldn't resolve their issues without a divorce. John refused, but Alexis asked if she could see me."

"Alone?"

"She didn't say. But I wasn't going there. I asked Corey to sit in on the sessions." Kent and I have already gone over this, but Mark wasn't present. "May 21st, Corey got stuck at school and was unable to be there. By the time she informed me, it was too late to contact Alexis. Dorothy, my secretary, wasn't present. So, when Alexis showed, I told her we'd have to reschedule. She had other ideas."

"You'll have to be more specific," Kent says. "If Simpson is unaware that Alexis lied, then you give her a chance to fill in the blanks however she wishes."

Heat steals up my neck. Alexis wasn't the first woman to make a pass. There's something about the pastoral position that gives some women a thrill. The first time it happened it was like I'd been stripped of what I thought was a protective shield. Some women have no boundaries.

I reposition my chair. "When she walked into my office, I stepped around my desk to escort her out. Instead of backing up, she moved in, snaked"—the most appropriate word— "her hands around my neck, and kissed me full on the mouth."

"And what did you do?" Kent says.

"I grabbed her wrists and removed her. Then I told her that she would not only need to find a new counselor, she'd need to find a new church. She was no longer welcome at Crossroads."

Mark leans forward, eyes wide. "What'd she do?"

"She got angry. Nasty is a better word." Vile woman. "She accused me of giving her signals for weeks, and said she knew

I couldn't possibly be satisfied at home." I can't look them in the eye with this one. It's a betrayal of Corey in some way.

"Anyone else witness this?" Kent says.

I shrug. "I thought I heard the outer office door open about the time she made her move, but there was no one there."

"Then it's your word against hers."

"I suppose."

Mark shakes his head. "A slam dunk."

"Why do you say that?" Kent asks.

"She's got a reputation." He points to me. "You're not the first."

"I didn't think I was." She was too practiced. Too slick.

Kent addresses Mark. "We don't want to turn this into a mudslinging contest, but if you have someone to back you up—"

"No," I say. Both Mark and Kent look at me like I've lost my mind. "If we do that, we're putting others in an awkward position. Someone might feel compelled to step in, but at what cost?" I shake my head. I let Corey leave to protect her from this. Why would I make someone else vulnerable to Alexis's lies?

A knock on the door draws our attention as Janice opens it. "Mr. Simpson and Ms. Andrews are here."

"Show them in," Kent says. He stands then looks at me. "You ready?"

"I better be."

I haven't had much experience with female manipulation. Not Corey's style, thank God—a fact I tuck away for later consideration. But when Alexis walks into the conference room, it's obvious she's setting the stage from the get-go. Playing a part with the pious church-like dress, hair pulled back, squeaky clean face. I've never seen her downplay her looks before, but when it suits her… Does she really think she's fooling anyone?

Kent throws me a look that says he knows what she's up to. Mark's smirk tells me he's onto her too. But it isn't us she needs to convince. It's Simpson, whose downturned mouth and stiff posture tell me he's already made up his mind, and it isn't in my favor.

"Appreciate the two of you meeting with us," I say, waiting for them to be seated before I resume my own position across from them. Mark sits at my right, Kent at the head of the table.

Simpson nods once—a silent acknowledgment.

Kent clears his throat. "We have a situation here—"

"Why's he here?" Alexis flicks a finger in Kent's direction, eyes on me.

"We thought it best to have an impartial participant."

Her eyes widen. "Impartial to who?"

"He has no stake in this," Mark says. "Everyone else in the room does."

"Let me understand," Simpson says, eyes drilling me. "The point to this meeting is you want to defend yourself against the allegations Alexis has made regarding inappropriate behavior."

I nod. "That's right. She's made accusations that are flat out untrue."

"So, what it comes down to is your word against hers."

"Yes."

"You have no proof that what you're saying is true and what she's saying isn't."

Kent rests his elbows on the table and leans forward. "His reputation is proof. There's nothing in Pastor Shaffer's history that makes these accusations suspect."

"The same can't be said for Ms. Andrews," Mark adds.

I grip his forearm and shake my head. No point in dredging up hearsay.

Alexis throws up a hand. "*My* past? You want to start flinging accusations, why don't we start with the pastor's wife?"

Heat flames my face. "You leave Corey out of this. Nothing we're discussing here has anything to do with her."

She jabs a finger toward me. "He made inappropriate advances toward me, and when I turned him down, he kicked me out of his precious church. You want to believe he's some sort of saint? There's a mess brewing in his household. Where do you think it all stems from?"

The silence that follows is heavy with tension.

"Unbelievable." It's the only coherent word I can find. My mind is exploding with a tirade of thoughts too scrambled to verbalize. Is this woman a raving paranoid schizophrenic? What possible reason can she have for targeting me?

Kent is the voice of reason. "Let's stick to the facts. Throwing around gossip and innuendo only muddles the truth." He looks at Alexis. "You claim Pastor Shaffer made advances toward you."

"Yes."

"When was this?"

She shrugs. "I don't know. Sometime last year."

Rubbing my forehead with shaky fingers, I flip through the notes I've made. "We had an appointment for marital counseling on May twenty-first of last year. That was the only time I ever met with her alone."

"Would you agree with that statement?" Kent asks Alexis.

"I guess."

"Good," Kent says. "Go ahead, Paul, and repeat for Ms. Andrews and Mr. Simpson what you've already told me about that meeting."

I make eye contact with both Alexis and Simpson and recount the events in question. Although Alexis interrupts with snorts and eye rolls, Simpson's focus remains on me. Does he hear the truth in my words? Or is he still taken in by Alexis's lies?

"I want to conclude with this," I say to Simpson at the end. "You're causing quite a stir in my church over what you perceive as questionable behavior. I can defend every one of those allegations and am willing to do so from the pulpit, if need be. I have *never* made inappropriate advances toward Alexis or any other woman."

Simpson squirms in his seat, eyes not meeting mine. What is it they say about a jury unwilling to meet the defendant's gaze? A guilty or *not* guilty verdict? Guess I'm about to find out.

∼

Corey

It's too cold to work outside, so I set up the dining room table with reading material, an algebra textbook, and an eighth-grade science book. Taylor's impromptu classroom.

"What's this?" She holds up the copy of *My Brother Sam is Dead* and wrinkles her nose. "I read this a long time ago."

I don't dare tell her that the eighth-grade reading book may be beyond her comprehension. "We're going to start slow and work our way up."

Flipping through the book, she plops into a chair. "This is a cinch."

Oh, I hope so. "Good. Then why don't you start from the beginning?"

Her eyes track the words, lips moving.

"Aloud, Tay. I need you to read to me."

Big sigh. "Fine." With the book flat on the table, she uses her index finger to track her progress, hair dangling over the words. "It was April, and...out...outside in the dark the rain whi...whip...ped aga...against the windows of our... tav...tavern."

She continues to struggle through the first page, and I hang on each word, laboring along with her. If she stumbles over the simple text of this eighth-grade-level historical fiction, how will she master pre-calc and physiology?

Then again, how many weeks has it been since she started talking? Six? Seven? And she's come so far.

"This is stupid." She flings the book aside, face red, tears swimming in her eyes. "I'm *never* going to grad...graduate."

Kneeling down next to her chair, I take her hands in mine. "I know it's hard, Tay. But think about how far you've come since the accident."

"I don't remember."

Tugging at her hands, I draw her eyes to mine. "No, but I do. I was just thinking about it. Six weeks ago, you couldn't read a word. Veronica would show you pictures of everyday things, and you couldn't even identify them. And now, you're reading."

"Junior high stuff." She swipes at the tears. "I want to go to college, Mom." Her voice cracks.

"Oh, sweetheart, you will. Your brain is working hard to reconnect."

She pins pained eyes on mine. "Why is God doing this to me?"

How do I answer? Telling her He's not isn't working. The question continues to plague her—and me. Why is God doing this to us? As I open my mouth to speak, uncertain what I'll say, the Lord puts on my heart my favorite verses from Proverbs. "'*Trust in the Lord with all your heart and do not lean on your own understanding. In all your ways acknowledge Him, and he will make straight your paths.*'"

Taylor sniffs and looks at me, eyebrows drawn together. "I don't get it."

"It's from Proverbs. Do you remember who wrote Proverbs?"

She shrugs. "Solomon?"

I nod.

"So?"

Standing, I lean my rear end on the table, facing her. "So, he was a very wise man. In fact, God gave him the gift of wisdom because it's what he asked for. He knew that in everything, God had a plan for his life. Sometimes, we don't know why things happen, but God does. We need to trust Him."

"Do you?"

From the mouths of babes. If God could speak through a donkey, it's no stretch to imagine Him speaking through Taylor. "Not like I should. Like you, I sometimes get caught up in the whys. Instead, I should be asking what? What is it He's trying to show me?"

"You think God's trying to show *me* something?"

"Oh, darling, I think he's trying to show us both something."

"What?"

"I don't know." Standing straight, I clap my hands together. "How about we move on to page two?"

With a big sigh, she retrieves the book just as my phone rings.

Checking the caller I.D., I hold it up. "It's Josh. You want to talk to him?"

Biting her lip, she reaches for it with shy smile.

"Only a few minutes. We have to get back to work."

Making myself scarce, I slip into the kitchen to put together a snack for Taylor. Her voice floats in as she regales Josh with our walks to the beach and her therapy sessions. She chatters non-stop, her voice on a steady rise, stuck on unimportant details.

What must Josh be thinking?

A few days before her accident, she and Josh were working

on an English project—a reader's theater script. Taylor was running circles around him.

"No," she'd said, cutting him off. "You have to remember that you only have dialogue and inflection to communicate emotions. That line *has* to be stronger."

"So, what do you suggest?"

"Hey, this is your project, I'm just coaching."

"Then it's fine the way it is."

"Seriously?"

I heard the drop of a pencil on the table and could imagine the eye roll she gave him. Peeling potatoes at the sink, I stifled a grin. So much like her father.

"Geez, Taylor. Why do you have to turn every assignment into a Pulitzer Prize winner. It's just a stupid English assignment."

"Don't you care what the other kids are going to think? You have to perform this, you know."

"Do you really think anyone in my class is going to give a rip about this? I'm probably the only one turning it in."

"Do you believe this, Mom?" She tossed the question at me.

"It *is* his assignment."

"And you call yourself a teacher."

I wished.

Now I listen as she jumps from one topic to the next—no rhyme or reason. It's too painful to watch. "Hey, Tay? Let's get back to work, okay?"

"Gotta go, Josh. I'll call you tomorrow, 'kay?" Smiling, she hits the end button.

College isn't looking too promising.

∾

Paul

I walk into an empty house. Not that long ago, I thought it'd be good to come home to blessed silence. And yet, now that I have it… I collect the mail, then sit at the dining room table. My office is too confining, only pointing out the isolation and quiet.

Ten minutes later, I have an excuse to call Corey. She answers on the third ring, her voice breathless.

"Paul?"

Her voice doesn't relieve the ache of loneliness, it only emphasizes it. "Hey, Corey. How's Taylor doing?"

"Oh, good I suppose."

"You don't sound so sure."

"Well…she's becoming aware of her limitations, and it's hard. The upside of it is that I see more and more of her old self peeking through."

"Giving you a hard time, is she?"

Corey laughs. "I should have brought my old copy of Dobson's book, *The Strong Willed Child* so I could bone up."

Come home, I want to tell her.

"But her speech therapist is wonderful, and I think she'll make better progress here without the distractions. How's Michael?"

Funny neither of us ask about each other but focus on the kids instead. "I'm guessing that strong-willed personality comes from your gene pool, not mine." The joke seems to fall flat when she doesn't respond. "Kidding, Cor."

"No, I know." But she doesn't sound it. Does she think I'm rubbing in her past?

I scramble to get levity back into our conversation. "I hold all the power, though. If he wants to eat, he has to talk to me."

"Spring break's next week," she says, as if just remembering.

"Something important about spring break?"

"N…no. Nothing."

Why don't I believe her? "Okay…" I draw the word out,

give her a chance to explain. Silence. "I got a reminder from your dentist in the mail. You have an appointment next week."

"I'll reschedule."

Has our marriage come down to this then? I want to tell her about the meeting with Simpson and Alexis, but how can I after months of keeping the whole mess to myself?

"So…" She sighs. "How's Michael doing. Aside from attitude?"

"He misses you." *So do I.* "He brought home another A in math."

"I'm not surprised."

"Look, Corey—"

"I have to go. Taylor's waiting for me to help her with a focus exercise her therapist assigned."

She can't get off the phone fast enough and…was she crying? Couldn't have been. It was her choice to leave.

I should have told her about the mess of dissension that's overtaken the church the last several months. Why have I waited so long? Truth is, I expected she'd bring it up herself.

To explain it all now on the phone with a wall between us —impossible. Maybe face to face…but we're not.

And what's settled? I figured it'd be a simple matter of the truth. The fact is, Alexis wasn't much interested in the truth. Suppose it puts her in a bad light, as it should. But I *did* detect a softening in Simpson's demeanor as he left, even if he said nothing. Is it enough? Only time will tell.

Chapter 28

Corey

The morning is bathed in a misty veil of fog when Taylor, Rambo, and I step outside for our walk to the beach. It's become routine. I'm good with routine. It keeps me from thinking too much. About things like how much I miss Paul or the distance that's grown between us. I somehow thought... well, I'm not sure what I thought. That he'd miss me so much when I left that our problems would seem trivial?

But we're strangers. And there's a part of me that fears it will never be any different.

I can't even pray with expectation, because I don't believe.

It's what motivated me to call Mr. Hamilton yesterday to accept the teaching position for next year. I promised an answer by spring break. That starts today.

I hug my hooded sweatshirt tight against my body and follow Taylor and Rambo down Tricia's bricked pathway. Will I ever get tired of the smell of the ocean?

Taylor stops at the end of the path and turns to me. "Which way?"

"Same as yesterday. Do you remember?"

She shrugs and gives an indistinguishable grunt.

"Think about it, Tay."

Rambo tugs at the end of the leash. He knows the way.

Without answering, Taylor heads south. It could be a lucky guess or proof her memory's getting better. I vote for the latter.

"What happened when I was in the accident?"

My step falters. "What do you mean?"

"Like did someone run into me? Or—" She shrugs. "Did you already tell me?"

This is the first she's mentioned it. "What do you remember?"

"Nothing, really. Just…was I mad at you?"

My heart pounds and my legs turn to concrete blocks that I have to drag down the root-exposed sidewalk. *I'm not ready for this, God.* Rather than look at her, I stall for time, untangling Rambo's leash from around his front leg.

"Are you okay, Mom?"

"I'm…" Drawing in a deep breath, I face her. To add another lie would only make it worse later. But to tell her the truth? It's not the time. For either of us. "We had an argument that afternoon. You were angry with me."

"I was angry with Mr. Johnson, too." She tugs on Rambo's leash and starts walking again. "Do you know why?"

"You have a lot of questions, Tay, but it might be better if we wait until your memory is a little clearer. I think at this point, it'll only be more confusing than helpful for me to fill in the blanks."

She stops and glares at me. "You *do* know why."

"I promise you, when the time is right, I'll tell you everything." And in that moment, I know it's true. I can't avoid it forever. I *won't* avoid it forever. But now's not the time.

"Fine." She steps over an exposed root and starts walking again. "But at least tell me if the accident was my fault."

"According to witnesses, you ran a stop sign."

She wrinkles up her nose. "I did?"

"Afraid so."

Eyes widening, she says, "Did someone get hurt? Oh, Mom." Tears well.

"No." I wrap an arm around her shoulder and hug her close. "You ran into a truck, but the man driving was fine. A few bruises, but otherwise—"

"You're telling the truth?"

"Honest, Tay. Dad's been to see him, and he's fine. He's even called a couple times to check on you."

The tension eases from her shoulders, and she raises a shaky hand to wipe her eyes. "Can I write him a letter? Do you think Dad would send it to him?"

"That's a great idea. Then you can let him know you're okay too."

We continue our walk in silence, me lost in my thoughts and, I imagine, Taylor lost in her own.

When we reach the beach, Taylor bends down to unleash an excited Rambo, laughing at his antics to gain his freedom. "What a dork," she says.

A golden retriever joins Rambo, and they race across the ice plant and down the dunes to the wet sand, Rambo having to work twice as hard with his shorter legs. Is that Jonas's—

"Seems Lexie's found herself a friend," a voice calls from behind us.

Taylor and I turn to find Jonas approaching, leash in hand.

Taylor points down the beach. "Is that your dog?"

He nods once, coming closer. "She is. Good morning, Corey."

"Morning."

"Beautiful day, isn't it?" His eyes crinkle when he smiles—a contagious smile.

"How do you know my mom?" Taylor looks from me to Jonas.

"You must be Taylor." He extends a hand to Taylor as he steps closer. "I'm Jonas. Your mother and I met last week."

Taylor shakes his hand. "Your dog is beautiful. How old is she?"

"Let's see now." He stares off for a moment, as if thinking. "Must be going on eleven this summer."

"Rambo's only five."

"Rambo, huh?" he says with a chuckle. "Someone has a sense of humor."

"My dad," she says. "He thought if we put a sign up in the yard that said 'Beware of Rambo' it might make people think we actually have a guard dog."

"Clever."

"Yeah." She laughs. "But it didn't work. Everyone knows Rambo."

"You must come from a small town." He looks at me, eyebrow raised in question.

"My dad's a pastor. It's like everyone watches to see if we'll mess up. Like my brother last year. He got into trouble, and boy, did everyone know about it." Her voice rises with excitement.

Heat steals up my neck, but there's no denying what Taylor's saying, even if my first instinct is to do so. Life in a fishbowl. Paul would be horrified to hear Taylor laying our dirty laundry out for a stranger. Part of me struggles with it, but there's a larger part that finds it refreshing.

No secrets. No lies.

"And now, the entire town of Carmel's privy to it, too," I say, making light of it.

Jonas waves a dismissive hand. "How're you enjoying our little seaside village, Taylor?"

Taylor turns away, as if searching for Rambo. "I'd like it better if I didn't have to go to rehab."

It's on the tip of my tongue to explain that Taylor's referring to rehab for TBI, not some kind of drug rehab. But why go there? Who cares if Jonas misunderstands the situation? Again, that would be Paul's concern, but it doesn't have to be mine.

"It's been nice chatting with you, Jonas." I take Taylor's elbow. "We're off for an invigorating walk."

"It's been a pleasure, ladies. I hope to run into you again sometime." He tips an imaginary hat, his sweet smile giving away nothing of his thoughts.

～

It's not lost on me, while coercing Taylor to go to bed, that I'm raising her all over again. Fighting over nap time and nagging her to complete her rehab assignments comes with a sense of déjà vu. We've done this before.

Taylor's supposed to attempt normal chores, like cooking a meal and doing the laundry. But each task is a battle of wills. To be honest, I don't really care if she remembers to put the ground beef in the spaghetti sauce, but Tricia deserves at least a decent meal for her generosity. And folding the clothes isn't all that important, but when I find Taylor's bra in the kitchen pantry, I have to draw the line.

Is it any wonder I'm exhausted by the end of the day?

Tricia trails behind me in the kitchen. "Let me at least help with the dishes. I didn't invite you here to be slave labor."

"Oh, please," I scoff, squirting liquid soap into a pot. "You'll be running for the Alka Seltzer anytime now."

"Leave these." Tricia nudges me aside to fill the kettle. "I'll make us some tea and we can sit out back and star gaze."

Ten minutes later, bundled in a throw, I follow Tricia out to the patio, a cup of herbal tea warming my hands. A mocha would be better. I can't quite remember the last time I indulged in one.

"Isn't this nice?" Tricia sets her mug on a teak side table and settles among the cushions of a wicker chair.

Joining her, I take a tentative sip of the hot tea. Yep, a mocha would be much better.

"So," she says. "What's bothering you?"

What is she, a mind reader? Taylor's questions this morning have been marching around inside my head like a band at half-time. "What makes you think anything's bothering me?"

"We've been friends since what? Sixth grade?"

"Fifth."

She nods. "That's right. Fifth." She blows on the tea, lowers her voice. "I bet I know you better than you know yourself."

She'd win that bet, too. "Taylor asked me this morning if she was angry with me the day of the accident."

"Oh?"

"What could I say?"

"What *did* you say?"

"I told her to give it a little more time and I'd answer her questions. She's not ready for the answers yet."

"Are you?"

I shake my head with a sigh. "I wish…"

"If wishes were horses, beggars would ride," she mutters.

"What?"

She smiles. "Something my mother would say whenever I said, 'I wish.' It used to really bug me, until I understood her point."

"Which was?"

"Wishing isn't going to make it so."

"Well, that's helpful."

"Sorry. I'm doing more than my fair share of wishing these days." She sets her mug down. "What do you wish?"

"I wish Paul and I were handling this together. Better yet, I wish I'd never gone to that stupid party eighteen years ago."

"Then you wouldn't have Taylor."

"Once she learns the truth, I may not have her anyway."

But a collage of past Taylor-starring scenarios flit through my head. There isn't one I'd want erased.

"Have you thought about talking to her therapist? Maybe she can help break it to Taylor."

I snort. "I can't bring myself to tell Taylor. How am I supposed to tell a complete stranger?"

"Sometimes I think it's easier to be open with a stranger."

"I suppose."

"You'll figure it out. How'd her rehab go today?"

"Well, let's see. She argued with Dottie over the necessity to write everything down, and she accused us of treating her like a baby. Then as we were leaving, Dottie informed me that Taylor would need to find some kind of volunteer position to help her re-enter normal life."

"Oh, that shouldn't be a problem. There are animal shelters, libraries, hospitals."

"All of which require finger printing, a background check, and a promise of at least a minimum three-month commitment."

"For the animal shelter?" She sounds as appalled as I felt when informed of this.

"Yep."

"Well, a three-month commitment isn't all that much, is it?"

"I can't stay here three months. And that's *after* the background check and fingerprinting come back."

"Hey," she says, sitting up. "I have the perfect solution. Taylor can work in my shop."

"Oh, Trish, I don't think that's a good idea. Did I tell you where I found Taylor's bra today?"

"It doesn't matter. She's my goddaughter, after all. I love her like my own." She rattles off one idea after another, and as her excitement grows, so does mine.

When she winds down, we sit in silence for a moment. "How did you manage to be so strong?"

"What?" Her laugh is whisper soft.

"No, I'm serious. If Paul died, like Steven—I mean look at you. A walking advertisement for the single, successful woman."

"I suppose that depends on how you define success." Her voice has a melancholy tone to it. "You don't give yourself enough credit, Corey. You never have."

"Credit for what?" I shake my head. "I'm standing on the brink of disaster, and I want to run in the worst way."

"But you won't. You've managed to raise two beautiful children while maintaining the kind of quiet peace I'd love to have."

Tears burn my eyes and nose. She doesn't know me after all. "It's not peace you see when you look at me. It's, I don't know, weakness."

A gasp floats out of the dark. "How can you say that?"

"It's true, Trish. It's much easier for me to ignore a problem than to face it."

"What are you talking about?"

"All of this." I wave my hand in the air. "Had I told Paul the truth all those years ago… *before* that night. My fear that he was like my father, how important teaching was to me. All those things that might have set us both on a different path. But at least it would have been an honest path."

"So you start from here."

"And expect Paul to accept this new reality after eighteen years? I might blame him for taking me for granted, but the truth is, I put myself in this position."

Chapter 29

Paul

Half a block from the house, I hear it—heavy metal garbage polluting the air. Is it...? Yes, it's blasting from the open windows of *my* house. I screech to a halt in the driveway and tangle with my seatbelt. With each *boom, boom, boom* of the bass, my temper rises until I'm slamming through the front door.

"Michael!" The television's on some music video channel. Black-clad, guitar-toting gyrators fill the flat screen, their so-called art pouring through the surround-sound speakers.

Michael comes out of the kitchen, a half-eaten sandwich in one hand, soda can in the other. "Hey." He bites into his snack.

I point a shaking finger at the television. "Turn off that garbage!"

Scowl in place, he sets the can on the coffee table and takes his sweet time with the remote, finishing off the sandwich and swallowing.

Blessed silence.

"It's not garbage. Just 'cause you don't get it—"

"The whole neighborhood just *got* it. What's the matter with you?" Even as the words spew from my mouth, I know better. Corey'd say I'm the adult here and I should act like it. "I heard it blaring from down the street."

"It's off now. No big deal." He snatches up the soda can and steps past me. The stale scent of cigarette smoke follows.

"Are you smoking?"

He turns back with a scowl. "What? No."

"I want the truth. You reek of it."

He turns away again. "What difference does it make? You won't believe me anyway."

"Don't walk away when I'm talking to you."

Facing me, he says, "I wish Mom was here."

You and me both. "Why? You think she'd be okay with the loud music and smoking?"

"I'm *not* smoking. I hung out with someone who does."

I'm not sure I believe him, but I take another tact. "You ever hear of guilt by association?"

He slurps at the soda.

"People see you hanging out with a smoker, they think you're smoking."

"So?"

"So, you already have one strike against you. You may not care what people think of you, but *I* do." Could I sound any more pompous?

"Who cares what people think? Just 'cause they believe something, doesn't make it true."

He's right about that. "Look, Michael. I know it's unfair, but people in this town are going to judge me by how you behave. They expect a pastor's family to be above reproach."

"I gotta behave, but you can do whatever you want."

"What are you talking about?"

He shakes his head. "Forget it."

"No, I won't forget it. If you have something to say, say it."

His jaw works for a moment, like he's fighting the words.

"All you care about is what people think. What about the truth? Isn't that more important?"

"Of course it is. But there are plenty of people out there who'll make up their own truth. We don't need to give them extra ammunition."

He mutters something I don't catch. "What'd you say?"

"I said you're a hypocrite. You're preaching one thing and doing another."

"Whatever you've heard—"

"I didn't have to *hear* it, I saw it for myself."

His accusation and anger are like a punch in the gut. "You better be darned sure of what you're saying, son."

"There you go again." He throws up a hand. "You say one thing but do another. It's okay for you to accuse me of doing something, like smoking. You want the truth, but then you do something worse than smoking and I'm supposed to be quiet."

"What do you—?" Alexis. He's heard her lies. "Are you referring to Ms. Andrews?"

He just glares.

"It's just vicious gossip, Michael. It's not true."

Shaking his head, he says, "Yeah, it is. I saw you with her."

That day in my office with Alexis, was that Michael I heard? What did he see? Whatever it was, he misconstrued it.

"I know how it looked, but if you'd stayed—"

"It made me sick. You with Josh's mom."

Shaking my head, I say, "You got it all wrong. It's not what it looked like."

His face contorts, eyes filling. "You were all over each other. How could you do that to Mom? You're supposed to be different."

"Why won't you believe me? Had you stayed even a few seconds more—"

"Why *should* I believe you?" he shouts. "You never believe me. You think I'm lyin' all the time."

"Are we back to the vandalism?"

He doesn't answer, just glares at me through watery eyes.

"You were caught red-handed."

"So were you."

"I swear to God, Michael, I—"

"Don't bother. I don't believe in God." He storms out of the room while my mouth works like a drowning fish.

I can't bring myself to go after Michael. I can't face the disgust in his eyes, even if it's misplaced. Instead, I slink into my office and hide away like a thief until I hear him leave for work. Did he mean it about not believing in God, or was that just a well-aimed slam? I have to head back to the church in an hour, make an appearance at a leadership meeting. It's the last thing I want to do.

First things first. Something to eat and a change of clothes.

The fridge holds a half gallon of expired milk, a wedge of moldy cheese, and a couple containers of Greek yogurt. I don't dare look in the crisper. No telling what's growing in there. Slamming the door, I turn to scowl at the dirty dishes in the sink and littering the countertop. Did I expect Michael to pick up the slack in Corey's absence? If so, I'm a fool.

I'll be lucky to find a clean pair of jeans, let alone a shirt to change into. I head to the bedroom a wiser man. But when I yank open the top dresser drawer, I freeze in shocked surprise. What's this? Clean boxers folded and stacked. I move to the next drawer—t-shirts lined up in somewhat neat rows. Not up to Corey's standards, but still... Did Michael do this?

I pick out a shirt, then jeans from the next drawer—also clean, folded and stacked—and change out of my work clothes. Is this Michael's strategy to change my mind about summer camp? I'm impressed. When did he learn to do laundry?

Checking my watch, I snatch up the phone receiver and punch in Corey's cell number. It rings four times, and I prepare a message in my mind for when her voicemail kicks on.

"Hello? Paul?"

I stumble over my surprise. "Oh, hey, Corey. I was expecting voicemail."

"No, it's me. Is everything okay?"

"When did Michael learn to do laundry?" Okay, that sounds accusatory. "I mean, did you teach him?"

She laughs. "Don't sound so surprised. It's not rocket science."

The humor in her voice reaches in and grabs my heart. "It was just unexpected. He's been moping around here since you left, and then to find clean clothes…well, you can imagine."

"There's hope for the kid."

"Yes." *I don't believe in God,* he'd said. "How are you and Taylor doing?"

She hesitates. Did her phone drop the call?

"Corey?"

"She…she's starting to remember." Her words are whisper-soft, but their impact isn't lost on me.

"Everything?"

"She wanted to know if she was angry with me before the accident."

Resentment and empathy battle in my mind. I want to hold her, tell her everything will be okay, but at the same time, she brought this on herself. *See to it that no one misses the grace of God and that no bitter root grows up to cause trouble and defile many.* How do I get rid of that bitter root?

Loving acts beget loving feelings. "What did you tell her?"

"I didn't know what to say. She's not ready."

"Are you sure about that?" *Or is it you're not ready?*

"Do you think she is?"

"Hard for me to say since I'm not around her."

A sigh drifts over the line. "So, Michael's attitude hasn't softened any?"

Okay, change of subject. "I came home this afternoon to his music blasting down the block. We kind of got into it."

"He's testing you."

"He said he doesn't believe in God."

"He's testing you."

"I don't know, Corey. He's so…angry. It's like he sees me as the enemy."

"Don't make too much of it."

Would she say that if she knew everything?

"Listen, Paul. I don't want you to take this the wrong way—"

I hate it when she prefaces something with those words. "What?"

"Lately, you've kind of been acting like his enemy. You two can't seem to be in the same room without drawing your weapons."

"So it's all *my* fault?"

"I'm not saying that. But you're—"

"The adult. Yeah, I know. All I ask is that he show some respect."

"No, Paul, that's not *all* you ask of him. I see him working so hard to get your attention."

"Because he wants something."

"Yes," she says. "He wants your love and acceptance."

"He wants to go to that summer camp program."

Her sigh sounds weary. "You're becoming a cynic, sweetheart."

I prefer realist. But after hanging up the phone, I try her words out for size. *He wants your love and acceptance.* Wasn't that what she'd said when Justine came to me all those years ago, pregnant and scared? If I'd I listened to her then, would things have been easier for Justine?

And had I not been so hard on Justine, would Corey have

seen me as more approachable—able to handle her fears about marrying me? I can place the blame on her until I'm blue in the face, but truth is, something had been off and I'd chosen to ignore it.

Two weeks before the wedding, Corey had a wedding shower in her parents' backyard. When I showed up that night for our date, she'd seemed edgy, distracted.

"I'll get my sweater." She slipped away before I could kiss her, leaving me at the door.

Stepping inside, I watched her jog up the stairs. It took an instant to realize her parents weren't there. The house was silent and dark beyond the entrance hall. I waited, listening to the ticking of the grandfather clock. Something about the house discouraged wandering. I'd never been upstairs and wouldn't dare tread on Richard's territory without permission.

Footsteps preceded Corey's appearance at the top of the stairs. "Where are we going?"

"How was the shower? Get lots of fun stuff?"

Reaching the last step, she slipped into the sweater. "It was fine. Are you hungry?"

"Hey, slow down." I put an arm around her as she passed me. "What's the big hurry? Show me what you got today."

Flicking a hand toward the stairs, she pulled away. "It's all up in my bedroom."

"You okay?"

The question stopped her at the door, one hand on the knob. She wouldn't hold my gaze. Instead, her eyes darted around, as if seeking someplace safe to land. "Yeah, I'm fine."

But she wasn't. A blind man could see that. "You're not nervous about the wedding, are you?"

"No, it's not—" Her eyes caught mine and she sighed. "You know what they say about people marrying their parents? I mean, a guy marries a woman like his mom, and… you know, a woman marries a guy like her dad."

"What're you saying? I'm like your dad?" I tried to make

light of it, but there was enough edge to my tone to shut her down. I'd known it then, even if I couldn't admit it.

And as the wedding drew closer, she seemed to pull farther away. Wedding jitters, that's what I told myself. She'd be fine once we were married. But something in Corey had died, and I hadn't tried to resurrect it. I hadn't even wanted to acknowledge it.

Until now.

Chapter 30

Corey

Entering Reflections, Tricia's shop, is like stepping into a fairy tale for grown-ups, and she's the fairy godmother. Every wall, every rack, every conceivable space is showcased with her impeccable taste in color, style, and texture. My fingers trail across faux suede, soft cashmere, and a light wool blend as I lead Taylor through the wonderland.

"Hi, Corey. Hi, Taylor." Jasmine, Tricia's assistant, appears. She reminds me of the Disney character with the same name—long sleek hair, exotic eyes, unreal figure. How is it possible to be that thin? "Tricia's in the back on the phone. She'll be out in a sec."

I catch my reflection in a full-length mirror and boy do I pale in comparison. Ill-fitting jeans, baggy t-shirt and—is that a stain from this morning's breakfast? —dull, unruly hair.

"I'm going to start working here today." Taylor plucks a lace camisole from a rack. "This is so cute." She holds it up against her. "What do you think?"

Jasmine snatches a light jacket from another rack. "Pair it

with this and a pair of skinny jeans. It'd look great. Especially that color."

I shake my head. "Not in our budget, kiddo."

Tricia emerges from the back room. "My goddaughter doesn't have a budget."

"No, but my *daughter* does." I give her a pointed look.

"We'll discuss it," she says dismissively. "How about I bring Taylor home around lunch time?"

"I want to work all day," Taylor says, breaking away from Jasmine.

There's no way she'll have the energy. "I don't know—"

"How about this?" Tricia says. "I'll bring you home for lunch, and if you feel up to it, I'll bring you back after."

She walks me to the door. "You know, Taylor's not the only one without a budget here."

"As beautiful as your clothes are, they aren't for me."

"Hmm. You'd be surprised."

I open my mouth to argue.

"We'll see you at lunch," she trills, closing the door behind me.

Stepping onto the sidewalk, I take a moment to soak in the sunshine breaking through a mist of high fog. With no agenda and no Taylor, I'm lost. It's Thursday morning. What would I be doing if I were home?

As I retrieve my car, I think back to my conversation with Paul the evening before. I don't know what I expected, opening up about Taylor's memory returning. Before everything fell apart, Paul was my best counsel. Godly, clearminded, maybe a little over-bearing. But it came with the territory.

And now?

With no destination in mind, I drive up and down the narrow streets of Carmel until I spot a charming little church tucked behind a few trees, its white steeple a beacon to my bruised soul. Oceanside Presbyterian Church, the wooden sign announces. I know as well as anyone that I don't need to be in church to pray. But God and I, we haven't been on the same wavelength lately. It's my fault. The reawakening of my sin's put a wedge between us. That same wedge that's been erected between Paul and me.

Pulling into the parking lot, I see only one other car, but it's enough to assure me the church is open. I park and climb out, taking a moment to bask in the warmth of the sun on my face, the faint whiff of cedar, and the uplifting notes of a bird's song. Contentment, even for such a brief moment, is a welcome relief.

The tall, narrow double doors are made of a dark wood, the handles black wrought iron. I grasp one and tug, revealing a foyer, and beyond that, straight rows of wooden pews, stained glass windows depicting Bible scenes, and the comforting musty tang of age. The altar is marble and wood, the wall behind taken up by a simple wooden cross.

Stepping inside, I glance around. Empty. Although the doors were unlocked, it feels as if I'm treading where I don't belong. If Paul were here, he'd march inside as if it were his right, and I suppose it is. This is God's house. Everyone belongs. Even so, I take tentative steps toward the back pew and ease into it. The bench is as hard as it looks, the wood smoothed and shaped by years of use. How many lost souls have found their way to this very same spot?

Closing my eyes, I struggle to find the words to pray. My cries for help get tangled up in a conscience entangled with guilt, shame, repercussions. *You made your bed.* It's not God who continually reminds me of my past. I know in my head that He doesn't hold an account of my sins. But how do I get my heart to take hold of it?

A rustling draws my attention to a door to the left of the alter. Someone exits—a man. Tall, slender, familiar. Dressed in black slacks, a gray shirt, and a clerical collar. It can't be.

"Jonas?"

"Well, isn't this a pleasant surprise." Jonas's grin is welcoming, but not surprised. Was he expecting me?

"Is this…are you the pastor here?"

He slips his hands into the front pockets of his slacks while moving down the middle aisle toward me. "I am. Been pastor here for going on twenty years now."

I think back to our two previous conversations. Was there anything he said that hinted at his occupation? No. Even when Taylor told him about Paul being a pastor, he gave no indication that he shared the same calling. But now, standing before me in the formal pastoral garb, it all fits.

"What brings you here on this beautiful morning?"

"I love old churches." Could I give a lamer excuse? "I mean, our church is modern. It doesn't have the same feel."

His eyes move about the room as if admiring a beautiful piece of art or a beloved child. "There is something quite comforting about them, isn't there? Maybe the spirit of those who've come before us seeking God's grace and forgiveness." His eyes land back on mine. "But of course, you'd know about that, being married to a pastor yourself."

"Yes," I murmur, unable to maintain eye contact. Grace and forgiveness. Two things that have been in short supply.

"I was getting ready to take a walk. Would you care to join me? Or," he indicates the pew, "am I disturbing your time with the Lord?"

"I'd like to walk with you. I'll slip back in here before leaving, if it's all right with you."

"That's why we're here."

I follow him out the doors I'd entered through not ten minutes earlier. Even so, I squint against the brightness of the sun as we pass fragrant gardenias and azaleas in full bloom. Evidence of God's abundant creation. The streets are quiet—midday, mid-week, away from the tourist traps. No shops or beaches here.

"Your daughter…Taylor, right?"

"Yes."

"She seems very sweet. Reminds me of my Rebecca. Of course, it's been quite a few years since she was a teenager."

"How many children do you have?"

"I had five. I lost a son to cancer when he was only sixteen." He shakes his head, eyes focused on the ground. "That was a hard year. Especially on my wife, Beth. I wasn't sure she'd ever recover. That's what brought us here to Carmel. Beth's always been partial to the ocean."

"And did she? Recover, I mean."

He chuckles. "She sure did. Give that woman a mission and watch out. Only thing she loves more than kids is the Lord. Practically ran the youth center single-handed for years." Pride and affection for his wife infuses his tone.

"How long have you been married?"

"Forty-six years this fall."

I hesitate to ask. "Beth, she's still with you then?"

His smile is sad. "In body. She's got Alzheimer's." He takes my elbow as we cross the street. "Enough about me. Tell me something about yourself. I know you're married to a pastor and you have a beautiful daughter. She said something about a brother."

My heart's still linked to Beth and the tragedy this poor man's suffered. Whatever I might say will be trivial in comparison. But then maybe Jonas needs to walk in someone else's shoes for a time. "Michael. He's fifteen."

"Are he and your husband here in Carmel with you?"

"No. I…" What? Pastor or not, I don't even know this man. To share my soap-opera-like life is unthinkable.

"You don't have to tell me if you don't want to. But I can see it in your eyes. Noticed it the first time we spoke."

"What?" I try to laugh it off.

"I've been there myself. Pain so deep, you don't know how to climb out of it."

Is it so obvious? Like Nathaniel Hawthorne's book, only

instead of a scarlet A, I have a scarlet S for shame. It takes a moment to find my voice. "Six months ago, if we had this conversation, I'd have convinced you that everything in my life was perfect. I might have even been able to convince myself."

"Nah." He looks at me and grins. "Hate to break it to you, but there's no such thing as perfection on this side of heaven."

"I suppose not. But for some of us, there's a wide chasm of sin separating us from God."

"Afraid I have to disagree with you again, Corey. Christ filled that chasm. *'For I am persuaded that neither death nor life, nor angels nor principalities nor powers, nor things present nor things to come, nor height nor depth nor any other created thing, shall be able to separate us from the love of God which is in Christ Jesus our Lord.'"*

As Jonas quotes the apostle Paul from Romans, my eyes fill, blurring my vision, and I stop. It sounds so simple in scripture, but in reality—

"You don't know what I've done."

"It doesn't matter. If you were Hitler himself, standing here in front of me, repentant, I'd tell you the same thing. Your sin is no better, no worse than anyone else's."

He leads me over to a bench. When did we enter a park? "You want to tell me what it is that was so awful? I guarantee you I've heard it all. Took part in quite a few of my own, too."

The slats of the bench press into the back of my thighs, and I shift to a more comfortable position before recounting the past several months. I share what only moments before seemed unthinkable to divulge, and with the confession comes relief. Jonas doesn't interrupt or allow his face to communicate his thoughts.

"So, here I am. A last-ditch effort to save my marriage and my relationship with Taylor."

"I see." He sighs, folds his arms, and rests against the bench back. "It seems you have quite a problem on your hands."

Finally, someone who agrees with me.

"You expect your husband and daughter to forgive you for something you aren't able to forgive yourself for?"

"No." What's he talking about? "That's not it."

"You don't expect them to forgive you?"

How can they? "I don't know. Of course, I *want* them to. It's just..."

"You don't think it's possible." Jonas's eyes soften and I have to look away.

"No, I suppose not."

"You have to forgive yourself first, Corey. Have you read First Corinthians thirteen?"

"Of course." My response comes without thought. "It's the most used scripture at weddings."

He nods. "True. But as often as it's used, those verses aren't speaking of the love of a husband and wife. I urge you to go back and reread First Corinthians thirteen five. We can read scripture from dawn till dusk, but if it doesn't penetrate our hearts..."

I tuck his words away for a later time, until I can retrieve them, study them, and pray that they'll take root. "It must seem crazy to you. A pastor's wife struggling with the basics of Christianity."

"Not crazy. Human."

Some of the guilt eases from my weary shoulders.

"It makes me a little curious, too." He seems focused on a little yellow-and-black bird hopping about the lawn not twenty feet from us. "What was, or is, your relationship with your father like?"

"My dad?" Where is this coming from?

"Often when we struggle with the idea of God's love and grace, it's in direct correlation to the lack of the same we had growing up."

He isn't telling me anything I don't already know. And it explains so much.

Chapter 31

Corey

Life away from home is taking on an eerie type of normal. Communication with Paul is handled with quick phone calls where neither of us says much of value and there is no progress toward changing the status quo. Michael prefers brief text messages—lots of exclamation points and all caps to get his point across. The bottom line? He and Paul aren't getting along. When am I coming home?

I spend a few days pondering my conversation with Jonas and how my relationship with my father plays into my disconnect with God. More accurately, how my relationship with my father makes it difficult for me to accept God's forgiveness for my past. How could I have been a pastor's wife for nearly two decades and never have dealt with this elemental issue?

And what Jonas said about sin—none better or worse than any other—sounds great in theory, but when I try to put it into practice, it feels more like I'm justifying my actions. Repentant? Yes, I couldn't be sorrier for my past mistakes. But that doesn't change how they are now affecting Taylor and Paul. And somewhere down the line, Michael as well.

I look up First Corinthians thirteen, a passage I've read a million times—a list of what God's love is: patient, kind, does not envy, does not boast, is not proud. Does not dishonor others, is not self-seeking, is not easily angered. But it's the last half of verse five Jonas was referring to—it keeps no records of wrongs. It's arrogant to think my sin is so great, Christ's sacrifice can't cover it. And yet, it's not my sin against God that has me stumbling, it's my sin against Paul and Taylor.

That Sunday, I talk Trish into attending services at Jonas's church with me. And while I sit in the bottom-worn pew between her and Taylor, I allow Jonas's message to take root in my heart. Perhaps if he were my father, I wouldn't be struggling with the issue of grace. Maybe I wouldn't have even experienced my Great Shame in the first place. Guilt follows with the speed of a whip, and an apology flits through my head before those thoughts have a chance to take hold. My choices cannot be blamed on anyone but me.

The next day, as Taylor and I are driving back to Trish's after the therapy appointment, Taylor asks, "Are you and Dad getting divorced?"

A sense of peace settles over me. Was it my talk with Jonas that prepared me for this moment? I'll never know. A week ago, my immediate answer would have been, "No!" But I don't know the answer to that question and am tired to the core of my heart pretending that I do.

"I hope not," I say instead.

"What?" Apparently, that's not the answer she expected. "Then that's why we're here? Because you guys are, like, separated?"

It only takes a quick glance to catch the crestfallen expression and sheen of tears. "I think it's time we had that talk."

Half a mile and two turns later, we're at the beach. I park the car and gather our sweatshirts, handing Taylor hers before climbing out. A high fog shrouds the day in gloom and the moist breeze has just enough bite to seep into the bones. But it's refreshing rather than intolerable.

The beach isn't deserted as expected, and I recognize a number of regulars as we slip off our shoes and navigate the shifting sand. Taylor's uncharacteristically quiet. Is that good or bad? I suppose I'll find out soon enough.

I point north. "Let's head this way." My shoes, tied together by the strings and hanging from my fingers, bump against my jeans, leaving a dusting of sand. I focus on my bare feet molding prints as we walk and remember the poem *Footprints in the Sand*. I have to believe God's carrying me through this, otherwise I couldn't be so calm.

I take Taylor's cold hand in mine. "You asked me last week if you were angry with me the day of your accident."

"What about you and Dad?" She slips her hand from mine, crosses her arms, and continues down the beach, head hanging.

"I'll get to that. What do you remember about that day?"

"I...I don't know. For some reason, I thought I was mad."

"You also mentioned being angry with Mr. Johnson."

Raising her head, eyebrows drawn together, the breeze swirls her hair around her face. "Yeah. But—" She sighs. "I don't remember why."

"Your class worked on a lab that day. Blood typing."

She stops, taking my arm to halt me, too. "Yeah."

"You thought your results were wrong."

"I did?"

She doesn't know. I could stop right now—no. I can't. It's the right thing to do. "Yes, sweetheart. You were upset with Mr. Johnson." I take her hand again, drawing in a breath before jumping. "But the results weren't wrong. When I tried to explain...you knew...I mean..." My explanation trails off into uncertainty. Not over whether I was going to finally tell her the truth, but *how*.

"I don't get it."

Be honest. "You knew that if the results were right, then you couldn't be Dad's biological daughter."

My heart beats heavy in my throat, and I can't breathe while I wait for her reaction.

She opens her mouth to speak, but nothing comes out. Nose scrunched up, she looks at me as if she must have misunderstood. Shaking her head, she stares at me, willing me to deny it with her eyes.

"It's the truth."

"But then…"

"I didn't know, Tay."

"No," she gasps. "I…but Dad…" Tears well and spill over, trailing down her wind-pinked cheeks.

"You were angry and took off in the car to go to Dad. But before you reached him, the accident happened."

"No. I'd remember. How could I forget that?"

"I'm sorry, sweetheart." I press my hand to my heart, as if that will ease the pain in my chest. Everything that happened to her is my fault.

"You…you cheated on Dad?"

I can't bear the look on her face, the same look of disgust that still haunts me. "It's not that simple."

Face red, tears coursing down her cheeks, she backs up. "I hate you. Do you *hear* me? I *hate* you," she screams, throwing her shoes down before taking off.

"Taylor." It takes a moment to get my legs to work. "Stop, Taylor." I chase after her but slip on the sand and land hard. Scrambling back up, I see the tail end of her sweatshirt as she reaches the parking lot.

It's like I'm reliving the day of her accident all over again.

～

Paul

"That's it then," I tell my staff. "It looks like we have a plan for VBS and the weekend camp-out. Any other questions? Concerns?"

Becky flicks a strand of blonde hair off her face and repositions herself. "Can we revisit this next week? I have to firm up a few things before I'll feel confident that it's under control."

"Sure." I look at Dorothy. "Can you add VBS onto next week's agenda?"

She nods.

"I guess we're done. I appreciate all the hard work."

Gathering up my notes and iPad, I say my good-byes as everyone files out of the room, leaving only Mark, me, and the lingering scent of greasy pizza behind.

"I guess we're all set." Mark snatches up the trash can and begins clearing the table of napkins and paper plates.

I grimace. "It seems that way. But every year, we scramble to be ready on time."

"Becky's on it this year. She's not dealing with so much personal stress."

"I hope so." I can relate to the marital issues that plagued her last year.

"So…" Mark draws out the word. "Have you heard from Drew Simpson?"

Just his name's enough to sour the pizza in my gut. "No. But remember when I thought someone came in that day?"

A look of confusion crosses his face.

"With Alexis?"

"Ah. Yeah."

"It was Michael."

"What?" His expression brightens. "But that's great. You have a witness."

Plopping my briefcase onto the table, I shake my head. "He only saw enough to incriminate me. Didn't stick around long enough."

"That's…rough. He knows you didn't do anything, though."

"Afraid not." I check my watch. "Look, I've got a meeting with his history teacher, so I gotta go."

"Must be tough filling in while Corey's gone."

"She'll be home soon." My stock answer whenever anyone brings her up. What else can I say? I have no idea when she's coming home? No idea *if* she's coming home?

The drive to school takes less than ten minutes, then another five to find Mr. McGinty's classroom. Corey'd know right where it is. I'm at a disadvantage. I've never met the man, let alone been to his classroom.

I check the room number on the door against my scribbled note. If I didn't have the room number right, I'd know I was in a history class the moment I entered. Posters line the walls: presidents recognizable by sight—Washington, Lincoln, Kennedy—Civil War battles, a history of the American flag. Desks form haphazard rows that appear to have been quickly abandoned, and the back wall is jammed with what appears to be textbooks.

What's the saying, youth's wasted on the young? How many kids get that the possibilities are endless? Instead, they take life for granted. I know I did.

"Are you Pastor Shaffer?" A man, Mr. McGinty, I assume, stands from behind an old oak desk, smile on his round face. Middle-age paunch, curling salt and pepper hair. Late 50s maybe?

"Mr. McGinty?"

Hand out, he walks toward me. "I don't think we've ever met. Bob's the name."

I return the handshake. "Paul. And no, I don't think we've met. My wife generally handles…" I flick my hand to indicate the school. "Anyway, she's out of town."

Bob nods. "So I heard. Have a seat." He motions to a chair beside his desk and resumes his previous position.

"How's Taylor doing? Michael tells me Corey took her to a friend's. Monterey, is it?"

"Carmel." I'm at a disadvantage here—the odd man out. "Taylor's recovering very well, thanks for asking. Do you know Corey well?"

He shrugs. "I had her substitute for me a few times. Wish we had more like her."

Had I ever given much thought to this side of Corey? Beyond the fact that it took time from what I needed from her? Beyond how it affected *me*?

"Taylor was in my class a couple years ago. I wish we had more like her, too."

"Yes, I'm sure. She's our easy kid." He probably doesn't need me to tell him. If he had Taylor, the comparison is a no brainer.

"Easy isn't always better."

The response surprises me. "Meaning?"

"I've been teaching almost thirty years. Michael's a stand-out."

Is that good or bad? "How so?"

"He's intelligent, funny, and has untapped potential."

"For?"

He shrugs. "Whatever he wants to do with his life. Right now, that's photography."

I smell setup. "Oh, I see. Michael's got you advocating for this asinine summer camp idea."

"Worse than that."

"Oh?"

"That asinine idea was mine in the first place."

It takes a moment to remove my size twelve foot from my big mouth. "Look, I appreciate your interest in my son, but you don't know what we've had to deal with over the last year."

He leans forward, folds his hands on the desk. "I know he

trashed an elementary school last year and that he's done everything short of truancy to flunk out of school."

"Then why are you so quick to advocate for him?"

"I'm sure you've noticed in your line of work that things aren't always what they seem."

"What are you getting at?"

"Michael won't tell me what precipitated last year's foray into delinquency except that he reacted out of anger toward you."

I close my eyes and blow out a breath as the truth hits me in the gut. How could I have not seen it? It's bad enough I didn't put two and two together last year, but after our argument the other night?

"I didn't ask you here to lay a guilt trip on you about camp. Just thought you should know what you're facing."

"And I appreciate it." I stand and extend my hand. "More than you can know."

Bob returns the proffered handshake. "He's a great kid."

"Yes, he is. It's just too bad I needed you to remind me."

As I walk back to the car, my mind replays every heated discussion Michael and I have had since last year. He never said outright that his attitude was in reaction to anger toward me, but had I been listening...had I stepped out of my own self-centered world long enough to make the connections—

"Paul?"

The exuberant greeting pulls me from my thoughts. Bill Hamilton crosses the parking lot toward me. "Hey, Bill. They let you out of the office now and again?"

"Only if I'm on my best behavior. I hear Taylor's doing well."

Retrieving the keys from my pocket, I nod. "We feel very blessed. It could have been so much worse."

He pats me on the back as he passes. "That's almost word for word what Corey said."

"You talked to Corey?"

Bill stops and turns. "Yeah. Last week when she called to accept the job offer. I can't tell you how thrilled I am to have her as part of the team."

Team? What team?

Corey

Panic lodges in my throat, cutting off my air supply, as I drive up one street and down another, eyes scanning for Taylor. Just this morning, as we left her rehab appointment, she'd walked out in front of a car speeding through the parking lot. I yanked her back and lectured her, yet again, on the importance of focus.

Who's going to pull her from danger now?

With trembling fingers, I wipe at the tears blurring my vision and turn right. *Oh, God, please keep her safe. I'll do anything You ask. Just please, please keep her safe. If something happens to her, I'll never forgive myself.*

My cell phone rings through the car speakers—Tricia—and I fumble to push the correct button on the steering wheel to connect it. My heart beats triple-time with hope. "Is she there?"

"No, Cor. Sorry. The police are, though. They say she has to be gone twenty-four hours. I tried to explain it to them, but—"

"Put 'em on the phone."

A rustling, then, "Mrs. Shaffer?"

"Yes. Who's this?"

"Officer Lambert. I appreciate your situation, but we can't—"

"You *can*, Officer Lambert." My voice cracks, and I swallow the tears down. "My daughter suffers from traumatic brain injury. She's supposed to have 24-hour supervision."

"Unless she's in immediate danger—"

"Are you not listening?"

"Excuse me?"

"Under the best of circumstances, she has focus issues. She received some devastating news, which is why she ran. She could get hit by a car or picked up by some pervert." Speaking it out loud makes it so much more real. More possible. More likely. "Please," I sob. "I need your help. If something happens to her—"

"Yes, ma'am," he says. "We'll see what we can do."

Voices mumbling, then Tricia's back on the line. "Corey?"

"Are they going to do something?"

"Yes, sweetie. They'll alert the patrolmen about her special circumstances and start an unofficial search. You must be more persuasive than I am. Maybe I should be out looking, too."

"No. If by some miracle she shows up at the house, you need to be there."

"Did...did you call Paul?"

I shudder at the thought. "Not yet. There's nothing he can do from there, so no sense in worrying him." Or in giving him more ammunition.

"But Taylor may call him."

"Then he'll know." My tone is sharper than intended. "I'm sorry, Trish. It's just...I'm so scared. What if—?"

"No sense going there. I scanned some copies of a picture I have of her and gave them to some friends. With all of us and the police—we'll find her."

"She's—"

"Hang on. There's a call coming through."

Silence fills the space and I reassess my strategy. What if she slipped into one of the shops? I'll never spot her from the car. Will the police do an on-foot search, or are we just covering the same ground? What are the chances—?"

"Corey? You there?"

"Yes." Is that excitement in Tricia's voice? "What's going on?"

"That was Jonas on the phone. Taylor's at his church. She's fine. Upset, but fine. She's not aware that he's called here."

Relief washes over me, at once both exhilarating and exhausting. But Jonas's? How would he even know to call Trish? It doesn't matter. "I'm on my way. Can you let the police know?"

"I'm on it."

Of course, Jonas's church is on the other side of town.

I take side streets and break about five traffic laws before pulling into the parking lot of Oceanside Presbyterian. My entire body's shaking as I climb out of the car, and I have to stop and take a few deep breaths. She won't be happy to see me. In fact, she might just bolt again.

I lock my purse in the car and pocket the keys. If this turns into a battle, I'd better be prepared. Taylor's got strength and youth on her side, but for the time being, I've got wit. Assuming Jonas and Taylor are in the sanctuary, using the front doors might not be the best idea. Instead, I walk around the side and test the door there. Unlocked.

I slip through and ease the door closed, wincing when it squeaks. Low voices reach my ears, but I can't decipher what they're saying. I peek into the sanctuary. Taylor sits about five feet from Jonas in the first pew. Her hair, loose from its scrunchie, veils her face. Shoulder's hunched, head down, she looks as dejected as I feel.

"You don't truly believe that, do you?" Jonas asks her. "That she's been manipulating you and your father since the day you were born?"

Taylor shrugs. "She lied to us."

"Have you ever lied?"

"No," she mumbles.

"Never?" Jonas's tone communicates disbelief. "You've

never told a friend that you like her new haircut, or her outfit, or her boyfriend when in fact you don't?"

"That's different."

"Afraid not. Not if we're using the biblical standards you claim as the measuring stick for your life. For your mother's life."

Taylor looks up, and I step back, so she doesn't spot me lurking in the back. "Lying to someone to spare their feelings isn't the same as lying about what she did. About who my dad is."

"You don't think your mother kept the secret to spare your feelings? Or maybe your dad's feelings?"

"No. I think she kept the secret because she knew we'd be upset with her if we knew the truth."

"And isn't that the motivation behind you lying to your friends? They'd be upset with you if they knew what you truly felt?"

Wow. He's good.

"You're confusing me."

"Your mother doesn't strike me as the self-serving type. And I know for a fact this whole mess is hurting her every bit as much as it is you. Maybe more so."

Taylor tucks a strand of hair behind her ear and glares up at Jonas. If I'm not mistaken, she's about to unsheathe her razor tongue. Time to take over.

I step into the sanctuary, drawing her gaze. "Hey, Tay. You gave me quite a scare."

She turns on Jonas. "You *called* her?"

Jonas doesn't bother to defend the accusation, but instead stands to greet me. "Are you okay?"

I nod. "I am now. Thank you."

"I'm not going with you," Taylor says.

"I'm afraid you don't have a choice."

"I want to go home."

"Good, that's the plan. Tricia's waiting for us."

"No. I mean *home*. With Dad." The defiance loses some of its heat when her voice cracks and she swipes at the tears coursing down her cheeks. "I mean, Paul."

"Oh, Tay. He *is* your dad. Always has been, always will be." I meet Jonas's eyes before he leaves us alone. "I know you're angry and confused. You have every right to be."

"You lied."

"I know."

"You cheated on Dad." She stares at me as if daring me to deny it.

"Yes."

"Why?"

"It happened before we were married."

"Why?"

I take Jonas's place on the pew. "I can't discuss that with you without your dad's permission."

"You mean Paul."

"No. I mean your dad."

"So…do you know who—?" She focuses on a jagged cuticle.

Better to get it all out in the open. "No. I…no."

Chapter 32

Paul

A warm breeze flows through the kitchen windows, hitting me with the scent of fresh-cut grass and flowers Corey planted before taking off. Same annuals she plants every spring, but I couldn't identify one for the life of me. Petunias, pansies, peonies. Whatever they are, they don't stand a chance of surviving if she doesn't come home soon.

I thought about calling her last night but needed time to cool down. How could she take a teaching position without discussing it with me? Maybe Hamilton was mistaken. Either way, it's best not to jump all over her.

Michael and I sit at the kitchen table, both of us pretending to eat the casserole I threw together. We're about pizza'd out, but my cooking's not much of a substitute.

"You cut the lawn." Instead of sounding pleasantly surprised, as intended, I sound suspicious.

Michael grunts a non-answer and moves the noodles around on his plate.

"I appreciate it. The backyard's beginning to look like a jungle."

No response.

"I met with your history teacher yesterday."

"Mr. McGinty?"

Do I detect interest? "Yes. You were off to work by the time I got home, or I would have told you about it then."

Another grunt.

"He thinks a lot of you."

"At least someone does."

"I thought, maybe—" My cell phone rings. I should just ignore it, but Michael snatches it up before I can react.

"Hey, Mom." There's the enthusiasm I'm looking for. "How's Taylor?"

I listen to the one-sided conversation as I clear the dishes from the table, Hamilton's revelation playing over in my head. What's become of our marriage. Okay, I blew it on my end—refusing to forgive, failing to tell her about Alexis, Drew, and the drama enfolding at the church—but to accept a teaching position when she knows how I feel about it? And how is that going to affect the charges at church when she already has a role to fill there?

"Mom wants to talk to you." Michael hands me the receiver and leaves.

"Corey?"

"Hey, Paul. Michael sounds good."

It's news to me. "Yeah. How's Taylor?"

A sigh floats through the line. "She's been better."

"Why? What happened?" The phone bites into my hand as I await her response.

"I told her the truth about the accident."

"Oh?" I retake my position at the table, now clear of dishes. "Did she…I mean…was she upset?" How could she not be?

"Let's put it this way, she's not talking to me right now."

Welcome to my world. I rub at a headache forming at the base of my neck. "Aren't we the poster children for parenting? Taylor's not talking to you, and Michael's not talking to me. Is she there? I'd like to talk to her, reassure her, you know?"

"She's asleep right now, but I'll have her call when she wakes up. I suppose my idea of divide and conquer wasn't such a good one, huh?"

"I thought you left because you were angry with me."

"That's funny," she says. "I thought I left because *you* were angry with *me*." But she doesn't sound like she's laughing.

"I had a meeting with Michael's history teacher yesterday."

"Bob?"

The familiarity irritates. "Yes. *Bob*. Anyway, it sounds like Michael's doing well. I didn't know it was he who suggested that summer camp idea."

"Oh, didn't you?"

Why is it I always feel like the outsider looking in? "No. There's something else I didn't know."

She doesn't respond for a moment. Probably waiting for me to continue. "What's that?"

"You've accepted a teaching position for next year." I can't seem to keep the accusation from my tone.

Again, no response.

"Or was Bill Hamilton mistaken?"

"When'd you talk to Bill?"

"What difference does it make?"

"Are you checking up on me?"

She's upset? What right does she have to be upset? "You're missing the point. Is this just more of the same—secrets?"

"You...you have a lot of nerve. Secrets? *Seriously*? You've been tiptoeing around a few of your own."

"This isn't about me, this is—"

"Of course, it's about you, Paul. It's *always* about you. You want to tell me what's been going on with Alexis Andrews? And what about Rebecca Simpson, huh? What about the clandestine phone calls with Mark, the moodiness over the last several months?"

"I—" *She's got you there, pal.*

"And furthermore." She takes a deep breath. I'm in for it now. "You've been on Michael about his attitude—well, where do you think he gets it? You want to preach forgiveness on Sunday and then refuse to offer it on Monday, be my guest. But if you think you can bully me into submission, you've got another thing coming."

And the line goes dead.

"Corey?" I check the screen—call ended.

The last time she hung up on me was…never. No, that's not true. An argument not a year into our marriage. Corey was pregnant with Taylor. It was the first week of September, and the temperature was hovering around a hundred. I was youth pastor for a mega church in Sacramento, working retail on the side to make ends meet. Even so, money was so tight we were consisting on beans and rice.

"I've got great news," Corey had told me over the phone.

I'd called on my dinner break—forty-five minutes and then back to selling electronics to kids who spent minimum wage-earnings on their toys. "We won the Lotto?"

She laughed. "Close. I was called in to substitute tomorrow. Isn't that great?" Her tone was tentative—as it should have been. She'd flat-out defied me.

"You mean you went ahead and filed the paperwork after we discussed it?"

"Please don't be upset, Paul. I just want to help. You're working all these crazy hours and—"

"And I told you I don't want you working. You're about to have a baby."

"In three months. I'm talking about working one day a week, two at the most."

"It's not appropriate."

Tension filled the silence.

"I'm looking out for what's best for you," I reminded her.

"No. You're looking out what's best for *you*. It's not my health you're worried about. It's how it'll look to Pastor Ray with your wife working. Because we all know a wife's place is in the home, barefoot and pregnant."

I couldn't deny the charge, but that was beside the point. "I'm not arguing with you about this, Corey, not over the phone. We can discuss it when I get home. If that—"

A click then dead silence.

And again tonight. Twice in eighteen years. Not a bad record. But Corey's not a temperamental person by nature. If she's angry enough to hang up on me, maybe it's time to take stock.

A half hour later, while I'm in the midst of answering emails, the phone rings again. Corey's number. But when I answer, it's a sleepy-sounding Taylor on the other end.

"Hey, kiddo."

"Dad? I mean...I don't know what—"

"It's Dad, Tay. It's always been Dad. It'll always be Dad." A deep sense of possessiveness takes hold of my heart.

"But Mom said...you know."

"It doesn't matter. You're my daughter. I fed you, walked you through colic and changed your diapers."

"Eww. Do you have to remind me?"

A grin takes hold. "Apparently."

"I don't want to be here with Mom. I hate her."

"No, you don't." The admonishment is automatic, but there's a part of me, deep inside, that celebrates Taylor's anger. It somehow justifies my own.

"She *cheated* on you."

Like I need a reminder. "That's between your mom and me. She's never done anything to you but be the best mom she knew how." The words burst forth, a defense of Corey. But they're true. When has Corey ever put herself before her children—or me, for that matter?

∼

Corey

"I'm really not in the mood to go out," I tell Tricia as I spot the five Italian flags waving over Little Napoli restaurant. "Let's pick up Chinese and take it back to your place."

"You can use a good meal." Tricia takes my arm and herds me across Delores Street. "I'd bet you've lost a good ten pounds in the last couple months."

"I should be home with Taylor." We step into the restaurant where garlic and Italian spices fill the air like a perfume. Despite my protests, my stomach rumbles in response.

"Reservations for two under the name Sewell," Tricia tells the hostess before leaning close to me. "Taylor's not talking to you right now, and the harder you push, the longer it'll take."

"But—"

"Jasmine's very responsible and promised to call if there are any problems."

Still, I hesitate when the hostess says, "Right this way."

Tricia starts to follow then steps back to reclaim my arm. "We're five minutes from home, Cor."

"But if she runs off again—"

"Which is more likely to happen with you hovering over her. Relax."

We follow the hostess to a small table in the back corner. It's busier than I'd expect for a Monday night. Vacationers or locals?

"How's this?" The hostess asks.

Tricia flashes her model-white smile. "Perfect."

I slip into my seat and accept a menu from the young woman.

"Your waitress will be right with you."

Tricia waves to someone across the room. "Now, isn't this nice?"

"Sure." Why is it I feel like a disgruntled teenager being dragged out by her mother?

"I haven't been here for ages. Steven and I used to come quite often."

"So, why are we here?"

"Excuse me?" Tricia fusses with her cloth napkin and rearranges her silverware.

"You have something to say, just say it."

"Well, aren't you the suspicious one?"

"Good evening, ladies." A chirpy waitress greets us, setting up bread, butter, and an olive oil/balsamic vinegar mix. "Can I get you anything to drink?"

"Water's fine," I say.

Tricia glances at the waitress. "Two waters."

"Let me tell you about our specials…" She regales us with dishes I can't pronounce, made all the more appetizing by their mystery. "I'll give you a few minutes to think it over."

Tricia loses herself in the over-large menu. "I heard you on the phone earlier with Paul," she murmurs.

So that's it. "I suppose you'd have to be deaf not to. You think Taylor heard?"

Tricia drops the menu. "She was sleeping off the excitement of the day. For the brief time you were on the phone, you sounded like the old Corey."

"What? A screeching harpy?"

"No. A woman who knows when to stand up for herself."

The menu's not such a bad place to lose oneself. I examine the pasta dishes with the intensity of a food connoisseur—which I'm not.

"Is everything okay?"

The question brings the unexpected well of emotion clogging my throat. "No."

"Have we decided, ladies?"

Tricia orders the lasagna and I choose a specialty salad.

The waitress collects our menus and leaves us alone. Or as alone as we can be in a crowded restaurant.

I take a piece of focaccia bread from the basket and tear it in half. "I shouldn't have yelled at him."

"I don't know. Sometimes that's the only way to get the point across. Men can be pretty dense."

"He has a right to be angry with me."

"You mean because you took that job without his knowledge or because of the past?"

"I cheated on him."

"Yes. And I'm partially to blame for that."

"What?" I lean over my bread plate. "You had nothing to do with it."

"You wouldn't have been at that party if it weren't for me."

"The party wasn't the issue, Trish. My getting married to Paul was." I sit back. "He's like my dad in more ways than I want to consider. I knew it even then. It scared me."

Tricia snorts. "He's nothing like your father."

Is she blind? "Judgmental, condescending, unapproachable."

"Loving, gentle, funny."

"I don't understand you," I say. "I thought you believed Paul was, I don't know, stuffy and unbending."

"He can be."

"This whole mess with Taylor," I flick a hand in the air, "it's my dad all over again."

Tricia shakes her head. "I don't think so."

"He's been punishing me, just like my dad would."

"*You*'ve been punishing you, Cor. You've been carrying this guilt around with you for so long it's like a cancer eating away at you—changing you."

"No." Tears burn my eyes and I swallow them back.

"Look at you." She waves a hand toward me. "I've

watched you change from a vivacious young woman to a drudge."

"I—"

"I'm sorry, sweetie, but your argument with Paul on the phone? It's the first time in a long while I've seen the old you."

"You don't understand."

"I do. You've been paying penance for far too long. How can Paul or Taylor forgive you when you can't forgive yourself?"

"Have you been talking to Jonas?"

"Jonas? What's he got to do with this?"

I wave a dismissive hand. "Never mind."

"Some women hide away behind a facade—you know, perfect hair, makeup, fashionable clothing. I'll admit, because it's only fair, that's what I do. But you do the opposite. Like you don't want anyone to notice you. That's not healthy, either."

"What are you talking about?"

"Well, look at you."

"I don't mean me. I mean you. You said you hide away behind a facade."

"Here we are, ladies." The waitress slips a plate of lasagna in front of Trish and my salad in front of me. "Can I get you anything else?"

I glance at Trish, who doesn't seem to have heard the waitress. "No, thanks. We're good."

The waitress leaves and I pick up my fork, waiting for Tricia to resume our conversation. When she doesn't, I say, "You can't just drop a bomb like that and then leave it."

"I—" She clears her throat and takes a sip from her water glass. "I didn't recognize it in you until the last few years."

"But you said—"

"I know. You all thought I was so heartbroken when Steven died. But the truth was, I was getting ready to leave him."

"What?"

"He was abusive, Cor." She looks at me, a sheen of tears in her green eyes. "I haven't remained single because I'm heartbroken. I've remained single because I'm terrified of making the same mistake again."

It takes a moment for her confession to sink in. How had I never seen it? "Oh, Trish. I'm so sorry. Why didn't you ever say anything?"

"I was ashamed." Her smile is sad. "So, you see, I know what it's like to carry shame around like a cancer. I've been there. I battle it every day. And that's why I know what I'm talking about when it comes to you."

I shake my head. "Aren't we a pair?"

Chapter 33

Corey

I'm persona non grata with Taylor. A cold front's blown in and huddles over our little habitat. She's all smiles with Trish —in fact, with anyone that isn't me—only making the issue more obvious. Tricia thinks we can remedy this with a girls' day out.

We start at the hair salon, to which I'm dragged kicking and screaming.

"There is nothing wrong with my hair," I mutter all the way to the salon chair.

Taylor, sitting in her own chair to my left, snorts. Not that her opinion matters. She'd argue the opposite out of spite.

"You're too young to go gray," Trish says from my right, while Chelsea, her hairdresser, digs through her roots.

"I'm not gray." I peer at myself in the much-too-large mirror surrounded by unflattering lights. It must be the lights, right? It couldn't be that I really look that drab.

"You have beautiful hair," Jacki, my hairdresser says. "With a little tweaking—"

"Tweaking?" I watch her in the mirror, hands raking through my hair, assessing. "What kind of tweaking?"

"Hmmm."

"I want purple streaks," Taylor says. "You can do that, right?"

I glance over at my daughter. "That's not—"

"Pick your battles," Tricia singsongs just loud enough for me to hear.

She's right. There's no point in turning every decision into a battle of wills. "That's not a bad idea," I say with a fake smile.

I receive Taylor's turned up nose in response.

"So, here's what I'm thinking," Jacki says, one hand on her hip, the other flicking a wide-tooth comb through my hair. "Cut up to about here." She brushes the comb to just above my shoulder. "And put some color back in. I'd say a shade or two darker than your daughter's."

"Color?" I catch her eye in the mirror. "I've never colored my hair."

Tricia's enthusiasm drowns out my protests. Even Taylor's eyes light up. I know when I'm beat.

Two hours later, we emerge from the salon. My head feels about five pounds lighter, and I have to admit, I look about five years younger. I was stealing glances at myself all the way out the door. Even as we walk down the street toward the car, I catch my reflection in shop windows. How could I have been so unaware of how my hair aged me?

Taylor's long brown hair now shapes her face, purple streaks strategically placed.

"Your hair looks nice," I tell her.

No response.

Tricia catches my eye and shrugs. "Next stop, Reflections."

"Hey," Taylor says. "I thought you weren't working today."

"I'm not. We're going shopping."

Protesting does no good. Has Tricia always been this stubborn?

After working in the shop all week, Taylor's got her new outfit all picked out. I'm suspicious. Did they have this little jaunt pre-planned?

"I'll help you try it on," Jasmine tells Taylor as they disappear to the back room.

"What do you think of this?" Tricia holds up a soft-pink silk shell top.

"I think it looks expensive."

"Nonsense." She slips into a dressing room and hangs it. "Let's see what we can find here."

"Trish, please. It's too much."

She turns from the rack of jeans and plants pleading eyes on me. "It's a drop in the bucket for me, Corey. I don't have anyone but you and your family. Let me spoil you a little."

Beautiful, sweet Trish. How did I not see that she's every bit as lost as I? "We're still pretty young, you know."

She smiles before turning back to the rack. "In our prime."

"Not even middle age by today's standards."

"These are perfect." She waggles a pair of faded, skinny jeans.

"For who?"

"You, silly."

I snort. "Yeah, if I was Pastor's Wife Barbie. Even if I could fit into those—"

"Bet you can."

"—and be able to breathe, they're not appropriate."

"Trust me, okay. I only carry *appropriate* clothing."

"So, back to the point I was trying to make."

She walks past me and hangs the jeans with the silk top. "Ah, yes. We're not even middle aged."

"You should have more than me and my family, Trish. You could get mar—"

The bell over the door tinkles, announcing three female customers.

"Good afternoon, ladies. How are you today?"

"Good," the chorus replies.

"Let me get Jasmine to assist you." She turns to me. "Be right back."

I swipe at my hair and throw a smile at the ladies, who are oohing and aahing over Tricia's inventory.

Jasmine emerges from the back, followed by Trish. "Good afternoon, ladies. May I help you find something?"

"One more thing." Trish grabs my arm and pulls me to a sales rack. "I had this great sweater—where is it?" Talking to herself, she riffles through the clothes.

"As I was *saying*…" Tricia's got the attention span of a two-year-old when it suits her. "You should think about remarrying."

"Ta da," she sings, holding up a cream-color sweater wrap. "Here it is."

"Are you listening to me?"

"This'll look great with those jeans. A pair of low-cut boots and we're good to go."

"Tricia!"

Wrapping an arm around my shoulder, she walks me to the dressing room. "I hear you, Cor. But really, who am I going to marry? Maybe if Jonas had a son, otherwise," she shrugs, "the pickin's are slim."

Paul

I pull into Craig's Pit 'n' Stop and tuck the bag of burgers and fries behind the passenger seat. Two chocolate shakes sit in the cup holders. Two minutes to five. Any later, I might have missed Michael. I'm perusing directions on the map app on my phone when he lumbers out of the garage. I'm close enough to catch the scowl.

He looks around, like he's scoping out an escape route, before heading to the car. Poking his head through the open passenger-side window he scowls again. "What're you doing here?"

"I thought we'd go for a ride."

"I'm going to the movies with Dan."

Hate to use the parent-card... Who am I kidding? I use it all the time. "It's not a request, son."

"Man," he moans, yanking the door open and plopping onto the seat. "Whatever happened to your rule about sticking to commitments?"

I offer my cell phone. "Do you need to call him?"

"No." He buckles up and slinks low in the seat. It's doubtful the belt will be much protection.

"You didn't have plans to go to the movies, did you?"

"What difference does it make? You're gonna make me go with you anyway."

"True." I reach behind his seat and snag the sack. "You hungry?"

He shrugs, but he doesn't turn down the meal.

I head toward Highway 49 as he distributes dinner. A burger for him, a burger for me, both orders of fries into the now-empty sack. He tears open two packets of salt, dumps them over the fries, closes the bag and shakes. He places the open bag on the middle console where we can both reach it. Like old times. How long's it been since we've done this? A year or more'd be my guess. Not since the school incident. Or more accurately, not since the Alexis incident.

"Where're we going?" he mumbles over a mouthful of fries.

"Georgetown." Keeping my eyes on the road, I try to maneuver the wrapper off my burger in my lap.

Michael sighs, snatches up my burger, pulls the wrapper down and hands it back to me.

"Thanks."

"Just trying to keep you from killing us."

We drive in silence, focused on our fast-food meal. Every now and then we reach for fries at the same time and our hands bump. It's not an unpleasant situation. At least we're not screaming at each other. Progress, right?

Ten minutes into our drive, Michael asks, "What's in Georgetown?"

"Possibilities."

"Cryptic."

"Cryptic?" I check to make sure it's my son in the seat.

"Vocab word. So, you don't want to tell me?"

"Nothing to tell. Yet. When I know, you'll know."

"And they say teenagers suck at communication."

"How's the job going?"

"It's going."

For the briefest moment, life's good. At least the hope of good. Dare I tread on that? "Look, Michael. I want to talk to you about what you saw with Ms. Andrews."

He wads the burger wrapper. "I knew it. You afraid I'll tell Mom?"

"No."

"So, did *you* tell her?"

He's got me there. "It's bigger than you realize."

"So, you *didn't* tell her."

"What you saw—it caught me by surprise. Had you stayed even one second more, we wouldn't be having this discussion." I glance at him. "You wouldn't have gotten into trouble."

He plucks his shake from the holder and focuses out his window. "I don't want to talk about it."

"Why didn't you tell me I was the reason you trashed the school?"

"Said I don't want to talk about it."

"Is it because you were trying to protect your mom?"

"Dad!" He turns to me. "Why can't we just drop it?"

"Because ignoring it won't make it go away."

No response.

"Do you believe me? About Ms. Andrews?"

He's silent for so long, I'm surprised when he finally answers. "I don't know."

"Do you *want* to believe me?"

"Yeah."

"Well then, that's a start."

We turn onto Highway 193 West, and he pulls his phone from his shirt pocket, plugs in ear buds, and tunes me out.

Fifteen minutes later, we pull into Georgetown and Michael sits up, like it's just getting interesting. I park the car in front of Community Church, and he yanks the wires to his earbuds.

"You're really not gonna tell me why we're here?"

The church is small, but looks historical—late 1800s maybe? There won't be a stage for worship or much space for Sunday school. Where do they hold church functions? A basement?

"Dad?"

"Hmmm?" I glance at Michael.

"I only have a couple more weeks of school."

"Yeah?"

"Can I go to Mom's?"

Mom's? Sounds so separate. "She might be home by then." God willing.

"I mean if she's not."

"You going to quit your job?" More to the point, are you leaving me, too?

"I can get a few days off."

A few days. That, I can handle. "I don't see why not. What d'you think of this church?"

He peers out his window. "It looks old."

Classic, is what I'm thinking. Couldn't seat more than a few hundred, tops. No possibility for much growth. But that might not be a bad thing.

Focus on what's in front of me, for a change.

Chapter 34

Corey

For the third day in a row, Taylor refuses to join me for our morning walk. The amount of time she's not talking to me is in direct correlation with how much she *is* talking to Paul. Their once-a-day phone calls have multiplied two or three times. She's using him as a weapon—not that it bothers me. Much. At least their relationship isn't suffering in the aftermath.

Tricia sends me off with a promise to get Taylor up and dressed in time for her rehab appointment.

"I guess it's just the two of us, Rambo." Clipping his leash, we make the five-minute walk to the beach. I use the silence to pray. At least God's not argumentative—not to my face, anyway. I'm sure He'll have some points to make when the time's right. For now, it's enough that we're talking again. Or I am.

When we reach the beach, I breathe in the briny, moist scent—will I ever tire of it? —and let Rambo loose. His short legs struggle with the sand until he hits the wet stuff. Such energy and enthusiasm. If only I could bottle it.

A golden retriever bounds toward Rambo. Lexie? I scan the beach in search of Jonas. I haven't seen him since I picked Taylor up from his church. Concern for him and his wife, Beth, has wriggled its way into my heart. Once I spot him, I'll know everything's fine. But then a middle-aged man whistles for the dog. He's too far from me to get a good look, but his hair is brown, instead of Jonas's shock of white. Maybe I'll stop by the church.

I call Rambo and we continue our hour-long walk down the beach and back. When I get to Tricia's, Taylor is dressed and waiting, as promised.

"You ready for rehab?" I pass her sitting on the couch and head for the kitchen. A piece of toast and a banana and I'll be ready to go.

She follows, arms crossed, and leans against the entrance. "I don't need you there."

Retrieving the whole wheat bread from the freezer, I glance at her. "Are you going to walk?"

"No. I mean I don't need you to come in with me."

"Sorry, kiddo, but you don't have a choice. I can't help with the assignments if I don't sit in on the instructions."

"They're stupid." Nostrils flared, eyebrows lowered, she glares at me. "I don't need to do rehab. There's nothing wrong with me."

Trish steps in through the French doors leading to the back patio. "What's going on?"

"Taylor doesn't seem to think she needs rehab. There's nothing wrong with her." I drop the bread into the toaster.

"Then what's this?" Trish holds up a toothbrush. "I found it in Rambo's water dish."

"I—" Taylor's face reddens. "I was brushing my teeth when I went out to feed Rambo. It's no big deal."

I pick through the bananas. "Weren't you looking for it last night?"

"She was," Trish says. "I had to give her a spare."

"Like you guys never make mistakes." She snatches the toothbrush from Tricia and stomps out with all the maturity of a two-year-old.

"Sorry," I say.

Trish shrugs. "Tantrum or not, just having you guys here makes my life much more interesting."

"Is she that forgetful at your shop?"

"Like I said, life's more interesting."

Twenty minutes later, the silent treatment continues as I park the car at the rehab center. "Do you have your day planner?"

Taylor holds up the leather-bound book, a bribe to get her excited about keeping copious notes on everything. Her definition of copious and mine differ by a mile.

"Let's go then."

"I don't want you in there."

"Like I said before, you don't have a choice." I drop the keys into my purse and open the door. "You want to be angry with me? Fine. But the longer you act like a spoiled three-year-old, the longer your recovery. No recovery, no high school graduation. And until you graduate, you're stuck with me."

She looks at me like I slapped her. "Dad said I can go home whenever I want."

Is Paul undermining me now? "So now he's Dad again?"

"Whatever," she mutters, pushing her door open.

She's too old for a swat on the butt, but I'm sorely tempted.

As we cross the parking lot, I follow a few paces behind, far enough to give her some semblance of independence, but close enough to step in if she walks in front of a car. We get to the elevator, and I step into the corner, hands behind my back.

"Well?" Raising her eyebrows, she gives a little head shake. A non-verbal "duh."

"You don't need me, remember?" I've stooped to her level. I'm not proud of it, but it feels good. There's a sense of release in not caring. I've made it too easy on her—which is why she doesn't think she needs me. Every time confusion shadows her face, I jump in and take over. No more.

Her finger hovers over the buttons.

An older couple step in, eyeing first Taylor, then me. The gentleman reaches past Taylor and hits 3. "What floor do you need, young lady?" He asks Taylor.

She throws panicked eyes in my direction.

He turns to me. "Ma'am?"

"We'll go to three too."

Silence descends as the elevator lurches its way up to the third floor. The doors open, and the couple steps out. Taylor follows. "This isn't the right floor."

"No." I wait for her to return.

"What floor?"

I shrug. "You don't need me, remember?"

"*Really*, Mom?"

I check my watch. We should be signing in by now. "You might want to check your day planner."

She folds her arms, the planner tucked against her chest. "I didn't put it in my planner."

"Didn't Dottie tell you to?"

"Can you just tell me what floor?" She makes eye contact for the first time in days. "Please?"

"Eight."

"Jeez," she mutters, punching 8. "Why do you have to make it so hard?"

"You ain't seen nothing yet, sweetheart."

"So, tell me." Dottie gathers up Taylor's chart. "How's the independent study going?"

"Good," Taylor says.

"How's your reading comprehension?"

"Really good."

Dottie looks at me, and I give her a slight head shake.

"I don't see why I can't graduate with my class."

Dottie folds her hands and places her elbows on the desk. "In less than two weeks? I hate to disappoint you, but I don't think that's going to happen."

"I was accepted to Sac State for next year." Taylor whips her head around to look at me. "I can't go to college if I don't graduate."

"College isn't going anywhere, sweetie. Let's just concentrate on one thing at a time."

"We'll talk more about it on Monday," Dottie says. "Our time's up for now."

When we step into the elevator, Taylor turns to me, eyes welling. "My friends. They already think I'm an idiot. Now they'll know."

"We both know you're not an idiot."

"I used to be smart," she whispers.

I put a hand out to pat her arm, but she shrugs me off. She's more like her dad than she realizes.

"This is your fault. My accident. If you hadn't cheated on Dad—"

"You wouldn't be here right now." Enough's enough.

"Yeah." She glares at me as the elevator doors open. "I'd be home, getting ready to graduate."

I step out ahead of her. "No, my dear. You wouldn't have been born."

"You wish." She stomps past me and pushes through the glass doors.

I pick up the pace. Leaving her to fail on her own is one thing; letting her walk in front of a moving vehicle is another. But we get to the car without incident, if you don't count childish sneers and glares. Maybe it's because I'm tired of beating myself up over Taylor's accident, or maybe Jonas's words have impacted me more than I realized, but I'm sick to death of the rain of judgment.

Buckling my seat belt, I turn to Taylor. "You have every right to be angry with me. I get it. But whatever I did or didn't do to your dad is between us. You don't get to throw it in my face again. Are we clear?"

Nostrils flaring, eyes hooded by drawn eyebrows, she stares through the windshield. "Whatever."

Oooh, I'm tempted to slap that snide look right off her face. With a deep breath and a quick prayer for patience, I start the engine. "If you don't mind, I'd like to take a detour before going home."

"And if I do?"

"Too bad."

Twenty minutes later, I pull the car into the parking lot of Oceanside Presbyterian. Relief eases the tension in my shoulders when I recognize Jonas's car. I've been worried over nothing. He's probably just been busy.

"Why are we here?"

"I want to check on Jonas. He hasn't been at the beach in the mornings."

"I'm not going in. I want to call Dad."

I hand her my cell phone. "Stay in the car."

The church doors are unlocked, the interior empty. It would be in poor taste to call out, but maybe—

"May I help you?" Jonas's voice comes from behind me. He must have been outside.

But when I turn, a stranger stands in the entrance. "Oh, I was looking for Jonas."

The smile he flashes is familiar. "He's in the basement. We're trying to de-clutter about twenty year's-worth of hoarding. Let me get him for you."

"And you are?" The question's out of my mouth before I think better of it. It's none of my business who he is.

"Dylan Crosby." He offers his hand. "Jonas's son."

"Corey Shaffer. It's nice to meet you."

"I know you." He waggles a finger at me, his smile a replica of Jonas's. "My dad's a little smitten with you, Mrs. Shaffer."

"Well, the feeling's mutual. I haven't seen him down at the beach the last few days. I've been a little worried. I know your mother's not well." How much do I reveal?

His smile fades. "No. It's tough on Dad. Tough on all of us."

"Do you live here or just visiting?"

"It looks like I'll be living here. I just got board approval to take over my dad's pastorship."

"Your Dad's—he's leaving?"

"Not leaving. Stepping down. He wants to spend more time with my mom."

I nod. "Smart man."

"I thought I heard voices up here." Jonas appears, a tired smile on his face, his hair mussed, a dirt smudge on his cheek. "Corey?" His eyes widen. "Well, look at you."

My face heats as I give my hair a self-conscious pat.

"It's good to see you. How's Taylor?"

I roll my eyes. "She's a work in progress. Just when I thought I'd never see the toddler years again…"

Dylan clears his throat. "If you'll excuse me. It was nice meeting you, Corey."

"You, too."

I watch him amble from the sanctuary then turn my eyes back to Jonas. "I hear you're leaving the church."

"Beth needs me. I'd have done it long before now, but we really wanted Dylan in place first."

"He seems nice."

"I think so."

"Married?"

Jonas barks out a laugh. "Mrs. Shaffer, are you angling for my son?"

"Depends."

His gaze sharpens. "You and your husband aren't parting ways, are you?"

"Not that I know of. But I do have a friend."

"Ah. Well, Dylan's not married, but he is divorced."

"You make it sound like a criminal offense."

"What his ex-wife did…" He grimaces. "Close enough as far as I'm concerned. So, you have a friend?"

"Tricia. She's been my best friend since grade school. Widowed."

"Hmmm. What did you have in mind?"

"How about dinner at her place? That's where I'm staying."

"He'd run at the first scent of a setup."

"Good. So would Tricia. We'll call it a thank you dinner— for your help with Taylor. Then we'll step back. If it's meant to be—"

"I'm a firm believer in leaving things in God's hands." He grins. "But there's nothing wrong with a little nudge now and again."

Chapter 35

Paul

A light rain dots the windshield, an occasional drop making its way through the open window. The late evening air's uplifting. Spring rain. Gentle, cleansing. Reminds me of God's grace. Too bad I need a reminder. I can't seem to hold onto it on my own.

I've just left the convalescent home. John Pendelton's improving, might even be released by the weekend. One of the more pleasant pastoral tasks—visiting recovering congregants. The worry and tension that aged Beverly has eased since the last time I saw her, and my heart's lighter than when I entered.

Dusk has our front porch in shadows as I pull up. No lights. And, thank God, no stereo blasting. Isn't Michael home? We agreed he'd let me know if he made plans. When I called to tell him I'd be late, he said nothing about going out.

I pull the car into the garage, cut the engine, and sit. I miss Corey and Taylor. I even miss Rambo and his enthusiastic greeting. My prayers have been more heartfelt. Nothing like loneliness to draw you closer to God. I want my family back.

And I want my church back. But the Lord seems to be moving me in some other direction. The desire for a simpler life.

Gathering my briefcase, I climb out of the car. What will await me inside? Emptiness or rebellion?

A light glows from the kitchen, but no one's there. No Michael and no dinner. But, what's this? A wad of cash sits in the middle of the table. Twenty, forty, sixty—two hundred dollars? I drop it back on the table and head for Michael's room.

He sits hunched over his computer, those ever-present ear-buds drowning out my arrival.

"Michael?"

No reaction.

I step in and tap him on the shoulder.

He jerks up, as if shocked, and turning, yanks out the earbuds. "You tryin' to give me a heart attack or something?"

I stifle a grin. "Sorry. I called your name, but—" I point to the buds in his hand. "You keep the music up that loud, you're going to go deaf before twenty. What are you working on?"

He turns back to the monitor and points. "Editing some pictures I took at school. I'm helping Dan with a collage. For the yearbook signing party."

Resting a hand on his desk, I lean in. Candid shots of kids and teachers portraying every emotion from hilarity to dejection. "These are great, Michael."

He shrugs. "Thanks."

When was the last time I showed interest in his photography?

"I did something like this with Mom and Taylor, too. Wanna see?"

"Yeah, I'd love to."

With a few clicks of his mouse, he pulls up another file. Taylor in the I.C.U., still as death, Corey at her side, the anguish in her eyes painful to see. Another of Taylor in her wheelchair, a blank look on her face, again, Corey at her side, eyes swimming with tears. Picture after picture depicts the journey Taylor took with Corey standing guard. The epitome of motherly devotion.

Emotion fills my chest, and I have to look away. "They're good. Really good." Corey'd show that same devotion for Michael or me. It's who she is. Why did I lose sight of that?

I clear my throat as I sit on his bed. "I found a couple hundred dollars on the kitchen table. Is that yours?"

"It's yours."

"No, I don't—"

"Restitution payment."

The last time he tried to give me money, I threw it back in his face and accused him of bribing me.

"You sure? I mean, you can make smaller payments."

"It's why I took the job."

"About that camp—"

"Forget it." His words hold no heat.

I point to his computer. "It's clear you have talent, Michael. But the fact is, we can't afford the tuition this year. Even though we have insurance, there have been some financial costs—"

"It's fine, Dad." He shrugs. "Really. It's too late now, anyway."

"You've worked hard to get your grades up. To make headway toward the restitution."

He nods, averting his eyes.

"I'm proud of you, son." His eyes meet mine and I hold the connection. "Real proud."

He drops his head and mumbles, "Thanks."

"So, I'm thinking if you keep your grades up next year and we plan ahead—"

He sits up straighter, eyes back on me.

"—maybe we can swing it for next summer. I know that sounds like a long way off—"

"Only forever."

"Just a thought. So." I slap my knee and stand. "Have you had dinner?"

"Peanut butter sandwich."

That sounds as appetizing as dog food. "We must have something more appealing."

"Good luck."

"You still hungry?"

"Yeah."

"I'm going to call your Mom, then I'll see what I can find."

I retrieve the phone, punch in her number, and sit at the dining room table to sort the mail. Most are from the hospital. Thank God for insurance.

"Hello?"

"Hey, Cor. You talking to me yet?"

"I think you've suffered my silence long enough."

"I'm sorry I upset you. It wasn't my intention."

"I know. It never is."

"Michael wants to come down for a visit when school gets out."

"Yeah?"

"I told him you might be coming home before then."

"Do you want me home?"

Pride rears its ugly head. "Do you want to come home?"

"Taylor's just making progress. With her speech therapist and with me. I figured out a new strategy."

I swallow down disappointment. "Oh? What's that?"

"Tough love."

"Is that strategy for Taylor or for me?"

"You didn't stop me from leaving when you had the chance."

"No."

"Is your reason still valid?"

"I wanted to protect you and Taylor."

"Does it have anything to do with Alexis Andrews?"

"It's not what you're thinking."

"How do you know what I'm thinking?"

"I don't. But I know what I'd be thinking if I were in your place."

"You didn't answer the question, Paul. Is your reason for wanting us gone still valid?"

I fight the urge to demand she come home. "Yes."

"Then I suppose we have nothing to talk about."

"Don't you even want to know what it is?"

"I wanted to know weeks ago. Now I just want to know that you're handling it."

"I'm trying." I blow out a breath. "I love you, Corey."

She hesitates before responding. "I love you too, Paul."

But is it enough? For the first time, I'm not so sure.

"Look, I have to go. There's another call coming in."

"Wait, Corey—" Too late. She's gone.

Again.

Corey

Chicken.

The only thing strong enough to get me to accept a call from my dad is the fear that I'll cower in the face of Paul's persistence. So, I choose the lesser of two evils. Grimacing at the caller ID, I flick a thumb to connect the call.

"Hello?"

"Corey?"

Wait. That's not the voice I expected. "Mom?"

"I've been trying to reach you for days. Didn't you get my messages?"

"Oh. I...I didn't. I mean, I thought it was Dad calling."

Why I made that assumption, I can't tell her. Guilt? My head's too far buried in the sand to think?

A sigh huffs over the line. "I've been worried sick. About you. About Taylor. If you didn't answer this time, I was going to call Paul again."

"Again? You've talked to Paul?" He could have warned me.

"And if you thought your dad was trying to reach you, why didn't you call back?"

Diversion is the best ploy at this point. "Is everything okay?"

"That's what I want to know. What's going on? Are you still at Tricia's?"

"Yes."

"You...you are? Are you and Paul...are you having marital problems?"

Hoots and hollers come from the back patio where Trish and Taylor are playing checkers. Taylor doesn't know it, but it's a therapy assignment. They're high fiving each other, so she must be doing well.

"Corey?"

"Yeah, Mom, I'm here. Sorry."

"Whenever I call the house, Paul or Michael just say you and Taylor are visiting Trish. But how long have you been there?"

"I put Taylor in outpatient therapy in Monterey, Mom, and she's doing so well. Her memory's coming back, she's able to retrieve words. She's even working at Tricia's shop."

"Wonderful. What a blessing. But you didn't answer me. Are you and Paul having marital problems?"

I flop onto the couch, and Rambo jumps up beside me. There's no evading the truth any longer. "I've made such a mess of things."

Her tone shifts to concern. "What's going on?"

How can I tell her? Even if I can stomach her knowing, the thought of Dad hearing it is enough to convince me to take it to my grave. "I can't tell you. You'll never understand."

"What a thing to say. How will you know if you don't give me a chance?"

"Even if you do, Dad won't. You know how he is."

"Your father loves you."

"There's a reason Brian moved to Japan, Mom."

"It had nothing to do with your father. That was a business decision..." She runs through the litany of reasons my big brother laid out— reasons meant to appease. But had his relationship with Dad been easier, would he have made such a drastic move? I don't think so.

"So, tell me what's going on."

"Not on the phone. Besides, I have to go. Taylor needs me." Lies, lies, lies. Here we go again. Will I ever learn?

"Can't I at least talk to her? I won't keep her long."

"Yes. Just a sec." I hesitate a moment. What if Taylor tells her about the blood test? *Then there will be no more secrets.* As the words settle over me, a peace follows. Whatever happens, happens.

"Best of three out of five," Tricia's saying as I open the French door.

"Taylor?" I waggle the phone. "Grandma would like to talk to you."

"'Kay." She pushes back from the table and snags the phone on her way into the house.

Tricia gathers checkers. "Want to take her place?"

"Are you letting her win?" I cross my arms, as if to ward off a chill—one that's coming from inside me.

"Listen, the kid's a checkers-shark. She doesn't need my charity."

"She's going to tell my mom about the blood test, I just know it."

A stack of red discs in her hand, Tricia watches as I take Taylor's seat. "What's the worst that could happen?"

"My dad never speaks to me again." I let loose the grasp on myself and reach for a black checker, fingering the ridge.

Trish snorts. "A blessing in disguise."

Ignoring the comment, I push the checker aside and change the subject. "I was on the phone with Paul before my mom called."

"And?" She starts laying the red discs on the board, each in its own square.

"I think he wants me to come home."

"That's good, isn't it?"

Is it? How can I be so wishy-washy? One minute I want him to want me, then when he does— "You know when you said you haven't seen the old me in a long time?"

"You mean the screeching harpy?"

I smile. "Yeah. Her. Even though I felt bad about yelling at him, there was something freeing about it, too. I spend so much time stuffing my thoughts and feelings, I've forgotten how to think and feel."

"And you're afraid when you go back to Paul…?"

I shrug. "Stuffing my thoughts and feelings again? It'll be like trying to shove an inflated air mattress back into its box."

"You're assuming Paul wants you…" She waves a hand around as if it'll help her retrieve the word she's looking for. "…stuffed."

"That's who he knows."

"But it's not who he fell in love with in the first place. Maybe he's just grown accustomed to you this way, the same way you have." She plops down onto the chair across from me and rests her chin in her hands.

"Or maybe our marriage has lasted this long because of who I've become." The idea is more than a little unsettling. "It's hard to live with a screeching harpy, you know."

Tricia smiles. "You're not a screeching harpy. It was that initial burst, like the pop of a champagne cork. Now that the pressure's off, you can ease into it some."

I snag a black checker and spin it between my thumb and forefinger. "I don't want to be the only one unstuffed. He's been hiding work issues from me for months. If we weren't communicating when we were living together, how can we fix it while we're apart?"

"All I can offer is this old adage." She takes my hand, checker and all, and squeezes it. "God works in mysterious ways."

Taylor steps out of the house, phone held toward me. "Grandma said she'll talk to you later. She's having trouble understanding how my science experiment proves that you cheated on Dad."

I drop my head in my free hand. What I wouldn't give for life to go back to boring.

Chapter 36

Corey

Staring in the mirror, I still can't believe it's me looking back. The jeans, the boots, the hair. The long sweater wrap hugs my new-found curves. Trish pushed enough makeup on me to service a chorus line. I opted for a touch of mascara and lip gloss, but even that's foreign to my minimalist taste. There was a time I had a heavier hand, but that was before I got it into my head that a pastor's wife should look...I don't know...pastorly.

"Let's see." Trish slips up behind me and I catch her eye in the mirror. "You look amazing. Didn't I tell you those jeans would fit?"

I pluck at the cream-colored sweater. "I don't know, Trish. I feel exposed."

"Exposed? Nonsense. You don't have an inch of skin showing. You look beautiful. Feminine."

"I feel like a fraud. At least you look like you."

The clingy, turquoise blouse she's wearing brings out the green in her eyes. "You're just out of practice. We find a few more outfits for you and you'll be back in the groove."

"My husband wouldn't recognize me."

"Sure he would. You look more like the woman he married now than you have since." She takes my place at the mirror and futzes with her hair. "What else needs to be done?"

"It's all under control. This is a thank you dinner for you and Jonas. I don't want you lifting a finger." I cock my head in an effort to discern where my daughter is. "Do you know what Taylor's doing?"

"She's out back trying to remember how to paint. That was a great idea, picking up those supplies for her."

"I hope she doesn't get anything on her clothes. I'm going to check on the lasagna and put the salad together."

I step out back on my way to the kitchen. Taylor's wearing an old dress shirt of Steven's over her clothes—her paint smock—and is staring at a blank canvas. "Hey, Tay? Did you feed Rambo?"

At the mention of his name, Rambo tears out of the house and spins in circles at my feet. When it comes to food, he speaks human.

"No. I'm trying to figure out what to paint." She turns to look at me and her eyes widen, but she doesn't say anything. Compliments might be misconstrued as forgiveness. We wouldn't want to make *that* mistake.

"Jonas will be here anytime. I need you to feed Rambo. Now." I step back inside.

Tricia walks through the dining room and does a double take. "Why are there five places set? Isn't it just you, Taylor, Jonas and me?"

"Oh, I guess I forgot to tell you. Jonas is bringing someone." Before she can respond, I slip into the Italian spice-scented kitchen. The garlic bread is cut, covered, and ready to pop into the oven. Now for the salad.

"Who's he bringing?" Trish stands in the entrance, suspicion lurking in her eyes.

"I told you about his wife, right?"

"Oh, he's bringing her?"

"Well, no." I stick my head in the fridge and root through it for the salad makings. "But Jonas is stepping down from the church to spend more time with her. He's bringing his replacement."

"Oh. Okay." Appeased, she leaves.

Ten minutes later, the suspicion is back in Tricia's eyes as I introduce Dylan to her. "This is Jonas's replacement."

"Oh, well." Is Tricia flustered? That's a first. "Nice to meet you, Dylan. Corey told me…well, I just assumed—" She looks at Jonas, her face reddening.

Jonas chuckles. "You thought he'd be some old geezer like me, did you?"

"Of course not. I mean, I wouldn't have used those words to describe you, Jonas. Won't you both come in?" She steps aside.

I take Jonas's arm and escort him into the living room and leave Tricia to figure out what to do with Dylan. Early evening light pours through the windows, framing the antipasti I set out.

Jonas glances around the room. "You have a beautiful home, Tricia."

"Thank you." She fusses with an earring and looks around, as if she's lost something. "Taylor's out back. I'll get her."

Dylan sits on one end of the cream-colored love seat, waggling a finger between Jonas and me. "What're you two up to?"

"I don't have any idea what you mean, son." He eases onto the couch, a devious smirk on his face. "Corey invited me over as a thank you. No one forced you to come along."

I snag a plate of antipasti and offer it to Dylan. "Pepper?"

He quirks an eyebrow at me, as if to say he isn't buying it. "Tell me about your husband's church."

Tricia returns with Taylor, who greets Jonas, then eyes Dylan with suspicion. She and Tricia are a matched pair.

"Dylan is Jonas's son," I say, and send up a quick prayer that her filtration system kicks in. No telling what'll come out of her mouth.

"Why—" My cell trills from the breakfast bar, and Taylor snatches it up. For once, her focus issue works in my favor. "It's Dad."

"So." Tricia addresses Jonas and sits on the arm of my chair, ignoring a perfectly good seat next to Dylan. "How is your wife doing?"

I'm distracted by the murmur of Taylor conversing with Paul. Unlike when she talks to me, there is no sarcasm or disdain dripping from her tone.

"How long are you staying in Carmel?" Dylan's question pulls me from my thoughts.

"It depends. Taylor's doing well in rehab here, so," I shrug, "we'll see." I look at Jonas. "Would you mind helping me get dinner on the table?"

Tricia jumps up. "I'll do that."

"Don't be silly." I snag her arm and force her into my chair. "You entertain Dylan. I have a few questions for Jonas."

We pass Taylor, who's saying, "—a pastor from the church we went to on Sunday, and I think the other guy is his son. When can I come home?"

Jonas follows me into the kitchen. "Have you and Taylor been able to work through her anger?"

"She's not as hateful as she was." I collect the salad from the fridge, along with a pint jar of dressing I made earlier. "That's progress, right?"

He takes the salad from me. "What did you want to ask me?"

"Ask you?" I turn the oven off and look at him.

"You told Tricia you had a few questions for me."

"It was a lie, I'm afraid. I was hoping if she was alone with Dylan—"

Taylor leans into the kitchen. "Michael's coming up next Friday. On the Greyhound."

"What time?"

She shrugs. "I forget." She slips out.

"Your son?"

"Yes. It'll be so good to see him."

"Then why don't you look too happy about it?"

Gathering up the hot mitts, I open the oven door. "He's a smart kid. He'll figure out the truth, then I'll have two angry kids on my hands."

Chapter 37

Paul

Male voices wake me in the middle of the night. I lie in the dark, listening to the silence. I don't have to be a psychologist to know the voices were all in my head. Talking to Taylor last weekend, those same male voices came through the line.

A pastor and his son.

Yeah, right.

I clear my schedule for the day. No sense paying for a bus ticket when I'm capable of driving Michael down to Carmel myself. Forget that VBS starts next week and I had to bail on a meeting. Forget that Michael would rather ride the bus.

Forget that I don't have the nerve to tell Corey.

We turn off Highway 1, windows rolled down. Cool ocean air beats air-conditioning. "Almost there." I'm talking to a rock. Michael's half asleep, earbuds drowning out anything I say.

I've only been to Tricia's a couple times, but that's what a map app is for. I park at the curb, my heart pounding in my ears. "We're here." I nudge Michael awake before climbing out, checking the house for activity.

What if they aren't here? Maybe the surprise approach isn't the right tack.

"Dad?" Taylor's voice calls out from the shadow of the porch before she emerges. Huge smile, arms open, she runs down the brick pathway. "I didn't know you were coming."

I get to the sidewalk before she about knocks me down with a hug. "Look at you." Her hair is different and...are those purple streaks?

She's on Michael's door before he can get it open. "Hey, butt head. It's great to see you."

Bleary-eyed, Michael climbs out and lets her hug him. "You too."

"Is your mom—" Rambo tears out of the house, Corey following, arms folded across her chest. Or at least I *think* it's Corey. She's thin. Her hair's shorter and—did she color it? What motivated this?

"Hi, Paul. I was just getting ready to head over to the bus station. You should have let me know you were coming."

"Did I interrupt your plans?"

As she passes me to greet Michael, confusion crosses her features at my abrupt tone. Not that I can blame her. I sound like a jealous husband. I *am* a jealous husband.

"Sweetheart." She pulls Michael in for a hug. "I've missed you."

When did Michael get taller than Corey?

"Yeah?" Michael steps back and looks her up and down. "Wow, Mom. You're, like, a different person."

Before I can agree with him, Taylor hugs my arm. "Can we get lunch and take it to the beach?"

"Oh, I don't know, Tay." I glance at Corey hugging herself. Snug tee-shirt and jeans, bare feet. I can't get over how different she looks. "Your mom might have other plans."

"No," Corey says. "That's fine. Unless you're in a hurry to get back."

"No hurry."

"I'll get a blanket and Rambo," Taylor says.

Corey looks down at her feet. "Shoes might be good, too."

We pile into the car, Rambo taking his place between Taylor and Michael in the back seat. The kids' conversation covers our awkwardness as we drive to a deli, order sandwiches, and head for the beach. We climb from the car and the sun breaks through a high fog, the moist breeze carrying the briny tang of the ocean. Corey's always loved the ocean. How often have I made a point of taking her? Three, four times in our marriage?

Was Corey right to be hesitant to marry me? I've never put her first. It wasn't intentional, but still...

We settle on the sand with our sacks of food. I can't help but look at Corey. The changes—what precipitated them?

"Lexie." Taylor stands, hands bracketing her mouth. "Here, Lexie."

A golden retriever, tail wagging, tongue hanging, skids into our picnic. It's obvious she and Rambo are fast friends.

"Jonas must be here," Corey says. She stands beside Taylor, but they don't touch. "Do you see him?"

Taylor points. "There he is. Hey, Jonas. Up here."

My gut churns. Jonas. The guy at Tricia's house last weekend. My competition? The man draws closer. He's wearing a ball cap, but the shock of white hair is still visible. He's got to be close to seventy. So, not my competition. But didn't Taylor say something about a son?

Corey takes his arm and turns to introduce him. "Jonas, this is my son, Michael, and my husband, Paul."

Jonas smiles, hand extended. "Michael, Paul. Nice to meet you at last. I've heard a lot about you both."

"Pleased to meet you too," I say. His handshake is firm for a guy his age.

"So, Michael. You'll be staying for a few days?"

"Yeah. 'Til Tuesday." A hank of hair blows across his eyes, and he swipes it aside. Must be time for another haircut.

"Well, I hope to see you in church on Sunday."

"Jonas is the pastor of Oceanside Presbyterian," Corey says. The smile she gives him is the first natural one I've seen since we landed in her camp.

"Ah. Not anymore. Former pastor," he says. "My son, Dylan, is now official. But I'll be there to support him."

"Join us for lunch," Corey says.

"Oh, no. I don't want to interrupt a family reunion." He grasps the dog's collar and backs away.

This might be my only chance. "You mind if I walk with you for a few minutes?"

Corey's suspicious. I can see it in her eyes.

"Not at all. Appreciate the chance to get to know you."

"I'll be back," I tell the family. They all look at me like I've lost it.

We slump across the shifting sand for about a hundred yards until we hit damp, firm sand, then head north. People are everywhere. Some set up with beach chairs, others walking. Almost as many dogs as people. "I want to thank you for helping Corey with Taylor. I understand you ended up with her when she ran off."

"God brought her to me. She didn't know where she was going." He's got an air of calm certainty.

"Have you been a pastor a long time?"

He glances at me, blue eyes bright in the sun. "Over forty years. Although I've only been here about half that time."

"Then I guess you've seen it all."

"Just about." He steps around a piece of driftwood. "You have a beautiful family."

More than I realized. "Thank you. It's been rough the last few months."

"Corey told me some of what's going on."

I stiffen.

"I hope you don't mind."

"No, of course not." Which is a lie. Wish she'd confided in me.

"Being a pastor's hard work."

"You can say that again." My tone sounds almost petulant, and heat steals up my neck at the realization.

"It's not for wimps."

I give him a stiff smile. "No."

"Sometimes it's easy to forget what's important. People are good at sucking the energy from you. And don't even get me started on Satan."

"I hear you."

"I've dealt with some loss in my life, like anyone." He shakes his head and sighs. "Life's too short. Makes you learn real quick what's important."

"And what've you discovered?" The question sounds casual, but how I long for words of wisdom. Something about his air of calm and peacefulness tells me he's got it going on.

He focuses on the rolling waves heading toward the beach. "God's most important work isn't happening within the four walls of a church. Anything that draws you away from God, well, that's just Satan doing his thing."

What's Corey told him? "Kind of hard to be a pastor and not get dragged into petty details."

"True. But we don't have to let it control us. You lose sight of God, what's the point? Who're we doing it for?"

Well, I got what I wanted—wise words. Now what do I do with them? "Is that why you're retiring? Tired of the petty details?"

"I should've retired long before now. My wife's got Alzheimer's. Don't know how much more time I have with her. You, better than most, know how fast life can change."

True. But I fear that lesson's come too late.

∾

Corey

Emotional exhaustion weighs on me. Hours spent with Paul, gauging, waiting, wondering. The look on his face when he saw me—what was that? Shock? Disappointment? He didn't say anything about the weight loss, haircut, clothes. Just stared as if he didn't know who I was.

Taylor went to bed early. If I feel overstimulated, I can only imagine how she's dealing. Tricia went out. She wouldn't say where. That's not at all like her. Maybe she and Dylan have a date. But then, why wouldn't she tell me?

I unroll Michael's sleeping bag on the couch. "Are you sure you don't mind camping out here?"

"No problem."

"Because I can always share Taylor's bed, and you can have my room."

He snorts. "Yeah, right."

"What's that supposed to mean?"

"I don't think she'd let you anywhere near her bed. Why's she so ticked at you?"

I whip open a flowered pillowcase, tuck the pillow between my chin and chest and maneuver it inside. "She's a teenage girl. Isn't that enough?"

He gives me the look—the one he's had down since the age of five. So like his father.

"It doesn't matter. She'll get over it."

"Will you and Dad get over it too?" He sits on the sleeping bag and pats the couch as an invitation to Rambo to jump up with him.

"Look, Michael—"

"Are you guys getting divorced?"

I gauge the worry in his eyes. There comes a time you can't protect your kids anymore. "I don't know."

He scratches Rambo's belly. "What if he says he's sorry? I mean, he told me he didn't even do it, so—"

"Do what?" Sitting on the other side of Rambo, I duck my head to catch Michael's eye.

His eyes flicker to mine before they drop again. "If you don't know, then why'd you leave?"

Secrets. More secrets. I'm sick to death of all of it. "Spit it out, son. What do you think you know?"

"I saw them. Dad and Josh's mom."

Alexis Andrews. I play it in my head again—maybe for the hundredth time—but it still doesn't work. "You must be mistaken."

He looks at me, eyes narrowed. Wondering if I'm gullible? "That's what Dad said. But I thought—I don't know. If he did something wrong, is he going to admit it?"

There may be something going on between Alexis and Paul, but it isn't an affair. "I'd bet my last meal that nothing happened between your dad and Ms. Andrews. Or your dad and *any* woman, for that matter."

"Why? Guys cheat all the time. Dan's dad? He cheated."

"Not your dad."

"Because he's a pastor?"

"No, of course not. Your dad has faults. I'm not blind. But that's not one of them."

"Then why?"

"Oh, Michael." I drop my head into my hands and rub my eyes. Mascara. That'll leave raccoon eyes. "Do we have to do this tonight? I'm so tired."

"No. No problem." His tone is hard. "No one wants to tell me what's going on around here. Not Dad, not you. Taylor's ticked at you. I've been ticked at Dad, and you guys are separated. But, hey, no problem. We'll talk about it later." He jumps up and fiddles with the sleeping bag.

"You want to tell me why you've been so upset with your Dad?"

"Why should I when you won't tell me anything?" He turns to me and crosses his arms—erecting walls.

"Okay, let's get this out in the open. You first."

Rambo hops off the couch and settles on the floor with a groan.

Michael relaxes his arms and plops back onto the couch. After days of Taylor's immovable anger, his ability to shift gears with such speed is a blessing. "Last year, I went to see Dad after school one day. No one was in the outer office, but Dad's door was open. I saw Ms. Andrews and Dad and they were kissing." His eyes drop like he doesn't want to see my reaction.

Okay, maybe I have been naive. "And then what?"

"I don't know. I got outta there."

"And your dad said what about it?"

"That I misread it. That if I stayed a second longer, I would have seen him kick her out."

Relief washes over me. Not so naive after all. "This is why you've been so angry? Why didn't you just ask him?"

He shrugs. "I was mad and cut through the elementary school on my way home."

The vandalism. Everything becomes clear. "Oh, Michael. What did you think you'd accomplish by trashing the school?"

"I wasn't thinking. I guess I wanted to get back at him."

I've had that feeling myself at times.

"Your turn. Why'd you leave if it wasn't because of Ms. Andrews?"

I check my watch—ten o'clock—and catch Michael's arched brows. He's not letting this go, and a promise is a promise. Once it's out, there will be no more secrets. The relief of it is almost enough to make me giddy.

"The week before your dad and I got married, I kind of freaked out."

"Why?"

"Your grandfather—"

"Grouchy Grandpa?"

"Yeah. Grouchy Grandpa. You think your dad's tough,

he's nothing compared to mine. But as the wedding date drew closer, I started seeing things about your dad that reminded me of *my* dad. It scared me. I thought I should call off the wedding."

"But you didn't. Obviously."

"No. Instead, I went to a party with Tricia and drank way too much. Of course, I'd never had much alcohol before, so it didn't take a lot." I draw in a deep breath and focus on my hands. How do I tell him something so shameful?

"What'd you do, sleep with someone?"

His words have my head snapping up. "I—how did you know?"

"Just a guess."

There is some relief in not having to say it out loud—to confess my sin to my own son. "I was so sick and ashamed of myself. I thought I could just put it behind me. Get married and forget it ever happened." I rub at my temple where a headache is forming. "When I found out I was pregnant with Taylor, I…I assumed—" My face heats and I can't bear to look at Michael. Another person raining judgment on me. Not that I don't deserve it.

"Dad isn't Taylor's dad?" Michael's voice is incredulous. "That can't be true. They're just alike. I mean, they like the same things and everything."

"I've never thought anything different until Taylor did that science experiment the day of her accident. She found out that her blood type didn't match up right with your dad's. She thought it was a mistake."

"You told Dad the truth?"

"No. I was going to, but Ms. Andrews found out from Josh that something was off about the experiment. She figured it out and told your dad."

"Why? What does she care?" His tone is laced with disgust.

"I don't know. I suppose it could have been to hurt your dad because he rejected her."

He's quiet for a moment, as if contemplating. "So, why'd you leave?"

"Your dad—he didn't seem to be able to forgive me."

"That's why you know, huh? I mean, about Dad not cheating on you."

"It would be pretty tough for him to be all righteous if he was having an affair. I'm sorry, Michael. This whole family's a mess because of me."

He nudges me with his shoulder. "It'll be okay, Mom."

I look at my son, sympathy in his eyes—his father's eyes—and I'm amazed. Is this what grace looks like?

Chapter 38

Paul

The house is too quiet. It never seemed all that large to me, but rattling around in it by myself, it's grown. Jonas's words hit hard. Not that I hadn't thought about the importance of family before. But it was confirmation. God speaking to me through someone older and wiser.

Much wiser.

After ten minutes of searching the shelves in my office, I pluck my old Bible from between Oswald Chambers' *My Utmost for His Highest* and a collection of Charles Spurgeon's sermons. With the flick of a switch, my desk lamp dispels the shadows of the late afternoon, and I sit at my desk, Bible in hand.

The leather-bound cover is creased with age, the tissue-thin pages well-worn. There's comfort in the heaviness of the book and the whisper-crackle of the pages as I turn them to the book of Proverbs. King Solomon was given the gift of great wisdom from God, and yet he still searched throughout his life for something other than his Creator to satisfy him. My only defense is that I've not been given great wisdom.

Thumbing to chapter eight, I smooth the pages and scan for verse thirteen. It's ingrained in my brain. *The fear of the Lord is to hate evil; pride and arrogance and the evil way and the perverse mouth I hate.* Pride and arrogance. The words may be ingrained in my brain, but the sin still found roots in my heart. When did that happen? And what do I do about it?

Humble yourself.

I flip back a few pages until I come to Proverbs 3:34. *God resists the proud but gives grace to the humble.*

I call Kent and ask if he can meet me at the cafe. Maybe give me a little more information on the church in Georgetown I disregarded without thought. If I'm not a pastor, then what am I? Where do I go from here? But how can I stay, when I know it's gotten all twisted up with my ego?

Kent's settled in a back booth when I arrive. Little Miss Sunshine points him out.

"Good to see you, Paul."

"Thanks for meeting me." I slide into the booth across from him. "How're things going?"

"Cheryl took the kids to visit her parents down south. Three days in Disneyland. There'll be no living with them when they get back. How do I compete with that?" Despite his words, he doesn't look concerned.

"I have a feeling it's not a problem for you. That daughter of yours looks at you like you're Santa Claus and Mickey Mouse all rolled into one."

"Yeah, well, the kid's easy to fool. Her older brothers are much wiser."

I doubt that. It used to be that way with Michael, but I've blown that.

Miss Sunshine appears, glass of water in one hand, order pad in the other. She slides the water to me, pulls a wrapped straw from her pocket, and slaps it on the table. "What can I get you fellas?"

"I'll have the burger and fries, June. And hold back a piece of that cherry pie, will you?"

"You got it, pastor. You?" She turns her watery blue eyes on me.

"Same, thanks."

"Only got one piece of cherry pie left. Got a nice peach, though." Is that a smile on her face?

"Perfect."

"You got it."

I watch her scamper off. "Think she's falling for me."

Kent laughs. "Look out." He pushes the utensils aside. "How's it going?"

"Let's see. Corey and Taylor are still gone, and it doesn't look like Corey's in a hurry to come home."

"I thought you encouraged her leaving."

"Yeah, well, it'd be good if she *wanted* to come home." The new Corey pops into my mind. Everything's changing.

"How's it going with Michael?"

"We're figuring it out. He's down in Carmel with Corey but'll be home tomorrow."

"Good." He raps his knuckles on the table. "That's good."

"I thought you could tell me if that opening up in Georgetown's still available."

Kent quirks an eyebrow. "You said you weren't interested."

"I've been doing some thinking. I—" Is that Drew Simpson coming our way? I look at Kent and tilt my head toward Drew.

"This ought to be interesting," Kent mumbles, then sits back and watches as Drew approaches.

Drew looks at us. "Pastors."

"Mr. Simpson," Kent says.

"Glad to run into you here, Paul. I was going to come see you tomorrow. Mind if I sit a moment?"

Startled, I don't answer at first. "Be my guest," I finally

respond. Peace settles with the realization that I don't have to give Simpson the power to ruin my day. Or my life.

"Would you like me to give you some privacy?" Kent starts to rise.

"No, stay. Please." Drew takes a chair from another table and sets it at the end of our booth. "You're involved in this too."

Kent and I make eye contact—what's this guy up to now?

Drew sits, elbows on the table, and looks at me. "I owe you an apology."

That's unexpected. "Oh?"

"I should never have caused a stir in your church. Not on the say so of one person."

I cross my arms. "You had a whole slew of accusations."

"Motivated by the lies of one woman."

Kent clears his throat. "And you know they're lies now how?"

"My wife. She heard some things, pushed me to check them out. I confronted Ms. Andrews and she finally confessed it was all a lie. She said you never did anything inappropriate. Also found out that she stirred up some pretty ugly stuff in your home."

My spine stiffens and I'm in defense mode once again. "We're not bringing my family into this."

"Not my intention, pastor. Just want you to know that her lies have been brought to light. You'll not have any more trouble from me or mine."

I draw in a deep breath and relax. "I appreciate that, Drew."

"Hope you'll accept my apology." He stands as June arrives with our order. "Enjoy the rest of your evening."

"Here we are, gentlemen. Let me know if I can get you anything else."

Kent reaches for the catsup. "What do you think?"

"About?"

"Still want to hear about the opportunity in Georgetown?"
Good question.

Corey

It's been a good day. While Taylor worked at the shop with Tricia, Michael and I went to the Monterey Bay Aquarium. It never ceases to amaze me what wonders God's created in this world. We learned about marine life, braved the shallow waters of an indoor tide pool, and observed sharks from the safe side of a glass partition.

"What do you want to do tonight?" I ask him as we do a slow crawl on Highway 1 back to Carmel.

"Let's rent a couple movies. Something we used to watch with you when we were kids."

"Are you sure?"

"Taylor's a sucker for sentiment. It might soften her up a little."

"She'll come around, Michael."

He hits the button to roll down the window, and the ocean tang fills the car. "I don't know what the big deal is anyway. It's not like anything's changed."

"She just needs time to process." I'm actually beginning to believe it, too.

Home from the video store, Michael goes out back to feed Rambo and I start on dinner. Meatloaf, Michael's favorite home-cooked meal. I take out the thawed hamburger and pork, gather up the other ingredients, and dump them all into a large bowl. Preparing to dig in with bare hands, I tug my wedding ring off. My eyes catch and hold on the simple gold band with the humble diamond in the center. It's the ring I wanted when we married, but more than that, it's what it symbolizes. To be true and faithful until death.

And I broke those vows before I even made them.

Some might say I wasn't accountable for that promise until I made it, but that's just semantics. I know in my heart that what I did was wrong. And I know in my head that my sin is forgiven. How do I get my heart to believe it? Because if I don't, then I disregard Jesus Christ's sacrifice on the cross—as if it wasn't enough for me. How arrogant.

With the ring clutched in my hand, I pray. *Help me, Lord, to accept the sacrifice of Your Son for my sins—past, present, and future. To let go and move forward and to offer the same grace He's given me to others.*

Laying the ring on the counter, I swipe at the tears on my cheeks. I'm tired of being separated from my husband, from my son, and even more so, from my God. Is it possible for Him to cleanse me of my guilt?

I'm knuckle deep in ground meat when the doorbell peals. "Michael," I call out. "Can you get that?"

No response. Where did that boy go?

I scrape what I can from my fingers as the doorbell peals again. Grabbing a towel, I jog through the house to the front door. In my haste, I forget to check the peephole and fling the door open.

It takes a moment to register. "Dad?"

"Good. I have the right address."

His stern countenance puts me on alert "What…what are you doing here?"

"Mind if I come in? It's been a long day of travel."

I step back to allow him entrance, then poke my head outside. "Is Mom with you?"

"Nope. I came by myself. It seems we have some things to talk about."

Hand on the knob, I fight the childish urge to take flight down the street. "Is she okay?"

"Yeah, she's fine." He homes in on me with a razor-sharp stare. "This isn't about her."

The back-door slams, then Michael calls out, "Hey, Mom, when's dinner ready? I'm starving."

"In here, Michael." I escort Dad into the family room, heart in my throat, as Michael appears.

"Grandpa? Hey, I didn't know you were coming."

"Hey, Michael." Dad reaches out and gives him a one-armed hug. "Your grandma said Taylor's here. I didn't know you were too."

"Just until tomorrow. Where's Grandma?" His glance moves past us toward the front door.

"She didn't come out with me this trip." He sits in the easy chair. "You all act like I can't travel by myself. I'm not *that* old yet."

They catch up, and I try to find my voice. Questions dance through my head until I'm dizzy with them.

"Can you give your mom and me a little time alone, son? We have a few things we need to talk about."

This can't be good. If Mom's okay, then this has to be about my marriage.

"Sure." But Michael looks at me as if asking permission.

I force a smile to let him know it's okay. "Maybe you could take Rambo down to the beach for a walk."

A few moments later, I'm facing my father. Alone. "You should have called first, Dad. I—"

"Don't worry. I got a hotel room, and I have a flight out in the morning." He waggles his hand toward the couch in a non-verbal command to sit.

I obey, perching on the edge, dishtowel in my hands. "I don't understand why you're here." But I'm afraid that's not true.

"No?" He leans forward, rests his elbows on his knees, and folds his hands. "I'm worried about you, kiddo. You're living here, away from your husband."

I focus on the towel I'm wringing in my hands. "I appreciate your concern, but—"

"I don't think you do."

"What?"

"You been lying to us for months. You didn't tell us how serious Taylor's accident was. Then you ignore your mom's phone messages."

"I thought it was you." The words escape before I can stop them, and they just hang there between us.

"So," he says. "It's not your mom you have a problem with."

His tone takes me back about thirty-five years, and it's irksome, which puts me on the defense. "Look, Dad. I'm sorry you felt the need to fly out here, but really, this is none of your business." My face heats as his eyes widen. What's gotten into me? I've never spoken to my father this way.

"Is that what your kids say when you question their lies?"

"Yes, as a matter of fact, they do. The difference is that they're just that—kids. I'm an adult—"

"Then it's time you start acting like one."

Words escape me. How dare he?

"I'm here because I'm concerned about you, Coraline. Can't you see that?"

Tears well and I shake my head. "No, I can't. My whole life, whenever I've messed up, you've been quick to judge me and find me guilty. I have enough guilt eating away at me right now without you adding to it."

"Is that what you think?"

"It's what I know." I swipe at my nose with the towel. "I messed up, Dad. A long time ago, I messed up. I can't change it. I'm trying to make it right, but—" I bury my face in the towel. Why won't he just go away?

The couch dips with his weight as he sits beside me. I'm ready to bolt, but then his arm slides around my shoulders and he pulls me close. The warmth of his embrace opens my emotions like a floodgate, and I sink into him, sobbing.

"It'll be all right, sweetheart. I promise."

Chapter 39

Corey

The bedroom is bathed in gray pre-dawn light when I wake. Too early to go for a walk, but there's no going back to sleep. Instead, I replay the events of the night before. After my crying jag, there was no time to talk—not with Tricia, Taylor, and Michael returning. Dad stayed for dinner and even sat through *The Princess Bride*.

Tricia watched me as if I were in the psycho ward on suicide watch. The kids were either not perceptive enough to see the evidence of my tears or chose to ignore it. Not Tricia. Twice, she tried to trap me in the kitchen for an explanation, but I'm nothing if not the queen of evasion.

There will be no putting her off this morning.

After Trish and the kids went to bed, Dad and I talked. I told him everything, as if daring him to judge me—baiting him to slip back to the man I thought I knew. It took me hours to fall asleep while I sifted through childhood memories, replaying each one to see if I'd missed some key ingredient of grace. But I could find none. Dad had changed. Where judgment once reigned, grace now prevailed.

I push the covers back and pad across the carpeted floor to the bathroom. Once done there, I make a beeline for the kitchen. And coffee. The glow of a light warns me that someone's beat me to it. Tricia. She sits at the kitchen table, bed-head hair, hands wrapped around a steaming, aromatic mug.

"Morning," I say in my soft, early-morning voice.

"You're up early."

Coffee pot in hand, I look at her. "I could say the same about you. Everything okay?"

She smiles. "You're asking *me*? It looked as if your dad put you through the emotional wringer yesterday."

I doctor my coffee and join her at the table. "Do your parents ever surprise you?"

"I don't suppose you're talking about my birthday or Christmas."

"You think you know someone…" I take a sip of coffee and close my eyes. "I told him, Trish."

"Everything?"

"Down to Taylor's blood type."

"Wow. That must've felt weird."

"That's just it, though. It didn't. He's different." Setting the mug on the table, I look at her. "I guess there's hope for Taylor."

"She's coming around."

"Not so you'd notice."

"The tough love thing is working. Stick with it. She mentioned you twice yesterday with no attitude. And I had her put together a fall ensemble on a mannequin. She said it'd look good on you."

"That's progress." Even so small a step lightens my mood. "I talked to her speech therapist about it."

"You did?"

"Not the exact situation, just that she's upset with me about something. Dottie reminded me that her focus issues will also be emotional. I just feel blessed that I didn't get any backlash from Michael."

"Yeah, what's up with that?"

I shrug. "I don't know, but I'm not questioning it."

We sip in silence for a moment, which gives me a chance to observe Tricia. Even with a smudge of mascara under her eyes and the rat's nest hair, she's glowing.

"Where were you the other night?"

"Hmmm?"

"Night before last." I narrow my eyes. "Did you have a date?"

"I had a business meeting."

"With who?"

"Whom," she corrects, lips pursing. "You're going to be teaching, so you should set a good example."

"You're evading."

She pushes up from the table. "What time does Michael need to be at the bus station?"

"It was Dylan, wasn't it?"

She doesn't answer. It *was* Dylan.

"Why didn't you tell me?" I quench the whoop of joy that climbs up my throat. No sense waking Michael.

She retrieves the coffee pot and refills our mugs. "It wasn't a date, Cor."

"You had a business meeting with Dylan? What kind of business?" I give her a smirk and she threatens to upend the coffee pot on my head.

"Ideas for community outreaches."

"Yeah, I'll bet."

Sitting back in her chair, she takes my hand. "Don't make more of it than it is." There's a furrow between her eyebrows. She's serious.

"Why? What are you afraid of?"

"I'm happy with my life. I don't need anything to come along and change that."

"You like him."

She drops her chin into her hands. "Yes. I like him. But I don't want to."

"It's your own fault, you know."

"How do you figure?"

"You did say if Jonas had a son—"

"I was *kidding*."

"Guess God didn't get the joke." I look at the microwave clock. "Hey, I gotta jump in the shower. I told my dad I'd take him to the airport this morning. Is Taylor going in with you, or should I get her up?"

"I've got Taylor."

"Thanks." I start to head out but turn back to Trish. "Do me a favor?"

"Sure."

"Don't close yourself off to possibilities."

She waves me away.

"No, Trish. I'm serious. Trust that God has a handle on it. He knows your heart."

"Wise words, my friend. When are you going to start believing them for yourself?"

Paul

Second day of Vacation Bible School is crazy. Two hundred kids, some we've never seen before, packing the church, classroom, and grounds. High energy Bible stories, kids' worship music and crafts. It'll take days for the staff and volunteers to recover, but it's worth it. This is the first year since Taylor was thirteen that she isn't part of it.

Mark drops onto the carpeted church floor and flops back. "What a zoo. We'll be scraping glue off the floor for weeks." His voice is raspy. Strained vocal cords, no doubt.

I continue picking up scraps of construction paper and popsicle sticks and things I can't identify. Don't *want* to identify. "You don't fool me. You love it."

"Do you think Taylor will want to help next year? The Collins girl is good, but Taylor's gifted with the kids."

"I don't know." Will we even be here next year?

Mark sits up but makes no move to help. "I saw Jenna McCarty pick up her son. How're they doing?"

"Two months ago, I'd have taken bets on a divorce date. But they're making headway. They would have done better with a marriage counselor."

"I saw the Pendletons in church on Sunday. John's looking good."

I gather the ends of the garbage bag and pull it from the can. "Guess God isn't done with him yet."

"Membership's going back up. Dorothy tells me collections are on the rise, too."

Slinging the sack over my shoulder, I look at Mark. Legs crossed, leaning back on his hands, he's the picture of relaxed. But I'm not buying it.

"What's with the inventory?" I drop the trash bag in the corner for pickup.

"You seem detached lately."

"Not detached. Busy." I check my watch. "In fact, I have to pick Michael up at the Greyhound station in half an hour."

"I thought you'd be thrilled over Simpson's concession."

"So did I."

Mark's eyebrows shoot up. "What's the deal?"

"It just doesn't seem all that important. At least, not as important as I made it out to be."

"No? So, what do you want?"

I drop onto the chair nearest Mark. "I want to know that what I'm doing makes a difference."

Mark pushes off from the floor and sits on the chair next to me. "Of course, it makes a difference. You're preaching

God's Word, counseling couples in trouble, bringing the Bible to life for kids. This is important stuff."

"The work's not enough if the motivation behind it isn't pure."

"Come on," Mark scoffs. "You're just overwhelmed with family stuff. Give it a few weeks and things'll be back to normal."

"That's what I'm afraid of." I shift in my seat. "For a long time now, I've been doing the work without feeling the Spirit. I've been disconnected. Detached, like you said, I suppose. It's infected my family, Mark. Don't you see that?"

Concern mars his brow. "No. What I see is a group of dissenters causing an uproar."

I shake my head. "They had a list of concerns, most of which were valid. It doesn't matter that it started with a lie. The rest, it was all true. I've been so busy trying to look good for them, I forgot who I was answering to."

"So, what're you saying?"

"I'm not sure. But I can't hold my wife back because the body feels she shouldn't work outside the home. I can't be hard on my boy because I fear how people will judge me when he messes up. And I can't see every past mistake as an end to my career." I rake a hand through my hair. "How's that teaching anybody about God's grace?"

"It didn't start out this way, you know?" I look at Mark, but he doesn't get it. "What made you want to be a pastor?"

He shrugs. "I don't know. I love God and His Word. It stands to reason I'd want to share it."

"You have a mission statement?"

"A mission statement?" He looks at me like I've grown a second head. "I'm beginning to think you were in that accident with Taylor."

I throw my hands up. "What's keeping you on track? How do you know you're still fulfilling God's purpose for your life?"

"I…I don't know. I guess I just feel it."

"But I *don't*. Don't you get it? I don't *feel* it anymore. All I feel is the stress of trying to keep everyone happy. This guy wants the music louder, that one not so loud. The message isn't biblical enough or it's too biblical. Too many services, not enough services. It never ends. And somewhere in the middle of it all, I allowed my ego to get the best of me. To actually believe that this church is about me when it's about everything but."

Mark sits back, shakes his head. "Then where do you go from here? I mean, what else is there? You going to chuck it all and see if you can get a job as a garbage collector? Maybe go back to school and find a new career?"

"Wouldn't be the worst thing."

"I'm *kidding*," Mark says, leaning toward me. "You're not seriously going to tell me you want a real do-over, are you?"

Starting from scratch never sounded so good.

Chapter 40

Corey

Life has been on hold for too long, and I'm reminded of that when Tess Holland calls to set up a meeting to plan out the next school year. I used the need-to-check-my-calendar excuse. What else could I say? The reality is that school starts in eight short weeks—and not just for me, but for Taylor, too. She'll need an Individual Education Plan, a new speech thera- pist, and an attitude adjustment if this is going to work.

And I need to find out where my marriage stands.

I call Paul's cell phone, but it goes to voicemail. "We need to talk. Can you call me back when you get this message?" I leave the same message on our home phone. Vague, maybe, but if Michael intercepts, I don't want him to worry.

I use the same line on Taylor as I pass the turn-off for Tricia's.

"About what?" Boredom infuses her tone. It's as if there's nothing I could say that would hold any appeal for her.

"Lots of things. But I don't want to do it in the car."

. She swings her head around to look behind us. "You missed the off thingy."

"It's such a beautiful day, I thought we'd park off the highway by the beach and take a walk."

She slumps back in her seat. I can feel her glare, even though I'm not looking at her. "I don't want to take a walk."

"It'll be good for you. Fresh air to build those neurons."

Her only response is a grunt.

A few miles of her silence and I find a parking space off the highway. The tide is out and the sun shimmers off the shallow waters and the wet, rippling sand several hundred feet out.

"Let's go."

We pull off our sandals before working down the bank and onto the white sand beach dotted with tourists and locals alike. Or at least I imagine those walking in a meditative state in worn beachwear are locals. Seagulls swoop and glide with an occasional squawk.

I reach for Taylor's hand, but she pulls away like a spoiled toddler. Enough is enough. "Do you intend to punish me forever? Because I have to say, it's getting old."

"You're a hypocrite." She slaps her sandals against her thigh, sand spraying from the soles, and stares ahead.

"In what way?"

"You've been telling me forever that I'm supposed to be good. You know, pure. But you weren't."

So true. "And I'm paying the price for it."

"So now I'm, like, your punishment?"

"It's not you, Taylor. It's the entire situation. I've hurt you and your dad and me. Granted, if I'd remained pure, you wouldn't be here right now. I can't regret that. But the rest of it?" I shake my head.

"Why'd you do it?"

"Do what?" A lame attempt at a stall tactic.

"Cheat on Dad. Did you, like, do that before?"

"Never. It was my intention to wait until I was married."

An unladylike snort escapes her mouth.

"It *was*. Then I got scared."

"Yeah? Of what?"

"Your dad—he was a good man. Is a good man. But there were times that he'd say something to me, and it was like I was looking at my own father. Judgmental, immoveable."

Taylor stops, her mouth opening in an O, eyes wide. "Like he is with Michael?"

Can she understand? "Yes. Just like with Michael. A week away from the wedding, I considered calling it off."

"Seriously?" She pushes a strand of purple hair from her face and leaves a smudge of sand behind.

"Just the thought of facing hi,"—I blow out a breath— "scared me to death. And facing my father after he'd paid for everything. The gifts were coming in, the honeymoon was paid for. Lame reasons, I know," I rush to say when she starts to interrupt.

"Did you even love him?"

I smile. "Yes, sweetheart. I loved him. But I was so torn and confused. One minute I'd decided to call it off and the next, I knew I couldn't."

"So, you slept with someone else?"

"That's not quite how it happened. Tricia saw I was upset and talked me into going to a party with her. Let it all go for one night. And I started drinking."

Taylor rolls her eyes. "Yeah, that's another lecture you guys give us."

"For good reason. Anyway, it felt good to forget. The more I drank, the more I forgot."

"Then what happened?"

I throw my hands up and shrug. "To be honest, Tay, I don't remember much else. It's like when you wake up remembering a dream, but after a while, all the details fade away until all that's left are illusive images."

"So, does Dad know all this?"

"Pretty much. Although, as angry as he was, I don't know what stuck. He was hurt. And he had every right to be."

"He didn't seem upset with you the other day. He could hardly take his eyes off you."

I stare out at the waves rolling up onto the sand. "Probably trying to figure what happened to the wife he's always known."

"I don't think so," she sing-songs, then giggles. "Maybe you should get a few more outfits from Tricia before we go home."

Home. How could I have forgotten? "Oh, Tay. That's why I brought you out here. To talk to you about going home."

"When?" Her eyes light up like a kid on Christmas morning. "Because Josh called yesterday and wants to know if I can go to a party with him."

I scrunch my nose up and shake my head. "Sorry, Charlie, but no parties for you. I know what can happen."

"Very funny." She giggles again, and I laugh in response.

"Seriously, though. We're going to have to figure a few things out."

"You are going back to Dad, aren't you?"

That's the million-dollar question. "I guess that depends on him."

~

Paul

"I don't get it." Michael looks out the window at Community Church. "Why're we here again?"

I roll the window down and breath in the warm, summer-scented air. "You said you wanted pizza for dinner."

"Yeah, I don't think we're getting pizza here."

"I have to meet with someone first." I check the rear-view

mirror as Kent parks behind me. Then I look at Michael. "I told you before that when I know, you'll know."

He throws up his hands, rolls his eyes. "Know *what?*"

I climb out of the car and turn to greet Kent. "Appreciate you coming out here."

"Glad to do it." His eyes narrow. "You look beat."

"Last day of VBS."

"Ah." He nods. "That'll be me next week. Who do we have here?" He extends his hand when Michael comes up beside me.

"Oh, that's right. You've never met my son. Pastor Kent, Michael."

"Good to meet you, Michael. I've heard a lot about you."

Michael flashes his crooked smile. "That can't be good."

Kent chuckles. "I assure you, it's all good."

"Well, it's nice to meet you, sir."

"So." Kent eyes me. "Are you ready to meet the board?"

I check my watch. "We have ten minutes before the meeting. Would you mind if I take that time to fill Michael in?"

"Not at all." He waves a hand at his car. "I'll be here working on Sunday's sermon. Let me know when you're ready."

With a hand on Michael's shoulder, I guide him across the street. Traffic is almost non-existent, and the old homes in the neighborhood are reminiscent of a simpler time. Just what we need. "Let's walk."

"What's going on, Dad?"

I tuck my hands in my pockets as we navigate the tree root-cracked sidewalk. "Do you know why God hates the sin of pride?"

Scrunching up his nose, he gives me a sideways look. "Huh?"

"Pride? You know?"

"Yeah, I know what pride is."

"In Proverbs sixteen seven, it's referred to as 'haughty

eyes,' but it's the same as pride or arrogance. One of the seven things that are an abomination to Him. And He hates it because it comes when we put ourselves above others. When we forget why we're here in the first place."

"Okay..." He draws the word out. Must think I've lost it.

"I've been guilty of that. Pride. For quite a while now. I feel like I've let so many things become more important than my family, more important than God, even."

"Is this about that thing with Josh's mom? 'Cause I talked to Mom about it last weekend, and she said she never believed that you did anything wrong."

"Oh, but I did."

His head snaps up. "You mean—"

"No." I grasp his upper arm. "I don't mean I did anything with Ms. Andrews. But I've been guilty of other things, worse in some ways."

"Like?"

Confession is good for the soul, or at least that's what I've heard. Michael deserves the truth. "I wanted accolades from the members of the church. You know what accolades are?"

"That was one of last year's vocab words, Dad."

"Yeah, okay. Well, I put that desire above everything else, including my relationship with God. I let it rule how I dealt with Ms. Andrews, how I dealt with the vandalism situation. Your mom, she's always wanted to teach, but I wouldn't allow it because members of the church thought she should focus on women's ministry."

"Which she doesn't like to do."

"No. And I owe her an apology. I owe her about ten apologies. But not just her, Michael. I owe you a few, too. I shouldn't have been so hard on you."

"It's done, Dad." The kid's much better at forgiveness than I've ever been. Smarter than I've given him credit for, too.

"I just want to be sure everything's cleared up."

"Okay." He swings his head around, as if to take in the

scenery. "But I don't get what that has to do with us being here."

I rub my hand over my face and take a deep breath. "I don't think, after everything that's happened at Crossroads, I can stay there. People there, well, they have expectations."

Shock registers on his face. "So, what're you going to do?"

We round the corner and are back on Church Street. "That church?" I point to Community. "They need a new pastor. It's a lot smaller than Crossroads, but they're looking for leadership."

Shock turns to panic. "You mean we're going to leave Placerville?" Just like a kid to home in on what's going to affect him.

"No, of course not. I mean, not if we're all in agreement that we want to stay in Placerville. I can commute. And your mom's accepted a teaching position there."

"She did? Cool."

"I'm sure you'd like to finish high school where you are. And Taylor—well, she'll need to finish high school one way or the other."

"So, you and Mom aren't getting divorced?"

"Not if I can help it." We arrive back at the church. "Anyway, I didn't want to meet with the board without telling you what's going on. After all, I promised."

"Have you talked to Mom about it?"

"Not yet." That should be an interesting conversation. "I won't commit to anything until I do, though."

Kent checks his watch and waves us over. "You ready?"

I slap Michael on the back. "You want to come in with me?"

"Me? But isn't this, like, a job interview?"

I nod. "Kind of. But they ought to know right up front that my family comes first, don't you think?"

Chapter 41

Corey

Traffic is light. Who else in their right mind is driving around on a Sunday morning at five a.m.? Taylor was asleep before I reached Highway 1, head cushioned by her pillow against the passenger side window. Rambo's spread out on the back seat like a king on his throne.

And I'm not quite sure what I'm doing. Last night, I was unsure of my next move. Do I go back to Paul and pretend nothing's changed? Do I turn down the teaching position, seek one out in the Monterey area and stay with Tricia? Or do I continue to pray that somehow, some way, God will intervene and restore my family?

"What do I do?" I'd asked Tricia as we cleared the dinner dishes from the table.

"I can't even figure out my own life, which is far less complicated than yours."

Opening the dishwasher, I glanced at her. "What's to figure out? I thought you were perfectly happy with the status quo."

She rested her hip on the counter and crossed her arms

with a sigh. "I *was* until you had to butt in and try your hand at matchmaking."

"No one's forcing you to go out with him, you know. And may I remind you that *you* started the whole thing?" I raised my voice to a falsetto. "If only Jonas had a son."

She snatched up a dishtowel and attempted to smack me with it. "I liked you better as the submissive little wife. The screeching harpy's hard to live with."

"Ha. Well, you better get used to it. I may never leave." I flicked my wet hands at her.

Wiping her face with the dishtowel, she shot me a smirk. "Aren't we just a pair? The picture of indecision."

"Do you like him? Dylan?"

"What's not to like? But I liked Steven, too. Look how that turned out."

I loaded the last plate into the dishwasher and closed the door. "So, you take it slow. He's a *pastor*, for goodness sake. We're talking church picnics and walks on the beach."

"True."

"And if there is a dark side to him, don't you think Jonas would have seen it?"

"Maybe."

"You know the warning signs now, don't you?"

"I think so."

"Look, Trish, don't make this to be more than it is. Give it some time, and I'm sure——"

"Hey, Mom?" Taylor poked her head into the kitchen and held out my cell phone. "I was on the phone with Rachel when butt head called. He says it's important."

I grimaced at her as I took the phone. "Maybe it's time you came up with a nicer nickname for your brother."

"Why?"

It must have been a rhetorical question, because she didn't wait for an answer.

"Hey, Michael. Everything all right?" Texts were more his style.

"You gotta come home." His tone was a little anxious, but not panicked.

"Your dad and I will talk in the next couple days—"

"No. Not the next couple days. Tomorrow. In time for church service."

"What? Why?"

"It's important, Mom."

"What's going on?" Tricia whispered. "Is everything okay?"

I shrugged. "I need more than that if you expect me to be on the road by," I count the hours in my head, "four-thirty."

"Can't you trust me? Please?"

We'd have to pack up that night. I'd need to call Jonas to tell him good-bye. And what about Taylor's therapy?

"You there, Mom?"

"Yeah." I looked at Trish and rolled my eyes. "This is important, huh?"

"It's the *epitome* of important."

It must have been for him to pull out a vocab word. "Okay then. I...I'll be there by nine."

"And Mom?"

Now what?

"Try not to let Dad see you until after, okay? I mean, stay in the foyer until worship is over."

Ten hours later, here we are on the road. Anxiety wars with exhaustion. It was a mad rush to call Jonas last night and pack up everything. Taylor was no help, focused on her own conflicting emotions. How would her friends react to her in person? They've all graduated, but she's, "like, the idiot freak unable to hold onto a thought longer than a minute." Of course, she then went into the facts she learned in fifth grade about the minuscule memory of a goldfish. Random thoughts that *had* to be vocalized.

The temperature rises the farther north we drive. A hazy gray sky greets us in Sacramento. Out of Carmel a few hours and I already miss the clean ocean air. I roll up my window and turn on the air. Taylor stirs and mumbles something incomprehensible. It wasn't that long ago that alien gibberish was her only mode of communication. A reminder to be thankful for God's mercy—even on this day wrought with uncertainty.

I pull into Placerville at eight-fifty. Twenty-five minutes until Paul will step up to the podium to give his message. Plenty of time to drop Rambo off at the house, wake Taylor, and freshen up a bit. Every conceivable reason Michael wants me here tumbles through my head, twisting and turning, yet never settling into anything that makes sense.

Your grace is sufficient, Lord. Your grace is sufficient, Lord. Your grace is sufficient, Lord. The prayer becomes a litany as I drive into the church lot and park the car. Attendance appears to be back up, if the number of vehicles is any indication. Or maybe there's something special happening today, and that's why Michael wants us here.

"Let's go." Taylor unbuckles her seat belt.

I latch onto her upper arm. "Wait a minute. Michael doesn't want your dad to see us." I check my watch. "When we go in, let's stay in the back. If there are empty seats, fine, but if not, we'll stand."

"But I want Dad to know I'm here."

"He will, sweetie. After. I promised your brother."

She rolls her eyes and sighs. "Fine. Whatever."

The ending strains of *How Great Thou Art* reach my ears as we step into the foyer. Wrapping an arm around Taylor's shoulders, I hold her back with me until I hear Paul's voice.

"Let's go. And remember, stay in the back with me."

∼

Paul

After a few deep breaths, I step up to the podium. I wouldn't admit it to anyone, but it's everything I can do to not lose what little food I have in my stomach. *Please, Lord, don't let me throw up.* Staring out over the sea of familiar faces, I hesitate over a few—John and Beverly Pendleton, Drew and Rebecca Simpson, Craig and Jenna McCarty, Mark and Brianna Lewis. And Michael, front and center, offering up an encouraging smile.

What did I ever do to deserve his loyalty?

Michael glances over his shoulder. Who's he looking for? I scan the back of the church, but the lights are too low to make out anyone. I clear my throat and lay my speech down on the podium. I rehearsed it in my office a dozen times last night but can't remember the first word.

"I figure I've stood before you all about five hundred times in the last ten years if you factor in the weeks I've been on vacation." My stomach does a precarious flip, and I breathe deep. *Please don't let me throw up.* The sea of faces in front of me blurs, and my head's pounding like a bass drum.

"When I first started here at the ripe old age of thirty-two, I thought I knew what it took to be lead pastor. I'd spent the previous ten years at three different churches in the capacity of youth or associate pastor. I watched lead pastors deal with every conceivable issue from dissension over music to abhorrent sexual sin." I pause to remind myself to breathe.

"But there's something I didn't factor into the equation— my own stinkin' thinkin'. What started out as a call to serve God by serving others became a call to serve myself." My words result in shocked expressions. I can just imagine what they're thinking. "Oh, I didn't pilfer money from the collections or give anyone cause to believe I was unfaithful to my wife. Although, if I'm going to be honest here, there were accusations made of which I was innocent. But my sin was worse, in many ways."

There's a shuffling in the body as members lean in, as if to hear better or turn to each other, eyes wide, while questions fill their minds.

"My sin was in wanting to receive the credit for my work —credit that rightly belonged to the Lord. Some might not see that as deserving a public confession but allow me to explain how that played out. First off, my son, Michael, gave me permission to share what many of you already know—last year he vandalized the elementary school. He did this out of anger toward me. I didn't know it at the time, nor did I bother to find out. I was too concerned with how his actions made *me* look and how it affected my position here."

I catch Michael's eye and he gives me a slight nod.

"Since that time, I've spent more energy defending my right to this position against eleven families who felt I should be removed. Rather, I should have been focusing on the multitude of you who weren't involved. I shirked my godly responsibilities in favor of a worldly reputation. I got caught up in the sin of pride and arrogance.

"Sadly, this didn't start just last year. It started when I first walked in those doors." I point to the back of the church. "When many members made it clear that my wife should be serving the church and not working outside our home, I stomped all over her dreams of teaching so my position would be secure. God first, then family, then work. I put work first, then it was a toss-up whether God or my family took second position."

No one's thrown out insults or demanded my blood. So far, so good. The churning in my gut eases and breathing becomes second nature again. Shuffling my notes, I find the passage I need.

"Proverbs six, sixteen through nineteen says, '*These six things the Lord hates, seven are an abomination to Him: a proud look, a lying tongue, hands that shed innocent blood, a heart that devises wicked plans, feet that are swift in running to evil, a false witness who speaks lies, and one who sows discord among brethren.'"*

I scan the body, catching a look here and there. But for the most part, eyes are down. Guilty consciences like mine? "It's humbling to note that I can see myself in most every one of these seven abominations. Although I've been guilty of not forgiving when I'm called to, I stand before you and humbly seek your forgiveness. None of us is sinless, but your pastor should be above reproach if at all possible. I've let you down. I've let my family down. And I've let my Lord down."

Gathering up my notes, I exit the stage, my steps much lighter than when I entered. There's something to be said for unburdening one's self.

Pushing through the side door with the intention of heading around to the foyer, I'm caught unawares by a woman's presence. I have to do a quick shuffle and grasp her shoulders to avoid running into her.

"Excuse me." I drop my hands and step back. It can't be. "Corey?"

Pushing her hair back with trembling fingers, she raises watery eyes to me.

"Why—how—I mean, what are you doing here?"

"Did you mean it?" She waves a hand toward the sanctuary. "What you said in there?"

"Yes, of course. But, I don't understand."

"Michael called last night."

"Mich—" I laugh. "Our son the conspirator."

She smiles and crosses her arms. "Now what?"

"I suppose that's up to you."

"No," she says. "It's up to us. I need you to forgive me and leave the past in the past. I don't want to relive it every time we disagree on something."

Reaching out a hand, I run a finger down her cheek until her eyes meet mine. "And I need my wife back. Someone to hold me accountable when I start thinking this life's about me."

She stands straight, looks me right in the eye. A challenge? "I want to teach."

"Good." I pull her in for a much-needed hug. "Because that speech I gave might have been my swan song. You just may be supporting us for a while."

EPILOGUE

Corey

What made me think life would be less chaotic once school got out? In a quest to find my planning book, I shuffle through the stacks of papers that cover the dining room table. Michael's photography portfolio, Taylor's Sac State class catalog, Paul's VBS material, and my freshman English curriculum.

"Hey, Mom," Michael shouts from the back of the house. "Where's my SOCAPA sweatshirt?"

"Everything's packed." Lifting *The Ancient World History* textbook, I thumb through the pages, breathing in the new book smell, my eyes catching the glossy, colorful pictures as they pass in a blur. My own classroom. My own students.

The clatter of Michael's suitcase being rolled down the hall precedes him. "I left my sweatshirt out for the airplane, but I can't find it."

"We have to leave in ten minutes if you want to make your flight. And hey, your portfolio's over there. Aren't you taking it with you?"

Grumbling, he snatches up the album from the table, lays

his suitcase down, and unzips it. "I was going to carry it on, but this'll be better."

"Are you nervous?"

"Nah." He looks up from the floor and grins. "Are you?"

"Just promise me you'll be careful."

"It's New York, Mom, not Afghanistan. I'd be more worried about Taylor going to college in September."

"What about me?" Taylor emerges from the hallway, Rambo at her heels, rubbing her eyes. The girl can still rival Rip Van Winkle when it comes to sleep.

"Hey." Michael stands and points at her. "That's my sweatshirt you're wearing."

Sure enough, SOCAPA blazes across her chest, black and red on gray.

She shrugs. "So?"

"So, give it back. I'm taking it with me."

"You've got a million sweatshirts. This one will keep me from missing you."

Michael snorts. "As if. I'm only going to be gone two weeks."

"How about you let me keep this one and I'll get you a Sac State sweatshirt when school starts?"

"No. Come on, Tay, it cost me twenty-five dollars. That's, like, almost three hours of pumping gas."

"Fine," she says with a moan. "Let me go change."

Glancing at the clock, I call out to her retreating back. "Better make it quick, Tay. Dad's going to want to leave soon. VBS starts today, remember?"

A door slams and Paul comes in from the garage. "You guys about ready?" He reaches for Michael's suitcase. "Let me load that for you."

I step up to him and take his wrist. "Michael's a big boy. He can load it himself."

"Got it, Dad, thanks."

Taking Paul's hand, I wait until Michael's in the garage. "It'll be fine, sweetheart."

"Oh, yeah, I know." He plants a quick kiss on the end of my nose. "This'll be a good experience for him."

"I mean VBS. I know Community Christian doesn't have the space you had at Crossroads, but—"

"Not even close."

"But you have a great team working with you."

He slips an arm around me. "I still wish you could be there today."

"Well, I'll be there tomorrow and the rest of the week. I want to try and get some planning done after I drop Michael at the airport. With church activities and Tricia's wedding in a few weeks, summer's going to be gone before we know it."

"I still can't believe you scored the sixth-grade teaching assignment."

I grin. "Me neither." When God opens doors, He doesn't mess around.

"What d'you think about staying down in Carmel for a week or so after Tricia's wedding?"

I step back to look at him. "Are you sure? We were just there."

"Babe, spring break was almost three months ago."

"What about church?"

He shrugs. "I'll see if I can get Mark to substitute, or maybe Kent."

"It'd be good to spend a little time with Jonas. I think he's covering for Dylan at church. Since Beth died, he seems so lost."

"Well, then it's good we can be down there for a few extra days."

"And hey, Tricia and Dylan will be on their honeymoon, maybe we can stay at their place."

"Sounds like a plan." He plants a kiss on my head and wraps his arms around me.

"Here you go, butt head," Taylor says, sweatshirt dangling from one finger. She looks around. "Where is he?"

Stepping away from Paul with a sigh, I glare at Taylor. "That's the last time I want to hear that come out of your mouth. You'll be starting college in a couple months. It's time you act like it."

"He knows I'm only kidding."

"Your mom's right, Tay. Grab some breakfast, we need to go."

Rolling her eyes, she passes us on the way to the kitchen, and I snatch the sweatshirt from her.

The door to the garage slams and Michael appears. "Okay, I'm ready to go."

Paul wraps an arm around his shoulders. "Have a great time and behave yourself."

"No worries, Dad. I don't think there're any elementary schools in the area."

Paul ruffles his hair and pulls him in for a hug. "Smart aleck. Do us proud."

"I'll do my best. I'm going to say goodbye to Tay." He lopes toward the kitchen.

"And Michael?"

Michael turns. "Yeah?"

"Be careful." Paul's voice comes out gruff, like he's fighting emotion.

"I will, Dad. Promise."

He turns and wraps his arms around me. "You be careful, too. No crazy driving."

"We're all prayed up," I remind him. "You prayed for everything under the sun last night at dinner. We ended up eating cold spaghetti."

Paul chuckles. "I'm not taking chances anymore. I know who's in charge."

Placing my hand on his cheek, I reach up on tip toes to

give him a kiss. Was it only a year ago I thought our marriage was over? And now, with God at the helm, I can't imagine anything could tear us apart.

ABOUT THE AUTHOR

Jennifer Sienes holds a bachelor's in psychology and a master's in education but discovered life-experience is the best teacher. She loves Jesus, romance and writing—and puts it altogether in inspirational contemporary fiction. Her daughter's TBI and brother's suicide inspired two of her three novels. Although fiction writing is her real love, she's had several non-fiction pieces published in anthologies including two in *Chicken Soup for the Soul*. She has two grown children and one very spoiled Maltese. California born and raised, she recently took a step of faith with her real-life hero and relocated to Tennessee.

Visit her at https://www.jennifersienes.com/

facebook.com/Jennifer-Sienes-Writer-186643172596

instagram.com/Jennifer_Sienes

goodreads.com/Jennifer_Sienes

ALSO BY JENNIFER SIENES

Surrendered (The Apple Hill Series Book One)

GILDED CAGE

AN APPLE HILL SHORT STORY

Chapter 1

Spring, 2002—Wheaton College, Illinois

It was that time in her life when possibilities seem endless and tragedies, unimaginable. A few short weeks and Tricia Sewell would be free to chase whatever adventures captured her imagination. No longer would she be confined to the expectations of her parents, nor obligated to garner their approval.

As she speed-walked across Wheaton College campus, giddiness bubbled up inside her chest, like the finest French champagne, desperate to be uncorked. Although a cool breeze had her pulling her sweater tighter across her body, dogwood, crabapple and redbud trumpeted the arrival of spring with riotous blossoms of white, pink and purple.

When Tricia reached the brick and columned library, she slowed her steps to a respectable pace. Late or not, good manners prevailed. A quick glance at her watch confirmed what she'd suspected, but Corey would wait—she always did. While Tricia had to remind herself to act appropriately, proper etiquette was ingrained in Corey from the time she could walk.

"There you are." Corey leaned against the wall just inside

the library doors. "I was beginning to think you changed your mind."

"Are you kidding? What could be more fun than helping with your wedding registry?" Sarcasm dripped from her tone. "Did you remind Paul that this is supposed to be *his* job?"

Corey hiked the strap of her purse higher onto her shoulder with a grimace. "As long as he's not too busy to show up for the ceremony…"

With a snort, Tricia did an about-face and pushed through the exit. "You need to work on raising your level of expectation—give him something to aim for." Once outside, she slipped her arm through Corey's, and they descended the steps. "You're sure you want to marry him? I mean, he's cute enough, but kind of old for someone so young. Wouldn't you rather live some before you get tied down?"

"You know, Tricia, being married and *living* aren't mutually exclusive." She looked up at the trees, eyes squinted against the sun, and took a deep breath.

"They are if you're marrying someone whose dream is to become a pastor. You'll be living like some kind of a pauper—Charles Dickens-style." They strolled through campus, toward the parking lot, arm in arm. Students milled about while others sat on the grass or on benches that lined the walkway. Corey was quiet for so long, Tricia thought maybe she'd finally gotten through to her. She and Corey had been friends since fifth grade, but if they were headed in totally opposite directions, they'd probably never see each other.

"I'm marrying him because I love him." Corey finally responded.

"Pu-*lease*. You're twenty-two years old. What'd you know about love? You had, like, one date in high school and the first guy you go out with in college puts a ring on your finger. You might as well have him put it in your nose and let him lead you around by it." Tricia couldn't imagine being tied down to anyone, let alone a guy who'd keep her confined to church-approval for the rest of her life.

"Said like a true romantic," Corey said with a laugh. "Just because I don't have your sense of adventure, doesn't mean I'm condemning myself to a life of boredom. I want to teach and have kids and serve the Lord. You talk big, but I don't see you making any life-altering plans for after graduation."

"I have plans, my friend. I'm going to intern this summer, and by this time next year, I'll be opening my own business. I'm not sure what exactly, but it'll come to me."

"From your lips to God's ears," Corey murmured.

"Listen." Tricia stopped and swung Corey around, so they were face-to-face, nearly knocking into a couple. "Sorry," she threw at them before focusing on Corey. "Next Saturday night, Todd Agnew's having a party at his parents' place in the City. Come with me. It might be the last chance we have to really hang out before graduation."

A shadow of annoyance passed over Corey's face. "Are you forgetting that my bridal shower is next Saturday?"

Tricia rolled her eyes. "Your shower is in the afternoon. The party isn't until that night."

"I already made plans with Paul for Saturday night."

Tricia sighed. "You know, you look like someone who belongs in a swimsuit ad, but you act like someone who belongs in a convent."

Corey threw her hands in the air and stepped away. "If you're really my friend, Tricia, you'll be happy for me instead of constantly belittling my choice. I'm marrying Paul. Either get on board or step back."

Tricia stepped back—literally. Sweet as pie or not, when Corey reached the end of her patience, there was no crossing her. But she vowed that no one would ever put *her* in a cage.

Chapter 2

Spring, 2015—Carmel-by-the-Sea, California

Whaler's Cove, at Point Lobos State Reserve, was the perfect spot to lick one's wounds. The turquoise waters below the cliffs appeared untouched by humanity, like something one would find in the Garden of Eden—if such a place ever existed. Tricia had her doubts. The sun glistened off the long bands of bull kelp dancing in the waves and a breeze tripped through the ancient cypress trees, bent over from years of lashing winds, like an old woman weighed down by age. Tricia could relate.

She sat on a bench and stared off in the distance, searching for sea life—playful otters or harbor seals. This late in spring, the gray whales were no longer migrating off the coastline and the blue whales had yet to arrive. Last year, she'd seen porpoises frolicking just off the cliffs—a beacon of hope she needed more than a heartbeat, today.

A gust of wind cooled the air, and she started to cross her arms against the sudden chill. Her eyes caught sight of the bruises on her wrists, now yellowing with age, and she tucked her hands into the sleeves of her sweatshirt before hugging them close to her body.

How had she gotten here? She tilted her head back to the sun and closed her eyes. *What should I do, Lord?* But He didn't answer. Not that she expected Him to; He'd only been silent for the last several years. The harder she strove for success and material wealth, the quieter He became.

With a deep sigh, she opened her eyes and rose from the bench. It was nearly ten o'clock, and although her not-so-loyal store manager would open the shop, she needed to at least pretend she was in control, if for no other reason than her dignity.

The drive up Highway 1 was uneventful until she turned onto Ocean Avenue in Carmel. Traffic during the day was often backed up, as this was where the tourists gravitated. But Tricia was in no hurry. Her name was on the business license, but it was all for show, like a fine piece of jewelry kept under lock and key until someone was around to impress. Soon enough, she pulled her BMW onto a side street and made her way to La Boutique.

The window display, which she'd finished at close of business the day before, had been changed. Nothing dramatic, but enough to let her know who had the upper hand—and it wasn't her. The scarf, which she'd taken great pains to drape stylishly over the mannequin was now knotted around the sleek, fiberglass neck. The handbag was switched, as well.

Manager Meghan struck again.

There were a few patrons riffling through the racks and another at the checkout desk with Diana, who gave Tricia a warm smile when their eyes met. Tricia maneuvered around the displays and slipped into the back. Meghan, long dark hair, runway-model makeup, and a dress that showed off every curve was looking through a box of new inventory.

"Tricia." She offered a smile that rivaled the display

window mannequin for authenticity. "I was wondering if you'd make an appearance today."

Tricia bit back a response. This was a game to Meghan, and she wasn't going to play it. Innuendo flirted with every word out of her mouth, yet to anyone not privy to the battle raging beneath the surface, it would sound like casual conversation.

"Meghan." She looked down at her own clothing—chic or not, her sweatshirt was still a sweatshirt. Her jeans, though by a famous Parisian designer, were still jeans. There was a time she would have taken more care with her appearance, but *not* doing so was her own little form of rebellion.

Meghan slipped a silk sheath onto a velvet hanger and placed it on the portable rack. "So, Steven flies home tomorrow."

Again, with the innuendo. The only way Meghan would know Steven was coming home was if he talked to her himself. Ten years of marriage and all she had to show for it was the illusion of success, verbal abuse, and the occasional bruises. Why did she continue this farce of a business—this farce of a marriage? From the moment Steven installed his mistress as manager, Tricia had been fighting for scraps. And for what? Steven was coming home, but he wouldn't be coming home for her.

Starting over on her own would be better than living in this gilded-cage-of-a-marriage. At least she could recapture some self-respect.

"So, tell me Meghan." Tricia kept her tone light, bordering on pleasant. Two could play this game.

"Hmmm?" Meghan slid another sheath onto a hanger.

"How long have you been sleeping with my husband?"

Meghan turned to her, eyebrow raised. "Hmm. Let me see now." She gazed past Tricia, as if giving the question serious thought. Then her eyes landed on Tricia's. "How long have I been manager of his shop?"

Tricia nodded. Meghan referred to La Boutique as *his* shop, just in case Tricia might be delusional enough to believe otherwise. "Yeah, that's what I thought. You're a beautiful girl. I imagine you could have anyone you choose. Am I right?"

The younger woman's mouth opened and closed, like a goldfish with its face pressed against a bowl. Was it shock that Tricia would say something so complimentary that robbed her of her voice?

"I…I don't know. I guess so," she finally managed.

Tricia shook her head and eyed Meghan with sympathy. She didn't even have to fake it. "So, why would you settle for being some guy's mistress? Prostituting yourself can't possibly have been your life's ambition."

Eyes hardened, she took a step toward Tricia, as though to put her in her place. "How dare——"

"Let me make it easy on you." Tricia swept her hands wide, lip curled. "He's all yours. You can have him."

"Wh…What?" The sheath in Meghan's hands slipped to the floor.

"I have to warn you, though. Once he gets tired of you— and believe me, he will—you'll be on *this* end of things. Personally, I'd rather wait tables." Which is what she just might end up doing. She'd have been smart to run the other way when Steven wanted a prenup. If a man has to protect his assets from his wife, he's up to no good.

Tricia walked from the back room and took what she assumed was her last look at La Boutique. Rage and self-pity warred within her. Steven would be home tomorrow, but she wouldn't be waiting for him with open arms. It's time this little birdie escaped.

Chapter 3

Tricia stood at the floor-to-ceiling windows that overlooked Carmel Beach but found no joy in the sun glistening off the waves or the antics of dogs, and their owners, that played along the pearly white sand. Instead, her focus was on what she was going to say to Steven when he arrived from the airport. Heart in her throat, she found it difficult to breathe. He should have been here at least a half hour ago. Did he stop by La Boutique first, hoping to steal a few minutes with Meghan? Just the thought of it strengthened her resolve.

"Miss Tricia?" Maria stood in the entryway, hands folded in front of her, a gentle smile on her face, graying hair pulled back into a bun. And wearing that ridiculous uniform. How Tricia detested the stamp of ownership—and all for show. Because everything Steven did was for show.

"Yes, Maria."

"I am going to the market. Is there anything you need that is not on the list?"

Maria's melodic accent pulled a smile from Tricia. More than anything, she would miss this sweet woman. But right now, what she needed was Maria's presence as a buffer. Steven wouldn't dare show his true colors with a witness around.

Tricia moved to Maria's side and put an arm around her shoulders. "Would you mind holding off until later this afternoon?" She started to give Maria an excuse but bit it back. She couldn't tell her the truth, but a lie was unacceptable.

"That will be fine, Miss Tricia. I have plenty to keep me busy until then."

Tricia couldn't imagine what needed attention, but after today, the care of this extravagant home would no longer be her concern. She watched Maria leave then retrieved her phone from her purse and punched in Corey's number.

"Hey, Trish. I was just thinking about you. Great minds and all that, huh?"

Tricia sank into the soft couch cushion at the sound of her friend's voice. Tears burned at the back of her eyes and she had to swallow before responding. After years of lying about her life, she couldn't lay it all out over the phone.

"Yeah, Cor, great minds." Her voice sounded strained even to her ears, and she took a deep breath to get it under control. "I was thinking of coming up for a spur-of-the-moment visit?" *Somewhere safe where I can figure out what I'm going to do with the rest of my life.*

"Funny you should say that, I was just telling Paul that we haven't seen you for a while. Of course, why would you want to come to Placerville when you live right there in paradise?"

Oh, if she only knew. Well, she would soon enough.

"When are you planning on heading up? I assume Steven's leaving on a business trip." Because that's the only time Tricia ever dared to visit. It was the only time she didn't live with the repercussions of Steven's insecurity.

Tricia cleared her throat and made a concentrated effort to keep her voice casual. "I thought I'd leave this afternoon."

"Oh." Tricia couldn't miss the surprise in her friend's voice. "That is last minute."

"Will that be a problem?" *Please, Lord, let her be okay with this. I have nowhere else to go.*

"Of course not, silly. You're family. Can we plan on you for dinner?"

"Better than that." Relief steadied Tricia's nerves. "Dinner's on me." She glanced at her purse where a fat cashier's check was hidden away. It may be her only source of income for some time, but she was allowed one celebratory dinner before she had to face the reality of homelessness and poverty.

"Well, we can discuss that when you get here," Corey hedged. "Just drive safely."

"I will, and—" The doorbell chimed, and dread hit Tricia's chest like an anvil. Steven. But no, he would come up from the garage.

Maria appeared at the top of the stairs. "I will get it, Miss Tricia."

"No need, Maria, I'm done here." She waved a hand at the maid. "Look, Corey, someone's at the door. I'll call somewhere from the road."

"Okay. Can't wait to see you."

"Same here, friend." Tricia slid her phone onto the glass-topped coffee table and crossed to the foyer. Two tall figures, dressed in dark clothing, were visible through the leaded glass, and their size gave her pause. Even in Carmel, one couldn't be too careful.

After unlocking the door, she eased it open enough to catch a glimpse of her visitors, and her breath caught. Policemen.

"Ma'am." The shorter of the two gave her a slight nod. "Are you Mrs. Neuvert?"

"Yes." The name grated on her, but it was pointless to inform them she'd kept her maiden name. It was the only thing she had that didn't belong to Steven.

"Would you mind if we come in?" The taller officer pointed inside. "We need to talk to you for a moment."

"May I see some ID?" She gave a cursory glance at the shields they produced, her mind chasing reasons they might have to be standing at her front porch. A robbery in the neighborhood? Vandalism? Or maybe they're just collecting for a policeman's fundraiser. If that's the case, they could certainly find a less intimidating way to request a donation.

"Miss Tricia?" Maria called from the top of the stairs. "Is everything okay?"

Tricia glanced up at the older woman, unsure if she should call her down or wave her away.

"Look, officers, if you're collecting for a fundraiser, this isn't really a good time. My husband should be arriving at any moment from a business trip. He really doesn't like to be bothered—"

"Mrs. Neuvert, please. There's been an…an accident, and we need to speak with you. Inside, if you don't mind."

"An accident?" Tricia stepped back to allow them to enter. "What kind of accident?"

Maria appeared and led the officers into the living room, while Tricia followed behind, her feet like lead. Call it a premonition or divine intervention, but she knew whatever they told her would change her life.

The taller officer turned to Tricia and flicked a hand toward the couch. "Maybe you should sit down."

Throat tight, Tricia wrapped her arms around herself. "And maybe you should just tell me why you're here. What do you mean by an accident?"

The officers glanced at each other before the shorter one said, "Your husband was driving Highway 17 southbound and was involved in a multi-car pile-up. I'm afraid he was killed at the scene."

Maria's gasp reached Tricia's ears as she dropped onto the couch.

Chapter 4

Three Weeks Later

Tricia parked her BMW under one of the crepe myrtle trees that lined Corey and Paul's street. The fuchsia-colored blooms announced spring in a way that reminded her of Wheaton College—and the stand-off she and Corey had over Corey's impending marriage.

What was it she'd vowed that day? *No one will ever put me in a cage.* She accused Meghan of prostituting herself to Steven, but hadn't Tricia done the same? She'd traded dignity and freedom for material wealth. Of course, it hadn't started that way, but to make that argument would just be splitting hairs.

She looked up at the house as tears welled. The last few weeks were some of the hardest she'd ever survived. Not because she lost her husband, but because the conflict warring inside her soul was exhausting. She'd wanted nothing more than to be free of Steven, but now that she was...well, grief was a funny thing. Somehow in death, memories of the man she'd fallen in love with, rather than the one who was killed on Highway 17, plagued her.

The one bright light in an otherwise gloomy few weeks

was the day she promoted Diana to manager. Meghan didn't hang around long enough to get fired, which saved them both a little embarrassment.

On the tail end of that thought, Tricia flipped the visor down to check her makeup and hair. Would Corey see past the mask she'd carefully applied to hide the shame lurking in her soul? Fresh highlights, and healthy color in her cheeks from walking along Carmel Beach, would help with the façade.

She climbed from the car, drew in a deep breath, and held it in her lungs for a heartbeat or two. The tang of pine flirted with fresh cut grass and a sweet tang of something blooming nearby—apple trees or maybe the crepe myrtle. So different from the briny sea air in Carmel.

"You're here." Corey's greeting pulled Tricia's gaze to the front porch where her friend waved before descending the few steps.

Eyes blinded by tears, Tricia waved back. "I'm here," she choked out, and quickly swiped away the moisture. Corey would assume she was still in the throes of grief, and in some ways she was, but it was pure joy that had her emotions running high in this moment.

Corey reached the sidewalk and Tricia pulled her in for a hug, her own Oscar de la Renta overpowering Corey's mild soap-and-water scent. Some things never changed.

Corey stepped back and gave Tricia a once over. "You *look* like the Tricia I know and love."

She squirmed under her friend's observation. "What's that supposed to mean?"

Dropping her hands, she shrugged. "The Tricia I used to know would've welcomed my friendship in her time of need. I guess I should've ignored your orders and come anyway. That's what you would have done had I lost Paul."

She dropped her eyes, lest Corey see her lies. "I'm sorry, Cor. I really needed some time alone to process."

"I could've helped put a service together."

"I didn't want a service." She stepped around Corey and hit her key fob to open the trunk. "Steven has no family to speak of, and it seemed pointless to have a service just for me and Maria."

"Surely he had friends." Corey slipped around her and retrieved a suitcase from the trunk. "What do you have in here? Rocks?"

"Gifts," she said, taking it from Corey. "I bought my God-children a few trinkets."

Corey snorted. "A few trinkets? The last time you bought Michael a trinket it turned out to be a Play Station 4. And Taylor about drove Paul out of his mind with that Karaoke machine you insisted she have."

She sighed. "Don't steel my joy, Cor. I don't have kids of my own—probably never will—so let me spoil them a little."

Corey grimaced. "I suppose when you put it that way…"

They hauled the two suitcases up the stairs and into the moderate house. Not high end, but not exactly the pauper-like accommodations Tricia predicted Corey would be stuck with by marrying a pastor. There's something to be said for inheriting a little money.

No one knew that better than Tricia.

"Let's get your stuff into the guest room and then we can have a little girl time before I have to pick the kids up from school."

Girl time. Just what Tricia looked forward to and, at the same time, dreaded. How would Corey react when she confessed the truth about her marriage? She did a mental cringe just remembering how arrogant she'd been on that day long ago, when Corey wanted nothing more than a little moral support. Instead, Tricia belittled her choice, as if she, the more worldly of the two, had all the answers.

What a joke that had turned out to be.

Aside from that brief moment when Corey got cold feet and danced on the precipice of the wild side, she'd been the more stable of the two. She knew what she wanted, stepped out in faith, and trusted God would deliver it. And look at her now. Two beautiful children, a handsome and godly (if not a little stuffy) husband, and a life she could boast about.

And what did Tricia have? Money. And whoever said "money can't buy happiness" knew what they were talking about.

Corey put on a fresh pot of coffee and rummaged around the kitchen cabinets until she found a bag of store-bought cookies. "It's not Mrs. Fields, but once you dunk them in the coffee, they're not half bad." She set everything up at the kitchen table and plopped into a chair across from Tricia. "Okay, girlfriend, spill it?"

For a brief moment, Tricia couldn't breathe. Did Corey already know the truth about her sordid life? No, she realized, able to draw air into her lungs once again. Corey was just giving her the opportunity to pour out her grief-stricken heart.

It was in that moment, staring into her best friend's sympathetic eyes, she knew she couldn't do it. Whether it was shame or pride, she wasn't sure. But regardless, she couldn't sully Corey's sweet, naive self with the ugly reality of living with abuse. And even if she could, how would Corey feel knowing Tricia had been hid behind lies for almost ten years.

What kind of a friend does that?

The street lights cast a warm glow along the sidewalk as Tricia parked her car along the curb. Taylor Schaffer, Corey's twelve-year-old daughter, was jabbering a mile a minute in the front seat, but Tricia had lost track of the conversation. Instead, she took comfort in the bantering between her and ten-year-old Michael, who sat behind her.

"You're making that up." After unlatching his seatbelt, Michael leaned his face between the bucket seats.

"No, I'm not." Taylor peered around her brother's head to look at Tricia. "Isn't that true, Aunt Trish?"

Oh boy, now she was going to have to confess her lack of attention. "Well, to tell the truth——"

"Never mind." Michael scrambled to open the door latch. "Mom and Dad are home now." He jumped out of the car and ran up to the open garage door.

Taylor shook her head. "He just doesn't want me to prove he's wrong." She shifted in her seat to look at Tricia. "Thanks for letting us ride with you, Aunt Trish. It's way cooler to ride in your car than Dad's." She didn't wait for a response but climbed out of the car and followed her brother at a more sedate pace.

Tricia sat in the sudden silence for a moment and gazed at the cozy home, porch light beckoning with its warmth. It brought to mind her childhood—white bread normal, bordering on dull. What she wouldn't give to get back to that place—family dinners that started with giving thanks, appreciation for the little things, church on Sundays and Wednesday nights. First thing in the morning, she was going to call her parents. It was time for a visit. Chicago was beautiful in the springtime.

More lights flicked on inside the house, and the kids' silhouettes crossed the family room's large picture window. This is what her world could have been like had she'd been wiser in her youth. Maybe, if she'd pursued ways to serve the Lord, as Corey had, her life would have reflected it. Instead, she was a thirty-five-year-old woman with more money than sense, trapped in an emotional cage from which she didn't know how to escape.

The front door opened, and Corey appeared under the glow of the porch light. She stood motionless for a moment, and then skipped down the three steps and crossed the lawn. Opening the passenger door, she stuck her head in the car. "Are you okay?"

The truth was, Tricia was tired to the bone. She could ease her seat back and sleep right here. "Just thinking."

Corey slipped into the car and shifted to face Tricia. "About Steven? I can't imagine how much you must miss him. If Paul..." She closed her mouth with a snap, as if she realized she'd said too much.

"It's okay, Cor." Tricia took her hand. "You don't have to tip-toe around it."

With a grimace, she squeezed Tricia's hand. They sat in silence for a few moments, both staring out the windshield. No words were necessary. One more hand squeeze, and Corey stepped out of the car, which forced Tricia to do the same. When they entered the house, Paul was perched on the edge of his recliner, Michael kneeling on the floor beside him. They had their heads bent together studying the gift Tricia had given him earlier.

"Is there a problem with the camera?" The reviews she'd read confirmed it was the best digital camera on the market, and for the price, it should take award-winning pictures, even for a novice such as her Godson.

Michael's head swiveled around. "Nope. Dad's just showing me how to change the aperture."

Okay, so maybe Michael's not such a novice after all. "The aperture, huh?" Tricia wasn't sure what that was, but it sounded pretty technical.

Paul handed the camera back to Michael as Tricia and Corey settled on the couch. "We can look at it more tomorrow, kiddo. I'm sure you have some homework to do before bed."

He nodded, held the camera in his arms like a prized possession and looked at Tricia. "Thanks again, Aunt Trish, for the camera."

"It's absolutely my pleasure, Michael. All I ask is you send me a few pictures every now and then."

Michael gave her a lopsided grin before scooting down the hall toward his bedroom.

Corey slipped off her shoes. "Where's Taylor?"

"Well," Paul said, standing. "She told me she was going to do her homework, but I imagine she's pouring over her new art studio." There was a reprimand in his tone.

"A few supplies, is all." Tricia wrinkled her nose. "How can she possibly know what medium she'll be good at if she doesn't have options?"

"You didn't give her options." Corey nudged Tricia with an elbow. "You gave her the entire art store."

"And that camera," Paul crossed his arms, "I know what they go for. I appreciate your generosity, Tricia, but don't you think it's a little much for a grown up, let alone a ten-year-old?"

"He'll grow into it."

Paul rolled his eyes and took a couple steps back. "I'm not going to argue with you, because I know how pointless it is. Thanks again for dinner and for the gifts you brought the kids. Now, if you'll excuse me, I have a sermon to work on. Maybe something along the lines of spoiling our children would be appropriate." If it was his intention to scold Tricia, the amused twitch of his lips ruined the affect.

Paul might be a little stuffy, but Tricia envied Corey, nonetheless. He wouldn't use intimidation, verbal abuse or brute strength to get his point across. And he was a loyal husband and father. Had Tricia been as wise as Corey in their youth... What was that saying her mom used to spout—*If wishes were horses then beggars would ride?*

Corey turned to Tricia. "Before I get too comfortable, do you want anything? Tea? Coffee? Dinner?"

"Dinner? We just had dinner."

"No," Corey said. "Paul, the kids and I had dinner. You barely touched your food. And I know it was good, because Bella Cucina is the best."

She grimaced. "I don't have much of an appetite since Steven died." Stress will do that to you.

Corey scooted back into the cushions and folded her legs beneath her as if preparing for a long conversation. "You're not sleeping, either."

So much for the mask of makeup.

Tricia drew in a deep breath and weighed her words with care. "I'm feeling very lost right now." It was an understatement, but all she was willing to confess.

Corey's eyes softened with sympathy. "I really can't imagine. If I lost Paul…well, you know." She leaned forward. "Is there anything I can do?"

Tricia's eyes took in the warm room—family pictures on the walls, a stack of mail sitting on the table next to Paul's recliner, and a layer of dust on the coffee table. A home that was lived in—not a showplace meant to impress. She needed such a place to redefine herself, to reclaim what had been lost in the mountain of shame she'd come to see as a normal existence.

What was the Bible scripture in Jude about being led astray? *They are like wild waves of the sea, churning up the foam of their shameful deeds. They are like wandering stars, doomed forever to blackest darkness.* She didn't want to be doomed forever to blackest darkness. She wanted to be in the light. Maybe she couldn't share her shame just yet, but she didn't have to be doomed to it, either.

There was a reason some seemingly long-lost scripture would pop into her mind so many years later. She may have abandoned God, but it was suddenly clear to her that He hadn't abandoned her. So, now what? She certainly wasn't going to find her way living in Steven's over-priced show piece.

"I'm going to sell the house." The moment she said it, she knew it was a positive first step. "It's extravagant, and there's no privacy. Do you have any idea what it's like living in a fish-bowl?"

"Are you kidding? I'm married to a pastor, remember? We can't sneeze without the whole congregation saying 'Gesund-heit.' But I thought you loved that house."

Tricia shook her head. "I love the ocean, and the view is beautiful, as long as the weather's good. But it doesn't reflect me. Or at least, the me I want to be."

A wrinkle formed between Corey's eyebrows, as if she was trying to decipher what Tricia just said. "You do know it's not always wise to make big decisions, like moving, while under emotional stress, right?"

"Would you believe me if I told you being in that house causes me emotional stress?" Before Corey could respond, Tricia flicked her hand in the air. "Never mind. I've never felt more certain of anything in my life. I can find a place a few blocks from the beach. Something small and cozy. Something that better reflects me." *The new and improved version.*

Corey threw her hands in the air. "Okay then. What can I do?"

"I just need you to be here for me, Cor, no questions asked."

Corey's face fell. "Is that it?" Disappointment laced her words.

"It's everything. I only wish I'd done the same for you when you needed me most." Of course, Corey's life turned out perfect, so no harm, no foul.

But she had no way of knowing that Corey, just like Tricia, held back the darkest part of her soul where the enemy lurked and awaited the perfect opportunity to strike.

Celebrate Lit Publishing
Is proud to endorse

Finding the pictures to capture your words

http://www.roseannawhitedesigns.com/